MRS. WARREN'S DAUGHTER

A Story of the Woman's Movement

SIR HARRY JOHNSTON

Mrs. Warren's Daughter

Sir Harry Johnston

© 1st World Library, 2007
PO Box 2211
Fairfield, IA 52556
www.1stworldlibrary.com
First Edition

LCCN: 2007927834

Softcover ISBN: 978-1-4218-4547-0
Hardcover ISBN: 978-1-4218-4463-3
eBook ISBN: 978-1-4218-4631-6

Purchase *"Mrs. Warren's Daughter"*
as a traditional bound book at:
www.1stWorldLibrary.com/purchase.asp?ISBN=978-1-4218-4547-0

1st World Library is a literary, educational organization
dedicated to:

- Creating a free internet library of downloadable ebooks

- Hosting writing competitions and offering book publishing
  scholarships.

1ˢᵗ World Library Literary Society

Giving Back to the World

"If you want to work on the core problem, it's early school literacy."

- James Barksdale, former CEO of Netscape

"No skill is more crucial to the future of a child, or to a democratic and prosperous society, than literacy."

- Los Angeles Times

"Literacy... means far more than learning how to read and write... The aim is to transmit... knowledge and promote social participation."

- UNESCO

"Literacy is not a luxury, it is a right and a responsibility. If our world is to meet the challenges of the twenty-first century we must harness the energy and creativity of all our citizens."

- President Bill Clinton

"Parents should be encouraged to read to their children, and teachers should be equipped with all available techniques for teaching literacy, so the varying needs and capacities of individual kids can be taken into account."

- Hugh Mackay

TO

MY JURY OF MATRONS:

WINIFRED JOHNSTON   ELLA HEPWORTH-DIXON
CATHERINE WELLS   ANGELA MOND
BEATRICE SANDS   MARGARET POWYS
ANNETTE HENDERSON   FLORENCE FELLOWES
MARY LEVY   RAY ROCKMAN-BRAHAM
FLORENCE TRAVERS   MAUD PARRY

THIS BOOK IS AFFECTIONATELY DEDICATED,
IN THE KNOWLEDGE THAT—IN THE MAIN—IT HAS
THEIR SYMPATHY AND APPROVAL.

H. H. JOHNSTON

POLING,
March, 1920

CONTENTS

PREFACE

The earlier part of Vivien Warren's life and that of her mother, Catherine Warren, was told by Mr. George Bernard Shaw in his play, "Mrs. Warren's Profession," published first in 1898.

(*Plays Pleasant and Unpleasant*: 1. *Unpleasant*. Constable and Co., 6th Edition.)

I have his permission to continue the story from 1898 onwards. To understand my sequel it is not necessary to have read the play which so brilliantly placed the Warren problem before us. But as most persons of average good education have found Mr. Shaw's comedies necessary to their mental furnishing, their understanding of contemporary life, it is probable that all who would be drawn to this book are already acquainted with the story of Mrs. Warren, and will be interested in learning what happened after that story was laid down by Mr. Shaw in 1897. I would in addition placate hostile or peevish reviewers by reminding them of the continuity of human histories; of biographies, real—though a little disguised by the sauce of fiction—and unreal—because entitled *Life and Letters, by His Widow*. The best novel or life-story ever written does not commence with its opening page. The real commencement goes back to the Stone ages or at any rate to the antecedent circumstances which led up to the crisis or the formation of the characters portrayed. Mr. Pickwick had a father, a grandfather; a mother in a mob-cap; in the eighteenth century. It is permissible to speculate on their stories and dispositions. Neither does a novel or a biography end with the final page of its convenient instalment.

When you lay down the book which describes the pathetic failure of Lord Randolph Churchill, you do so with curiosity as to what will become of Winston. With a pre-knowledge of the Pickwick Club, one may usefully employ the imagination in tracing out the possible careers of Sam Weller's chubby little boys; grown into old men, and themselves, perchance, leaving progeny that may have married into the peerage from the Turf, or have entered the War Cabinet at the beckoning of Mr. Lloyd George.

I know of descendants of Madame de Brinvilliers in England who have helped to found the Y.W.C.A.; and collateral offshoots from the Charlotte Corday stock who are sternly opposed to the assassination of statesmen-journalists.

So, I have taken on myself the continuation of the story outlined twenty-three years ago by Mr. Shaw in its late Victorian stage. *He* had a prior claim to do so; just as he might have shown us the life—but not the letters, for she was illiterate—of Catherine Warren's mother, the frier of fish and letter of lodgings on Tower Hill in the 'forties and 'fifties of the last century; and of the young Lieutenant Warren of the Tower garrison who lodged and cohabited with her at intervals between 1850 and 1854, when he went out to the Crimea and there died of frost-bite and neglected wounds. Mr. Shaw has waived such claims, having, as Vivie's grandmother would have said, "other fish to fry." But for this I should not have ventured to take up the tale, as I hold an author while he lives has a prescriptive right to his creations.

I shall feel no bitterness in Nirvana if, after my death, another continues the story of Vivie or of her friends and collateral relations, under circumstances which I shall not live to see.

In justice to Mr. Shaw I should state that the present book is entirely my own, and that though he has not renounced a polite interest in Vivie he is in no way responsible for her career and behaviour. He may even be annoyed at both.

H. H. JOHNSTON.

CHAPTER I

VIVIE AND NORIE

The date when this story begins is a Saturday afternoon in June, 1900, about 3 p.m. The scene is the western room of a suite of offices on the fifth floor of a house in Chancery Lane, the offices of *Fraser and Warren*, Consultant Actuaries and Accountants. There is a long window facing west, the central part of which is open, affording a passage out on to a parapet. Through this window, and still better from the parapet outside, may be seen the picturesque spires and turrets of the Law Courts, a glimpse here and there of the mellow, red-brick, white-windowed houses of New Square, the tree-tops of Lincoln's Inn Fields, and the hint beyond a steepled and chimneyed horizon of the wooded heights of Highgate. All this outlook is flooded with the brilliant sunshine of June, scarcely dimmed by the city smoke and fumes.

In the room itself there are on each of the tables vases of flowers and a bunch of dark red roses on the top of the many pigeon-holed bureau at which Vivien Warren is seated. The walls are mainly covered with book-shelves well filled with consultative works on many diverse subjects. There is another series of shelves crowded with neat, green, tin boxes containing the papers of clients. A dark green-and-purple portiere partly conceals the entry into a washing place which is further fitted with a gas stove for cooking and cupboards for crockery and provisions. At the opposite end of the room is a door which opens into a small bedroom. The fireplace in the main room is fitted with the best and least smelly kind of gas stove obtainable in 1900.

There are two square tables covered with piles of documents neatly tied with green tape and ranged round the central vase of flowers; a heavy, squat earthenware vase not easily knocked over; and there is a second bureau with pigeon-holes and a roll top, similar to the one at which Vivien Warren is seated. This is for the senior partner, Honoria Fraser. Between the bureaus there is plenty of space for access to the long west window and consequently to the parapet which can be used like a balcony. Two small arm-chairs in green leather on either side of the fireplace, two office chairs at the tables and a revolving chair at each bureau complete the furniture of the partners' room of *Fraser and Warren* as you would have seen it twenty years ago.

The rest of their offices consisted of a landing from which a lift and a staircase descended, a waiting-room for clients, pleasantly furnished, a room in which two female clerks worked, and off this a small room tenanted by an office boy. You may also add in imagination an excellent lavatory for the clerks, two telephones (one in the partners' room), hidden safes, wall-maps; and you must visualize everything as pleasing in colour—green, white, and purple—flooded with light; clean, tidy, and admirably adapted for business in the City.

Vivien Warren, as already mentioned, was, as the curtain goes up, seated at her bureau, reading a letter. The letter was headed "Camp Hospital, Colesberg, Cape Colony, May 2, 1900"; and ran thus:—

DEAREST VIVIE,—

Here I am still, but my leg is mending fast. The enteric was the worse trouble. That is over and done with, though I am the colour of a pig-skin saddle. My leg won't let me frisk just yet, but otherwise I feel as strong as a horse.

When I was bowled over three months ago and the enteric got hold of me, on top of the bullet through my thigh, I lost my self-control and asked the people here to cable to you to come and nurse me. It was silly perhaps—the nursing here is quite efficient—and if any one was to have come out on my account it ought to have been the poor old mater, who wanted to very much. But somehow I could only think of *you*. I wanted you more than I'd ever done before. I hoped somehow your heart might be touched and you might come out and nurse me, and then out of pity marry me. Won't you do so? Owing to my stiff leg I dare say I shall be invalided out of the Army and get a small wound pension. And I've a project which will make lots of money—up in Rhodesia—a tip I've had from a man in the know. I'm going to take up some land near Salisbury. Ripping country and climate and all that. It would suit you down to the ground. You could put all that Warren business behind you, forget it all, drop the name, start a new career as Mrs. Frank Gardner, and find an eternally devoted husband in the man that signs this letter.

I've been out here long enough to be up to all the ropes, and I'd already made a bit of money in Rhodesia before the war broke out and I got a commission. At any rate I've enough to start on as a married man, enough to give you a decent outfit and your passage out here and have a honeymoon before we start work on our future home. Darling Vivie! Do think about it. You'd never regret it. I'm a very different Frank to the silly ass you knew in the old Haslemere days.

Now here's a five pound note to cover the cost of a full cable to say "yes," and when you'll be ready to start. When I get your answer—somehow I feel it'll *be* "yes"—I'll send you a draft on a London bank to pay for a suitable trousseau and your passage from London to Cape Town, and *of course* I'll come and meet you there, where we can be married. I shan't sleep properly till I get your "yes."

Your ever loving and always faithful
FRANK.

P.S. There's a poor fellow here in the same ward dying—I should say—of necrosis of the jaw—Vavasour Williams is his name or a part of his name. His father was at Cambridge with my old man, and—isn't it rum?—he was a pupil of *Praddy's*!! He mucked his school and 'varsity career, thought next he'd like to be an architect or a scene painter. My dad recommended Praddy as a master. He worked in the Praed studio, but got the chuck over some foolery. Then as he couldn't face his poor old Governor, he enlisted in the Bechuanaland Border police, came out to South Africa and got let in for this show. The doctors and nurses give him about a month and he doesn't know it. He can't talk much owing to his jaw being tied up—usually he writes me messages, all about going home and being a good boy, turning over a new leaf, and so on. I suppose the last person you ever see nowadays is the Revd. Sam Gardner? You know they howked him out of Woodcote? He got "preferment" as he calls it, and a cure of souls at Margate. Rather rough on the dear old mater—bless her, *always*—She so liked the Hindhead country. But if you run up against Praddy you might let him know and he might get into touch with Vavasour Williams's people—twig?—F.G.

Vivie rose to her feet half-way through this letter and finished it standing by the window.

She was tall—say, five feet eight; about twenty-five years of age; with a well-developed, athletic figure, set off by a smart, tailor-made gown of grey cloth. Yet although she might be called a handsome woman she would easily have passed for a good-looking young man of twenty, had she been wearing male costume.

Her brown-gold hair was disposed of with the least ostentation possible and with no fluffiness. Her eyebrows were too well furnished for femininity and nearly met when she frowned—a too frequent practice, as was the belligerent look from her steely grey eyes with their beautiful Irish setting of long dark lashes. She had a straight nose and firm rounded chin, a rather determined look about the mouth—lower lip too much drawn in as if from perpetual self-repression. But all this severity disappeared when she smiled and showed her faultless teeth. The complexion was clear though a little tanned from deliberate exposure in athletics. Altogether a woman that might have been described as "jolly good-looking," if it had not been that whenever any man looked at her something hostile and forbidding came into the countenance, and the eyebrows formed an angry bar of hazel-brown above the dark-lashed eyes. But her "young man" look won for her many a feminine friendship which she impatiently repelled; for sentimentality disgusted her.

The door of the partners' room opened and in walked Honoria Fraser. She was probably three years older than Vivie and likewise a well-favoured woman, a little more matronly in appearance, somewhat after the style of a married actress who really loves her husband and has preserved her own looks wonderfully, though no one would take her for less than twenty-eight.

At the sight of her, Vivie lost her frown and tossed the letter on to the bureau.

Honoria Fraser had been lunching with friends in Portland Place.

Honoria: "What a swotter you are! I *thought* I should find you here. I suppose the staff departed punctually at One? I've come back expressly from the Michael Rossiters to carry you off to them—or rather to Kew. They're going to have tea with the Thiselton-Dyers and then revel in azaleas and roses. I shall go out and charter a hansom and we'll drive down ... it'll be some compensation for your having worked extra hard whilst I've been away....

"I met such a delightful man at the Rossiters'!" (slightly flushing) "Don't look at me so reproachfully! There *are* delightful men—a few—in existence. This one has been wounded in South Africa and he's so good-looking, though the back of his head is scarred and he'll always walk with a limp.... Now then! Why do you look so solemn? Put on your hat..."

Vivie: "I look solemn because I'm just considering a proposal of marriage—or rather, the fewest words in which I can refuse it. I don't think I want to go to Kew at all ... much sooner we had tea together, here, on the roof..."

Norie: "I suppose it's Frank Gardner again, as I see his handwriting on that envelope. Well I'm sorry about Kew—I should have enjoyed it..."

Vivie (bitterly): "I expect it's that 'delightful man' that attracts you."

Norie: "Nonsense! I'm vowed to virginity, like you are ... I really don't care if I never see Major Armstrong again ... though he certainly *is* rather a darling ... very good-looking ... and, d'you know, he's almost a Pro-Boer, though the Boers ambushed him.... Says this war's a beastly mistake....

"Well: I'll have tea here instead, if you like, and we can talk business, which we haven't done for a fortnight. I must get out of the way of paying visits in the country. They make one so discontented with the City afterwards. I've had a feeling lately I should like to have been a farmer.... Too much of the work of the firm has been thrown on you.... But there's lots and lots I want to talk over. I abandon Kew, willingly, and as to Major Armstrong.... However he can always find my address if he cares to..."

Vivie (sits down in one of the arm chairs and Norie takes the other): "Oh don't pity me. I love hard work and work which interests me. And as to working for *you*, you know there's nothing I wouldn't..."

Norie: "Oh stow that!... You've been a full-fledged partner for a year and ought to be getting callous or suspicious ... I *did* take some money out of the petty cash yesterday. I must remember to put it down. I took quite a lot ... for theatre tickets ... and you may be suspecting Bertie Adams ... we can't call this an Adamless Eden, can we? I wonder why we keep an office boy and not an office girl? I suppose such things will soon be coming into being. We've women clerks and typewriteresses ... Adams, I notice, is growing, and he has the trace of a moustache and is already devoted to you ... dog-like..."

Vivie: "He's still more devoted to cricket, fortunately; and as soon as Rose and Lilian had gone he was off too.... Only, I fancy, he discards Regent's Park now in favour of Hendon or Herne Hill..."

Norie: "Now, about Frank Gardner..."

Vivie: "Yes, that cablegram.... Let's frame it and send it off as soon as we can; then get tea ready. Talking of tea: I was just thinking before Frank's letter came how much good you'd done me—in many other ways than setting me up in business."

Norie: "Shut up!..."

Vivie: "How, when we first worked together, I used to think it necessary to imitate men by drinking an occasional whiskey and soda—though I loathe spirits—and smoking a cigar—ugh!—And how you drew me back to tea and a self-respecting womanliness—China tea, of course, and cigarettes. Why *should* we have wanted to be like men?... much better to be the New Woman....

"As to Frank's cablegram..." (Goes to bureau, tries over several drafts of message, consults Postal Guide as to cable rates *per* word, and reads aloud) ... "How's this? 'Captain Frank Gardner Camp Hospital Colesberg Cape Colony. Sorry must say no Best wishes recovery writing. Vivie.' That'll cost just Two pounds and out of the balance I shall buy a good parcel of books to send him, and some strawberries and cakes for our tea." (Therewith she puts on hat carefully—for she is always very particular, in a young-gentlemanly way, about her appearance—goes out to send off cablegram from Chancery Lane post-office, buy strawberries and cakes from Fleet Street shops, and so back to the office by four o'clock. Meantime Norie is reading through some of the recent correspondence on the file.)

Vivie (on her return): "Pouf! It *was* hot in Fleet Street! I'm sorry for poor Frankie, because he seems so to have set his heart on marrying me. But I do hope he will take this answer as *final*."

Norie: "I suppose you are not refusing him for the same old reason—that vague suggestion that he might be your half-brother?"

Vivie: "Oh *no*! Besides I pretty well know for a fact he isn't, he simply couldn't be. I'm absolutely sure my father wasn't Sam Gardner, any more than George Crofts was. I believe it was a young Irish seminarist, some student for the priesthood whom my mother met in Belgium the year before I was born. If I ever find out more I will tell you. *You* haven't seen 'Soapy Sam,' the Vicar of Woodcote, or that beast, George Crofts; but if you *had*, you'd be as sure as I am that neither of them was *my* father—thank goodness! As to Frank—yes—for a short time I *was* fond of him—till I learnt about my mother's 'profession.' It was rather a silly sort of fondness. He was two years younger than I; I suppose my feeling for him was half motherly ... I neither encouraged him nor did I repel him. I think I was experimenting ... I rather wanted to know what it felt like to be kissed by a man. Frank was a nice creature, so far as a man can be. But all those horrid revelations that broke up our summer stay at Haslemere four years ago—when I ran away to you—gave me an utter disgust for marriage. And what a life mine would have been if I had married him then; or after he went out to South Africa! *Ghastly*! Want of money would have made us hate one another and Frank would have been sure to become patronizing. Because I was without a father in the legitimate way he would have thought he was conferring a great honour on me by marrying me, and would probably have expected me to drudge for him while he idled his time away.... Oh, when I think what a life I have led here, with you, full of interesting work and bright prospects, free from money anxieties—dearest, dearest Norie—I can't thank you enough. No, I'm not going to be sentimental—the New Woman is never that. I'm going to get the tea ready; and after we've had tea on the balcony we really must go into business matters.

Your being away so much the last fortnight, things have accumulated that I did not like to decide for myself..."

Norie (speaking rather louder as Vivie is now busy in the adjoining roomlet, boiling the kettle on the gas stove and preparing the tea): "Yes. And I've got *lots* to talk over with you. All sorts of plans have come into my head. I don't know whether I have been eating anything more than usually brain stimulating—everything has a physical basis—but I have come back from this scattered holiday full of new ideas."

Presently they are seated on camp-stools sipping tea, eating strawberries and cakes, under the striped sun-blind.

Norie continues: "Do you remember Beryl Clarges at Newnham?"

Vivie: "Yes—the pretty girl—short, curly hair, brown eyes, rather full lips, good at mathematics—hockey ... purposely shocked you by her outspokenness—well?"

Norie: "Well, she's had a baby ... a month ago ... awful rumpus with her people ... Father's Dean Clarges ... Norwich or Ely, I forget which ... They've put her in a Nursing Home in Seymour Street. Mother wears a lace mantilla and cries softly. Beryl went wrong, as they call it, with an architect."

Vivie: "Pass your cup ... Don't take *all* the strawberries (*Norie*: "Sorry! Absence of mind—I've left you three fat ones") Architect? Strange! I always thought all architects were like Praddy—had no passions except for bricks and mortar and chiselled stone and twirligig iron grilles ... perhaps just a thrill over a nude statue. Why, till you told me this I'd as soon have trusted my daughter—if I had one— with an architect as with a Colonel of Engineers—You know! The kind that believes in the identity of the Ten Lost

Tribes with the British and is a True Protestant! Poor Beryl!
But how? what? when? why?"

Norie: "I think it began at Cambridge—the acquaintance
did ... Later, it developed into a passion. He had already one
wife in Sussex somewhere and four children. He took a flat
for her in Town—a studio—because Berry had given up
mathematics and was going in for sculpture; and there,
whenever he could get away from Storrington or some such
place and from his City office, he used to visit Beryl. This
had been going on for three years. But last February she had
to break it to her mother that she was six months gone. The
other wife knows all about it but refuses to divorce the
naughty architect, and at the same time has cut off
supplies—What *cowards* men are and how *little* women
stand by women! And then it's a poor deanery and Beryl has
five younger brothers that have got to be educated. Her
sculpture was little more than commissions executed for her
architect's building and I expect that resource will now
disappear ... I half think I shall bring her in here, when she is
well again. She's got a very good head-piece and you know
we are expanding our business ... She'd make a good House
Agent ... She writes sometimes for *Country Life*..."

Vivie: "Ye-es.... But you can't provide for many more of our
college-mates. Any more gone wrong?"

Norie: "It depends how you qualify 'wrong.' I really don't see
that it is 'wronger' for a young woman to yield to 'storge' and
have a baby out of wedlock than for a man to engender that
baby. Society doesn't damn the man, unless he is a Cabinet
Minister or a Cleric; but it does its best to ruin the woman ...
unless she's an actress or a singer. If a woman likes to go
through all the misery of pregnancy and the pangs of
delivery on her own account and without being legally tied
up with a man, why can't she? Beryl, at any rate, is quite

unashamed, and says she shall have as many children as her earnings support ... that it will be great fun choosing their sires—more variety in their types.... Is *she* the New Woman, I wonder?"

Vivie: "Well the whole thing bores me ... I suppose I am embittered and disgusted. I'm sick of all this sexual nonsense.... Yes, after all, I approve of the marriage tie: it takes away the romance of love, and it's that romance which is usually so time-wasting and so dangerous. It conceals often a host of horrors ... But I'm a sort of neuter. All I want in life is hard work ... a cause to fight for.... Revenge ... revenge on Man. God! How I hate men; how I despise them! We can do anything they can if we train and educate. I have taken to your business because it is one of the crafty paths we can follow to creep into Man's fastnesses of the Law, the Stock-Market, the Banks and Actuarial work...."

Norie: "My dear! You have quite a platform manner already. I predict you will soon be addressing audiences of rebellious women.... But I am more the Booker Washington of my sex. I want women to work—even at quite humble things— before they insist on equal rights with man. At any rate I want to help them to make an honest livelihood without depending on some one man.... Business seems to be good, eh? If the first half of this year is equalled by the second, I should think there would be a profit to be divided of quite a thousand pounds?"

Vivie: "Quite. Of course we are regular pirates. None of the actuarial or accountancy corporations will admit women, so we can't pass exams and call ourselves chartered actuaries or incorporated accountants. But if women clients choose to consult us there is no law to prevent them, or to make our giving advice illegal. So we advise and estimate and do accounts and calculate probabilities. Then although we can't call ourselves Solicitors we can—or at any rate we do—give legal advice. We can't figure on the Stock Exchange, but we can advise clients about their investments and buy and sell stock and real estate (By the bye I want you to give me your opinion on the tithe question, the liability on that Kent fruit farm). We are consulted on contracts ... I'm going to start a women authors' branch, and perhaps a tourist agency. Some day we will have a women's publishing business, we'll set up a women's printing press, a paper mill.... Of course as you know I am working hard on law ... not only to understand men's roguery in every direction, but so that if necessary I can add pleading in the courts to some other woman's solicitor work. That's going to be my first struggle with Man: to claim admittance to the Bar.... If we can once breach that rampart the Vote must inevitably follow. Oh *how* we have been dumb before our shearers! The rottenness of Man's law.... The perjury, corruption, waste of time, special pleading that go on in our male courts of *in*justice, the verdicts of male juries!"

Norie: "Just so. But can't you find a little time to be social? Why be so morose? For instance, why not come and be introduced to Michael Rossiter? He's a dear—amazingly clever—a kind of prophet—Your one confidant, Stead, thinks a lot of him."

Vivie: "*Dear* Norie—I can't. I swore two years ago I would drop Society and run no risk of being found out as 'Mrs. Warren's daughter.' That beast George Crofts revenged himself because I wouldn't marry him by letting it be known here and there that I *was* the daughter of the 'notorious Mrs. Warren'; whereupon several of the people I liked—you remember?—dropped me—the Burne-Joneses, the Lacrevys. Or if it wasn't Crofts some other swine did. But for the fact that it would upset our style as a firm I could change my name: call myself something quite different....

"D'you know, I've sometimes thought I'd cut my hair short and dress in men's clothes, and go out into the world as a man ... my voice is almost a tenor—*Such* a lark! I'd get admitted to the Bar. But the nuisance about that would be the references. I'm an outlaw, you see, through no fault of mine.... I couldn't give *you* as a reference, and I don't know any man who would be generous enough to take the risk of participating in the fraud.... unless it were Praed—good old Praddy. I'm sure it's been done now and again. They call Judge FitzSimmons 'an old woman.' Well, d'you know, I believe he *is* ... a wise old woman."

Norie: "Well: bide a wee, till our firm is doing a roaring business: I can pretend then to take in a male partner, p'raps. Rose and Lilian are very hard-working and we can't afford to lose them yet. If you appeared one morning dressed as a young man they might throw up their jobs and go elsewhere..."

Vivie: "You may be quite sure I won't let *you* down. Moreover I haven't the money for any vagaries yet, though I have an instinct that it is coming. You know those Charles Davis shares I bought at 5*s*. 3*d*.? Well, they rose to 29*s*. whilst you were away; so I sold out. We had three hundred, and that, less commissions, made about L350 profit; the boldest coup we have had yet. And all because I spotted that new find of emery powder in Tripoli, saw it in a Consular Report....

"I want to be rich and therefore powerful, Norie! Then people will forget fast enough about my shameful parentage."

Norie: "How *is* she? Do you ever hear from or of her now?"

Vivie: "I haven't heard *from* her for two years, since I left her letters unanswered. But I hear *of* her every now and again. No. Not through Crofts. I suppose you know—if you take any interest in that wretch—that since he married the American quakeress he took his name off the *Warren Hotels Company* and sold out much of his interest. He is now living in great respectability, breeding race horses. They even say he has given up whiskey. He has got a son and has endowed six cots in a Children's hospital. No. I think it must be *mother* who has notices posted to me, probably through that scoundrel, Bax Strangeways ... generally in the *London Argus* and the *Vie-de-Paris*—cracking up the Warren Hotels in Brussels, Berlin, Buda-Pest and Roquebrune. *What* a comedy!...

"There's my Aunt Liz at Winchester—Mrs. Canon Burstall—won't know me—I'm too compromising. But I'm sure her money-bags have been filled at one time—perhaps are still—out of the profits on mother's 'Hotels.'"

Norie: "I didn't remember your aunt was married ... or rather I suppose I did, but thought she was a widow, real or *soi-disant...*"

Vivie: "So she is, after four years of happy married life! My 'uncle' Canon Burstall—Oh what a screaming joke the whole thing is!... I doubt if he was aware he had a niece.... Don't you remember he was killed in the Alps last autumn?..."

Norie: "I remember your going down to see your aunt after you broke off relations with your mother in—in—1897...?"

Vivie: "Yes. I wanted to see how the land lay and not judge any one unfairly. Besides I—I—didn't like being dependent entirely on you—at that time—for support: and Praed was in Italy. I knew that Aunt Liz, like mother, was illegitimate—and guessed she had once made her living in the higher walks of prostitution—she was a stockbroker's mistress at one time—. But she had married and settled down at Winchester ... She met her Canon—the Alpine traveller ... in Switzerland. I felt if she took no money from mother's 'houses,' I could perhaps make a home with her, or at any rate have *some* kith and kin to go to. She had no children.... But—I must have told you all this years ago?—she almost pushed me out of her house for fear I should stay till the Canon came in from the afternoon service; denied everything; threatened me as though I was a blackmailer; almost looked as if she could have killed me and buried me in the garden of the Canonry....

"I've examined the business of the *Warren Hotels Ltd.* since then, but it's a private company, and all its doings are so cleverly concealed.... Aunt Liz doesn't figure amongst the shareholders any more than Crofts does. That horrid Bax holds most of the shares now, and mother the rest.... Yet Aunt Liz must be rich and she certainly didn't get it from the Canon, who only left a net personality of under L4,000.... I read his will at Somerset House.... She has had her portrait in the *Queen* because she gave a large subscription to the underpinning of Winchester Cathedral and the restoration of Wolvesey as a clergy house.... Mother must be very rich, I should judge, from certain indications. I expect *she* will retire from the 'Hotels,' some day, wipe out the past, and buy a new present with her money.... She'll have *her* portrait in the *Queen* some day as a Vice-President of the Girls' Friendly Society!... And yet she's such a gambler and a rake that she *may* get pinched over the White Slave traffic.... I was on tenterhooks over that Lewissohn case the other day, fearing every moment to see mother's name mixed up with it, or else an allusion to her 'Hotels.' But I fancy she has been wise enough—indeed I should guess that Aunt Liz had long ago warned her to leave England alone as a recruiting ground and to collect her chambermaids, waitresses, musicians, typists from the Continent only—Austria, Alsace, Bohemia, Belgium, Italy, the Rhineland, Paris, Russia, Poland. Knowing what we British people are, can't you almost predict the *bias* of Aunt Liz's mind? How she would solace herself that her dividends were not derived from the prostitution of English girls but only of 'foreigners'?..."

Norie: "You seem to have studied the geography of the business pretty thoroughly!..."

Vivie (bitterly): "Yes. I have talked it over with Stead from time to time. I believe he has only spared mother and the Warren Hotels out of consideration for me ... He wants me to change my surname and give myself a chance..."

Norie: "I see" (pausing). "Of course it is rather an idea, as you refuse to disguise yourself by marriage. You'd change your name and then listen with equanimity to fulminations against the Warren Hotels. But there would be an awkwardness in the firm. We oughtn't to change our title just as we are getting a good clientele.... I must think ... If only we could pretend you'd been left some property—but that sort of lie is soon found out!—and had to change your name to—to—to. Oh well, we could soon think of some name beginning with a W—Walters, Waddilove—Waddilove is a delicious name in cold weather, suggesting cotton-wool or a warm duvet—or Wilson—or Wilberforce. But I'm afraid the staff—Rose Mullet and Lily Steynes and the amorous Bertie Adams—would think it odd, put two and two together, and guess right. Warren, after all, is such a common name. And we've got so used to our three helpers, we could hardly turn them off, and take on new people whom perhaps we couldn't trust.... We must think it over....

"Now I must go back to Queen Anne's Mansions and sit a little while with Mummy. Come and dine with us? There'll

only be us three ... no horrid man to fall in love with you....
You needn't put on a low dress ... and we'll go to the dress
circle at some play afterwards."

Vivie: "But those papers on my desk? I must have your
opinion for or against..."

Norie: "All right. It's half-past five. I'll give them half an
hour's study whilst you wash up the tea things and titivate.
Then we'll take a hansom to Quansions: the Underground is
so grimy."

CHAPTER II

HONORIA AND HER FRIENDS

The story of Honoria Fraser was something like this: partly guesswork, I admit. Although I know her well I can only put her past together by deductions based on a few admitted facts, one or two letters and occasional unfinished sentences, interrupted by people coming in. Is it not *always* thus with our friends and acquaintances? I long to know all about them from their birth (including date and place of birth and parentage) onwards; what the father's profession was and why on earth he married the mother (after I saw the daguerreotype portrait), and how they became possessed of so much money, and why she went back to live with *her* mother between the birth of her second child and the near advent of her third. But in how very few cases do we know their whole story, do we even care to know more than is sufficient for our purpose in issuing or accepting invitations? There are the Dombeys—the Gorings as they're now called, who live near us. I've seen the tombstone of Lucilla Smith in Goring churchyard, but I don't know *for a fact* that Lord Goring was the father of Lucilla's son (who was killed in the war). I guess he was, from this and that, from what Mrs. Legg told me, and what I overheard at the Sterns'. If he wasn't, then he has only himself to thank for the wrong assumption: I mean, from his goings-on.

Then again, the Clementses, who live at the Grange. I feel instinctively they are *nice* people, but I haven't the least idea who *she* was and how *he* made his money, though from his acreage and his motors I am entitled to assume he has a large income. She seems to know a lot about Spain; but I don't feel encouraged to ask her: "Was your father in the wine trade? Is *that* why you know Xeres so well?" Clements himself has in his study an enlarged photograph of a handsome woman with a kind of mourning wreath round the frame—beautifully carved. Is it the portrait of a former wife? Or of a sister who committed suicide? Or was it merely bought in Venice for the sake of the carving? Perhaps I shall know some day—if it matters. In a moment of expansion during the Railway Strike, Mrs. Clements will say: "*That* was poor Walter's first. She died of acute dyspepsia, poor thing, on their marriage tour, and was buried at Venice. Don't ever allude to it because he feels it so dreadfully." And my curiosity will have been rewarded for its long and patient restraint. Clements' little finger on his left hand is mutilated. I have never asked why—a lawn-mowing machine? Or a bite from some passionate mistress in a buried past? I note silently that he disapproves of palmistry—

But about Honoria Fraser, to whom I was introduced by Mr. George Bernard Shaw twenty years ago: She was born in 1872, as *Who's Who* will tell you; also that she was the daughter and eldest child of a famous physician (Sir Meldrum Fraser) who wrought some marvellous cures in the 'sixties, 'seventies and 'eighties, chiefly by dieting and psycho-therapy. (He got his knighthood in the first jubilee year for reducing to reasonable proportions the figure of good-hearted, thoroughly kindly, and much loved Princess Mary of Oxford.) He—Honoria's father—was married to a beautiful woman, a relation of Bessie Rayner Parkes, with inherited advanced views on the Rights and Position of Woman. Lady Fraser was, indeed, an early type of Suffragist and also wrote some poetry which was far from bad. They had two children: Honoria, born, as I say, in 1872; and John (John Stuart Mill Fraser was his full name—too great a burden to be borne) four years later than Honoria, who was devoted to him, idolized him, as did his mother and father. Honoria went to Bedford College and Newnham; John to one of the two most famous of our public schools (I need not be more precise), with Cambridge in view afterwards.

But in the case of John a tragedy occurred. He had risen to be head of the school; statesmen with little affectation applauded him on speech days. He had been brilliant as a batsman, was a champion swimmer, and *facile princeps* in the ineptitudes of the classics; and showed a dazzling originality in other studies scarcely within the school curriculum. Further he was growing out of boy gawkiness into a handsome youth of an Apolline mould, when, on the morning of his eighteenth birthday, he was found dead in his bed, with a bottle of cyanide of potassium on the bed-table to explain why.

All else was wrapt in mystery ... at any rate it was a mystery I have no wish to lay bare. The death and the inquest verdict, "Suicide while of unsound mind, due to overstudy," broke his father's heart and his mother's: in the metaphorical meaning of course, because the heart is an unemotional pump and it is the brain and the nerve centres that suffer from our emotions. Sir Meldrum Fraser died a year after his son. He left a fortune of eighty thousand pounds. Half of this went at once to Honoria and the other half to the life-use of Lady Fraser with a reversion to her daughter.

Honoria after her father's death left Cambridge and moved her mother from Harley Street to Queen Anne's Mansions so that with her shattered nerves and loss of interest in life she might have no household worries, or at any rate nothing worse than remonstrating with the still-room maids on the twice-boiled water brought in for the making of tea; or with the culinary department over the monotonous character of the savouries or the tepid ice creams which dissolved so rapidly into fruit-juice when they were served after a house-dinner.[1] Honoria herself, mistress of a clear two thousand pounds a year, and more in prospect, carried out plans formed while still at Newnham after her brother's death. She, like Vivien Warren, her three-years-younger friend and college-mate, was a great mathematician—a thing I never could be and a status I am incapable of understanding; consequently one I view at first with the deepest respect. I am quite astonished when I meet a male or female mathematician and find they require food as I do, are less quick at adding up bridge scores, lose rather than win at Goodwood, and write down the "down" train instead of the "up" in their memorabilia. But there it is. They have only to apply sines and co-sines, tangents and logarithms to a stock exchange quotation for me to grovel before their superior wisdom and consult them at every turn in life.

[Footnote 1: This, of course, was twenty, years ago.— H.H.J.]

Honoria had resolved to turn her great acquirements in Algebra and the Higher Mathematics to practical purposes. Being the ignoramus that I am—in this direction—I cannot say how it was to be done; but both she and Vivie had grasped the possibilities which lay before exceptionally well-educated women on the Stock Exchange, in the Provision markets, in the Law, in Insurance calculations, and generally in steering other and weaker women through the difficulties and pitfalls of our age; when in nine cases out of thirteen (Honoria worked out the ratio) women of large or moderate means have only dishonest male proficients to guide them.

Moreover Honoria's purpose was two-fold. She wished to help women in their business affairs, but she also wanted to find careers for women. She, like Vivien Warren, was a nascent suffragist—perhaps a born suffragist, a reasoned one; because the ferment had been in her mother, and her grandmother was a friend of Lydia Becker and a cousin of Mrs. Belloc. John's death had been a horrible numbing shock to Honoria, and she felt hardly in her right mind for three months afterwards. Then on reflection it left some tarnish on her family, even if the memory of the dear dead boy, the too brilliant boy, softened from the poignancy of utter disappointment into a tender sorrow and an infinite pity and forgiveness.

But the tragedy turned her thoughts from marriage to some mission of well-doing. She determined to devote that proportion of her inheritance which would have been John's share to this end: the liberation and redemption of women.

She was no "anti-man," like Vivie. She liked men, if truth were told, a tiny wee bit more than women. But she wished in the moods that followed her brother's death in 1894 to be a mother by adoption, a refuge for the fallen, the bewildered, the unstrung. She helped young men back into the path of respectability and wage-earning as well as young women. She was even, when opportunity offered, a matchmaker.

Being heiress eventually to L4,000 a year (a large income in pre-war days) and of attractive appearance, she had no lack of suitors, even though she thought modern dancing inane, and had little skill at ball-games. I have indicated her appearance by some few phrases already; but to enable you to visualize her more definitely I might be more precise. She was a tall woman rather than large built, like the young Juno when first wooed by Jove. Where she departed from the Junonian type she turned towards Venus rather than

Minerva; in spite of being a mathematician. You meet with her sisters in physical beauty among the Americans of Pennsylvania, where, to a stock mainly Anglo-Saxon, is added a delicious strain of Gallic race; or you see her again among the Cape Dutch women who have had French Huguenot great grandparents. It is perhaps rather impertinent continuing this analysis of her charm, seeing that she lives and flourishes more than ever, twenty years after the opening of my story; not very different in outward appearance at 48, as Lady Armstrong—for of course, as you guess already, she married Major—afterwards Sir Petworth—Armstrong—than she was at twenty-eight, the partner, friend and helper of Vivien Warren.

Being in comfortable circumstances, highly educated, handsome, attractive, with a mezzo-soprano voice of rare beauty and great skill as a piano-forte accompanyist, she had not only suitors who took her rejection without bitterness, but hosts of friends. She knew all the nice London people of her day: Lady Feenix, who in some ways resembled her, Diana Dombey, who did not *quite* approve of her, being a little uncertain yet about welcoming the New Woman, all the Ritchies, married and unmarried, Lady Brownlow, the Duchess of Bedford (Adeline), the Michael Fosters, most of the Stracheys (she liked the ones I liked), the Hubert Parrys, the Ripons (how she admired Lady Ripon, as who did not!), Mrs. Alfred Lyttelton, Miss Lena Ashwell, the Bernard Shaws, the Wilfred Meynells, the H.G. Wellses, the Sidney Webbs; and—leaving uninstanced a number of other delightful, warm-blooded, pleasant-voiced, natural-mannered people—the Rossiters.

Or at least, Michael Rossiter. For although you could tolerate for his sake Mrs. Rossiter, and even find her a source of quiet amusement, you could hardly say you liked her—not in the way you could say it of most of the men and women I have specified. Michael Rossiter, who comes into this story, ought really if there were a discriminating wide-awake, up-to-date Providence—which there is not—to have met Honoria when she was twenty. (At nineteen such a woman is still immature; and moreover until she was twenty, Honoria had not mastered the Binomial Theorem.) Had he married her at that period he would himself have been about twenty-seven which is quite soon enough for a great man of science to marry and procreate geniuses. But as a matter of fact, when he came down to Cambridge in—? 1892—to deliver a course of Vacation lectures on embryology, he was already two years married to Linda Bennet, an heiress, the daughter and niece (her parents died when she was young and she lived with an uncle and aunt) of very rich manufacturers at Leeds.

So, though his eye, quick to discern beauty, and his brain tentacles ready to detect intelligence combined with a lovely nature, soon singled out Honoria Fraser, amongst a host of less attractive girl-graduates, he had no more thought of falling in love with her than with a princess of the blood-royal. He might, long since, within a month of his marriage have found out his Linda to be a pretty little simpleton with a brain incapable of taking in any more than it had learnt at a Scarborough finishing school; but he was too instinctive a gentleman to indulge in any flirtation, any deviation what-ever from mental or physical monogamy. For he remem-bered always that it was his wife's money which had enabled him to pursue his great researches without the heart-breaking delays, limitations and insufficiencies involved in Govern-ment or Royal Society grants; and that Linda had not only endowed him with all her worldly goods—all but those he had insisted in putting into settlement—but that she had given him all her heart and confidence as well.

Still, he liked Honoria. She was eager to learn much else

beyond the hard-grained muses of the square and cube; she was the daughter of a prosperous and boldly experimental physician, whose wife was a champion of women's rights. So he pressed Honoria to come with her mother and make the acquaintance of himself and Linda in Portland Place.

Why was Michael Rossiter wedded to Linda Bennet when he was no more than twenty-five, and she just past her coming of age? Because fresh from Edinburgh and Cambridge and with a reputation for unusual intuition in Biology and Chemistry he had come to be Science master at a great College in the North, and thus meeting Linda at the Philosophical Institute of Leeds had caused her to fall in love with him whilst he lectured on the Cainozoic fauna of Yorkshire. He was himself a Northumbrian of borderland stock: something of the Dane and Angle, the Pict and Briton with a dash of the Gypsy folk: a blend which makes the Northumbrian people so much more productive of manly beauty, intellectual vivacity, bold originality than the slow-witted, bulky, crafty Saxons of Yorkshire or the under-sized, rugged-featured Britons of Lancashire.

Linda fell in love all in one evening with his fiery eyes, black beard, the Northumbrian burr of his pronunciation, and the daring of his utterances, though she could scarcely grasp one of his hypotheses. Her uncle and aunt being narrowly pietistic she was bored to death with the Old Testament, and Rossiter's scarcely concealed contempt for the Mosaic story of creation captured her intellect; while the physical attraction she felt was that which the tall, handsome, resolute brunet has for the blue-eyed fluffy little blonde. She openly made love to him over the tea and coffee served at the "soiree" which followed the lecture. Her slow-witted guardian had no objection to offer; and there were not wanting go-betweens to urge on Rossiter with stories of her wealth and the expanding value of her financial interests. He wanted to marry; he was touched by her ill-concealed passion, found her pretty and appealingly childlike. So, after a short wooing, he married her and her five thousand pounds a year, and settled down in Park Crescent, Portland Place, so as to be near the Zoo and Tudell's dissecting rooms, to have the Royal Botanic gardens within three minutes' walk, and the opportunity of turning a large studio in the rear of his house into a well-equipped chemical and dissecting laboratory. One of his close pursuits at that time was the analysis of the Thyroid gland and its functions, its over or under development in British statesmen, dramatic authors and East End immigrants.

CHAPTER III

DAVID VAVASOUR WILLIAMS

It is in the spring of 1901. A fine warm evening, but at eight o'clock the dusk is already on the verge of darkness as Honoria emerges from the lift at her Chancery Lane Office (near the corner of Carey Street), puts her latch-key into the door of the partners' room, and finds herself confronting the silhouette of a young man against the western glow of the big window.

Norie (inwardly rather frightened): "Hullo! Who are *you* and what are you doing here?"

Vivie (mimicking a considerate, cringing burglar): "Sorry to startle you, lidy, but I don't mean no 'arm. I'll go quiet. Me name's D.V. Williams..."

Norie: "You absurd creature! But you shouldn't play such pranks on these respectable premises. You gave me a *horrid* start, and I realized for the first time that I've got a heart. I really must sit down and pant."

Vivie: "I am sorry, dearest. I had not the slightest notion you would be letting yourself into the office at this hour—8 o'clock—and I was just returning from my crammers..."

Norie: "I came for those Cranston papers. Mother is ill. I may have to sit up with her after Violet Hunt goes, so I thought I would come here, fetch the bundle of papers and plans, and go through them in the silent watches of the night, *if* mother sleeps. But do you mean to say you have already started this masquerade?"

Vivie: "I do. You see Christabel Pankhurst has been turned down as a barrister. They won't let her qualify for the Bar, because she's a woman, so they certainly won't let *me* with my pedigree; just as, merely because we are women, they won't let us become Chartered Actuaries or Incorporated Accountants. After we had that long talk last June I got a set of men's clothes together, a regular man's outfit. The suit doesn't fit over well but I am rectifying that by degrees. I went to a general outfitter in Cornhill and told a cock-and-bull story—as it was an affair of ready cash they didn't stop to question me about it. I said something about a sea-faring brother, just my height, a trifle stouter in build—lost all his kit at sea—been in hospital—now in convalescent home—how I wanted to save him all the fatigue possible—wouldn't want more than reach-me-downs at present, etc., etc. They rather flummoxed me at first by offering a merchant service uniform, but somehow I got over that, though this serge suit has rather a sea-faring cut. I got so unnecessarily explanatory with the shopman that he began to pay me compliments, said my brother must be a good-looking young chap if he was at all like me. However, I got away with the things in a cab, and told the cab to drive to St. Paul's station, and on the way re-directed him here.

"Last autumn I began practising at night-time after all our familiars had left these premises. Purposely I did not tell you because I feared your greater caution and instinctive respectability might discourage me. Otherwise, nobody's spotted me, so far. I'd intended breaking it to you any day now, because I've gone too far to draw back, for weal or woe. But either we have been rushed with business, or you've been anxious about Lady Fraser—How is she?" (Norie interpolates "Very poorly.") "So truly sorry!—I was generally just about to tell you when Rose or Lilian—tiresome things!—would begin most assiduously passing in and out with papers. Even now I mustn't keep you, with your mother so ill..."

Norie (looking at her wrist-watch): "Violet has very kindly promised to stay with mother till ten.... I can give you an hour, though I must take a few minutes off that for the firm's business as I haven't been here much for three days..." (They talk business for twenty minutes, during which Norie says: "It's really *rather* odd, how those clothes change you! I feel vaguely compromised with a handsome young man bending over me, his cheek almost touching mine!"—and Vivie retorts "Oh, *don't* be an ass!")

Norie: "So you really *are* going to take the plunge?"

Vivie: "I really *am*. As soon as it suits your convenience, Vivie Warren will retire from your firm and go abroad. You must either replace her by Beryl Clarges or allow Mr. Vavasour Williams" (Honoria interpolates: "*Ridiculous* name! How did you think of it?") "to come and assist in the day-time or after office hours. You can say to the winds that he is Vivie's first cousin, remarkably like her in some respects.... Rose Mullet is engaged to be married and is only—she told me yesterday with many blushes—staying on to oblige us. Lilian Steynes said the other day that if we were making any changes in the office, much as she liked her work here, her mother having died she thought it was her duty to go and live with her maternal aunt in the country. The aunt thinks she can get her a post as a brewery clerk at Aylesbury, and she is longing to breed Aylesbury ducks in her spare time.—There is Bertie Adams, it's true. There's something so staunch about him and he is so useful that he and Praed and Stead are the three exceptions I make in my general hatred of mankind..."

Norie: "He will be very much cut up at your going—or seeming to go."

Vivie: "Just so. I think I shall write him a farewell note, saying it's only for a time: I mean, that I may return later on—dormant partnership—nothing really changed, don't you know? But that as Rose and Lilian are going, Mrs.—what does she call herself, Claridge?"—(Norie interpolates: "Yes, that was her idea: she doesn't want to blazon the name of Clarges as the symbol of Free Love, 'cos of the dear old Dean; yet Claridge will not be too much of a surrender and is sure to invoke respectability, because of the Hotel")—"Mrs. Claridge, then, is coming in my stead—He's to help her all he can—and my cousin, who is reading for the Bar, will also look in when you are very busy. I shall, of course, see about rooms in one of the Inns of Court—the Temple perhaps. I have been stealthily watching Fig Tree Court. I *think* I can get chambers there—a man is turning out next month—got a Colonial appointment—I've put my new name down at the lodge and I shall have to rack my brains for references—you will do for one—or perhaps not—however that I can work out later. Of course I won't take the final plunge till I have secured the rooms. Meantime I will use my bedroom here but promise you I will be awfully prudent..."

Norie: "I couldn't possibly have Beryl 'living in,' with a child hanging about the place; so I think if you *do* go I shall turn your bedroom into an apartment which Beryl and I can use for toilet purposes but where we can range out on book-shelves a whole lot of our books. Just now they are most inconveniently stored away in boxes. It's rather tiresome about Beryl. I believe she's going to have *another* child. At any rate she says it may be four months before she can come to work here regularly. I asked her about it the other day, because if mother gets worse I may be hindered about coming to the office, and I didn't want you to get overworked,—so I said to Beryl.... That reminds me, she referred to the coming child and added that its father was a policeman. Quite a nice creature in his private life. Of course she's only kidding. I expect it's the architect all the time. You know how she delighted in shocking us at Newnham. I wish she hadn't this kink about her. P'raps I'm getting old-fashioned already—You used to call me 'the Girondist.' But if the New Woman *is* to go on the loose and be unmoral like the rabbits, won't the cause suffer from middle-class opposition?"

Vivie: "Perhaps. But it may gain instead the sympathies of the lower and the upper classes. Why do you bother about Beryl? I agree with you in disliking all this sexuality..."

Norie: "Does one *ever* quite know why one likes people? There is *something* about Beryl that gets over me; and she *is* a worker. You know how she grappled with that Norfolk estate business?"

Vivie: "Well, it's fortunate she and I have not met since Newnham days. You must tip her the story that I am going away for a time—abroad—and that a young—young, because I look a mere boy, dressed up in men's clothes—a young cousin of mine, learned in the law, is going to drop in occasionally and do some of the work..."

Norie: "I'm afraid I'm rather weak-willed. I *ought* to stop this prank before it has gone too far, just as I ought to discourage Beryl's babies. Your schemes sound so stagey. Off the stage you never take people in with such flimsy stories and weak disguises—you'll tie yourself up into knots and finally get sent to prison.... However.... I can't help being rather tickled by your idea. It's vilely unjust, men closing two-thirds of the respectable careers to women, to bachelor women above all..." (A pause, and the two women look out on a blue London dotted with lemon-coloured, straw-coloured, mauve-tinted lights, with one cold white radiance hanging over the invisible Piccadilly Circus)—"Well, go ahead! Follow your star! I can be confident of one thing, you won't do anything mean or disgraceful. Deceiving Man while his vile laws and restrictions remain in force is no crime. Be prudent, so far as compromising our poor little firm here is concerned, because if you bring down my grey hairs with sorrow to the grave we shall lose a valuable source of income. Besides: any public scandal just now in which I was mixed up might kill my mother. Want any money?"

Vivie: "You generous darling! *Never, never* shall I forget your kindness and your trust in me. You have at any rate saved one soul alive." (Honoria deprecates gratitude.) "No, I don't want money—yet. You made me take and bank L700 last January over that Rio de Palmas coup—heaps more than my share. Altogether I've got about L1,000 on deposit at the C. and C. bank, the Temple Bar branch. I've many gruesome faults, but I *am* thrifty. I think I can win through to the Bar on that. Of course, if afterwards briefs don't come in—"

Norie: "Well, there'll always be the partnership which will go on unaltered. I shall pretend you are only away for a time and your share shall be regularly paid in to your bank. Of course I shall meet Mr. Vavasour Williams now and again and I can tell him things and consult with him. If we think Beryl, after she is installed here as head clerk—of course I shan't make her a partner for *years* and *years*—not at all if she remains flighty—if we think she is unsuspicious, and Bertie Adams likewise, and the new clerks and the housekeeper and her husband, there is no reason why you should not come here fairly often and put in as much work as you can on our business."

Vivie: "Yes. Of course I must be careful of one predicament. I have studied the regulations about being admitted to the English Bar. They are very quaint and medieval or early Georgian. You mayn't be a Chartered Accountant or Actuary—the Lord alone knows why! I suppose some Lord Chancellor was done in the eye in Elizabeth's reign by an actuary and laid down that law. Equally you mayn't be a clergyman. As to that we needn't distress ourselves. It's rather piteous about the prohibiting Accountants, because as women we are not allowed to qualify in *any* capacity as Accountants or Actuaries; and work here is only permissible by our not pretending to belong to any recognized body like the Institute of Actuaries. So that in coming to work for you I must not seem to be in any way doing the business of Accountants or Actuaries. Indeed it might be awkward for my scheme if I was too openly associated with Fraser and Warren.

"I already think of myself as Williams—I shall pose of course as a Welshman. My appearance *is* rather Welsh, don't you think? It's the Irish blood that makes me look Keltic—I'm sure my father was an Irish student for the priesthood at Louvain, and certain scraps of information I got out of mother make me believe that *her* mother was a pretty Welsh girl from Cardiff, brought over to London Town by some ship's captain and stranded there, on Tower Hill.

"However, I have still the whole scheme to work out and when I'm ready to start on it—which will be very soon—I'll let you know. Now, though I'd love to discuss all the other details, I mustn't forget your mother will be wanting you—I wish *I* had a mother to tend—I wonder" (wistfully) "whether

I was too hard on mine?

"D'you mind posting these letters as you go out? I shall change back to Vivie Warren in a dressing gown, give myself a light supper, and then put in two hours studying Latin and Norman French. Good night, dearest!"

Two months after this conversation Vivie decided to pay a call on an old friend of her mother's, Lewis Maitland Praed, if you want his full name, a well-known architect, and one of the few male friends of Catherine Warren who had not also been her lover. Why, he never quite knew himself. When he first met her she was the boon companion, the mistress—more or less, and unattached—of a young barrister, a college friend of Praed's. Kate Warren at that time called herself Kitty Vavasour; and on the strength of having done a turn or two on the music halls considered herself an actress with a right to a professional name. It was in this guise that the "Revd." Samuel Gardner met her and had that six months' infatuation for her which afterwards caused him so much disquietude; though it preceded the taking of his ordination vows by quite a year, and his marriage to his wife—much too good for him—in 1874. [The Revd. Sam, you may remember, was the father of the scapegrace Frank who nearly captured Vivie's young affections and had written from South Africa proposing marriage at the opening of this story.]

Kate Vavasour in 1872 was an exceedingly pretty girl of nineteen or twenty; showily dressed, and quick with her tongue. She was good-natured and jolly, and though Praed himself was the essence of refinement there was something about her reckless mirth and joy in life—the immense relief of having passed from the sordid life of a barmaid to this quasi-ladyhood—that enlisted his sympathies. Though she was always somebody else's mistress until she developed her special talent as a manageress of high-class houses of accommodation, "private hotels" on the Continent, chiefly frequented by English and American *roues*—Praed kept an eye on her career, and occasionally rendered her, with some cynicism, unobtrusive friendly services in disentangling her affairs when complications threatened. He was an art student in those days of the 'seventies, possessed of about four hundred a year, beginning to go through the aesthetic phase, and not decided whether he would emerge a painter of pictures or an architect of grandiose or fantastic buildings. To his studio Miss Kitty Vavasour or Miss Kate Warren would often come and pose for the head and shoulders, or for some draped caryatid wanted for an ambitious porch in an imaginary millionaire's house in Kensington Palace Gardens. When in 1897, Vivie had learnt about her mother's "profession," she had flung off violently from all her mother's "friends," except "Praddy." She even continued to call him by this nickname, long ago bestowed on him by her mother. At distant intervals she would pay him a visit at his house and studio near Hans Place; when Honoria's advice and assistance did not meet the case of some grave perplexity.

So one afternoon in June, 1901, she came to his little dwelling with its large studio, and asked to have a long talk to him, whilst his parlour-maid—he was still a bachelor—denied him to other callers. They had tea together and Vivie plunged as quickly as possible into her problem.

"You know, Praddy dear, I want to be a Barrister. But as a female they will never call me to the Bar. So I'm going to send Vivien Warren off for a long absence abroad—the few who think about me will probably conclude that money has carried the day and that I've gone to help my mother in her business—and in her absence Mr. Vavasour Williams will take up the running. David V. Williams—don't interrupt me—will study for the Bar, eat through his terms—six dinners a year, isn't it?—pass his examinations, and be called to the English Bar in about three years from now. Didn't you once have a pupil called Vavasour Williams?"

Praed: "What, David, the Welsh boy? Yes. His name reminded me of your mother in one of her stages. David Vavasour Williams. I took him on in—let me see? I think it was in 1895 or early 1896. But how did you hear about him?"

Vivie: "Never mind, or never mind for the moment. Tell me some more about him."

Praed: "Well to sum him up briefly he was what school boys and subalterns would call 'a rotter.' Not without an almost mordid cleverness; but the Welsh strain in him which in the father turned to emotional religion—the father was Vicar or Rector of Pontystrad—came out in the boy in unhealthy fancies. He had almost the talent of Aubrey Beardsley. But I didn't think he had a good influence over my other pupils, so before I planned that Italian journey—on which you refused to accompany me—I advised him to leave my tuition—I wasn't modern enough, I said. I also advised him to make up his mind whether he wanted to be a sane architect—he despised questions of housemaids' closets and sanitation and lifts and hot-water supply—or a scene painter. I think he might have had a great career at Drury Lane over fairy palaces or millionaire dwellings. But I turned him out of my studio, though I put the fact less brutally before his father—said I should be absent a long while in Italy and that I feared the boy was too undisciplined. Afterwards I think he went into some South African police force..."

Vivie: "He did, and died last year in a South African hospital. Had he—er—er—many relations, I mean did he come of well-known people?"

Praed: "I fancy not. His father was just a dreamy old Welsh clergyman always seeing visions and believing himself a descendant of the Druids, Sam Gardner told me; and his mother had either died long ago or had run away from her husband, I forget which. In a way, I'm sorry David's dead. He had a sort of weird talent and wild good looks. By the way, he wasn't altogether unlike *you*."

Vivie: "Thank you for the double-edged compliment. However what you say is very interesting. Well now, my idea is that David Vavasour Williams did *not* die in a military hospital; he recovered and returned, firmly resolved to lead a new life.—Is his father living by the bye? Did he believe his son was dead?"

Praed: "Couldn't tell you, I'm sure. I never took any further interest in him, and until you mentioned it—I don't know on whose authority—I didn't know he was dead. On the whole a good riddance for his people, I should say, especially if he died on the field of honour. But what lunatic idea has entered your mind with regard to this poor waster?"

Vivie: "Why my idea, as I say, is that D.V.W. got cured of his necrosis of the jaw—I suppose it is not invariably deadly?—came home with a much improved morale, studied hard, and became a barrister, thinking it morally a superior calling to architecture and scene painting. In short, I shall be from this day forth Vavasour Williams, law-student! Would it be safe, d'you think, in that capacity to go down and see his old father?"

Praed: "*Vivie*! I *did* think you were a sober-minded young woman who would steer clear of—of—crime: for this impersonation would be a punishable offence..."

Sir Harry Johnston

Vivie: "*Crime*? *What* nonsense! I should consider I was justified in a Court of Equity if I burnt down or blew up the Law Courts or one of the Inns or broke the windows of the Chartered Institute of Actuaries or the Incorporated Law Society. All these institutions and many others bar the way to honourable and lucrative careers for educated women, and a male parliament gives us no redress, and a male press laughs at us for our feeble attempts to claim common rights with men. Instead of proceeding to such violence I am merely resorting to a very harmless guile in getting round the absurd restrictions imposed by the benchers of the Inns of Court, namely that all who claim a call to the Bar should not be *accountants*, *actuaries*, *clergymen* or *women*. I am going to give up the accountancy business—or rather, the law has never allowed either Honoria or me to become chartered accountants, so there is nothing to give up. To avoid any misapprehension she is going to change the title on our note paper and brass plate to 'General Inquiry Agents.' That will be sufficiently non-committal. Well then, as to sex disqualification, a few weeks hence I shall become David Vavasour Williams, and I presume he was a male? You don't have to pass a medical examination for the Bar, do you?"

Praed: "Really, Vivie, you are *unnecessarily* coarse..."

Vivie: "I don't care if I am, poor outlaw that I am! Every avenue to an honest and ambitious career seems closed to me, either because I am a woman or—in women's careers—the few that there are—because I am Kate Warren's daughter. *I* am not to blame for my mother's misdeeds, yet I am being punished for them. That beast of a friend of yours—that filthy swine, George Crofts—set it about after I refused to marry him that I was 'Mrs. Warren's Daughter,' and the few nice people I knew from Cambridge days dropped me, all except Honoria and her mother."

Praed: "Well, *I* haven't dropped you. *I'll* always stick by you" (observes that Vivie is trying to keep back her tears). "Vivie—*darling*—what do you want me to do? Why not marry me and spend half my income, take the shelter of my name—I'm an A.R.A. now—You needn't do more than keep house for me.... I'm rather a valetudinarian—dare say I shan't trouble you long—we could have a jolly good time before I went off with a heart attack—travel—study—write books together—"

Vivie (recovering herself): "Thanks, dear Praddy; you are a brick and I really—in a way—have quite got to love you. Except an office boy in Chancery Lane and W.T. Stead, I don't know any other decent man. But I'm not going to marry any one. I'm going to become Vavasour Williams—the name is rotten, but you must take what you can get. Williams is a quiet young man who only desires to be left alone to earn his living respectably at the Bar, and see there if he cannot redress the balance in the favour of women. But there is something you *could* do for me, and it is for that I came to see you to-day—by the bye, we have both let our tea grow cold, but *for goodness' sake* don't order any more on my account, or else your parlour-maid will be coming in and out and will see that I've been crying and you look flushed. What I wanted to ask was this—it's really very simple—*If Mr. Vavasour Williams, aged twenty-four, late in South Africa, once your pupil in architecture* or scene painting or whatever it was—*gives you as a reference to character, you are to say the best you can of him.* And, by the bye, he will be calling to see you very shortly and you could lend further verisimilitude to your story by renewing acquaintance with him. You will find him very much improved. In every way he will do you credit. And what is more, if you don't repel him, he will come and see you much oftener than his cousin—I'm not ashamed to adopt her as a cousin—Vivie Warren could have done. Because Vivie, with her deplorable parentage, had

Sir Harry Johnston

your good name to think of, and visited you very seldom; whereas there could be raised *no* objection from your parlour-maid if Mr. D.V. Williams came rather often to chat with you and ask your advice. Think it over, dear friend— Good-bye."

Early in July, Norie and Vivie were standing at the open west window in their partners' room at the office, trying to get a little fresh air. The staff had just gone its several ways to the suburbs, glad to have three hours of daylight before it for cricket and tennis. Confident therefore of not being overheard, Vivie began: "I've got those rooms in Fig Tree Court. I shall soon be ready to move my things in. I'll leave some of poor Vivie Warren's effects behind if you don't mind, in case she comes back some day. Do you think you can rub along if I take my departure next week? I want to give myself a fortnight's bicycle holiday in Wales—as D.V. Williams—a kind of honeymoon with Fate, before I settle down as a law student. After I come back I can devote much of the summer recess to our affairs, either openly or after office hours. You could then take a holiday, in August. You badly need one. What about Beryl?"

Norie: "Beryl is well over her accouchement and is confident of being able to start work here on August 1.... It's a boy this time. I haven't seen it, so I can't say whether it resembles a policeman more than an architect. Besides babies up till the age of six months only resemble macrocephalic idiots.... I shall be *wary* with Beryl—haven't committed myself— ourselves to any engagement beyond six months. She's amazingly clever, but I should say quite heartless. Two babies in three years, and both illegitimate—the real Mrs. Architect very much upset, no doubt, Mr. Architect getting wilder and wilder in his work through trying to maintain two establishments—they say he left out all the sanitation in Sir Peter Robinson's new house and let the builders rush up the walls without damp courses—and it's killing her father, the Dean. It's not as though she hid herself away, but she goes out so much! They are talking of turning her out of her club because of the things she says before the waitresses..."

Vivie: "What things?"

Norie: "Why, about its being very healthy to have babies when you're between the ages of twenty and thirty; and how with this twilight sleep business she doesn't mind how often; that it's fifty times more interesting than breeding dogs and cats or guinea-pigs; and she's surprised more single women don't take it up. I think she must be detraquee.... I have a faint hope that by taking her in hand and interesting her in our work—which *entre nous deux*—is turning out to be very profitable—I may sober her and regularize her. No doubt in 1950 most women will talk as she does to-day, but the advance is too abrupt. It not only robs *her* parents of all happiness, but it upsets *my* mother. She now wrings her hands over her own past and fears that by working so strenuously for the emancipation of women she has assisted to breach the dam—Can't you imagine the way the old cats of both sexes go on at her?—the dam which held up female virtue, and that Society now will be drowned in a flood of Free Love..."

Vivie: "Well! We'll give her a six months' trial here, and see if our mix-up of advice in Law, Banking, Estate management, Stock-and-share dealing, Divorce, Private Enquiries, probate, etc., does not prove *much* more interesting than an illicit connection with a hare-brained architect.... If she proves impossible you'll pack her off and Vivie shall return and D.V. Williams go abroad.... Don't you think there is something that ought to win over Providence in that happily chosen name? *D.V.* Williams? And my mother once actually called herself 'Vavasour.'"

"Well, then, barring accidents and the unforeseen, it's agreed I go on my holiday next Saturday, to return never no more—perhaps—?"

Norie (with a sigh): "Yes!"

Vivie: "How's your mother?"

Norie: "Oh, as to her, I'm glad to say '*much* better.' When I can get away, after the new clerks and Beryl are installed and everything is going smoothly, I shall take her to Switzerland, to a deliciously quiet spot I know and nobody else knows up the Goeschenenthal. The Continent won't be so hot for travelling if we don't start till the end of August..."

Vivie: "*Then*, dearest ... in case you don't come to the office any more this week, I'll say good-bye—for—for some time..."

(They grip hands, they hesitate, then kiss each other on the cheek, a very rare gesture on either's part—and separate with tears in their eyes.)

The following Monday morning, Bertie Adams, combining in his adolescent person the functions of office boy, junior clerk, and general factotum, entered the outer office of Fraser and Warren and found this letter on his desk:—

Fraser and Warren
Midland Insurance Chambers,
General Inquiry Agents
88-90, Chancery Lane, W.C.
July 12, 1901.

DEAR BERTIE—

I want to prepare you for something. If you had been an ordinary Office boy, I should not have bothered about you or confided to you anything concerning the Firm. But you are by now almost a clerk, and from the day I joined Miss Fraser in this business, you have helped me more than you know—helped me not only in my work, but to understand that there *can* be good, true, decent-minded, trustworthy ... you won't like it if I say "boys" ... young men.

I am going away for a considerable time, I cannot say how long—probably abroad. But Miss Fraser thinks I can still help in the work of her firm, so I remain a partner. A cousin of mine, Mr. D.V. Williams, may come in occasionally to help Miss Fraser. I shall ask him to keep an eye on you. Miss Rose Mullet and Miss Steynes are likewise leaving the service of the firm. I dare say you know Miss Mullet is getting married and how Miss Steynes is going to live at Aylesbury. Two other ladies are coming in their place, and much of my own work will be undertaken by a Mrs. Claridge, whom you will shortly see.

It is rather sad this change in what has been such a happy association of busy people, nobody treading on any one else's toes; but there it is! "The old order changeth, giving place to the new ... lest one good custom should corrupt the world"—you will read in the Tennyson I gave you last Christmas. Let's hope it won't be when I return: "Change and Decay in all around I see" ... as the rather dismal hymn has it.

Sometimes change is a good thing. You serve a noble mistress in Miss Fraser and I am sure you realize the importance of her work. It may mean so much for women's careers in the next generation. I shan't quite lose touch with you. I dare say Miss Fraser, even if I am far away, will write to me from time to time and give me news of the office and tell me how you get on. Don't be ashamed of being ambitious: keep up your studies. Why don't you—but perhaps you do?—join evening classes at the Polytechnic?—or at this new London School of Economics which is close at hand? Make up your mind to be Lord Chancellor some day ... even if it only carries you as far as the silk gown of a Q.C. I suppose I ought now to write "K.C." A few years ago we all thought the State would go to pieces when Victoria died. Yet you see we are jogging along pretty well under King Edward. In the same way, you will soon get so used to the new Head Clerk, Mrs. Claridge, that you will wonder what on earth you saw to admire in

VIVIEN WARREN.

This letter came like a cricket ball between the eyes to Bertie Adams. His adored Miss Warren going away and no clear prospect of her return—her farewell almost like the last words on a death-bed.... He bowed his head over his folded arms on his office desk, and gave way to gruff sobs and the brimming over of tear and nose glands which is the grotesque accompaniment of human sorrow.

He forgot for a while that he was a young man of nineteen with an unmistakable moustache and the status of a cricket eleven captain. He was quite the boy again and his feeling for Vivien Warren, which earlier he had hardly dared to characterize, out of his intense respect for her, became once more just filial affection.

His good mother was a washerwoman-widow, in whom Honoria Fraser had interested herself in her Harley Street girlhood. Bertie was the eldest of six, and his father had been a coal porter who broke his back tumbling down a cellar when a little "on." Bertie—he now figured as Mr. Albert Adams in the cricket lists—was a well-grown youth, rather blunt-featured, but with honest hazel eyes, fresh-coloured, shock-haired. Vivie had once derided him for trying to woo his frontal hair into a flattened curl with much pomade ... he now only sleeked his curly hair with water. You might even have called him "common." He was of the type that went out to the War from 1914 to 1918, and won it, despite the many mistakes of our flurried strategicians: the type that so long as it lasts unspoilt will make England the predominant partner, and Great Britain the predominant nation; the type out of which are made the bluejacket and petty officer, the police sergeant, the engine driver, the railway guard, solicitor's clerk, merchant service mate, engineer, air-pilot, chauffeur, army non-commissioned officer, head gardener, head game-keeper, farm-bailiff, head printer; the trustworthy manser-vant, the commissionaire of a City Office; and which in other avatars ran the British World on an average annual income of L150 before the War. When women of a similar educated lower middle class come into full equality with men in opportunity, they should marry the Bertie Adamses of their acquaintance and not the stockbrokers, butchers, drapers, bookies, professional cricketers or pugilists. They would then become the mothers of the salvation-generation of the British people which will found and rule Utopia.

However, Bertie Adams was quite unconscious of all these possibilities, and thought of himself modestly, rather cheaply. Swallowing the fourth or fifth sob, he rose from his crouching over the desk, wiped his face with a wet towel, smoothed his hair, put straight his turn-over collar and smart tie, and went to his work with glowing eyes and cheeks; resolved to show Miss Warren that she had not thought too highly of him.

Nevertheless, when Miss Mullet arrived and giggled over the details of her trousseau and Lily Steynes discussed the advertisements of Aylesbury ducks in the current *Exchange and Mart*, he was reserved and rather sarcastic with them both. He intimated later that he had long been aware of the coming displacements; but he said not a word of Vivie's letter.

CHAPTER IV

PONTYSTRAD

On a morning in mid-July, 1901, Mr. D.V. Williams bicycled to Paddington Station from New Square, Lincoln's Inn. The brown canvas case fitted to the frame of his male bicycle contained a change of clothes, a suit of paijamas, a safety razor, tooth-brush, hair-brush and comb. He himself was wearing a well-cut dark grey suit—Norfolk jacket, knickerbockers and thick stockings.

Having had his bicycle labelled "Swansea," he entered a first-class compartment of the South Wales express. Though not lavish on his expenditure he was travelling first because he still felt a little uneasy in the presence of men—mostly men of the rougher type. Perhaps there was a second class in those days; there may be still. But I have a distinct impression that Mr. Vavasour Williams, law student, travelled "first" on this occasion: for this was how he met a person of whom his friend, Honoria Fraser, had often spoken —Michael Rossiter.

He did not of course—till after they had passed Swindon— know the name of his travelling companion. Five minutes before the train left Paddington there entered his compartment of the corridor carriage a tall man with a short, curly

Sir Harry Johnston

black beard and nice eyes—eyes like agates in colour. There was a touch of grey about the temples, otherwise the head hair, when he changed from a hard felt hat to a soft travelling cap, showed as dark as the beard and moustache. His frame was strong, muscular and loosely built, and he had clever, nervous hands with fingers somewhat spatulate. His clothes did not much suggest the tourist—they seemed more like a too well-worn town morning suit of dark blue serge; as though he had left home in an absent-minded mood intent on some hurriedly conceived plan. He cast one or two quick glances at David; once, indeed, as they got out into full daylight, away from tunnels and high walls, letting his glance lengthen into a searching look. Then he busied himself with a number of scientific periodicals he had brought to read in the train.

Impelled, he knew not why, to provoke conversation, David asked (quite needlessly), "This *is* the South Wales express, I mean the Swansea train, is it not?"

Blackbeard was struck with the unusualness of the voice—a very pleasant one to come from the lips of a man—and replied: "It is; at least I got in under that impression as I am intending to go to Swansea; but in any case the ticket inspector is sure to come along the corridor presently and we'll make sure then. We stop at Swindon, I think, so if we've made a mistake we can rectify it there."

Then after a pause he resumed: "I think you said you were going to Swansea? Might I ask if you are bound on the same errand as I am? I mean, are you one of Boyd Dawkins's party to examine the new cave on the Gower coast?"

D.V.W.: "Oh no—I—I am going inland from Swansea to—to have a bicycling tour. I'm going to a place on the river—I don't know how to pronounce it—at least I've forgotten. The river's name is spelt Llwchwr."

Blackbeard: "You should change your mind and turn south—come and see these extraordinary caves. Are you interested in palaeontology?" (David hesitates) "What careless people call 'prehistoric animals' or 'prehistoric man.' They have been ridiculously misled by comic artists in *Punch* who imagine a few thousand years of Prehistory would take us back to the Cretaceous period; really four or five million years before Man came into existence, when this country and most other lands swarmed with preposterous reptiles that had become extinct long before the age of mammals. However, I don't suppose this interests you. I only spoke because I thought you might be one of Boyd Dawkins's pupils ... or one of mine."

David: "On the contrary, I am very, very much interested in the subject, but I am afraid it has lain rather outside my line of studies so far—p'raps I will turn south when I have seen something of the part of Glamorgan I am going to. I'm really Welsh in origin, but I know Wales imperfectly because I left it when I was quite young" ("This'll be good practice," Vivie's brain voice was saying to herself) ... "I've returned recently from South Africa."

Blackbeard: "What were you doing there?"

David: "I—I—was in the army ... at least in a police force ... I got wounded, had to go into hospital—necrosis of the jaw ... I came home when I got well..."

Blackbeard: *"Necrosis of the jaw!* That was a bad thing. But you seem to have got over it very well. I can't see any scar from where I am..."

David: "Oh no. It was only a *slight* touch and I dare say I exaggerate ... I've left the Army however and now I'm reading Law..."

Blackbeard thinks at this point that he has gone far enough in cross-examination and returns to his periodicals and pamphlets. But there's something he likes—a wistfulness—in the young man's face, and he can't quite detach his mind to the presence of palaeolithic man in South Wales. At Swindon they both get out—there was still lingering the practice of taking lunch there—have a hasty lunch together and more talk, and share a bottle of claret.

On returning to their compartment, Rossiter offers David a cigar but the young man prefers smoking a cigarette. By this time they have exchanged names. D.V.W. however is reticent about the South African War—says it was all too horrible for words, and should never have taken place and he can't bear to think about it and was knocked out quite early in the day. Now all he asks is peace and quiet and the opportunity of studying law in London so that he may become some day a barrister. Rossiter says—after more talk, "Pity you're going in for the Bar—we've too many lawyers already. You should take up Science"—and as far as the Severn Tunnel discourses illuminatingly on biology, mineralogy, astronomy, chemistry as David-Vivien had never heard them treated previously. In the Severn Tunnel the noise of the train silences both professor and listener, who willingly takes up the position of pupil. Between Newport and Neath, David thinks he has never met any one so interesting. It has been his first real induction into the greatest of all books: the Book of the Earth itself. Rossiter on his part feels indefinably attracted by this young expatriated Welshman. David does not say much, but what he does contribute to the conversation shows him a quick thinker and a person of trained intelligence. Yet somehow the professor of Biology in the University of London—and many other things beside—F.R.S., F.Z.S., F.L.S., Gold Medallist of this and that Academy and University abroad—does not "see" him as a soldier or a non-commissioned officer in the British Army: law-student is a more likely qualification. However as they near Swansea, Michael Rossiter gives Mr. D.V. Williams his card (D.V.W. regrets he cannot reciprocate but says he has hardly settled down yet to any address) and—though as a rule he is taciturn in trains and cautious about making acquaintances—expresses the hope he will call at 1, Park Crescent some afternoon—"My wife and I are generally at home on Thursdays"—when all are back in town for the autumn. They separate at Swansea station.

David spends the night at Swansea, employing some of his time there by enquiring at the Terminus Hotel as to the roads that lead up the valley of the Llwchwr, what sort of a place is Pontystrad ("the bridge by the meadow"), whether any one knows the clergyman of that parish, Mr.... er ... Howel Vaughan Williams. The "boots" or one of the "bootses," it appears, comes from the neighbourhood of Pontystrad and knows the reverend gentleman by sight—a nice old gentleman—has heard that he's aged much of late years since his son ran away and disappeared out in Africa. His sight was getting bad, Boots understood, and he could not see to do all the reading and writing he was once so great at.

After a rather wakeful night, during which D.V. Williams is more disturbed by his thoughts and schemes than by the continual noises of the trains passing into and out of Swansea, he rises early and drafts a telegram:—

Revd. Howel Williams, Vicarage, Pontystrad, Glamorgan. Hope return home this evening. All is well.

DAVID.

Then pays his bill and tries to mount his bicycle the wrong way to the great amusement of the Boots; then remembers the right way and rides off, with the confidence of one long accustomed to bicycling, through the crowded traffic of Swansea in the direction of Llwchwr.

It was a very hot ride through a very lovely country, now largely spoilt by mining and metallurgy, along a road that was constantly climbing up steeply to descend abruptly. David of course could have travelled by rail to the Pontyffynon station and thence have ridden back three miles to Pontystrad. But he wished purposely to bicycle the whole way from Swansea and take in with the eye the land of his fathers. He was postponing as long as possible the test of meeting his father, the father of the young n'eer-do-weel who had been lying for months in a South African field hospital the year before. He halted for a cup of tea at Llandeilotalybont ... Wales has many place names like this ... and being there not many miles from Pontystrad was able to glean more recent and more circumstantial information about the man he proposed to greet as "father."

At half-past six that evening, having perspired and dried, perspired and dried, strained a tendon and acquired a headache, he halted before the gate of the Vicarage garden at Pontystrad, having been followed thither to his secret annoyance by quite a troop of village boys of whom he had imprudently asked the way. As they talked Welsh he could not tell what they were saying, but conjectured that his telegram had arrived and that he was expected.

Standing under the porch of the house was an old man with a long white beard like a Druid in spectacles shading his eyes and expectant...

A bicycle might prove an incumbrance in the ensuing

interview, so David hastily propped his against a fuchsia hedge and hurried forward to meet the old man, who extended hands to envelop him, not trusting to his eyes. An old, rosy-cheeked woman in a sunbonnet came up behind the old man, shrieked out "Master David!" and only waited with twitching fingers for her own onslaught till the father had first embraced his prodigal son. This was done at least three times, accompanied with tears, blessings, prayers, the uplifting of poor filmy eyes to a cloudless Heaven—"Diolch i Dduw!"—ejaculations as to the wonder of it—"Rhyfeddol yw yn eiholl ffyrdd"—God's Providence—His ways are past finding out! "Ni ellir olrain ei Ragluniaeth!"—"My own dear boy! Fy machgen annwyli!"

Then the old woman took her turn: "Master David! Eh, but you're changed, mun!"—then a lot of Welsh exclamations, which until the Welsh can agree to spell their tongue phonetically I shall not insert—"Five years since you left us! Eh, and I never thought to see you no more. Some said you wass dead, others that you wass taken prisoner by the Wild Boars. But here you are, and welcome—indeed—" Then Master David between the embraces was scanned, a little more critically than by the purblind father, but with distinct approval.

At last David stood apart in the stone-flagged hall of the Vicarage. His abundant hair was rumpled, his face was stained by other people's tears, his collar, tie, dress disordered, and his heart touched. It was a rare experience in his twenty-four years of life—he guessed that should be his age—to find himself really taken on trust, really desired and loved. Honoria's friendship was a pure and precious thing, but in its very purity carefully restrained. Praddy's kindness, and the office boy's worship had both been gratifying to Vivie's self-esteem, but both had to be kept at bay. Somehow the love of a father and of an old nurse were of a different category to these other contacts.

All these thoughts passed through David's brain in thirty seconds. He shook himself, straightened himself, smiled adequately, and tried to live up to the situation.

"Dear father! And dear ... Nannie! (A bold but successful deduction). How sweet of you both—greeting me like this. I've come home a very different David to the one that left you—what was it? Five—six years ago?—to go to Mr. Praed's studio. I've learnt a lot in the interval. But I'm so sick of the past, I don't want to talk about it more than I can help, and I've been in very queer health since I got ill—and—wounded—in—South Africa. My memory has gone for many things—I'm afraid I've forgotten all my Welsh, Nannie, but it'll soon come back, that is, if I may stay here a bit." (Exclamations from father and nurse: "This is your *home*, Davy-bach!") "I'm not going to stay too long this time because I've got my living to earn in London....

"Did you never hear anything about me from ... South Africa ... or the War Office—or—your old college chum, Mr. Gardner?"

"I heard—my own dear boy—" said the Revd. Howel, again taking him in his arms in a renewed spasm of affection. "I heard you were wounded and very ill in the camp hospital at Colesberg. It was a nursing sister, I think, who sent me the information. I wrote several times to the War Office, my letters were acknowledged, that was all. Then Sam Gardner wrote to me from Margate and said his son had been in the same hospital with you. Later on I saw in a Bristol paper that this hospital—Colesberg—had fallen into the hands of the Boers and the Cape insurgents. Then I said to myself 'My poor boy's been taken prisoner' and as time went on, 'My poor boy's dead, or he would have written to me.'"

Here the Revd. Howel stopped to wipe his eyes and blow his nose. David touched through his armour of cynicism, said—Nannie retiring to prepare the evening meal—"Father dear, though I don't want to refer too often to the past, I behaved disgracefully some time ago and the Colonies seemed my only chance of setting myself right. I did manage to get away from the Boers, but I had not the courage to present myself before you till I had done something to regain your good opinion. I have got now good employment in London and I'm even reading up Law. We will talk of that by and bye but I tell you now—from my heart—I am a different David to the one you knew, and you shall never regret taking me back."

Both father and son were crying now, for emotion especially in Wales is catching. But the father laughed through his tears; and incoherently thanked God for the return of the prodigal—a fine upstanding lad—whole and sound. "No taint about *you*, Davy, *I'll* be bound. Why your voice alone shows you've been a clean liver. It's music in my ears, and if I could see as well as I can hear I'd wager you're a handsome lad and have lost much of your foolishness. Davy, lad" (lowering his voice) "you've no cause to be anxious about Jenny. She—she—had a boy, but we got her married to a miner—I made it right with him. She has another child now, but they're being brought up together. We won't refer to it again. She lives twenty miles from here, at Gower—and ... and ... there's an end of it...."

"Now you won't run away back to London till you're obliged? Where's your luggage? At Pontyffynon?"

"No," said David, a little non-plussed at evidences of his dissolute past and this unexpected fatherhood assumed on his account. "I haven't more luggage than what is contained in my bicycle bag. But don't let that concern you. I'll go over to

Swansea one day or some nearer town and buy what may be necessary, and I'll stay with you all my holidays, tell you all my plans, and even after I go back to London I'll always come down here when I can get away. For the present I'm going simply to enjoy myself for the first time in my life. The last four years we'll look on as a horrid dream. What a paradise you live in." His eye ranged over the two-storeyed, soundly-built stone house facing south, with mountains behind and the western sun throwing shafts of warm yellow green over the lawn and the flower beds; over clumps of elms in the middle, southern distance, that might have been planted by the Romans (who loved this part of Wales). Bees, butterflies and swallows were in the air; the distant lowing of kine, the scent of the roses, the clatter in the kitchen where Nannie aided by another female servant was preparing supper, even the barking of a watch dog; aware that something unusual was going on, completed the impression of the blissful countryside. "What a paradise you live in! How *could* I have left it?"

"Ay, dear lad; I doubt not it looks strange and new to you since you've been in South Africa and London. But it'll soon seem homelike enough. And now you'll like to see your room, and have a wash before supper. Tom, the gardener, shall take in your bicycle and give it a rub over. I've still got the old one here in the coach-house which you left behind. Tom's new, since you left. He's not so clever with the bees as your old friend Evan was, but he's a steadier lad. I fear me Evan led you into some of your scrapes. The fault was partly mine. I shouldn't have let you run wild so much, but I was so wrapped up in my studies—Well, well!"

David was careful to play his part sufficiently to say when shown into his old bedroom, "Just the same, father; scarcely a bit altered—but isn't the bed moved—to another place?"

"You're right, my boy—Ah! your memory can't be as bad as you pretend. Yes, we moved it there, Bridget and I, because the Archdeacon came once to stay and complained of the draught from the window."

"The deuce he did!" said David. "Well, *I* shan't complain of anything."

His father left him and he then proceeded to lay out the small store of things he had brought in his bicycle bag, giving special prominence to the shaving tackle. He had just finished a summary toilet when there was a tap on the door, and, suppressing an exclamation of impatience—for he dearly wanted time and solitude for collected thought—he admitted Bridget.

"Well, Nannie," he said, "come for a gossip?"

"Yess. I can hardly bear to take my eyes off you, for you've changed, you *have* changed. And yet, I don't know? You don't look much older than you wass when you went off to London to be an architect. Your cheek—" (lifting her hand and stroking it, while David tried hard not to wince) "Your cheek's as soft and smooth as it was then, as any young girl's. Wherever you've been, the world has not treated you very bad. No one would have dreamt you'd been all the way to South Africa to them Wild Boars. But some men wear wonderful well. I suppose your father giv' you a bit of a shock? He's much older looking; and he wassn't suffering, to speak of, from his sight when you went away. And now he can hardly see to read even with his new spectol. Old Doctor Murgatroyd can't do nothing for him—Advises him to go to see some Bristol or London eye-doctor. But after you seemed to disappear in Africa he had no heart for trying to get his sight back. He'd sit for hours doing nothing but think and talk, all about old Welsh times, or Bible times. Of course he knows hiss services by heart; hiss only job wass with the Lessons.... But you see, he'd often only have me and the girl and Tom in church. There's a new preacher up at Little Bethel that's drawn all the village folk to hear him. But your father'll be a different man now—you see, he'll be like a boy again. And if you could stay long enough, you might take him to Bristol—or Clifton I think it wass—to see if they could do anything about his eyes....

"The past's the past and we aren't going to say no more about it, and now you've turned over a new leaf—somehow I *can't* feel you're the same person—don't go worrying yourself about that slut Jenny. *She's* all right. After your baby was born at her mother's, she went into service at Llanelly and there she met a miner who's at work on the new coal mine in Gower. He wasn't a bad sort of chap and when he'd heard her story he said for a matter of twenty pound he'd marry her and take over her baby. So your father paid the twenty pounds, and if she'll only keep straight she'll be none the worse for what's happened. I always said it wass my fault. It wass the year I had to go away to my sister, and your father had to go to St. David's, and after all, if it hadn't 'a-been you, it 'd 'a-been young Evan. Why there's bin some girls in the village have had two and even three babies before they settled down and got married. Now we must dish up supper. I've given you lots and lots of pancakes and the cream and honey you wass always so fond of—you bad boy—" She ventured a kiss on the smooth cheek of her nursling and heavily descended the stairs.

David had a very bad night, because to please his old nurse he had eaten too many of her pancakes with cream and honey. In fact, he had at last to tip-toe down through a sleeping house cautiously to let himself out and relieve his feelings by pacing the verandah till the nausea passed off. After that he lay long awake trying to size up the situation.

He got his thoughts at last into some such shape as this:—

"It's clear I was a regular young rake before I was sent up to London to be Praddy's pupil. Apparently I seduced the housemaid or kitchenmaid—my father's establishment seems to consist of Nannie who is housekeeper and cook, and a maid who does housework and helps in the kitchen—and this unfortunate girl who fell a prey to my solicitations—or more likely misled me—afterwards gave birth to a child attributed either to my fatherhood or the gardener's. But the matter has been hushed up by a payment of twenty pounds and the girl is now married and respectable and ought to give no further trouble. I suppose that was a climax of naughtiness on my part and the main reason why I was sent away. The two people who matter most have received me without doubt or question, but the one to be wary about is the old nurse, whose very affection makes her inconveniently inquisitive. *Mem.* get up and lock my door, or else she may come in with hot water or something in the morning and take me by surprise.

"The original David is evidently dead and well out of the way. There can be no harm in my taking his place, at any rate for a few years: it may give the old man new life and genuine happiness, for I shall play my part as a good son, and certainly shall cost him nothing. I'll begin by taking him to an oculist and finding out what is wrong with his eyes.... Probably only cataract. It may be possible to effect a cure and he can then finish his book on the history of Glamorganshire from earliest times. Must remember, by the bye, that the Welsh change most of the old *m's* into *f's* and that this country is called Forganwg, with the *w* pronounced like *oo*, and the *f* like *v*. Must learn some Welsh. What a nuisance. But nothing is worth doing if it isn't done well. If I can keep this deception up this would be a jolly place to come to for occasional holidays, and I simply couldn't have a better reference to respectability, sex and station with the benchers of Lincoln's Inn than 'my father,' the Revd. Howel Williams, Vicar of Pontystrad. They'll probably want a second or a third reference. Can I rely on Praddy? Is it possible I might work up my acquaintance with that professor whom I met in the train? I'll see. Perhaps I could attend classes of his if he lectures in London."

Then the plotting David fell asleep at last and woke to hear the loud tapping on his door at eight o'clock, of Bridget, rather surprised to find the door locked, but entering (when he had garbed himself in his Norfolk jacket and opened the door), with hot water for shaving and a cup of tea.

It was a hot July morning, and while he dressed, the southern breeze came in through the open window scented by the roses and the lemon verbena growing against the wall. His father was pacing up and down the hall and the verandah restlessly awaiting him, fearing lest the whole episode of the day before might not have been one of his waking dreams. His failing sight made reading almost a torture and writing more a matter of feeling than visual perception. Time therefore hung wearisomely on his hands; Bridget was not a good reader, besides being too busy a housekeeper to have time for it. Had David really returned to him? Would he sometimes read aloud and sometimes write his letters, or even the finish of his History? Too good to be true!

But there was David coming down the stairs, greeting him with tender affection. "Read and write for you, father? Of course! But before I go back to London—and unfortunately I *must* go back early in August—I'm going to take you to see an oculist—Bristol or Clifton perhaps—and get your sight restored."

After breakfast, however, the father decided he must take

David round the village, to see and be seen. David was not very anxious to go, but as the Revd. Howel looked disappointed he gave in.

It had to be got over some time or other. So they first visited the church, a building in the form of a cross, with an imposing battlemented tower. Here David asked to inspect the registers and found therein (while the old gentleman silently prayed or sat in mute thankfulness in a sunny corner)—the record of his father's marriage to Mary Vavasour twenty-six years before (Mary was twenty-three and the Revd. Howel forty at the time) and of his own baptism two years afterwards.

Then issuing from the church, father and son walked through the village, the father pointing out the changes for better or worse that had taken place in four years, and not noticing the vagueness of his son's memories of either persons or features in the landscape. The village, like most Welsh villages, was of white-washed cottages, slate-roofed, but it was embowered with that luxuriance of foliage and flowers which makes Glamorganshire—out of sight of the coal-mining— seem an earthly paradise. Every now and then the Revd. Howel would nudge his son and say: "That man who spoke was old Goronwy, as big a scoundrel now as he was five years ago," or he would introduce David to a villager of whom he thought more favourably. If she were a young woman she generally smirked and looked sideways; if a man he grunted out a Welsh greeting or only gave a nod of surly recognition. Several professed fluent recognition but some said in Welsh "he wasn't a bit like the Mr. David *they* had known." Whereupon the Revd. Howel laughed and said: "Wait till you have been out to South Africa fighting for your king and country and see if *that* doesn't change *you*!"

The visit to the Clifton oculist resulted in a great success.

The oculist after two or three days' preparation in a nursing home performed the operation and advised David then to leave his father for a few days (promising if any unfavourable symptoms supervened he would telegraph) so that he might pass the time in sleep as much as possible, and with no mental stimulation. During this interval David transferred himself and his bicycle to Swansea, and thence visited the Gower caves where he ran up against Rossiter once more and spent delightful hours being inducted into palaeontology by Rossiter and his companions. Then back to—by contrast—boresome Clifton (except for its Zoological Gardens). After another week his father was well enough to be escorted home. In another fortnight he might be able to use his eyes, and soon after that would be able to read and write—in moderation.

But David could not wait to see his intervention crowned with complete success. He must keep faith with Honoria who would be wanting a long holiday in Switzerland; and their joint business must not suffer by his absence from London. There were, indeed, times when the peace and comfort and beauty of Pontystrad got hold of him and he asked himself: "Why not settle down here for the rest of his life, put aside other ambitions, attempt no more than this initial fraud, leave the hateful world wherein women had only three chances to men's seven." Then there would arise once more fierce ambition, the resolve to avenge Vivien Warren for her handicaps, the desire to keep tryst with Honoria and to enjoy more of Rossiter's society. Besides, he ran a constant risk of discovery under the affectionate but puzzled inspection of the old nurse. In her mind, residence amongst the "Wild Boars," service in an army, travel and adventure generally during an absence of five years, as well as emergence from adolescence into manhood, accounted for much change in physical appearance, but not sufficiently for the extraordinary change in *morale*: the contrast between the vicious, untidy, selfish, insolent boy that had gone off to London with ill-concealed glee in 1896 and this grave-mannered, polite, considerate, pleasant-voiced young man who had already managed to find good employment in London before he revealed himself anew to his delighted father.

These doubts David read in Nannie's mind. But he would not give them time and chance to become more precise and formulated. Gradually she would become used to the seeming miracle. In the meantime he would return to London, and if his father's recovery was complete he would not revisit "home" till Christmas. As soon as he was able to write, his father would forward him the copy of his birth-certificate, and he would likewise answer in the sense agreed upon any letters of reference or enquiry: would state the apprenticeship to architecture with Praed A.R.A., and then the impulse to go out to South Africa, the slight wound—David insisted it was slight, a fuss about nothing, because he had enquired about necrosis of the jaw and realized that even if he had recovered it would have left indisputable marks on face and throat. In fact there were so many complications involved in an escape from the Boers, only to be justified under the code of honour prevailing in war time, that he would rather his father said little or nothing about South Africa but left him to explain all that. A point of view readily grasped by the Revd. Howel, who to get such a son back would even have not thought too badly of desertion—and the negative letters of the War Office said nothing of that.

So early in September, after the most varied, anxious, successful six weeks in his life—so far—David Vavasour Williams returned to Fig Tree Court, Inner Temple.

CHAPTER V

READING FOR THE BAR

It had been a hot, windless day in London, in early September. Though summer was in full swing in the country without a hint of autumn, the foliage in the squares and gardens of the Inns of Court was already seared and a little shrivelled. The privet hedges were almost black green; and the mould in the dismal borders that they screened looked as though it had never known rain or hose water and as if it could no more grow bright-tinted flowers than the asbestos of a gas stove which it resembled in consistency and colour. It was now an evening, ending one of those days which are peculiarly disheartening to a Londoner returned from a long stay in the depths of the country—a country which has hills and streams, ferny hollows, groups of birches, knolls surmounted with pines, meadows of lush, emerald-green grass, full-foliaged elms, twisted oaks, orchards hung with reddening apples, red winding lanes between unchecked hedges, blue mountains in the far distance, and the glimpse of a river or of ponds large enough to be called a mere or even a lake. The exhausted London to which David Williams had returned a few days previously had lost a few thousands of its West-end and City population—just, in fact, most of its interesting if unlikable folk, its people who mattered, its insolent spoilt darlings whom you liked to recognize in the

Carlton atrium, in Hyde Park, in a box at the theatre: yet the frowsy, worthy millions were there all the same. The air of its then smelly streets was used up and had the ammoniac strench of the stable. It was a weary London. The London actors had not returned from Cornwall and Switzerland. Provincial companies enjoyed—a little anxiously owing to uncertain receipts at the box office—a brief license on the boards of famous play-houses. The newspapers had exhausted the stunt of the silly season and were at their flattest and most yawn-provoking. The South African War had reached its dreariest stage....

Bertie Adams on this close September evening had out-stayed the other employes of *Fraser and Warren* in their fifth floor office at No. 88-90 Chancery Lane. He had remained after office hours to do a little work, a little "self-improvement"; and he was just about to close the outer office and leave the key with the housekeeper, when the lift came surging up and out of it stepped a young man in a summer suit and a bowler hat who, to Bertie's astonishment, not only dashed straight at the door of the partners' room, but opened its Yale lock with a latch-key as though long accustomed to do so. "But, sir!..." exclaimed the junior clerk (his promotion to that rank had tacitly dated from Vivie Warren's departure). "It's all right," said the stranger. "I'm Mr. David Williams and I've come to draw up some notes for Mrs. Claridge. I dare say Miss Fraser has told you I should work in the office every now and then whilst my cousin—Miss Warren, you know—is away. You needn't wait, though you can close the outer office before you go; and, by the bye, you might fetch me *Who's Who* for the present year." All this was said a little breathlessly.

Bertie brought the volume, then only half the size of its present bulk, because it lacked our new nobility and gave no heed to your favourite recreation. D.V. Williams stood in the yellow light of the west window, reading a letter... "Cousin? No! Twin brother, perhaps; but had she one?..." mused Bertie... and then, that never-to-be-forgotten voice ... "Here's 'Oo's Oo—er—Hoo's Hoo, I mean.... Miss..." He only added the last word as by some sub-conscious instinct.

"*Mister* Williams," said Vivien-David-Warren Williams, facing him with resolute eyes. "Be quite clear about that, Adams; *David Vavasour Williams*, Miss Warren's cousin."

"Indeed I will be, Miss ... Mister ... er ... Sir..." said the transfigured Bertie (his brain voice saying over and over again in ecstasy ... "*I* tumble to it! *I* tumble to it!"). And then again "*Indeed* I will, Mr. Williams. I'm a bit stupidlike this evenin' ... readin' too much.... May I stay and help you, Sir? I'm pretty quick on the typewriter, Miss Warren may have told you ... Sir ... and I ain't—I mean—*I am not*—half bad with me shorthand.... You know—I mean, *she* would know I'd joined them evenin' classes..."

"Thank you, Adams; but if you have joined the evening classes you oughtn't to interrupt your attendance there. I can *quite* manage here alone and you need not be afraid: I shall leave everything properly closed. You could give up the key of the outer office as you go out. You may often find me at work here after office hours, but that need not disturb you ... and I need hardly say, after all Miss Fraser and Miss Warren have told me about you, I rely on you to be at all times thoroughly discreet and not likely to discuss the work of this firm or my share in it with any one?"...

"Indeed you may ... Mr. Williams ... indeed you may.... Oh! I'm so happy.... Good-night ... Sir!"

And Adams's heart was too full for attendance at a lecture on Roman law. He went off instead to the play. He himself belonged now to the world of romance. He knew of things—and wild horses and red-hot tweezers should not tear the knowledge from him, or make him formulate his deductions—he knew of things as amazing, as prodigal of developments as anything in the problem play enacted beyond the pit and the stalls; he was the younger brother of Herbert Waring and the comrade of Jessie Joseph: at that moment deceiving the sleuth hounds of Stage law by parading in her fiance's evening dress and going to prison for his sake.

Beryl Claridge had taken up much of Vivie Warren's work on the 1st of August in that year, while Honoria Fraser was touring in Switzerland. Miss Mullet and Miss Steynes were replaced (Steynes staying on a little later to initiate the new-comers) by two young women so commonplace yet such efficient machines that their names are not worth hunting up or inventing. If I have to refer to them I will call them Miss A. and Miss B.

Beryl Claridge was closely scanned by Bertie Adams, and frequently compared in his mind with the absent and idealized Vivie. He decided that although she was shrewd and clever and very good-looking, he did not like her. She smoked too many cigarettes for 1901. She had her curly hair "bobbed" (though the term was not invented then). She put up her feet too high and too often; so much so that the scandalized Bertie saw she wore black knickerbockers and no petticoats under her smart "tailor-made." She snapped your head off, was short, sharp and insolent, joked too much with the spectacled women clerks (who became her willing slaves); then would ask Bertie about his best girl and tell him he'd got jolly good teeth, a good biceps and quite a nice beginning of a moustache.

But she was a worker: no doubt of that! Of course, in the

dead season there were not many clients to shock or to win over by her nonchalant manners, only a few women who required advice as to houses, stocks, and shares, law, or private enquiries as to the good faith of husbands or fiances. Such as found their way up in the lift were a little disappointed at seeing Beryl in Vivie's chair or at not being received by their old friend Honoria Fraser. But Beryl was too good a business woman to put them off with any license of speech or manners. For the rest she spent August and early September in "mugging up" the firm's business. Although deep down in her curious little heart, under all her affectation of hardness and insolent disdain of public or family opinion she firmly loved her architect and the children she had borne him, she desired quite as passionately to be self-supporting, to earn a sufficient income of her own, to be dependent on no one. She might have her passing caprices and her loose and flippant mode of talking, but she wasn't going to be a failure, a cadger, a parasite, a "fallen" woman. She fully realized that in England no woman *has* fallen who is self-supporting, whose income meets her expenses and who pays her way. Given those guarantees, all else that she does which is not actually criminal is eventually put down to mere eccentricity.

So Honoria's offer and Honoria's business provided her with a most welcome opening. She realized the opportunities that lay before this Woman's Office for General Inquiries, established in the closing years of the nineteenth century— this business that before Woman's enfranchisement nibbled discreetly at the careers and the openings for profit-making hitherto rigidly reserved for Man. She wasn't going to let Honoria down. Honoria, she realized, was in herself equivalent to many thousands of pounds in capital. Her reputation was flawless. She was known to and esteemed by a host of women of the upper middle class. Her Cambridge reputation for learning, her eventual inheritance of eighty thousand pounds were unexpressed reasons for many a woman of good standing preferring to confide her affairs to the judgment of *Fraser and Warren*, in preference to dealing with male legal advisers, male land agents, men on the Stock Exchange, men in house property business.

So Beryl became in most respects a source of strength to Honoria Fraser, deprived for a time of the overt co-operation of her junior partner.

Beryl in the first few weeks of her stay evinced small interest in the departure of Vivien Warren and her reasons for going abroad. She had a scheme of her own in which her architect would take a prominent part, for providing women—authoresses, actresses, or the wives of the newly enriched—with week-end cottages; the desire for which was born with the Twentieth century and fostered by the invention of motors and bicycles. Cases before the firm for opinions on intricate legal problems Beryl was advised to place before the consideration of one of Honoria's friends, a law student, Mr. D.V. Williams, who would shortly be back from his holiday and who had agreed to look in at the office from time to time and go through such papers as were set aside for him to read. Beryl had remarked—without any intention behind it—on seeing some of his notes initialled V.W. that it was rum he should have the same initials as that Vivie girl whom she remembered at Newnham ... who was "so silent and standoffish and easily shocked." But she noticed later that when Mr. Williams got to work his initials were really three and not two—D.V.W. One thing with the other: her departure from the office at the regular closing hour—five—so that she might see her babies before they were put to bed; Williams's habit of coming to work after six; kept them from meeting till the October of 1901. When they did meet after Honoria's return from Switzerland, Beryl scanned the law student critically; decided he was rather nice-looking but

Sir Harry Johnston

very pre-occupied; perhaps engaged to some girl whose parents objected; rather mysterious, *quand meme*; she had heard some one say this Mr. David Williams was a cousin or something of Vivie Warren ... what if he were in love with Vivie and she had gone away because she had some fad or other about not wanting to marry? Well! All this could be looked into some other time, if it were worth bothering about at all. Or could Williams be spoony on Honoria? After her money? He was much younger—evidently—but young men adored ripe women, and young girls idolized elderly soldiers. *C'etait a voir* (Beryl ever since she had been to Paris on a stolen honeymoon with the architect liked saying things to herself in French).

Towards the end of October, David received at Fig Tree Court a letter from his father in Glamorganshire.

Pontystrad Vicarage,
October 20, 1901.

MY DEAR SON,—

The improvement in my sight continues. I can now read a little every day, by daylight, without pain or fatigue, and write letters. I feel I owe you a long one; but I shall write a portion each day and not try my eyes unduly.

I am glad to know you are now settled down in chambers at Fig Tree Court in the Temple and have begun your studies for the Bar. You could not have taken up a finer profession. What seems to me so wonderful is that you should be able to earn your living at the same time and be no charge on me. I accept your assurances that you need no support; but never forget, my dear Son, that if you *do*, I am ready and willing to help. You sowed your wild oats—perhaps we both exaggerated the sins of the wild years—at any rate you have made a noble reparation. What a splendid school the Colonies must be! What a difference between the David who left me five years ago for Mr. Praed's studio and the David who returned to me last summer! I can never be sufficiently thankful to Almighty God for the change He has wrought in you! No lip religion, but a change of heart. I presume you explained everything to the Colonial Office after you got back to London and that you are now free to take up a civil career? The people out there never sent me any further information; but the other day one of my letters to you (written after I had received the sad news) returned to me, with the information that the hospital you were in had been captured by the Boers and that you could not be traced. I enclose it. You can now finish up the story yourself and let the authorities know how you got away and returned home.

The other day that impudent baggage Jenny Gorlais came and asked to see me ... she said her husband was out of work and refused to give her enough money to provide for all her children, that he had advised her to apply to *you* for the maintenance of *your* son! Relying on what you had told me I sent for Bridget and we both told her we had made every enquiry and now refused absolutely to believe in her stories of five years ago—that we were sure you were *not* the father of her eldest child. Bridget, for example, believed the postman was its father. Jenny burst into tears, and as she did not persist in her claim my heart was moved, and I gave her ten shillings, but told her *pretty plainly* that if she ever made such a claim again I should go to the police. You should have heard Bridget defending you! *Such* a champion. If you want a witness to character for your references you should call *her*! She is loud in your praise.

October 22.

There is one thing I want to tell you; and it is easier to write it than say it. Your mother did not die when you were three years old—much worse: she left me—ran away with an engineer who was tracing out the branch railway. He seemed a nice young fellow and I had him often up at the Vicarage, and *that* was the way he repaid my hospitality! He wrote to me a year afterwards asking me to divorce her. As though a Clergyman of the Church of England could do such a thing! I had offered to take her back—not then—it would have been a mockery—but by putting advertisements into the South Wales papers. But after her paramour's letter—which I did not answer—I never heard any more about her....

["Damn it all," said David to himself at this juncture of the letter—he was training himself to swear in a moderate, gentlemanly way—"Damn it all! Whatever I do, it seems I *cannot* come from altogether respectable stock."...]

You grew up therefore without a mother's care, though good Bridget did her best. When you were a child I fear I rather neglected you. I was so disappointed and embittered that I sought consolation in the legends of our beloved country and in Scriptural exegesis. You were rather a naughty boy at Swansea Grammar School and somewhat of a scamp at Malvern College—Well! we won't go over all that again. I quite understand your reticence about the past. Once again I think the blame was mine as much as yours. I ought to have interested myself more in your pursuits and games ... what a pity, by the bye, that you seem to have lost your gift of drawing and painting! I do remember how at one time we were drawn together over the old Welsh legends and the very clever drawings you made of national heroes and heroines—they seemed to come on you as quite a surprise when I took them out of the old portfolio.

But about your mother—for it is necessary you should know all I can tell you in case you have to answer questions as to your parentage. Your mother's name was, as you know, Mary Vavasour. It is a common name in South Wales though it seems to be Norman French. She came to our Pontystrad school as a teacher in 1873. Her father was something to do with mining at Merthyr. I fell in love with her—she had a sweet face—and married her in 1874. You were born two years afterwards. Bridget had been my housekeeper before I was married and I asked her to stay on lest your mother should be inexperienced at first in the domestic arts. They never got on well together and when Mary had recovered from her confinement and seemed disposed to take up housekeeping I sent away poor Bridget reluctantly and only took her back after your mother's flight. Bridget was a second mother to you as you know, though I fear you never showed her much affection till these later days.

October 23.

My eyes seem to be improving instead of getting tired with the new delights of reading and writing. I owe all this to you and to the clever oculist at Clifton. Dr. Murgatroyd from Pontyffynon looked in here the other day, to ask about your return. He seemed almost to grudge me my restored sight because I had got it from other people's advice. Said *he* could have advised an operation only he never believed my heart would stand it. When I told him they had mixed the anaesthetic with oxygen he became quite angry—and exclaimed against these new-fangled notions. But I must not use up my new found energy writing about him. I want to finish my letter in a business-like fashion so that you may know all that is necessary to be known about yourself and your position. You may have at any moment to answer questions before you get called to the Bar, and with your defective memory—I am glad to hear things in the past are becoming clearer to you—I am sure with God's grace you will wholly recover soon from the effects of your wound and your illness—What was I writing? I meant to say that you ought to know the main facts about your family and your position.

I was an only son. Your grandfather was a prosperous farmer and auctioneer. You have distant cousins, Vaughans and Williamses, and some others living at Shrewsbury named Price. I have written to none of them about your return because they never evinced any interest in me or my concerns. Your mother's people, her Vavasour relations at Cardiff—did not seem to me to be very respectable, though her father was a well-educated man for his position. He died—I heard—in a mine accident.

I am not poorly off for a Welsh clergyman. My mother—a Price of Ystrwy—wanted me to go into the Church and prevailed on your grandfather to send me first to Malvern and next to Cambridge. It was at Cambridge that I met your comrade's father—Sam Gardner, I mean. He was rather wild in his college days and to tell you the truth, I never cared to keep up with him much—he had such very rowdy friends. My mother died while I was at Cambridge and in his later years your grandfather married again—his housekeeper—and rather muddled his affairs, because at one time he was quite well off.

After I was ordained he purchased for me the advowson of this living. All that came to me from his estate, however, was a sum of about eleven thousand pounds. This used to bring me in about five hundred pounds a year, and in addition to that was the fluctuating two hundred and fifty pounds income from my benefice. I took about three thousand pounds out of my capital to pay the debts you ran up, to article you to Mr. Praed; and, I must admit, to get my "Tales from Taliessin" and "Legends of the Welsh Saints" privately printed at Cardiff. I am afraid I wasted much good money on the desire to see my Cymraeg studies in print.

Well: there I am! with about eight or nine thousand pounds to leave. I have not altered my will—leaving it all to you, subject to an annuity of L50 a year to your faithful Nannie. I was projecting an alteration in case of your death, when you most happily returned. I may live another ten years yet. You have put new life into me. One charge, however, I was going to have laid on you; while you were with me I could not bear to speak of these matters. If at any time after I'm gone you should come across your unhappy mother and find her in distressed circumstances, I bid you provide for her, but how much, I leave entirely to your judgment. Meantime, here I am with an income of nearly L700 a year. I live very simply, as you see, but I give away a good deal in local charity. The people are getting better wages now; in any case they are usually most ungrateful. I feel I should be happier if I diverted some of this alms-giving to you. You must find this preparatory life very expensive. You must let me send you twenty-five pounds every half-year for pocket money. Here is a cheque on the South Wales Bank for the first instalment. And remember, if you are in *any* difficulty about your career that a little money can get over do not hesitate to apply to me.

Your loving father,
HOWEL VAUGHAN WILLIAMS.

P.S. I have taken five days to write this but see how steady the handwriting is. It is a pleasure to me to look on my own handwriting again. And I feel I owe it all to you! I also forgot in the body of the letter to tell you one curious thing. You know we are here on the borders of an interesting vein of limestone which runs all round the coal beds. I dare say you remember as a boy of fifteen or so spraining your ankle in Griffith's Hole? Well Griffith's Hole turns out to be the entrance into a wonderful cave in the limestone. Hither came the other day a party of scientific men who think that majestic first chapter of Genesis to be a Babylonian legend! It appears they discovered or thought they discovered the remains of Ancient man in Griffith's Hole. I invited them to tea at the Vicarage and amongst them was a very learned gentleman quite as wise as but less aggressive than the others. He was known as "Professor Rossiter"; and commenting on the similarity of my name with that of a "very agreeable young gentleman" whom he had recently seen in Gower, it turned out that you were an acquaintance of his. He thinks it a great pity that you are reading for the Bar and wishes you had taken up Science instead. At any rate he hopes you will go and see him in London one day—No. 1 Park Crescent. Portland Place.

H. V. W.

Several times in reading this letter the tears stood in David's eyes. So much trust and kindness made him momentarily sorry at the double life he was leading. If it were possible to establish the death of the wastrel he was personating he would perhaps allow his "father" to live on in this new-found happiness; but if the real D.V.W. were alive some effort must be made to help him out of the slough—perhaps to bring him back. He would try to find out through Frank Gardner.

Some time before Vivie Warren had taken her departure, she had left behind in Honoria Fraser's temporary care a Power of Attorney duly executed in favour of David Vavasour

Williams; and reciprocally D.V.W. had executed another in favour of Vivien Warren. Both these documents lay securely in the little safe that David had had fitted into the wall of his sitting-room in Fig Tree Court. Also David had opened an account in his own name after he got back from Wales, at the Temple Bar Branch of the C. &. C. Bank. Into this he now paid the cheque for twenty-five pounds which his father had sent as pocket money.

A few days afterwards, Vivie Warren reappeared—in spirit —and indited a letter to Frank Gardner's agents in Cape Town. She was careful to give no address at the head of the letter and to post it at Victoria Station. In it she said she was starting on a tour abroad, but asked him to do what he could to trace the boy who had lain so grievously ill in the hospital at Colesberg. Had he recovered after the Boers had taken Colesberg? As a rumour had reached her that he had, and had even returned to England. She wanted to know, and if they ever met again would tell him why. Meanwhile if he got any news would he address it to *her*, care of Honoria Fraser, Queen Anne's Mansions, St. James's Park; as her own address would be quite uncertain for the present. Or it would do quite as well if he wrote to Praddy; but *not* to his father, which might only needlessly agitate the old clergyman down in Wales, whom Vivie by an unexpected chance had come to know.

The first result of this letter a year later was a statement of Frank's belief, almost certainty, that his acquaintance of the hospital *had* died and been buried while the Boers held possession of Colesberg; and that indeed was the utmost that was ever learnt about the end of the ill-fated son of Howel Vaughan Williams and Mary his wife, who were wedded in sunshine and with fair prospects of happiness in the early summer of 1874.

The new-born David Vavasour Williams having by November settled all these details, having arranged to pay the very modest rent of fifty-five pounds for his three rooms at Fig Tree Court, and twenty-five pounds a year to the housekeeper who was to "do" for him and another gentleman on the same floor—a gentleman who was most anxious to be chummy with the new tenant of the opposite chambers but whose advances were firmly though civilly kept at bay— having likewise passed his preliminary examination (since he could not avow that inside his clothes he was a third wrangler), having satisfied his two "godfathers" of the Bar that he was a fit person to recommend to the Benchers; having arranged to read with a barrister in chambers, and settled all other preliminaries of importance: decided that he would pay an afternoon call on the Rossiters in Portland Place and see how the land lay there.

Already a strange exhilaration was spreading over David's mind. Life was not twice but ten times more interesting than it had appeared to the prejudiced eyes of Vivien Warren. It was as though she—he—had passed through some magic door, gone through the looking-glass and was contemplating the same world as the one Vivie had known for—shall we say fifteen?—years, but a world which viewed from a different standpoint was quite changed in proportions, in colour, in the conjunction of events. It was a world in which everything was made smooth and easy before the semblance of manhood. What a joy to be rid of skirts and petticoats! To be able to run after and leap on to an omnibus, to wear the same hat day after day just stuck on top of her curly head. Not, perhaps, to change her clothes, between her uprising and her retirement to bed, unless she were going out to dine. No simpering. No need to ask favours. No compliments. It is true she felt awkward in the presence of women, not quite the same, even with Honoria. But with men. What a difference! She felt she had never really known men before.

At first the frank speech, the expletives, the smoking-room stories made her a little uncomfortable and occasionally called forth an irrepressible blush. But this was not to her disadvantage. It made her seem younger, and created a good impression on her tutors and acquaintances. "A nice modest boy, fresh from the country—pity to lead him astray—won't preserve his innocence long—" was the vaguely defined impression, contact with her—him, I mean—made on most decent male minds. Many a lad comes up from the country to commence his career in London who knew far less than the unfortunate Vivie had been compelled to know of the shady side of life; who is compelled to lead a somewhat retired life by straitness of means; whose determination towards probity and regularity of life is respected by the men of law among whom he finds himself.

But David having decided—he did not quite know why—to pursue his acquaintance with Professor Rossiter; having written to ask if he might do so (as a matter of fact he frequently saw Rossiter walking across the gardens of New Square to go to the museum of the Royal College of Surgeons: he recollected him immediately but Rossiter did not reciprocate, being absent-minded); and having received a card from "Linda Rossiter" to say they would be at home throughout the winter on Thursdays, between 4 and 6: went on one of those Thursdays and made definite progress with the great friendship of his life.

Sir Harry Johnston

CHAPTER VI

THE ROSSITERS

The Rossiters' house in Park Crescent was at the northern end of Portland Place, and its high-walled garden—the stables that were afterwards to become a garage—and Michael Rossiter's long, glass-roofed studio-laboratory—abutted on one of those quiet, deadly-respectable streets at the back that are called after Devon or Dorset place names.

The house is now a good deal altered and differently numbered, a portion of it having been destroyed in one of the 1917 air-raids, when the Marylebone Road was strewn with its broken glass for twenty yards. But in the winter of 1901-2 and onwards till 1914 it was a noted centre of social intercourse between Society and Science. The Rossiters were well enough off—he made quite two thousand a year out of his professorial work and his books, and her income which was L5,000 when she first married had risen to L9,000 after they had been married ten years; through the increase in value of Leeds town property. Mrs. Rossiter had had two children, but were both dead, her facile tears were dried, she satisfied her maternal instinct by the keeping of three pug dogs which her husband secretly detested. She also had a scarlet-and-blue macaw and two cockatoos and a Persian cat; but these last her husband liked or tolerated for their colour or their biological interest; only, as in the case of the dogs, he objected (though seldom angrily, out of consideration for his wife's feelings) to their being so messily and inopportunely fed.

Linda Rossiter was liable to lose her pets as she had lost her two children by alternating days of forgetfulness with weeks of lavish over-attention. But as she readily gave way to tears on the least remonstrance, Michael in the course of eleven years of married life remonstrated as little as possible. A clever, tactful parlour-maid and two good housemaids, a manservant who was devoted to the "professor" and a taxidermist who assisted him in his experiments did the rest in keeping the big house tolerably tidy and presentable. Rossiter himself was too intent on the stars, the gases of decomposition, the hidden processes of life, miscegenation in star-fish, microbic diseases in man, beasts, birds and bees, the glands of the throat, the suprarenal capsules and the chemical origin of life to care much for aesthetics, for furniture and house decoration. He was the third son of an impoverished Northumbrian squire who on his part cared only for the more barbarous field-sports, and when he could take his mind off them believed that at some time and place unspecified Almighty God had dictated the English bible word for word, had established the English Church and had scrupulously prescribed the functions and limitations of woman. His wife—Michael Rossiter's tenderly-loved mother—had died from a neglected prolapsus of the womb, and the old rambling house in Northumberland situated in superb scenery, had in its furniture grown more and more hideous to the eye as early and mid-Victorian fashions and ideals receded and modern taste shook itself free from what was tawdry, fluffy, stuffy, floppy, messy, cheaply imitative, fringed and tasselled and secretive.

Michael himself from sheer detestation of the surroundings

under which he had grown to manhood favoured the uncovered, the naked wood or stone or slate, the bare floor, the wooden settee or cane-bottomed chair, the massive sideboard, the bare mantelpiece and distempered wall. On the whole, their house in Portland Place satisfied tolerably well the advanced taste in domestic scenery of 1901. But your eye was caught at once by the additions made by Mrs. Rossiter. Linda conceived it was her womanly mission to lighten the severity of Michael's choice in furniture and decorations. She introduced rickety and expensive screens that were easily knocked over; photographs in frames which toppled at a breath; covers on every flat surface that could be covered—occasional tables, tops of grand pianos. If she did not put frills round piano legs, she placed tasselled poufs about the drawing-room that every short-sighted visitor fell over, and used large bows of slightly discoloured ribbon to mask unneeded brackets. In the reception rooms food-bestrewn parrot stands were left where they ought never to be seen; and there were gilt-wired parrot cages; baskets for the pugs lined with soiled shawls; absurd ornaments, china cats with exaggerated necks, alabaster figures of stereotyped female beauty and flowerpot stands of ornate bamboo. She loved portieres, and she would fain have mitigated the bareness of the panelled or distempered walls; only that here her husband was firm. She unconsciously mocked the few well-chosen, well-placed pictures on the walls (which she itched to cover with a "flock" paper) by placing in the same room on bamboo easels that matched the be-ribboned flower-stands pastel, crayon, or *gouache* studies of the worst possible taste.

Michael's library alone was free from her improvements, though it was sometimes littered with her work-bags or her work. She had long ago developed the dreadful mistake that it "helped" Michael at his work if she brought hers (perfectly futile as a rule) there too. "I just sit silently in his room, my dear, and stitch or knit something for poor people in

Marrybone—I'm told you mayn't say Mary-le-bone. I feel it *helps* Michael to know I'm there, but of course I don't interrupt him at his *work*."

As a matter of fact she did, confoundedly. But fortunately she soon grew sleepy or restless. She would yawn, as she believed "prettily," but certainly noisily; or she would wonder "how time was going," and of course her twenty-guinea watch never went, or if it was going was seldom within one hour of the actual time. Or she would sneeze six times in succession—little cat-like sneezes that were infinitely disturbing to a brain on the point of grasping the solution of a problem. Throughout the winter months she had a little cough. Oh no, you needn't think I'm preparing the way for decease through phthisis—it was one of those "kiffy" coughs due in the main to acidity—too many sweet things in her diet, too little exercise. She *thought* she coughed with the greatest discretion but to the jarred nerves of her husband a few hearty bellows or an asthmatic wheeze would have been preferable to the fidgety, marmoset-like sounds that came from under a lace handkerchief. Sometimes he would raise his eyes to speak sharply; but at the sight of the mild gaze that met his, the perfect belief that she was a soothing presence in this room of hard thinking and close writing—this superb room with its unrivalled library that he owed to the use of her wealth, his angry look would soften and he would return smile for smile.

Linda though a trifle fretful on occasion, especially with servants, a little petulant and huffy with a sense of her own dignity and importance as a rich woman, was completely happy in her marriage. She had never regretted it for one hour, never swerved from the conviction that she and Michael were a perfect match—he, tall, stalwart, black-haired and strong; she "petite"—she loved the French adjective ever since it had been applied to her at

Scarborough by a sycophantic governess—petite—she would repeat, blonde, plump, or better still "potelee" (the governess had later suggested, when she came to tea and hoped to be asked to stay) *potelee*, blue-eyed and pink-cheeked. Dresden china and all the stale similes applied to a type of little woman of whom the modern world has grown intolerant.

It was therefore into this *milieu* that David found himself introduced one Thursday at the end of November, 1901. He had walked the short distance from Great Portland Street station. It was a fine day with a red sunset, and a lemon-coloured, thin moon-crescent above the sunset. The trees and bushes of Park Crescent were a background of dull blue haze. The surface of the broad roads was dry and polished, so his neat, patent-leather boots would still be fit for drawing-room carpets.

A footman in a very plain livery—here Michael was firm—opened the massive door. David passed between some statuary of too frank a style for Linda's modest taste and was taken over by a butler of severe aspect who announced him into the great drawing-room as Mr. David Williams.

He recognized Rossiter at once, standing up with a tea-cup and saucer, and presumed that a fluffy, much be-furbelowed little lady at the main tea-table was Mrs. Rossiter, since she wore no hat. There was besides a rather alarming concourse of men and women of the world as he kept his eyes firmly fixed on Mrs. Rossiter for his immediate goal.

Rossiter met him half-way, shook hands cordially and introduced him to his wife who bowed with one of her "sweet" looks. For the moment David did not interest her. She was much more interested in trying to give an impression of profundity to Lady Feenix who was commenting on the professor's discoveries of the strange properties of the thyroid gland. A few introductions were effected—Lady Towcester, Lady Flower, Miss Knipper-Totes, Lady Dombey, Mr. Lacrevy, Professor Ray Lankester, Mr. and Mrs. Gosse—and naturally for the most part David only half caught their names while they, without masking their indifference, closed their ears to his ("Some student or other from his classes, I suppose—rather nicely dressed, rather too good-looking for a young man"); and Rossiter, who had been interrupted first by Mrs. Rossiter asking him to observe that Lady Dombey had nothing on her plate, and secondly by David's entrance, resumed his discourse. Goodness knew that he didn't *want* to discourse on these occasions, but Society expected it of him. There were quite twenty—twenty-two—people present and most of them—all the women—wanted to go away and say four hours afterwards:

"We were (I was) at the Rossiters this afternoon, and the Professor was fascinating" ("great," "profoundly interesting," "shocking, my dear," "scandalous," "disturbing," "illuminating," "more-than-usually- enthralling-only-she-*would*-keep-interrupting-why-*is*-she-such-a-fool?") according to the idiosyncrasy of the diner-out. "He talked to us about the thyroid gland—I don't believe poor Bob's got one, between ourselves—and how if you enlarged it or reduced it you'd adjust people's characters to suit the needs of Society; and all about chimpanzi's blood—I believe he *vivisects* half through the night in that studio behind the house—being the same as ours; and then Ray Lankester and Chalmers Mitchell argued about the caeca—caecums, you know—something to do with appendicitis—of the mammalia, and altogether we had a high old time—I *always* learn something on their Thursdays."

Well: Rossiter resumed his description of an experiment he was making—quite an everyday one, of course, for there were at least three men present to whom he wasn't going to give away clues prematurely. An experiment on the motor biallaxis of dormice.

[Mrs. Rossiter had six months previously bought a dormouse in a cage at a bazaar, and after idolizing it for a week had forgotten all about it. Her husband had rescued it half starved; his assistant had fed it up in the laboratory, and they had tried a few experiments on it with painless drugs with astonishing results.]

The recital really was interesting and entirely outside the priggishness of Science, but it was marred in consecutive-ness and simplicity by Mrs. Rossiter's interruptions. "Michael dear, Lady Dombey's cup!" Or: "Mike, could you cut that cake and hand it round?" Or, if she didn't interrupt her husband she started stories and side-issues of her own in a voice that was quite distinctly heard, about a new stitch in crochet she had seen in the *Queen*, or her inspection of the East Marrybone soup kitchen.

However when all had taken as much tea and cakes and *marrons glaces* as they cared for—David was so shy that he had only one cup of tea and one piece of tea-cake—the large group broke up into five smaller ones. The few gradually converged, and dropping all nonsense discussed biology like good 'uns, David listening eager-eyed and enthralled at the marvels just beginning to peep out of the dissecting and vivisecting rooms and chemical laboratories in the opening years of the Twentieth century. Then one by one they all departed; but as David was going too Rossiter detained him by a kindly pressure on the arm—a contact which sent a half-pleasant, half-disagreeable thrill through his nerves.

"Don't hurry away unless you really *are* pressed for time. I want to show you some of my specimens and the place where I work."

David followed him—after taking his leave of Mrs. Rossiter who accepted his polite sentences—a little stammered—with a slightly pompous acquiescence—followed him to the library and then through a curtained door down some steps into a great studio-laboratory, provided (behind screens) with washing places, and full of mysteries, with cupboards and shelves and further rooms beyond and a smell of chloride of lime combined with alcoholic preservatives and undefined chemicals. After a tour round this domain in which David was only slightly interested—for lack of the right education and imagination—so far he—or—she had only the mind of a mathematician—Rossiter led him back into the library, drew out chairs, indicated cigarettes—even whiskey and soda if he wanted it—David declined—and then began to say what was at the back of his mind:—

"We met first in the train, the South Wales Express, you remember? I fancy you told me then that you had been in South Africa, in this bungled war, and had been either wounded or ill in some way. In fact you went so far as to say you had had 'necrosis of the jaw,' a thing I politely doubted because whatever it was it has left no perceptible scar. Of course it's damned impertinent of me to cross-examine you at all, or to ask *why* you went to and why you left South Africa. But I don't mind confessing you inspire me with a good deal of interest.

"Now the other day—as you know—I made the acquaintance of your father in Wales—at Pontystrad. I told him I had shown a young fellow some of those Gower caves and how his name was—like your father's, 'Williams.' Of course we soon came to an understanding. Then your father spoke of you in *high* praise. What a delightful nature was yours, how considerate and kind you were—don't blush, though I admit it becomes you—Well you can pretty well guess how he went on. But what interested me particularly was his next admission: how different you were as a lad—rather more than the ordinary wild oats—eh? And how completely an absence in South Africa had changed you. You must forgive my cheek in dissecting your character like this. My excuse is that you yourself had rather vaguely referred to some wound or blood poisoning or operation, on the jaw or the throat. Not to beat about the bush any more, the idea came into my mind that *if* in some way the knife or the enemy's bullet had interfered with your thyroid gland—Twig what I mean? I mean, that if your old man has not been exaggerating and that the difference between the naughty boy whom he sent up to London in—what was it? 1896?—and the perfectly behaved, good sort of chap that you are *now* is no more than what usually happens when young men lose their cubbishness, *why—why*—do you take me?—I ask myself whether the change had come about through some interference with the thyroid gland. Do you understand? And I thought, seeing how intensely interesting this research has become, you might have told me more about it. Just what *did* happen to you; where you were wounded, who attended to you, what operation was performed on the throat—only the rum thing is there seems to be no scar—well: now *you* help me out, that is unless you feel more inclined to say, 'What the *hell* does it matter to *you*?'"...

David by this time has grown scarlet with embarrassment and confusion. But he endeavoured to meet the situation.

"My character *has* changed during the last five years, and especially so since I came back from South Africa. But I am quite sure it was not due to any operation, on the throat or anywhere else. I really don't know *why* I told you that silly falsehood in the train—about necrosis of the jaw. The fact is that when I was in hospital—at—Colesberg, a friend of mine in the same ward used—to chaff me—and say I was going to have necrosis. I had got knocked over one day—by—the—wind of a shell and thought I was done for, but it really was next to nothing. P'raps I had a dose of fever on top. At any rate they kept me in hospital, and one morning the doctors disappeared and the Boers marched in and when I got well enough I managed to escape and get away to—er—Cape Town and so returned—with some money—my friend Frank Gardner lent me." (At this stage the sick-at-heart Vivie was saying to herself, "*What* an account I'm laying up for Frank to honour when he comes back—if he *does* come back.") "I don't know *why* I tell you all this, except that I ought never to have misled you at the start. But *if* you are a kind and good man"—David's voice broke here—"You will forget all about it and not upset my father, I can *assure* you I haven't done *anything* really wrong. I haven't deserted—some day—perhaps—I can tell you all about it. But at present all that South African episode is just a horrid dream—I was more sinned against than sinning" (tears were rather in the voice at this stage). "I want to forget all about it—and settle down and vex my father no more. I want to read for the Bar—a soldier's life is the very *opposite* to what I should choose if I were a free agent. But you will trust me, won't you? You will believe me when I say I've done *nothing* wrong, nothing that you, if you knew all the facts, would call wrong...?"

Speech here trailed off into emotion. Despite the severest self-restraint the bosom rose and fell. A few tears trickled down the smooth cheeks—it was an ingratiating boy on the verge of manhood that Rossiter saw before him. He hastened to say:

"My *dear* chap! Don't say another word, unless you like to blackguard me for my impertinence in putting these questions. I *quite* understand. We'll consider the whole thing erased from our memories. Go on studying for the Bar with all your might, if you must take up so barren a profession and won't become my pupil in biology—Great openings, I can tell you, coming now in that direction." (A pause.)

"But if it's of any interest to you, just come here as often as you like in your spare time—either to tea with Mrs. Rossiter or to see me at work on my experiments. I've taken a great liking to you, if you'll allow me to say so. I think there's good stuff in you. A young man reading for the Bar in London is none the worse for a few friends. He must often feel pretty lonely on a Sunday, for example. And he may also—now I'm going to be impertinent and paternal again— he may also pick up undesirable acquaintances, male—and female. Don't you get feeling lonely, with your home far away in Wales. Consider yourself free of this place at any rate, and my wife and I can introduce you to some other people you might like to know. I might introduce you to Mark Stansfield the Q.C. Do you know any one in London, by the bye?"

"Oh yes," said David, smiling with all but one tear dried on a still coloured cheek. "I know Honoria Fraser—I know Mr. Praed the architect—"

"The A.R.A.? Of course; you or your father said you had been his pupil. H'm. Praed. Yes, I visualize him. Rather a dilettante—whimsical—I didn't like what I heard of him at one time. However it's no affair of mine. And Honoria Fraser! She's simply one of the best women I know. It's curious she wasn't here—At least I didn't see her—this afternoon. She's a friend of my wife's. I knew her when she was at Newnham. She had a great friend—what was it? Violet? No, Vera? Vivien—yes that was it, *Vivien* Warren. Of course! Why that business she started for women in the City somewhere is called *Fraser and Warren*. She was always wanting to bring this Vivien Warren here. Said she had such a pretty colouring. I own I rather like to see a pretty woman. But she didn't come" (pulls at his pipe and thrusts another cigarette on David). "Went abroad. Seemed rather morose. Some one who came with Honoria said she had a bad mother, and Honoria very rightly shut him up. By the bye, *where* and *how* did you come to meet Honoria first?"

(David was on the point of saying—he was so unstrung— "Why we were at Newnham together." Then resolved to tell another whopper—Indeed I am told there is a fascination in certain circumstances about lying—and replied): "Vivien Warren was my cousin. She was a Vavasour on her mother's side—from South Wales—and my mother was a Vavasour too—" And as the disguised Vivie said this, some inkling came into her mind that there *was* a real relationship between Catharine Warren *nee* Vavasour and the Mary Vavasour who was David's mother. A spasm of joy flashed through her at the possibility of her story being in some slight degree true.

"I see," said Rossiter, satisfied, and feeling now that the interview had lasted long enough and that there would be just time to glance at his assistant's afternoon work before he dressed for dinner....

"Well, old chap. Good-bye for the present. Come often and see us and look upon me—I must be fifteen years older than you are—What, *twenty-four*? Impossible! You don't look a day older than twenty—in fact, if you hadn't told me you'd been in South Africa—However as I was saying, look on me as *in loco parentis* while you *are* in London. I'll show you the way out into the hall. Shall they call you a cab? No? You're quite right. It's a splendid night for January. Where do you live? Here, write it down in my address book.... '7 Fig Tree Court, Temple'—What a jolly address! Are there fig trees in the Temple ... still? P'raps descended from cuttings or layers the poor Templars brought from the Holy Land."

David returned to Fig Tree Court and his studies of criminology. But his body and mind thrilled with the experiences of the afternoon; and the musty records in works of repellent binding and close, unsympathetic print of nineteenth century forgery, poisoning, assaults-on-the-person, and cruelty-to-children cases for once failed to hold his close attention. He sat all through the evening after a supper of bread and cheese and ginger beer in his snug, small room, furnished principally with well-filled book-shelves. The room had a glowing fire and a green-shaded reading lamp. He sat staring beyond his law books at visions, waking dreams that came and went. The dangers of exposure that opened before him were in these dreams, but there were other mind-pictures that filled his life with a glow of colour. How different from the drab horizons that encircled poor Vivie Warren less than a year ago! Poor Vivie, whom even FitzJohn's Avenue at Hampstead had rejected, who had long since been dropped—no doubt on account of rumours concerning her mother—by the few acquaintances she had made at Cambridge, who had parents living in South Kensington, Bayswater, and Bloomsbury. Here was Portland Place receiving her in her guise as David Williams with open arms. Men and women looked at her kindly, interestedly, and she could look back at them without that protective frown. At night she could walk about the town, go to the theatre, stroll along the Embankment and attract no man's offensive attentions. She could enter where she liked for a meal, a cup of tea, frequent the museum of the Royal College of Surgeons when she would without waiting for a "ladies" day; stop to look at a street fight, cause no sour looks if she entered a smoking compartment on the train, mingle with the man-world unquestioned, unhindered, unnoticed, exciting at most a pleasant off-hand camaraderie due to her youth and good looks.

Should she go on with the bold adventure? A thousand times

yes! David should break no law in Vivie's code of honour, do real wrong to no one; but Vivie should see the life best worth living in London from a man's standpoint.

David however must be armed at every point and have his course clearly marked out before his contemplation. He must steep himself in the geography of South Africa—Why not get Rossiter to propose him as a fellow of the Royal Geographical Society? That *would* be a lark because they wouldn't admit women as members: they had refused Honoria Fraser. David must read up—somewhere—the history of the South African War as far as it went. He had better find out something about the Bechuanaland Police Force; how as a member of such a force he could have drifted as far south as the vicinity of Colesberg; how thereabouts he could have got sick enough—he certainly would say nothing more about a wound—to have been put into hospital. He must find out how he could have escaped from the Boers and come back to England without getting into difficulties with the military or the Colonial Office or whoever had any kind of control over the members of the Bechuanaland Border Police....

But the whole South African episode had better be dropped. Rossiter, after his appeal, would set himself to forget and ignore it. It must be damped down in the poor old father's mind as of relative unimportance—after all, his father was a recluse who did not have many visitors ... by the bye, he must remember to write on the morrow and explain why he could not come down for Christmas or the New Year ... would promise a good long visit in the Easter holidays instead—Must remember that resolution to learn up some Welsh. What a nuisance it was that you couldn't buy anywhere in London or in South Wales any book about modern conversation in Welsh. The sort of Welsh you learnt in the old-fashioned books, which were all that could be got, was Biblical language—Some one had told David that if you went into Smithfield Market in the early morning you might meet the Welsh farmers and stock-drivers who had come up from Wales during the night and who held forth in the Cymric tongue over their beasts. But probably their language was such as would shock Nannie.... Supposing Frank Gardner did come to England? In that case it might be safer to confide in Frank. He was harum-scarum, but he was chivalrous and he pitied Vivie. Besides he was a prime appreciator of a lark. Should she even tell Rossiter? No, of *course* not. That was just one of the advantages of being "David." As "David" she could form a sincere and inspiring friendship with Rossiter which would be utterly beyond her reach as "Vivie." How pale beside the comradeship of Honoria now appeared the hand-grips, the hearty male free-masonry of a man like Rossiter. How ungrateful however even to make such an admission to herself....

At present the only people who knew of her prank and guessed or knew her purpose were Honoria and Bertie Adams. Honoria! what a noble woman, what a true friend. Somehow, now she was David, she saw Honoria in a different light. Poor Norie! She too had her wistful leanings, her sorrows and disappointments. What a good thing it would be if her mother decided to die—of course she would, could, never say any such thing to Norie—to die and set free Honoria to marry Major Petworth Armstrong! She felt Norie still hankered after him, but perhaps kept him at bay partly because of her mother's molluscous clingings—No! she wouldn't even sneer at Lady Fraser. Lady Fraser had been one of the early champions of Woman's rights. Very likely it was a dread of Vivie's sneers and disappointment that had mainly kept back Norie from accepting Major Armstrong's advances. Well, when next they met she—Vivie—or better still David—would set that right.

CHAPTER VII

HONORIA AGAIN

7, Fig Tree Court, Temple.
March 20, 1902.

DEAR HONORIA,—

I am going down to spend Easter with my people in South Wales. Before I leave I should so very much like a long talk with you where we can talk freely and undisturbed. That is impossible at the Office for a hundred reasons, especially now that Beryl Claridge has taken to working early in her new-found zeal, while Bertie Adams deems it his duty to stay late. I am—really, truly—grieved to hear that your mother is so ill again. I would not ask to meet her—even if she was well enough to receive people—because she does not know me and when one is as ill as she is, the introduction to a stranger is a horrid jar. But if you *could* fit in say an hour's detachment from her side—is it "bed-side" or is she able to get up?—and could receive me in your own sitting-room, why then we could have that full and free talk I should like on your affairs and on mine and on the joint affairs of *Fraser and Warren.*

Sir Harry Johnston

Yours sincerely,
D. V. W.

DEAR DAVID,—

Come by all means. The wish for a talk is fully reciprocated on my side. Mother generally tries to sleep in the afternoon between three and six, and a Nurse is then with her.

Yours sincerely,
H. F.

"Mr. David Williams wishes to see you, Miss," said a waiter, meeting Honoria on a Thursday afternoon, as she was emerging into their tiny hall from her mother's room.

"Show him up, please.... Ah *there* you are, *David*. We must both talk rather low as mother is easily waked. Come into my study; fortunately it is at the other end of the flat."

*   *   *   *   *

They reach the study, and Honoria closes the door softly but firmly behind them.

"We never do kiss as a rule, having long ago given up such a messy form of greeting; but certainly we wouldn't under these circumstances lest we could be seen from the opposite windows and thought to be 'engaged'; but though I may seem a little frigid in greeting you, it is only because of the clothes you are wearing'—You understand, don't you—?"

"Quite, dearest. We cannot be too careful. Besides we long ago agreed to be modern and sanitary in our manners."

"Won't you smoke?"

"Well, perhaps it would be more restful," said David, "more manly; but as a matter of fact of late I have been rather 'off' smoking. It is very wasteful, and as far as I am concerned it never produced much effect—either way—on the nerves. Still, it gives one a nice manly flavour. I always liked the smell of a smoking-room.... And your mother: how is she?"

"Very bad, I fear. The doctor tells me she can't last much longer, and hypocritical as the phrase sounds I couldn't wish her to, unless these pains can be mitigated, and this dreadful distress in breathing.... I wonder if some day *I* shall be like that, and if behind my back a daughter will be saying she couldn't wish me to live much longer, unless, etc. I shall miss her *frightfully*, if she does die.... Armstrong has been more than kind. He has got a woman's heart for tenderness. He thinks every day of some fresh palliative until the doctors quite dislike him. Fortunately his kindness gives mother a fleeting gleam of pleasure. She wants me to marry him—I don't know, I'm sure.... Whilst she's so bad I don't feel I could take any interest in love-making—and I suppose we *should* make love in a perfunctory way—We're all of us so bound by conventions. We try to feel dismal at funerals, when often the weather is radiant and the ride down to Brookwood most exhilarating. And love-making is supposed to go with marriage ... heigh-ho! What should you say if I *did* marry—Major Armstrong...? Did you ever hear of such a ridiculous name as Petworth? I should have to call him 'Pet' and every one would think I had gone sentimental in middle age. How *can* parents be so unthinking about Christian names? He can't see the thing as I do; it is almost the only subject on which he is 'huffy.' *You* are the other, about which more anon. He says the Petworth property meant *everything* to the Armstrongs, to *his* branch of the Armstrongs. But for that, they might have been any other kind of Armstrong—it always kept him straight at school and in the army, he says, to remember he was an Armstrong of Petworth. They have

Sir Harry Johnston

held that poor little property (*I* call it) alongside the Egmonts and the Leconfields for three hundred years, though they've been miserably poor. His second name is James—Petworth James Armstrong. But he loathes being called 'Jimmy.'"

"Of course, dear, I've no illusions. I'm not bad to look at—indeed I sometimes quite admire my figure when I see myself after my bath in the cheval glass—but I'm pretty well sure that one of the factors in Pet's admiration for me was my income. Mother, it seems, has a little of her own, from one of her aunts, and if the poor darling is taken—though it is simply horrid considering that *if*—only that she has talked so freely to Army—I think I like 'Army' far better than 'Pet'—Well I mean she's been trying to tell him ever since he first came to call that when she is gone I shall have, all told, in my own right, Five thousand a year. So I took the first opportunity of letting *him* know that Two thousand a year of that would be held in reserve for the work of the firm and for the Woman's Cause generally.... Look here, I won't babble on much longer.... I know you're dying to make *me* confidences.... We'll ring for tea to be sent in here, and whilst the waiter is coming and going—Don't they take *such* a time about it, when they're *de trop*?—we'll talk of ordinary things that can be shouted from the *house tops*.

"I haven't been to the Office for three days. Does everything seem to be going on all right?"

David: "Quite all right. Bertie Adams tries dumbly to express in his eyes his determination to see the firm and me through all our troubles and adventures. I wish I could convey a discreet hint to him not to be so *blatantly* discreet. If there were a Sherlock Holmes about the place he would spot at once that Adams and I shared a secret.... But about Beryl—" (Enter waiter....)

Honoria (to waiter): "Oh—er—tea for two please. Remember it must be China and the still-room maids *must* see that the water has been fresh-boiled. And buttered toast—or if you've got muffins...? You have? Well, then muffins; and of course jam and cake. And—would you mind—you always try, I know—bringing the things in very quietly—here—? Because Lady Fraser is so easily waked..."

(The Swiss waiter goes out, firmly convinced that Honoria's anxiety for her lady mother is really due to the desire that the mother should not interrupt a flirtation and a clandestine tea.)

Honoria: "Well, about Beryl?"

David: "Beryl, I should say, is going to become a great woman of business. But for that, and—I think—a curious streak of fidelity to her vacillating architect ('How happy could I be with either,' don't you know, *he* seems to feel—just now they say he is living steadily at Storrington with his wife No. 1, who is ill, poor thing) ... but for that and this, I think Beryl would enjoy a flirtation with me. She can't quite make me out, and my unwavering severity of manner. Her cross-questioning sometimes is maddening—or it might become so, but that with both of us—you and me—retiring so much into the background she has to lead such a strenuous life and see one after the other the more important clients. Of course—here's the tea..."

(Brief interval during which the waiter does much unnecessary laying out of the tea until Honoria says: "Don't let me keep you. I know you are busy at this time. I will ring if we want anything.") David continues: "Of course I come in for my share of the work after six. On one point Beryl is firm; she doesn't mind coming at nine or at eight or at half-past seven in the morning, but she *must* be back in Chelsea by half-past five to see her babies, wash them and put them to bed. She has a tiny little house, she tells me, near Trafalgar Square, and fortunately she's got an excellent and devoted nurse, one of those rare treasures that questions nothing and is only interested in the business in hand. She and a cook-general make up the establishment. Before Mrs. Architect No. 1 became ill, Mr. Architect used to visit her there pretty regularly, and is assumed to be Mr. Claridge.... Well: to finish up about Beryl: I think you—we—can trust her. She may be odd in her notions of morality, but in finance or business she's as honest—as—a man."

"My dear Vivie—I mean David—what a strange thing for *you* to say! I suppose it is part of your make-up—goes with the clothes and that turn-over collar, and the little safety pin through the tie—?"

David: "No, I said it deliberately. Men are mostly hateful things, but I think in business they're more dependable than women—think more about telling a lie or letting any one down. The point for you to seize on is this—if you haven't noticed it already: that Beryl has become an uncommonly good business woman. And what's more, my dear, you've improved *her* just as you improved *me*" (Honoria deprecates this with a gesture, as she sits looking into the fire). "Beryl's talk is getting ever so much less reckless. And she takes jolly good care not to scandalize a client. She finds Adams—she tells me—so severe at the least jest or personality that she only talks to him now on business matters, and finds him a great stand-by; and the other day she told Miss A.—as you call the senior clerk—she ought to be ashamed of herself, bringing in a copy of the *Vie Parisienne*. The way she settled Mrs. Gordon's affairs—you remember, No. 3875 you cata-logued the case—was masterly; and Mrs. G. has insisted on paying 5 per cent. commission on the recovered property. And it was Beryl who found out that leakage in the 'Variegated Tea Rooms' statement of accounts. I hadn't spotted it. No. I think we needn't be anxious about Beryl, especially whilst I am in Wales and you are giving yourself up—as you ought to do—to your mother. But it's coming to *this*, Honoria—" (Enter waiter. David says "Oh, damn," half audibly. Waiter is confirmed in his suspicions, but as he likes Honoria immensely resolves to say nothing about them in the Steward's room. She is such a kind young lady. He explains he has come to take the tea things away, and Honoria replies "Capital idea! Now, David, you'll be able to have the whole table for your accounts!").... "It's coming to *this*, Honoria," says David, clearing his throat, "that you will soon be wanting not to be bothered any more with the affairs of *Fraser and Warren*, and after I really get into the Law business I too shall require to detach myself. Let us therefore be thankful that Beryl is shaping so well. I rather think this summer you will have to get more office accommodation and give her some more responsible women to help her.... *Now* finish what you were saying about Major Armstrong."

Honoria: "Of *course* I shall marry him some day. I suppose I felt that the day after I first met him. But it amuses me to be under no illusion. I am sure this is what happened two years ago—or whenever it was he came back wounded from your favourite haunt, South Africa. Michael Rossiter—who likes 'Army' enormously—I think they were at school or college together—said to Linda, his wife: 'Here's Armstrong. One of the best. Wants to marry. Wife must have a little money, otherwise he'll have to go on letting Petworth Manor. And here's Honoria Fraser, one of the finest women I've ever met. Getting a little long in the tooth—or will be soon. Let's bring 'em together and make a match of it.'"

"So we are each convoked for a luncheon, with a projected adjournment to Kew—which *you* spoilt—and there it is. But joking apart, 'Army' is a dear and I am sure by now he wants me even more than my money—and I certainly want him.

I'm rising thirty and I long for children and don't want 'em to come to me too late in life."

David: "You said he didn't like *me*..."

Honoria: "Oh that was half nonsense. When we all met last Sunday at the Rossiters he became very jealous and suspicious. Asked who was that whipper-snapper—I said you neither whipped nor snapped, especially if kindly treated. He said then who was that Madonna young man—a phrase it appears he'd picked up from Lord Cromer, who used to apply it to every new arrival from the Foreign Office—Armstrong was once his military secretary. I was surprised to hear he thought you womanish—I spoke of your fencing, riding,—was just going to add 'hockey,' and 'croquet': then remembered they might be thought feminine pastimes, so referred to your swimming. Military men always respect a good swimmer; I fancy because many of them funk the water.... I was just going on to explain that you were a cousin of a great friend of mine and helped me in my business, when a commissionaire came from Quansions in a hansom to say that mother was feeling very bad again. 'Army' and I went back in the hansom, but I was crying a little and being a gentleman he did not press his suit..."

Enter Lady Fraser's nurse on tiptoe. Says in a very hushed voice "Major Armstrong has called, Miss Fraser. He came to ask about Lady Fraser. I said if anything she was a bit better and had had a good sleep. He then asked if he might see you."

Honoria: "Certainly. Would you mind showing him in here? It will save my ringing for the waiter."

Enter Major Armstrong. At the sight of David he flushes and looks fierce.

Honoria: "So glad you've come, dear Major. I hear mother has had a good nap. I must go to her presently. You know David Vavasour Williams?—Davy! You really *must* leave out your second name! It gets so fatiguing having to say it every time I introduce you."

Armstrong bows stiffly and David, standing with one well-shaped foot in a neat boot on the curb of the fireplace, looks up and returns the bow.

Honoria: "This won't do. You are two of my dearest friends, and yet you hardly greet one another. I always determined from the age of fifteen onwards I would never pass my life as men and women in a novel do—letting misunderstandings creep on and on where fifty words might settle them. *Army!* You've often asked me to marry you—or at least so I've understood your broken sentences. I never refused you in so many words. Now I say distinctly 'Yes'—if you'll have me. Only, you know quite well I can't actually marry you whilst mother lies so ill..."

Major Armstrong, very red in the face, in a mixture of exultation, sympathy and annoyance that the affairs of his heart are being discussed before a whipper-snapper stranger—says: "*Honoria!* Do you *mean* it? Oh..."

Honoria: "Of course I mean it! And if I drew back you could now have a breach-of-promise-of-marriage action, with David as an important witness. D.V.W.—who by the bye is a cousin of my *greatest friend*—my friend for life, whether you like her—as you ought to do—or not—Vivie Warren.... David is reading for the Bar; and besides being your witness to what I have just said, might—if you deferred your action long enough—be your Counsel.... Now look here," (with a catch in the voice) "you two dear things. My nerves are all to bits.... I haven't slept properly for nights and nights. David, dear, if you *must* talk any more business before you go down to Wales, you must come and see me to-morrow.... Darling mother! I can't *bear* the thought you may not live to see my happiness." (David discreetly withdraws without a formal good-bye, and as he goes out and the firelight flickers up, sees Armstrong take Honoria in his arms.)

CHAPTER VIII

THE BRITISH CHURCH

David had read hard all through Hilary term with Mr. Stansfield of the Inner Temple; he had passed examinations brilliantly; he had solved knotty problems in the legal line for *Fraser and Warren*, and as already related he had begun to go out into Society. Indeed, starting from the Rossiters' Thursdays and Praed's studio suppers, he was being taken up by persons of influence who were pleased to find him witty, possessed of a charming voice, of quiet but unassailable manners. Opinions differed as to his good looks. Some women proclaimed him as adorable, rather Sphynx-like, you know, but quite fascinating with his well-marked eye-brows, his dark and curly lashes, the rich warm tints of his complexion, the unfathomable grey eyes and short upper lip with the down of adolescence upon it. Other women without assigning any reason admitted he did not produce any effect on their sensibility—they disliked law students, they said, even if they were of a literary turn; they also disliked curates and shopwalkers and sidesmen ... and Sunday-school teachers. Give them *manly* men; avowed soldiers and sailors, riders to hounds, sportsmen, big game hunters, game-keepers, chauffeurs—the chauffeur was becoming a new factor in Society, Bernard Shaw's "superman"—prize-fighters, meat-salesmen—then you knew where you were.

Similarly men were divided in their judgment of him. Some liked him very much, they couldn't quite say why. Others spoke of him contemptuously, like Major Armstrong had done. This was due partly to certain women being inclined to run after him—and therefore to jealousy on behalf of the professional lady-killer of the military species—and partly to a vague feeling that he was enigmatic—Sphynx-like, as some women said. He was too silent sometimes, especially if the conversation amongst men tended towards racy stories; he was sarcastic and nimble-witted when he did speak. And he was not easily bullied. If he encountered an insolent person, he gave full effect to his five feet eight inches, the look from his grey eyes was unwavering as though he tacitly accepted the challenge, there was an invisible rapier hanging from his left hip, a poise of the body which expressed dauntless courage.

Honoria's stories of his skill in fencing, riding, swimming, ball-games, helped him here. They were perfectly true or sufficiently true—*mutatis mutandis*—and when put to the test stood the test. David indeed found it well during this first season in Town to hire a hack and ride a little in the Park—it only added one way and another about fifty pounds to his outlay and impressed certain of the Benchers who were beginning to turn an eye on him. One elderly judge—also a Park rider—developed an almost inconvenient interest in him; asked him to dinner, introduced him to his daughters, and wanted to know a deal too much as to his position and prospects.

On the whole, it was a distinct relief from a public position, from this increasing number of town acquaintances, this broader and broader track strewn with cunning pitfalls, to lock up his rooms and go off to Wales for the Easter holidays. Easter was late that year—or it has to be for the purpose of my story—and David was fortunate in the weather and the temperature. If West Glamorganshire had looked richly, grandiosely beautiful in full summer, it had an exquisite, if quite different charm in early spring, in April. The great trees were spangled with emerald leaf-buds; the cherries, tame and wild, the black-thorn, the plums and pears in orchards and on old, old, grey walls, were in full blossom of virgin white. The apple trees in course of time showed pink buds. The gardens were full of wall-flowers—the inhabited country smelt of wall-flowers—purple flags, narcissi, hyacinths. The woodland was exquisitely strewn with primroses. In the glades rose innumerable spears of purple half-opened bluebells; the eye ranged over an anemone-dotted sward in this direction; over clusters of smalt-blue dog violets in another. Ladies'-smocks and cowslips made every meadow delicious; and the banks of the lowland streams were gorgeously gilded with king-cups. The mountains on fine days were blue and purple in the far distance; pale green and grey in the foreground. Under the April showers and sun-shafts they became tragic, enchanted, horrific, paradisiac. Even the mining towns were bearable—in the spring sunshine. If man had left no effort untried to pile hideosity on hideosity, flat ugliness on nauseous squalor, he had not been able to affect the arch of the heavens in its lucid blue, all smokes and vapours driven away by the spring winds; he had not been able to neutralize the vast views visible from the miners' sordid, one-storeyed dwellings, the panorama of hill and plain, of glistening water, towering peaks, and larch forests of emerald green amid the blue-Scotch pines and the black-green yews.

David in previous letters, looking into his father's budget, had shown him he could afford to keep a pony and a pony cart. This therefore was waiting for him at the little station with the gardener to drive. But in a week, David, already a good horseman, had learnt to drive under the gardener's teaching, and then was able to take his delighted father out for whole-day trips to revel in the beauties of the scenery.

They would have with them a wicker basket containing an ample lunch prepared by the generous hands of Bridget. They would stop at some spot on a mountain pass; tether the pony, sit on a plaid shawl thrown over a boulder, and feast their eyes on green mountain-shoulders reared against the pale blue sky; or gaze across ravines not unworthy of Switzerland. Or they would put up pony and cart at some village inn, explore old battlemented churches and church-yards with seventeenth and eighteenth century headstones, so far more tasteful and seemly than the hideous death memorials of the nineteenth century. And ever and again the old father, looking more and more like a Druid, would recite that charming Spring song, the 104th Psalm; or fragments of Welsh poetry sounding very good in Welsh—as no doubt Greek poetry does in properly pronounced Greek, but being singularly bald and vague in its references to earth, sea, sky and flora when translated into plain English.

David expressed some such opinions which rather scanda-lized his father who had grown up in the conventional school of unbounded, unreasoning reverence for the Hebrew, Greek and Keltic classics. From that they passed to the great problems, the undeterminable problems of the Universe; the awful littleness of men—mere lice, perhaps, on the scurfy body of a shrinking, dying planet of a fifth-rate sun, one of a billion other suns. The Revd. Howel like most of the Christian clergy of all times of course never looked at the midnight sky or gave any thought to the terrors and mysteries of astronomy, a science so modern, in fact, that it only came into real existence two or three hundred years ago; and is even now only taken seriously by about ten thousand people in Europe and America. Where, in this measureless universe—which indeed might only be one of several universes—was God to be found? A God that had been upset by the dietary of a small desert tribe, who fussed over burnt sacrifices and the fat of rams at one time; at another objected to censuses; at another and a later date wanted a human sacrifice to placate his wrath; or who had washed out the world's fauna and flora in a flood which had left no geological evidence to attest its having taken place. "Did you ever think about the Dinosaurs, father?" said David at the end of some such tirade—an outburst of free-thinking which in earlier years might have upset that father to wrath and angry protest, but which now for some reason only left him dazed and absent-minded. (It was the Colonies that had done it, he thought, and the studio talk of that dilettante architect. By and bye, David would distinguish himself at the Bar, marry and settle down, and resume the orthodox outlook of the English—or as he liked to call it—the British Church.)

"The Dinosaurs, my boy? No. What were they?"

David: "The real Dragons, the Dragons of the prime, that swarmed over England and Wales and Scotland, and Europe, Asia, and North America—and I dare say Africa too. One of the most stupendous facts of what you call 'creation,' though perhaps only one amongst many skin diseases that have afflicted the planet—Well the Dinosaurs went on developing and evolving and perfecting—so Rossiter says—for three million years or so—Then they were scrap-heaped. What a waste of creative energy!..."

Father: "Ah it's Rossiter who puts all these ideas into your head, is it?"

David (flushing); "Oh dear no! I used to think about them at (is about to say 'Newnham,' but substitutes 'Malvern')—at Malvern—"

Father (drily): "I'm glad to hear you thought about

something—serious—at any rate—then, in the midst of your scrapes and truancies—but go on, dear boy. It's a delight to me to hear you speak. It reminds me—I mean your voice does—of your poor mother. You know I loved her very tenderly, David, and though it is all past and done with I believe I should forgive her *now*, if she only came back to me. I'm sometimes *so* lonely, boy. I wish you'd marry and settle down here—there's lots of room for you—some nice girl—and give me grandchildren before I die. But I suppose I must be patient and wait first for your call to the Bar. What a dreary long time it all takes! Why can't they, with one so clever, shorten the term of probation? Or why wait for that to marry? I could give you an allowance. As soon as you were called you could then follow the South Wales circuit—well, go on about your Dinosaurs. I seem to remember Professor Owen invented them—but *he* never wavered in his faith and was the great opponent of that rash man, Darwin. Oh, *I* remember now the old controversies—what a stalwart was the Bishop of Winchester! They couldn't bear him at their Scientific meetings—there was one at Bath, if I recollect right, and he put them all to the right-about. What about your Dinosaurs? I'm not denying their existence; it's only the estimates of time that are so ridiculous. God made them and destroyed them in the great Flood, of which their fossil remains are the evidence—"

David however would desist from pursuing such futile arguments; feel surprised, indeed, at his own outbreaks, except that he hated insincerity. However new and disturbing to his father were these flashes of the New Learning, in his outward conduct he was orthodox and extremely well-behaved. The spiritual exercises of the Revd. Howel had become jejune, and limited very much by his failing sight. The recovery after the operation had come too late in life to bring about any expansion of public or private devotions. Family prayers were reduced to the recital from memory of an exhortation, a confession, and an absolution, followed by the Lord's Prayer and a benediction. Services in the church were limited to Morning and Evening prayers, with Communion on the first Sunday in the month, and a sermon following Morning prayer. There was no one to play the organ if the schoolmistress failed to turn up—as she often did. David however scrupulously turned the normal congregation of five—Bridget, the maid of the time-being, the gardener-groom, the sexton, and a baker-church-warden—into six by his unvarying attendance. In the course of half his stay the rumour of his being present and of his good looks and great spiritual improvement attracted quite a considerable congregation, chiefly of young women and a few sheepish youths; so that his father was at one and the same time exhilarated and embarrassed. Was this to be a Church revival? If so, he readily pardoned David his theories on the Dinosaurs and his doubts as to the unvarying evidence of Divine Wisdom in the story of Creation.

If any other consideration than a deep affection for this dear old man and repentance for his unwise ebullitions of Free Thought had guided David in the matter it was an utter detestation of the services and the influence of the Calvinist Chapel in the village, the Little Bethel, presided over by Pastor Prytherch, a fanatical blacksmith, who alternated spells of secret drunkenness and episodes of animalism by orgies of self-abasement, during which he—in half-confessing his own lapses—attributed freely and unrebukedly the same vices to the male half of his overflowing congregation. These out-pourings—"Pechadur truenus wyf i! Arglwydd madden i mi!"—extempore prayers, psalms chanted with a swaying of the body, hymns sung uproariously, scripture read with an accompaniment of groans, hysteric laughter, and interjections of assent, and a rambling discourse—lasting fully an hour, were in the Welsh language; and David on his three or four visits—and it can be imagined what a sensation *they* caused! The Vicar's son—himself perhaps about to confess his sins!—understood very little of the subject matter, save from the extravagant gestures of the participants. But he soon made up his mind that religion for religion, that expressed by the English—"Well, father, you are right—the 'British'"—Church in Wales was many hundred times superior in reasonableness and stability to the negroid ebullitions of the Calvinists. As a matter of fact they were scarcely more followers of the reformer Calvin than they were of Ignatius Loyola; it was just a symptomatic outbreak of some prehistoric Iberian, Silurian form of worship, something deeply planted in the soil of Wales, something far older than Druidism, something contemporary with the beliefs of Neolithic days.

Eighteen years ago, much of Wales was as enslaved by whiskey as are still Keltic Scotland, Keltiberian Ireland, Lancashire, London and wicked little Kent. It was only saved from going under completely by decennial religious revivals, which for three months or so were followed by total abstinence and a fierce-eyed continence.

Just about this time—during David's extended spring holiday in Wales (he had brought many law books down with him to read)—there had begun one of the newspaper-made-famous Revivals. It was led by a young prophet—a football half-back or whatever they are called, though I, who prefer thoroughness, would, if I played football, offer up the whole of my back to bear the brunt—who saw visions of Teutonically-conceived angels with wings, who heard "voices," was in constant communication with the Redeemer of Mankind and on familiar terms with God, had a lovely tenor voice and moved emotional men and hysterical, love-sick women to tears, even to bellowings by his prayers and songs. He had for some weeks been confined in publicity to half-contemptuous paragraphs in the South Wales Press. Then the

Daily Chronicle took him up. Their well-known, emotional-article writer, Mr. Sigsbee, saw "copy" in him, and—to do him justice (for there I agreed with him)—a chance to pierce the armour of the hand-in-glove-with-Government distillers, so went down to Wales to write him up. For three weeks he became more interesting than a Cabinet Minister. Indeed Cabinet Ministers or those who aspired to become such at the next turn of the wheel truckled to him. Some were afraid he might become a small Messiah and lead Wales into open revolt; others that he might smash the whiskey trade and impair the revenue. Mr. Lloyd George going to address a pro-Boer meeting at Aberystwith (was it?) encountered him at a railway junction, attended by a court of ex-footballers and reformed roysterers, and said in the hearing of a reporter "I must fight with the Sword of the Flesh; but you fight with the Sword of the Spirit"—whatever that may have meant—and I do not pretend to complete accuracy of remembrance—I only know I felt very angry with the whole movement at the time, because it delayed indefinitely the *Daily Chronicle's* review of my new book. Well this Evan—in all such movements an Evan is inevitable—Evan Gwyllim Jones—with the black eyes, abundant black hair, beautiful features (he was a handsome lad) and glorious voice, addressed meetings in the open air and in every available building of four walls. Thousands withdrew their names from foot-ballery, nigh on Two Millions must have taken the pledge—and not merely an anti-whiskey pledge but a fierce renunciation of the most diluted alcohol as well; and approximately two hundred and fifty thousand confessed their sins of unchastity and swore to be reborn Galahads for the rest of their lives. It was a spiritual Spring-cleaning, as drastic and as overdone as are the domestic upheavals known by that name. But it did a vast deal of good, all the same, to South Wales; and though it was a seventh wave, the tide of temperance, thrift, cleanliness, bodily and spiritual, has risen to a higher level of average in the beautiful romantic

Principality ever since. Evan Gwyllim Jones, however, overdid it. He had to retire from the world to a Home—some said even to a Mental Hospital. Six months afterwards he emerged, cured of his "voices," much plumper, and—perhaps—poor soul—shorn of some of his illusions and ideals; but he married a grocer's widow of Cardiff, and the *Daily Chronicle* mentioned him no more.

The infection of his meetings however penetrated to the agricultural district in which Pontystrad was situated. Five villages went completely off their heads. The blacksmith-pastor had to be put under temporary restraint. Quite decent-looking, unsuspected folk confessed to far worse sins than they had ever committed. There arose an aristocracy of outcasts. Three inns where little worse than bad beer was sold were gutted, respectable farmers' wives drank Eau-de-Cologne instead of spirits, several over-due marriages took place, there were a number of premature births, and the membership of the football clubs was disastrously reduced. Such excitement was generated that little work was done, and the illegitimate birth rate of west Glamorganshire—always high—for the opening months of 1903 became even higher.

David was enlisted by the employers of labour, the farmers, chemical works, mining and smelting-works managers, squires, and postmasters to restore order. He preached against the Revivalists. Not with any lack of sympathy, any apology for the real ills which they denounced. He spoke with emphasis against the loosening of morality, recommended early marriage, and above all *education*; denounced the consumption of alcohol so strenuously and convincedly that then and there as he spoke he resolved himself henceforth to abstain from anything stronger than lager beer or the lighter French and German wines. But he threw cold water resolutely on the fantastical nonsense that accompanied these emotional outbursts of so-called religion; invited his hearers to study—at any rate elementarily—astronomy and biology; did not run down football but advised a moderate interest only being taken in such futile sports; recommended volunteering and an acquaintance with rifles as far preferable, seeing that we always stood in danger of a European war or of a drastic revival of insolent conservatism.

Then he made his appeal to the women. He spoke of the dangers of this hysteria; the need there was for level-headed house-keeping women in our councils; how they should first qualify for and then demand the suffrage, having already attained the civic vote. (Here some of the employers of labour disapproved, plucked at his arm or hem of his reefer jacket, and one squire lumbered off the platform.) But he held on, warming with a theme that hitherto had hardly interested him. His speeches were above the heads of his peasant audiences; but they were a more sensitive harp to play on than the average Anglo-Saxon audience. Many women wept, only decorously, as he outlined their influence in a reformed village, a purified Principality. The men applauded frantically because, despite some prudent reserves, there seemed to be a promise of revolt in his suggestions. David felt the electric thrill of the orator in harmony with his audience; who for that reason will strive for further triumphs, more resounding perorations. He introduced scraps of Welsh—all his auto-intoxicated brain could remember (How physically true was that taunt of Dizzy's—"Inebriated with the exuberance of his own verbosity!").

And the delighted audience shouted back "You're the man we want! Into Parliament you shall go, Davy-bach" and much else. So David restored the five villages to sobriety in life and faith, yet left them with a new enthusiasm kindled.

Before he departed on his return to London and the grind of his profession, he had effected another change. Because he had spoken as he had spoken and touched the hearts of emotional people, they came trickling back to his father's church, to the "British" Church, as David now called it. Little Bethel was empty, and the pastor-blacksmith not yet out of the asylum at Swansea. The Revd. Howel Williams trod on air. His sermons became terribly long and involved, but that was no drawback in the minds of his Welsh auditory; though it made his son swear inwardly and reconciled him to the approaching return to Fig Tree Court. The old Druid felt inspired to convince the hundred people present that the Church they had returned to *was* the Church of their fathers, not only back to Roman times, when Glamorganshire was basking in an Italian civilization, but further still. He showed how the Druids were rather to be described as Ante-Christian than Anti—with an *i*; and played ponderously on this quip. In Druidism, he observed—I am sure I cannot think why, but it was his hobby—you had a remarkable foreshadowing of Christianity; the idea of the human sacrifice, the Atonement, the Communion of Saints, the mystic Vine, which he clumsily identified with the mistletoe, and what not else. He read portions of his privately-published *Tales of Taliessin*. In short such happiness radiated from his pink-cheeked face and recovered eyes that David regretted in no wise his own lapses into conventional, stereotyped religion. The Church of Britain might be stiff and stomachered, as the offspring of Elizabeth, but it was stately, it was respectable—as outwardly was the great virgin Queen—and it was easy to live with. Only he counselled his father to do two things: never to preach for more than half-an-hour—even if it meant keeping a small American clock going inside the pulpit-ledge; and to obtain a curate, so that the new enthusiasm might not cool and his father verging on seventy, might not overstrain himself. He pointed out that by letting off most of the glebe land and pretermitting David's "pocket-money" he might secure a young and energetic Welsh-speaking curate, the remainder of whose living-wage would—he felt sure—be found out of the diocesan funds of St. David's bishopric.

The Revd. Howel let him have his way (This was after David had returned to Fig Tree Court) and by the following June a stalwart young curate was lodged in the village and took over the bulk of the progressive church work from the fumbling hands of the dear old Vicar. He was a thoroughly good sort, this curate, troubled by no possible doubts whatever, a fervent tee-totaller, a half-back or whole back—I forget which—at football, a good boxer, and an unwearied organizer. Little Bethel was sold and eventually turned into a seed-merchant's repository and drying-room. The curate in course of time married the squire's daughter and I dare say long afterwards succeeded the Revd. Howel Vaughan Williams when the latter died—but that date is still far ahead of my story. At any rate—isn't it *droll* how these things come about?—David's action in this matter, undertaken he hardly knew why—did much to fetter Mr. Lloyd George's subsequent attempts to disestablish the British Church in Wales.

What did Bridget think of all this, of the spiritual evolution of her nursling, of his identity with the vicious, shifty, idle youth whose uncanny gift of design seemed to have been completely lost after his stay in South Africa? David Vavasour Williams had left home to the relief of his father and the whole village, if even to the half-pitying regret of his old nurse, in 1896. He had spent a year or more in Mr. Praed's studio studying to be an architect or a scene painter. Then somehow or other he did not get on with Mr. Praed and he enlisted impulsively in a South African Police force (in the Army, it seemed to Bridget). He had somehow become involved in a war with a South African people, called by Bridget "the Wild Boars"; he is wounded or ill in hospital; is little heard of, almost presumed dead. Throughout all these five years he scarcely ever writes to his forgiving father; maintains latterly a sulky silence. Then, suddenly in the summer of 1901, returns; preceded only by a telegram but apparently vouched for by this Mr. Praed; and announces himself as having forgotten his Welsh and most of the events of his youth, but having acquired a changed heart, and an anxiety to make up for past ill-behaviour by a present good conduct which seems almost miraculous.

Well: miracles were easily believed in by Bridget. Perhaps his father's prayers had been answered. Providence sometimes meted out an overwhelming boon to really good people. David was certainly a Vavasour, if there was nothing Williamsy about his looks.... His mother, in Mrs. Bridget Evanwy's private opinion, had been a hussy.... Was David his father's son? Hadn't she once caught Mrs. Howel Williams kissing a young stranger behind a holly bush and wasn't that why Bridget had really been sent away? She had returned to take charge of the pretty, motherless little boy when she herself was a widow disappointed of children, and the child was only three. Would she ever turn against her nursling now, above all, when he was showing himself such a son to his old father? Not she. He might be who and what he would. He was giving another ten years of renewed life to the dear old Druid and the continuance of a comfortable home to his old Nannie.

They talked a great deal up at Little Bethel of a "change of heart." Perhaps such things really took place, though Bridget Evanwy from a shrewd appraisement of the Welsh nature doubted it. She would like to, but couldn't quite believe that an angel from heaven had taken possession of David's body and come here to play a divine part; because David sometimes talked so strangely—seemed not only to doubt the existence of a heavenly host, but even of Something beyond, so awful in Bridget's mind that she hardly liked to define it in words, though in her own Welsh tongue it was so earthily styled "the Big Man."

However, at all costs, she would stand by David ... and without quite knowing why, she decided that on all future visits she herself would "do out" his room, would attend to him exclusively. The "girl" was a chatterer, albeit she looked upon Mr. David with eyes of awe and a most respectful admiration, while David on his part scarcely bestowed on her a glance.

Sir Harry Johnston

CHAPTER IX

DAVID IS CALLED TO THE BAR

1902 was the year of King Edward's break-down in health but of his ultimate Coronation; it was the year in which Mr. Arthur Balfour became premier; it was the year in which motors became really well-known, familiar objects in the London streets, and hansoms (I think) had to adopt taximeter clocks on the eve of their displacement by taxi-cabs. It was likewise the year in which the South African War was finally wound up and the star of Joseph Chamberlain paled to its setting, and Mrs. Pankhurst and her daughter Christabel founded the Women's Social and Political Union at Manchester.

In 1903, the Fiscal controversy absorbed much of public attention, the War Office was once more reformed, women's skirts still swept the pavement and encumbered the ball-room, a Peeress wrote to the *Times* to complain of Modern Manners, Surrey beat Something-or-other at the Oval, and modern Cricket was voted dull.

In 1904, the Russo-Japanese War was concluded, and *Fraser and Warren* received a year's notice from the Midland Insurance Co. that they must vacate their premises on the fifth floor of Nos. 88-90 Chancery Lane. The business of *F.*

and W. had grown so considerable that, as the affairs of the Midland Insurance Co. had slackened, it became intolerable to hear the lift going up and down to the fifth floor all through the day. The housekeeper also thought it odd that a well-dressed young gentleman should steal in and up, day after day, after office hours to work apparently alone in *Fraser and Warren's* partners' room. *Fraser and Warren* over the hand of its junior partner, Mrs. Claridge, accepted the notice. Their business had quite overgrown these inconveniently situated offices and a move to the West End was projected. Mrs. Claridge's scheme for week-end cottages had been enormously successful and had put much money not only into the coffers of *Fraser and Warren* but into the banking account of that clever architect, Francis Brimley Storrington.

[I find I made an absurd mistake earlier in this book in charging the too amorous architect with a home at "Storrington." His home really was in a midland garden city which he had designed, but his name—a not uncommon one—was Storrington.]

In the autumn of 1902, poor Lady Fraser died. In January, 1903, Honoria married the impatient Colonel Armstrong. In January, 1904, she had her first baby—a boy.

At the close of 1904 Beryl Claridge made proposals to Honoria Fraser relative to a change in the constitution of *Fraser and Warren*. Honoria was to have an interest still as a sleeping partner in the concern and some voice in its management and policy. But she was to take no active share of the office work and "Warren" was to pass out of it altogether. Beryl pointed out it was rather a farce when the middle partner—she herself had been made the junior partner a year before—was perpetually and mysteriously absent, year after year, engaged seemingly on work of her own abroad. Her architect semi-husband moreover, who if not in the firm was doing an increasing share of its business, wanted to know *more* about Vivien Warren. "Was she or was she not the daughter of the 'notorious' Mrs. Warren; because if so..." He took of course a highly virtuous line. Like so many other people he compounded for the sins he was inclined to by being severe towards the misdoings of others. *His* case—he would say to Beryl when they were together at Chelsea—was *sui generis*, quite exceptional, they were really in a way perfectly good people—*Tout savoir c'est tout pardonner, etc.*; whereas the *things* that were *said* about Mrs. Warren!... And though Vivien was nothing nearer sin than being her daughter, still if it were known or known more widely that *she* was the Warren in *Fraser and Warren*, why the wives of the wealthier clergy, for example, and a number of Quakeresses would withdraw their affairs from the firm's management. Whereas if only his little Berry could become the boss, *he* knew where to get "big money" to put behind the Firm's dealings. The idea was all right; an association for the special management on thoroughly honest lines of women's affairs. They'd better get rid of that hulking young clerk, Bertie Adams, and staff the entire concern with capable women. He himself would always remain in the background, giving them ideas from time to time, and if any were taken up merely being paid his fees and commissions.

David Vavasour Williams, privately consulted by Norie, put forward no objection. He disliked Beryl and was increasingly shy of his rather clandestine work on the fifth floor of the Midland Insurance Chambers; besides, if and when he were called to the Bar, he would have to cease all connection with *Fraser and Warren*. The consent of Vivie was obtained through the Power of Attorney she had left behind. A new deed of partnership was drawn up. Honoria insisted that Vivien Warren must be bought out for Three Thousand pounds, which amount was put temporarily to the banking account of David Vavasour Williams; she herself received another Three Thousand and a small percentage of the future profits and a share in the direction of affairs of THE WOMEN'S CO-OPERATIVE ASSOCIATION (*Fraser and Claridge*) so long as she left a capital of Five Thousand pounds at their disposal.

So in 1905 David with Three Thousand pounds purchased an annuity of L210 a year for Vivien Warren. That investment would save Vivie from becoming at any time penniless and dependent, and consequently would subserve the same purpose for her cousin and agent, David V. Williams.

Going to the C. and C. Bank, Temple Bar branch, to take stock of Vivie's affairs, he found a Thousand pounds had been paid in to her current account. Ascertaining the name of the payee to be L.M. Praed, he hurried off at the first opportunity to Praed's studio. Praed was entertaining a large party of young men and women to tea and the exhibition of some wild futurist drawings and a few rather striking designs for stage scenery and book covers. David had perforce to keep his questions bottled up and take part in the rather vapid conversation that was going on between young men with *glabre* faces and high-pitched voices and women with rather wild eyes.

[It struck David about this time that women were getting a little out of hand, strained, over-inclined to laugh mirthless laughter, greedy for sensuality, sensation, sincerity, sweet-meats. Something. Even if they satisfied some fleeting passion or jealousy by marrying, they soon wanted to be de-married, separated, divorced, to don male costume, to go on the amateur stage and act Salome parts on Sunday afternoons that most ladies of the real Stage had refused; while the men that went about with them in these troops from restaurant to restaurant, studio to studio, music hall to cafe chantant,

Brighton to Monte Carlo, Sandown to Goodwood, were shifty, too well-dressed, too near neutrality in sex, without defined professions, known by nicknames only, spendthrifts, spongers, bankrupts, and collectors of needless bric-a-brac.]

However this mob at last quitted Praddy's premises and he and David were left alone.

Praed yawned, and almost intentionally knocked over an easel with a semi-obscene drawing on it of a Sphynx with swelling breasts embracing a lean young man against his will.

David: "Praddy! why do you tolerate such people and why prostitute your studio to such unwholesome art?"

Praed: "My dear David! This is *indeed* Satan rebuking sin. Why there are three designs here—one I've just knocked over—beastly, wasn't it?—that *you* left with me when you went off at a tangent to South Africa.... Really, we ought to have *some* continuity you know....

"But I agree with you.... I'm sick of the whole business of this Nouvel Art and L'Art Nouveau, about Aubrey Beardsley and the disgusting 'nineties generally—But what *will* you? If Miss Vivie Warren had condescended to accept me as a husband she might have brought a wholesome atmosphere into my life and swept away all this ... inspired me perhaps with some final ambition for the little that remains of my stock of energy.... Heigh-ho! Well: what is the quarrel now? The life I lead, the people who come here?"

David: "No. I hardly came about that; though dear old Praddy, I wish I had time to look after you ... Perhaps later.... No: what I came to ask was: what *did* you mean the other day by paying in a Thousand Pounds to Vivie Warren's account at her bank? She's not in want of money so far as I know, and you can't be so very rich, even though you design three millionaire's houses a year. Who gave you the money to pay in to my—to Vivie's account?"

Praed: "Well, when Vivie herself comes to ask me, p'raps I'll tell; but I can't see how it concerns *you*. Why not stop and dine—a l'imprevu, but I dare say my housekeeper can rake something together or it may not be too late to send out for a pate. We can then talk of other things. When are you going to get your call?"

David: "Sorry, dear old chap, but I can't stay to dinner. I'm not going anywhere else but I've got some papers I *must* study before I go to bed. But I'll stop another half-hour at any rate. Don't ring for lights or turn up the electric lamps. I would sooner sit in the dark studio and put my question. Who has given me that thousand pounds?"

Praed: "That's *my* business: *I* haven't! I shan't give or lend Vivie a penny till she consents to marry me. As to the rest, take it and be thankful. You're not certain to get any more and I happen to know it had what you would call a 'clean origin.'"

David: "You mean it didn't come from those 'Hotels'?"

Praed: "Well, at any rate not directly. Don't be a romantic ass, a tiresome fool, and give me any trouble about it. A certain person I imagine must have heard that *Fraser and Warren* had been wound up and couldn't bear the thought of your being hard up in consequence ... doesn't know you got a share of the purchase-money..."

* * * * *

David decided at any rate for the present to accept the addition to his capital—you can perhaps push principle *too* far; or, once you plunge into affairs, you cease to be quite so high-souled. At any rate nothing in David's middle-class mind was so horrible as penury and the impotence that comes with it. How many months or years would lie ahead of him before fees could be gained and a professional income be earned? Besides he wanted to take Bertie Adams into his service as a Clerk. A barrister must have a clerk, and David in his peculiar circumstances could only engage one acquainted more or less with his secret.

So Bertie Adams fulfilled the ambition he had cherished for three years—he felt all along it was coming true. And when David was called to the Bar—which he was with all the stately ceremonial of a Call night at the Inner Temple in the Easter term of 1905, more elbow room was acquired at Fig Tree Court, and Bertie Adams was installed there as clerk to Mr. David Vavasour Williams, who had residential chambers on the third floor, and a fair-sized Office and small private room on the second floor. Bertie's mother had "washed" for both Honoria and Vivie in their respective dwellings for years, and for David after he came to live at Fig Tree Court. A substantial douceur to the "housekeeper" had facilitated this, for in the part of the Temple where lies Fig Tree Court the residents do not call their ministrants "laundresses," but "housekeepers." Curiously enough the accounts were always tendered to the absent Vivie Warren, but Mrs. Adams noted no discrepancy in their being paid by her son or in an unmarried lady living in the Temple under the name of David Williams.

Installed as clerk and advised by his employer to court one of the fair daughters of the housekeeper (Mrs. Laidly) with a view to marriage and settling down in premises hard-by, Bertie Adams (who like David had spent his time well between 1901 and 1905 and was now an accomplished and serviceable barrister's clerk) soon set to work to chum up with other clerks in this clerical hive and get for his master small briefs, small chances for defending undefended cases in which hapless women were concerned.

But before we deal with the career of David at the Bar, which of course did not properly commence—even as a brilliant junior—till the early months of 1906, let us glance at the way in which he had passed the intervening space of time between his return from Wales in May, 1902, and the spending of his Long Vacation of 1905 as an Esquire by the Common Law of England called to the Bar, and entitled to wear a becoming grey wig and gown.

He had begun in 1900 by studying Latin, Norman French— so greatly drawn on in law terms—and English History. In the summer of 1901, by one of those subterfuges winked at then, he had obtained two rooms, sublet to him by a member of the Inn, in Fig Tree Court, Inner Temple. In the autumn of that year, having made sure of his parentage and his finance, he had approached the necessary authorities with a view to his being admitted a member of the Inner Temple, which meant filling up a form of declaration that he, David Vavasour Williams, of Pontystrad, Glamorgan, a British subject, aged twenty-four, son of the Revd. Howel Vaughan Williams, Clerk in Holy Orders, of Pontystrad in the County of Glamorgan, was desirous of being admitted a Student of the Honourable Society of the Inner Temple for the purpose of being called to the Bar or of practising under the Bar; and that he would not either directly or indirectly apply for or take out any certificate to practise directly or indirectly as a Pleader, Conveyancer or Draftsman in Equity without the special permission of the Masters of the Bench of the said Honourable Society of the Inner Temple.

Further, David declared with less assurance but perhaps within the four corners of the bare truth that he had not acted directly or indirectly in the capacity of a Solicitor, Attorney-at-law, Writer to the Signet or in about thirteen other specified legal positions; that he was not a Chartered, Incorporated or Professional Accountant ("A good job we changed the device of the Firm," he thought), a Land Agent, a Surveyor, Patent Agent, Consulting Engineer, or even as a clerk to any such officer. Which made him rather shivery about what he *had* been doing for *Fraser and Warren*, but there was little risk that any one would find out—And finally he declared that he was not in Trade or an undischarged bankrupt.

The next and most difficult step was to obtain two separate Certificates from two separate barristers each of five years' standing, to the effect that he was what he stated himself to be. This required much thinking out, and was one of the reasons why he did not go down as promised and spend his Christmas and New Year with his father.

Instead he wrote to Pontystrad explaining how important it was he should get admitted as a Student in time to commence work in Hilary term. Did his father know any such luminary of the law or any two such luminaries? His father regretted that he only knew of one such barrister of over five years' standing: the distinguished son of an old Cambridge chum. To him he wrote, venturing to recall himself, the more eagerly since this son of an old friend was himself a Welshman and already distinguished by his having entered Parliament, served with the Welsh Party, written a book on Welsh history, and married a lady of considerable wealth.

Next David applied to Rossiter with the result—as we have seen—that he got an introduction to Mr. Stansfield. So he obtained from Mr. Price and Mr. Stansfield the two certificates to the effect that "David Vavasour Williams has been introduced to me by letter of introduction from the Revd. Howel Williams" (or "Professor Michael Rossiter, F.R.S.") "and has been seen by me; and that I, Mark Stansfield, Barrister-at-law, King's Counsel" (or "John Price, Barrister-at-law, Member of Parliament") "believe the said David Vavasour Williams to be a gentleman of respectability and a proper person to be admitted a Student of the Honourable Society of the Inner Temple with a view to being called to the Bar."

Copies of the letters of introduction accompanied the two certificates. These of course were not obtained without several visits to the unsuspicious guarantors; or at least one to Mr. Price in Paper Buildings, for whom it was enough that David claimed to be Welsh and showed a very keen interest in the Welsh tongue and its Indo-German affinities, and three or four to Mr. Mark Stansfield, K.C., one of the nicest, kindliest and most learned persons David had ever met, whom he grieved deeply at deceiving. Stansfield had a high opinion of Rossiter. The fact that he recommended David was quite sufficient to secure his "guarantee." But apart from that, he felt himself greatly drawn towards this rather shy, grave, nice-looking young fellow with the steady eyes and the keen intelligence. He had him to dine and to lunch; drew him out—as far as David thought it prudent to go—and was surprised David had never been to a University ("Only to Malvern—and then I studied with an architect in London— Who? Mr. Praed, A.R.A.—but then I travelled for a bit, and after that I felt more than ever I wanted to go in for the Bar"—said David, with a charming smile which lit up his young face ordinarily so staid). Stansfield consented that David should come and read with him, and in many ways facilitated his progress so materially and so kindly that more than once the compunctious young Welshman thought of discarding the impersonation; and might have done so had not this most estimable Stansfield died of pneumonia in the last year of David's studenthood.

Of course the preliminary examination was easily and quickly passed. David translated his bit of Caesar's commentaries, answered brilliantly the questions about Alfred the Great, the Anglo-Norman kings, the Constitutions of Clarendon, Magna Charta and Mortmain, Henry the Eighth and the Reformation, the Civil War and Protectorate of Cromwell, the Bill of Rights and the Holy Alliance. He paid his fees and his "caution" money; he ate the requisite six dinners—or more, as he found them excellent and convenient—in each term, attended all the lectures that interested him, and passed the subsidiary examinations on them with fair or even high credit; and finally got through his "Call-to-the-Bar" examination with tolerable success; at any rate he passed. A friend of the deceased Stansfield—whose death was always one of the scars in Vivie's memory—introduced him to one of the Masters of the Bench who signed his "call" papers. He once more made a declaration to the effect that he was not a person in Holy Orders, that he was not a Solicitor, Attorney-at-law, Writer to the Signet, etc., etc., a Chartered, Incorporated or Professional Accountant; and again that if called to the Bar, he would never become a member of the abhorred professions over and over again enumerated; and was duly warned that without special permission of the Masters of the Bench of the Inner Temple he might not practise "under the Bar"—whatever that may mean (I dare say it is some low-down procedure, only allowed in times of scarcity). Then after having his name "screened" for twelve days in all the Halls of the four Inns, and going in fear and trembling that some one might turn up and object, he finally received his call to the Bar on April 22 (if April 22 in that year was on a Sunday, then on the following Monday) and was "called" at the Term Dinner where he took wine with the

Masters. He remembered seeing present at the great table on the dais, besides the usual red-faced generals and whiskered admirals, simpering statesmen, and his dearly loved friend, Michael Rossiter—representing Science,—a more sinister face. This was the well-known philanthropist and race-horse breeder, Sir George Crofts, Bart., M.P. for a Norfolk borough. Their eyes met, curiously interlocked for a moment. Sir George wondered to himself where the dooce he had seen that, type of face before, those grey eyes with the dark lashes. "Gad! he reminds me of Kitty Warren! Well, I'll be damned" (he was eventually) "I wonder whether the old gal had a son as well as that spitfire Vivie?!"

Michael whispered a word or two to one of the Masters, and David was presently summoned to attend the Benchers and their distinguished guests in the inner chamber to which they withdrew for wine and dessert. Rossiter made room for him, and he had to drink a glass of port with the Benchers. Every one was very gracious. Rossiter said: "I was a sort of godfather to him, don't you know. David! you must do me credit and make haste to take silk and become a Judge." Crofts moved from where he sat next to a Bishop. ("Damn it all! I like bein' respectable, but why *will* they always put me next a Bishop or an Archdeacon? It spoils all my best stories.") He came over—dragging his chair—to Rossiter and said "I say! Will you introduce me to our young friend here?" He was duly introduced. "H'm, Williams? *That* doesn't tell me much. But somehow your face reminds me awfully of—of—some one I used to know. J'ever have a sister?" "No," said David.

Crofts, he noticed, had aged very much in the intervening eight years. He must now be no more than—58? But he had become very stout and obviously suffered from blood pressure without knowing it. He moved away a little, and David heard him talking to a Master about Lady Crofts, who had come up to London for the season and how they were both very anxious about his boy—"Yes, he had two children, a boy and a girl, bless 'em—The boy had been ill with measles and wasn't makin' quite the quick recovery they expected. What an anxiety children were, weren't they? Though we wouldn't be without 'em, would we?" The Bencher assented out of civility, though as a matter of fact he was an old bachelor and detested children or anything younger than twenty-one.

David after his call was presented with a bill to pay of L99. 10s. His father hearing of this, insisted on sending him a cheque for L150 out of his savings, adding he should be deeply hurt if it was not accepted and no more said about it. How soon was David coming down to see South Wales once more gloriously clothed with spring?

[Much of this review of the years between 1901 and 1905, many of these sweet remembrances are being taken from Vivie's brain as she lies on a hard bed in 1913, musing over the past days when, despite occasional frights and anxieties, she was transcendently happy. Oh "Sorrow's Crown of Sorrow, the remembering happier days!" She recalled the articles she used to write from the Common Room or Library of the Inn; how well they were received and paid for by the editors of daily and weekly journals; what a lark they were, when for instance she would raise a debate in the *Saturday Review*: "Should Women be admitted to the Bar?" Or an appeal in the *Daily News* to do away with the Disabilities of Women. How poor Stansfield, before he died, said he had never met any young fellow with a tenderer heart for women, and advised him to marry whilst he still had youth and fire. She remembered David's social success at the great houses in the West End. How he might have gone out into Society and shone more, much more, only he had to consider prudence and expense; the curious women who fell in love with him, and whom he had gently, tactfully to keep at arm's length. She remembered the eager discussions in the Temple Debating Society, or at the "Moots" of Gray's Inn, her successes there as an orator and a close reasoner; how boy students formed ardent friendships for her and prophesied her future success in Parliament, would have her promise to take them into the Cabinet which David was to form when an electorate swept him into power and sent the antiquated old rotters of that day into the limbo of deserved occlusion.

She saw and heard once more the amused delight of Honoria Armstrong over her success, and the latent jealousy of the uxorious Colonel Armstrong if she came too often to see Honoria in Sloane Street: And she remembered—Oh God! *How* she remembered—the close association in those three priceless years with her "godfather" Michael Rossiter; Rossiter who shaped her mind—it would never take a different turn—who was patient with her stupidity and petulance; an elder brother, a robust yet tactful chaffer; a banisher of too much sensibility, a constant encouragement to effort and success. Rossiter, she knew, with her woman's instinct, was innocently in love with her, but believed all the time he was satisfying his craving for a son to train, a disciple who might succeed him: for he still believed that David when he had been called to the Bar and had flirted awhile with Themis, would yet turn his great and growing abilities to the service of Science.

And Mrs. Rossiter in those times: Vivie smiled at the thought of her undefined jealousy. She was anxious to be civil to a young man of whom Michael thought so highly. She sympathized with his regret that they had no children, but why could he not take up with one of her cousin Bennet's boys from Manchester, or Sophy's son from Northallerton, or one of his own brother's or sister's children? How on earth did he become acquainted with this young man from South

Wales? But she was determined not to be separated in any way from her husband, and so she sat with them as often and as long as she could in the library. The studio-laboratory she could not stand with its horrid smell of chemicals; she also dreaded vaguely that vivisection went on there—Michael of course had a license, though he was far too tender-hearted to torture sentient creatures. Still he did odd things with frogs and rats and goats and monkeys; and her dread was that she might one day burst in on one of these sacrifices to science and see a transformed Michael, blood-stained, wielding a knife and dangerous if interrupted in his pursuit of a discovery.

But as the long talks and conferences of the two friends—really not so far separated in age as one of them thought—generally took place in the library, she assisted at a large proportion of them. Rossiter would not have had it otherwise, though to David she was at times excessively irksome. Her husband had long viewed her as a lay figure on these occasions. He rarely replied to her flat remarks, her inconsequent platitudes, her yawns and quite transparent signals that it was time for the visitor to go. Sometimes David took her hints and left: he had no business to make himself a bore to any one. Sometimes however Michael at last roused to consciousness of the fretful little presence would say "What? Sweety? *You* still up. Trot off to bed, my poppet, or you'll lose the roses in your cheeks."

The roses in Mrs. Rossiter's cheeks at that time were beginning to be a trifle eczematous and of a fixed quality. Nevertheless, though she tossed her head a little as she took up her "work" and swished out of the great heavy door—which David opened—she was pleased to think that Michael cared for her complexion and was solicitous about her rest.

And Vivie's eyes swam a little as she thought about the death of Mark Stansfield, and the genuine tears that flowed down the cheeks of his pupils when they learnt one raw February morning from the housekeeper of his chambers that he had died at daybreak. "A better man never lived" they agreed. And they were right.

And she smiled again as she thought of some amongst those pupils, the young dogs of those days, the lovers of actresses of the minor order—ballet girls, it might have been; of the larks that went on sometimes within and without the staid precincts of the Temple. Harmless larks they were; but such as she had to withdraw from discreetly. She played lawn tennis with them, she fenced surprisingly well; but she had refused to join the "Devil's Own"—the Inns of Court Volunteers, for prudent reasons; and though it had leaked out that she was a good swimmer—that tiresome impulsive Honoria had spread it abroad—she resolutely declined to give proofs of her prowess in swimming baths. Her associates were not so young as the undergraduates she had met in Newnham days: they were an average ten years older. Their language at times made David blush, but they had more discretion and reserve than the University student, and they respected his desire to withdraw himself into himself occasionally, and to abstain from their noisier amusements without questioning his camaraderie.

At this point in her smiling reminiscences, the wardress clanged open the door and slammed down a mug of cocoa and a slab of brown bread; and rapped out some orders in such a martinet utterance that they were difficult to understand. (Don't be alarmed! She isn't about to be executed for having deceived the Benchers of the Inner Temple in 1905; she is only in prison for a suffragist offence).]

I can't wind up this chapter somehow without more or less finishing the story of Beryl Claridge. She has been a source of anxiety to my wife—who has read these chapters one by one as they left my typewriter. "Was it wise to bring her in?" "Well, but my dear, she was rather a common type of the New Woman in the early nineteen hundreds." "Yes—but—"

Of course the latent anxiety was that she might end up respectably. And so she did. In 1906, the first Mrs. Storrington died at Ware (Ware was where the architect husband had his legitimate home). She had long been ill, increasingly ill of some terrible form of anaemia which had followed the birth of her fourth child. She slowly faded away, poor thing; and about the time David was returning from a triumphant Christmas and New Year at Pontystrad— the Curate and his young wife had made a most delightful partie carree and David had kissed the very slightly protesting Bridget under the native mistletoe—Mrs. Storrington breathed her last, while her faithless yet long forgiven Francis knelt by her bedside in agonies of unavailing grief.

Well: she died and was buried, and her four children, ranging from nine to sixteen, sobbed very much and mourned for darling Mummie without the slightest suspicion ("'twas better so," she had always thought) that Dad had poisoned her wells of happiness ever since he took up with that minx at Cambridge in the very year in which long-legged Claribel was born. A few months after the poor lady was consigned (under a really lovely cenotaph designed by her husband) to Ware Churchyard—no, it was to Ware cemetery; Dad introduced them all to a very sprightly and good-looking widow, Mrs. Claridge, who had also been bereaved years ago and left with two perfect ducks of children, four and five years old, to whom Claribel took instinctively (the elder ones sniffed a little, disliking "kids").

Then about Christmas time, 1906, Dad told them that Mrs. Claridge was going to make him happy by coming to tend his motherless children; was going to be his wife. Francis, the eldest, stomped about the garden at Ware and swore he would go back to Rugby during the holidays; Elspeth, the gaunt girl of fourteen and Agnes, a dreamy and endearing child, cried themselves to sleep in each other's arms. Claribel, however, quite approved. And whether they liked it or not, in January, 1907, the marriage took place—at the Registrar's—and Beryl came to live for a short time at Ware, bringing ducksome Margery and adorable Podge. In less than a month Beryl had won over all her step-children, except Francis, who held out till Easter, but was reduced to allegiance by the hampers she sent to him at Rugby—; in three months they had all moved to a much sweller house on the Chelsea Embankment. Father—Beryl voted "Dad" a little lower-middle class—Father had somehow become connected with some great business establishment of which Mother was the head. Together they were making pots of money. Francis would go to Sandhurst, Elspeth to a finishing school in Paris (her ambition), and the others would spend the fine months of the year rollicking with Margery and Podge on the Sussex coast.

In 1907, also, they became aware that their new mother was not alone in the world. A stately lady whose eyes seemed once to have done a deal of weeping (they were destined alas! to do much more, for three of her gallant, handsome sons were killed in the War, and *that* finally killed the poor old Dean of Thetford), who wore a graceful Spanish mantilla of black lace when in draughty places, came to see them after they had moved to Garden Corner on the Chelsea Embankment. She turned out to be the mother of Mrs. Beryl and was quite inclined to be their grandmother as well as Margery's and Podge's. But her husband the Dean was—it appeared—too great an invalid to come up to town.

The second Mrs. Storrington, who was a woman of

Sir Harry Johnston

boundless energy, could work all day with secretaries, and could dance all night, gave brilliant parties in the season at her large Chelsea house. But she never invited to them Mr. David Vavasour Williams, that rising young barrister who had become so famous as a pleader of the causes of friendless women.

CHAPTER X

THE SHILLITO CASE

In the autumn of 1905, increase among women of the idea of full citizenship made rapid strides. There was a feeling in the air that Balfour must soon resign or go to the country, that a Liberal Ministry would succeed to power, and that being Liberal it could scarcely, in reason or with any logic, refuse to enlarge the franchise to the advantage of the female half of the community. These idealizers of the Liberal Party, which had really definitely ceased to be Liberal in 1894, had a rude awakening. Annie Kenney and Christabel Pankhurst dared to act as if they were men, and asked Sir Edward Grey at his Manchester meeting in October, 1905, if a Liberal Administration would give Votes to Women, should it be placed in power at the next Election. Answer they had none, from the platform; but the male audience rose in their hundreds, struck these audacious hussies in the face, scratched and slapped them (this was the role of the boys), and hustled them out into the street, bleeding and dishevelled. Here for attempting to explain the causes of their expulsion they were arrested by the police, and the following morning were sent to prison, having declined to pay the fines illegally imposed on them.

This incident made a great impression on the

newspaper-reading public, because at that time the Press boycott on the Woman Suffrage movement had not set in. It gave David much to think about, and he found Honoria Fraser and several of his men and women friends had joined the Woman Suffrage movement and were determined that the new Liberal Government should not shirk the issue; an issue on which many members of Parliament had been returned as acquiescent in the principle. On that account they had received the whole-hearted support of many, women owing allegiance to the Liberal Party.

At first of course the new Government was too busy in allotting the loaves and fishes of Office and in handing out the peerages, baronetcies, knighthoods, Governorships, private secretaryships, and promotions among the civil servants which had—not to put too fine a point on it—been purchased by large and small contributions to the Party Chest.

[Such a procedure seems to be inseparable from our present Party system. In this respect the Conservatives are no better than the Liberals; and it is always possible that in a different way the Labour Party when It comes into power will be similarly inclined to reward those who have furnished the sinews of war. The House of Commons in the last Act which revised the conditions of elections of members of Parliament was careful to leave open many avenues along which Money might attain to the heart of things.]

But at length all such matters were settled, and the Cabinet was free to face the steady demand of the women leaders of the Suffrage movement; a demand that at any rate *some* measure of enfranchisement should be granted to the women of the British Isles without delay.

We all know how this demand was received by the leading

men of the Liberal Party and by the more prominent Liberals among their supporters in the House; with evasions, silences, sneers, angry refusals, hasty promises given to-day (when Ministers were frightened) and broken to-morrow; with a whole series of discreditable tongue-in-the-cheek tricks of Parliamentary procedure; till at last the onlooker must have wondered at and felt grateful for our British phlegm; surprised that so little actual harm was done (except to the bodies of the Suffragists), that no Home Secretary or Police Inspector or magistrate, no flippant talker-out of would-be-serious Franchise Bills was assassinated, trounced, tarred and feathered, kidnapped, nose-tweaked, or even mud-bespattered. (I am reproducing here the growing comprehension of the problem as it shaped in Vivie's mind, under the hat and waistcoat of David Williams.)

Honoria, faithful to her old resolve, continued to devote the greater part of the Two Thousand a year she had set aside for the Woman's Cause to financing the new Suffrage movement; and incidentally she brought grist to David's mill by recommending him as Counsel to many women in distress, arrested Suffragists. In 1906, 1907 and 1908 he made himself increasingly famous by his pleadings in court on behalf of women who with dauntless courage and at the cost of much bodily pain and even at the risk of death had forcibly called attention to this grave defect in the British polity, the withholding of the ordinary rights of tax-paying citizens from adult women.

Where the Suffragist was poor he asked no fee, or a small fee was paid by some Suffragist Association. But he gained much renown over his advocacy; he became quite a well-known personality outside as well as inside the Law Courts and Police-stations by 1908. His pleadings were sometimes so moving, so passionate that—*teste* Mrs. Pankhurst—"burly policemen in court had tears trickling down their faces" as he described the courage, the flawless private lives, the selfless devotion to a noble cause of these women agitating for the rights of their sex—rich and poor, old and young. Juries flinched from the verdict which some bitter-faced judge enjoined; magistrates swerved from executing the secret orders of the Home Office; policemen—again—for they are most of them decent fellows—resigned their positions in the Force, sooner than carry out the draconian policy of the Home Secretary.

But of course concurrently he lost many a friend and friendship in the Inns of Court. There were even growls that he should be disbarred—after this espousal of the Suffrage cause had been made manifest for three years. He might have been, but that he had other compeers, below and above his abilities and position; advocates like Lord Robert Brinsley, the famous son of the Marquis of Wiltshire. If Williams was to be disbarred, why they would have to take the same course with a Brinsley who also defended women law-breakers, fighting for their constitutional rights. And of course such a procedure as *that* was unthinkable. Yet where a Brinsley sailed unhampered, undangered over these troubled waters, poor David often came near to crashing on the rocks. "To hear the fellow talk," said one angry K.C. in the Library at the Inner Temple, "you'd think he was a woman himself!" "Egad" said his brother K.C.—yes, he really *did* say "Egad," the oath still lingers in the Inns of Court—"Egad, he looks like one. No hair on his face and I'll lay he doesn't shave."

There were of course other briefs he held, for payment or for love of justice; young women who had killed their babies (as to these he was far from sentimental; he only defended where the woman had any claim to sympathy or mitigation of the unreal death sentence); breach of promise actions where the woman had been grossly wronged; affiliation cases in high life—or the nearest to high life that makes a claim on the man for his fatherhood. He was a deadly prosecutor in cases where women had been robbed by their male trustees, or injured in any other way wherein, in those days, the woman was at a disadvantage and the marriage laws were unjust.

One way and another, with the zealous aid and business-like care of his interests by his clerk, Albert Adams, David must have earned between 1906 and the autumn of 1908, an average Three hundred a year. As he paid Adams L150 a year and allowed him certain perquisites, and lived within his own fixed income (from his annuity and investments) of L290 a year, this meant a profit of about L500. This was raised at a leap to L1,500 by the fees and the special gift he received for defending Lady Shillito.

The "Shillito Case," an indictment for murder, was tried at the winter assize of the North-eastern Circuit, January or February, 1909. I dare say you have forgotten all about it now: Lady Shillito changed her name, married again (eventually), and was lost in the crowd—she may even, eleven years afterwards, be reading this novel at the riper age of forty and be startled out of her well-fed apathy by the revival of acute memories.

There have been not a few similar cases before and since of comparatively young, beautiful women murdering their elderly, objectionable husbands in a clever cattish way, and of course getting off through lack of evidence or with a short term of imprisonment. (They were always treated in prison far more tenderly than were Suffragettes, and the average wardress adored them and obtained for them many little alleviations of their lot before the Home Secretary gave way and released them.) Nowadays the War and the pressing necessities of life, the coal famine, the milk famine, the railway strikes have robbed such cases of all or nearly all their interest. I could quite believe that women in similar circumstances continue to murder their elderly husbands, and the doctors and coroners and relations on "his" side tacitly agree not to raise a fuss in the presence of much graver subjects of apprehension.

I can also understand why these beautiful-women-elderly-husband cases scarcely starred our Island story prior to the 'fifties of the last century. It was only when chemical analysis had approached its present standard of perfection that the presence of the more subtle poisons could be detected in the stomach and intestines, and that the young and beautiful wife could be charged with and found guilty of the deed by the damning evidence of an analytical chemist.

It was Rossiter who secured for David the conduct of Lady Shillito's defence. Arbella[1] Shillito was his second cousin, a Rossiter by birth, and would fain have married Michael herself, only that he was not at that time thinking of marriage, and when his thoughts turned that way—the very day after, as it were—he met Linda Bennet and her thousands a year. But he retained a half humorous liking for this handsome young woman.

[Footnote 1: An old Northumbrian variant of Arabella.]

Arbella, disappointed over Michael—though she was a mere slip of a girl at the time—next decided that she must marry money. When she was twenty-one she met Grimthorpe Shillito, an immensely rich man of Newcastle-on-Tyne, whose foundries poured out big guns and many other things made of iron and steel combined with acids and brains. Grimthorpe was a curious-looking person, even at forty; in appearance a mixture of Julius Caesar, several unpleasant-featured Doges of Venice, and Voltaire in middle age. His looks were not entirely his fault and doubtless acquired for him, in his moral character, a worse definition than he deserved. He had travelled much in his pursuit of metallurgy and chemistry; at forty he saw rising before him the prospect of a peerage, due either for his extraordinary discoveries and inventions in our use of steel, or easily purchasable out of his immense wealth. What is the good of a peerage if it ends with your life? He was not without his vanities, though one of the most cynical men of his cynical period.

He arrived therefore at the decision that he would marry some young and buxom creature of decent birth and fit in appearance to be a peeress, and decided on Arbella Rossiter.

After a gulp or two and several *moues* behind his back, she accepted him. A brilliant marriage ceremony followed, conducted by a Bishop and an Archdeacon. And then Arbella was carried off to live in a Bluebeard's Castle he possessed on the Northumbrian coast.

In the three years following her marriage she gave him two boys, with which he was content, especially as his own health began to fail a little just then. At the end of four years of marriage with this cynical, Italianate tyrant, Arbella got very sick of him and thought more and more tenderly of a certain subaltern in the Cavalry whom she had once declined to marry on L500 a year. This subaltern had returned from the South African war, a Colonel and still extremely good-looking. They had met again at a garden party and fallen once more deeply in love. If only her tiresome old Borgia would die—was the thought that came too often into the mind of Arbella, now entering the "thirties" of life, and with the least possible misgiving of her Colonel's constancy if she became presently "*un peu trop mure.*"

She noticed at this time that Grimthorpe Shillito went on

several occasions to London to consult a specialist. He complained of indigestion, was rather thin, and balder than ever, and difficult to please in his food and appetite.

This was her opportunity. She would have said, had she been convicted, that he had driven her to it by his cruelties: that's as may be.—She consulted the family doctor who attended to the household of Bluebeard's Castle; suggested that Sir Grimthorpe (they had just knighted him) might be the better for a strychnine tonic; she had read somewhere that strychnine did wonders for middle-aged men who had led rather a rackety life in their early manhood.

The family doctor who disliked her and suspected her, as you or I wouldn't have done, but doctors think of everything, feigned to agree; and supplied her with little phials of *aqua distillata* flavoured with quinine. He himself was puzzled over Sir Grimthorpe's condition but was a little offended at not being personally consulted.

The fact was that Sir G. had a very poor opinion of his abilities in diagnosis and being naturally secretive and generally cussed, preferred consulting a London specialist. He wasn't then Sir Grimthorpe, the specialist wasn't very certain that it *was* cancer on the liver, and amid his multitude of consulters did not, unless aroused, remember very clearly the case of a Mr. Shillito from somewhere up in the North.

But Shillito pondered gravely over the specialist's carefully guarded phrases about "growths, possibly malign, but at the same time—difficult to be sure quite so soon—perhaps harmless, might of course be merely severe suppressed jaundice." When the pains began—he hated the idea of operations, and knew that any operation on the liver only at best staved off the dread, inevitable end for a year or a few months—When the pains began, he had grown utterly tired of life; so he compounded a subtle poison—he was a great chemist and had—only his wife knew not of this—a cabinet which contained a variety of mineral, vegetable, and acid poisons; and kept the draught in a secret locker in his bedroom. Meantime Arbella, who after all was human, was tortured at the sight of his tortures. She felt she must end it, or her nerves would give way. She trebled, she quintupled the dose of *aqua distillata* embittered with quinine. One night when the night nurse was sleeping ("resting her eyes," she called it) the wretched man stole from his bed to the night nursery and kissed both his boys. He then swiftly took the phial from its hiding place and drank the contents and died in one ghastly minute.

When the night nurse awoke he was crisped in a horrible *rigor*. On the night table was the phial with the remains of the draught. She had noticed in the last day or two Lady Shillito fussing a good deal about the sick man, pressing on him doses of a colourless medicine. *What if she had stolen in while the nurse was asleep and placed a finally fatal draught by the bedside?* From that she proceeded to argue (when she had leisure to think it out) that she *hadn't* been to sleep, had merely been resting her eyes. And she was now sure that whilst she had closed those orbs she had heard—as indeed she had, only it was Sir Grimthorpe himself—some one stealing into the room.

She communicated her suspicions to the doctor. The latter knew his patient had not died of anything he had prescribed, but concluded that Lady Shillito, wishing to be through with the business, had prepared a fulminating dose obtained elsewhere; and insisted on autopsy with a colleague, to whom he more than hinted his suspicions. Together they found the strychnine they were looking for—not very much, but the proportion that was combined by Shillito with less traceable drugs to make the death process more rapid—and quite overlooked the signs of cancer in the liver.

The outcome was that Lady Shillito at the inquest found herself "in a very unpleasant position" and was placed under arrest, and later charged with the murder of her husband.

Believing herself guilty she summoned all her resolution to her aid, admitted nothing, appealed to Michael Rossiter and others for advice. Thus David was drawn into the business.

[But this doesn't sound very credible, you will say. "If the husband felt he could not face the agony of death by cancer, why didn't he leave a note saying so, and every one would have understood and been quite 'nice' about it?" I really can't say. Perhaps he wished to leave trouble for her behind him; perhaps he divined the reason why she thought a day nurse unnecessary, and insisted on giving him his day medicines with her own fair hands. Perhaps he hoped for an open verdict. Perhaps he wasn't quite right in his mind. I have told you the story as I remember it and my memory is not perfect. Personally I've always been a bit sorry for Grimthorpe. It is quite possible that all those hints as to his "queerness" were invented by his wife to excuse herself. I only know that Science benefited greatly from his researches, and that he bequeathed some priceless collections to both branches of the British Museum. Some one once told me he had a heart somewhere and had loved intensely a sister much younger than himself and had only begun to be "queer" and secretive and bald after her premature death. I think also that in the last year of his life he was greatly embittered at not getting the expected peerage; after the trouble and disagreeableness he had gone through to obtain heirs for this distinction this poor little attempt at immortality which it is in the power of a Prime Minister to bestow.]

The Grand Jury returned a true bill against Lady Shillito.

David had been studying the case from the morrow of the inquest, that is as soon as Rossiter had learnt of the coming trouble. The latter though he regarded Cousin Arbella as a rather amusing minx, an interesting type in modern psychology (though really her type is as old as—say—the Hallstadt period) had no wish to see her convicted of murder. Furthermore he was getting so increasingly interested in this clever David Williams that he would have liked to make his fortune by helping him to a sensational success as a pleader, to one of those cases which if successfully conducted mark out a path to the Bench. So he insisted that David Williams be briefed for the defence, and well fee'ed, in order that he might be able to devote all his time to the investigation of the mystery. David had an uphill task. He went down to the North in November, 1908, conferred with Lady Shillito's solicitors, and at great length with the curiously calm, ironly-resolved Lady Shillito herself. The evidence was too much against her for him to prevent her being committed for trial and lodged in reasonably comfortable quarters in Newcastle jail, or for the Grand Jury to find no true bill of indictment. But between these stages in the process and the actual trial for murder in February, 1909, David worked hard and accumulated conclusive evidence (with Rossiter's help) to prove his client's innocence of the deed of which she believed herself guilty. To punish her as she deserved he allowed her to think herself guilty till his defence of her began.

The prospect of a death on the gallows did not perturb Lady Shillito in the least. She was perfectly certain that if found guilty her beauty and station in life would avail to have the death penalty commuted to a term of imprisonment which she would spend in the Infirmary. Still, that would ruin her life pretty conclusively. She would issue from prison a broken woman, whom in spite of her wealth—if she retained any—no impossibly-faithful Colonel would marry at the age of forty-five or fifty. So she followed the opening hours of the trial with a dry mouth.

With the help of Rossiter and of many and minute researches David got on the track of the consultation in Harley Street, the warning given of the possible cancer. He found in Sir Grimthorpe's laboratory sufficient strychnine to kill an army. He was privately informed by the family doctor (who didn't want to press matters to a tragedy) that although he fully believed Arbella capable of the deed, she certainly had—so far as the doctor's prescriptions were concerned—obtained nothing from him which could have killed her husband, even if she had centupled the dose.

Lady Shillito appeared in the dock dressed as much as possible like Mary, Queen of Scots on her trial; and was attended by a hospital nurse with restoratives and carminatives. The Jury retired for a quarter of an hour only, and returned a verdict of *Not Guilty*. The Court was rent with applause, and the Judge commented very severely on such a breach of decorum, apparently unknown to him in previous annals of our courts of justice. Lady Shillito fainted and the nurse fussed, and the Judge in his private room sent for Mr. Williams and complimented him handsomely on his magnificent conduct of the case. "Of course she *meant* to poison him; but I quite agree with the Jury, she didn't. He saved her the trouble. Now I suppose she'll marry again. Well! I pity her next husband. Come and have lunch with me."

And in the course of the meal, His Ludship spoke warmly to Mr. Williams of the bright prospects that lay before him if he would drop those foolish Suffragette cases.

David returned to London with Rossiter and remained silent all the way. His companion believed him to be very tired, and refrained from provoking conversation, but surrounded him with a quiet, fatherly care. Arrived at King's Cross Rossiter said: "Don't go on to your chambers. My motor's here. It can take your luggage on with mine to Portland Place. You can have a wash and a rest and a talk when you're rested; and after we've dined and talked the motor shall come round and take you back to Fig Tree Court."

Mrs. Rossiter was there to greet them, and whilst David went to wash and rest and prepare himself for dinner, she chirrupped over her big husband, and asked endless and sometimes pointless questions about the trial and the verdict. "Did Michael believe she really *had* done it? She, for one, could believe anything about a woman who obviously dyed her hair and improved her eyebrows. (Of course Michael said he didn't, or the questions, as to why, how, when might have gone on for hours). Was Mr. Williams's defence of Arbella so very wonderful as the evening papers said? Why could he not have gone straight home and rested *there*? It would have been so much nicer to have had Mike all to herself on his return, and not have this tiresome, melancholy young man spending the evening with them ... really *some* people had *no* tact ... could *not* see they were *de trop*. Why didn't Mr. Williams marry some nice girl and make a home for himself? Not well enough off? Rubbish! She had known plenty young couples marry and live very happily on Two hundred and fifty a year, and Mr. Williams must surely be earning that? And if he must always be dining out and spending the evening with other people, why did he not make himself more 'general?' Not *always* be absorbed in her husband. Of course she understood that while Arbella's fate hung in the balance they had to study the case together and have long confabulations over poisons in the Lab'rat'ry...!" (This last detestable word was a great worry to Mrs. Rossiter. Sometimes she succeeded in suppressing as many vowels as possible; at others she felt impelled to give them fuller values and call it "laboratorry.") And so on, for an hour or so till dinner was announced.

David sat silent all through this meal, under Mrs. Rossiter's mixture of mirthless badinage: "We shall have you now proposing to Lady Shillito after saving her life! I expect her husband won't have altered his will as she didn't poison him, and she must have had quite thirty thousand pounds settled on her.... They do say however she's a great *flirt*..." Indiscreet questions: "How much will you make out of this case? You don't know? I thought barristers had all that marked on their briefs? And didn't she give you 'refreshers,' as they call them, from time to time? What was it like seeing her in prison? Was she handcuffed? Or chained? What did she wear when she was tried?" And inconsequent remarks: "I remember my mamma—she died when I was only fourteen—used to dream she was being tried for murder. It distressed her very much because, as she said, she couldn't have hurt a fly. What do *you* dream about, Mr. Williams? Some pretty young lady, I'll be bound. I dream about such *funny* things, but I nearly always forget what they were just as I am going to tell Michael. But I did remember one dream just before Michael went down to Newcastle to join you ... was it about mermaids? No. It was about *you*—wasn't that funny? And you seemed to be dressed as a mermaid—no, I suppose it must have been a mer*man*—and you were trying to follow Michael up the rocks by walking on your tail; and it seemed to hurt you awfully. Of course I know what it all came from. Michael had wanted me to read Hans Andersen's fairy stories—don't you think they're pretty? I do; but sometimes they are about rather silly things, skewers and lucifer matches ... and I had spent the afternoon at the Zoo. Michael's a fellow, of course, and I use his ticket and always feel quite at home there ... and at the Zoo that day I had seen one of the sea-lions trying to walk on his tail.... Oh, *how* I laughed! But what made me associate the sea-lion with you and mermaids, I cannot say, but then as poor papa used to say, 'Dreams are funny things'..."

David's replies were hardly audible, and to his hostess's pressing entreaties that he would try this dish or not pass that, he did not answer at all. He felt, indeed, as though the muscles of his throat would not let him swallow and if he opened his mouth wide enough to utter a consecutive speech he would burst out crying. A great desire—almost unknown to Vivie hitherto—seized him to get away to some lonely spot and cry and cry, give full vent to some unprecedented fit of hysteria. He could not look at Rossiter though he knew that Michael's eyes were resting on his face, because if he attempted to reply to the earnest gaze by a reassuring smile, the lips would tremble and the tears would fall.

At last when the dessert was reached and the servants—*do* they never feel telepathically at such moments that some one person seated at the table, crumbling bread, wishes them miles away and loathes their quiet ministrations?—the servants had withdrawn for a brief respite till they reappeared with coffee, David rose to his feet and stammered out something about not being well—would they order the motor and let him go? And as he spoke, and tried to speak in a level, "society" voice, his aching eyes saw the electric lamps, the glinting silver, Mrs. Rossiter's pink, foolish face and crisp little flaxen curls, Rossiter's bearded countenance with its honest, concerned look all waltzing round and round in a dizzying whirl. He made the usual vain clutches at unreal supports, and fainted into Rossiter's arms.

The latter carried him with little effort into the cool library and laid him down on a couch. Mrs. Rossiter followed, full of exclamations, vain questions, and suggestions of inapplicable or unsuitable remedies. Rossiter paid little heed to her, and proceeded to remove David's collar and tie and open his shirt front in order to place a hand over the heart.

Suddenly he looked up and round on his wife, and said with a peremptoriness which admitted of no questioning: "Go and see that one of the spare bedrooms is got ready, a fire lit, and so on. Get this done *quickly*, and meantime leave him to me. I have got restoratives here close at hand."

Mrs. Rossiter awed into silence summoned the housemaid and parlour-maid and hindered them as much as possible in the task of getting a room ready.

Meantime the sub-conscious David sighed a great deal and presently wept a great deal in convulsive sobs, and then opened his eyes and saw the tourbillon of whirling elements settling down into Rossiter's grave, handsome face—yes, but a gravity somehow interpenetrated by love, a love not ashamed to show itself—bending over him with great concern. The secret had been guessed, was known; and as they held each other with their eyes as though the world were well lost in this discovery, their lips met in one kiss, and for a minute Vivie's arms were round Michael's neck, for just one unforgettable moment, a moment she felt she would cheerfully have died to have lived through.

They were soon unlaced, for sharp little high-heeled footsteps on the tiled passage and the clinketing of trinkets announced the return of Mrs. Rossiter.

Vivie became David once more, but left behind her the glad tears of relief that were coursing down David's cheeks.

Mrs. Rossiter thought this was a very odd way for a barrister to celebrate his winning a great case at the criminal courts, and turned away in delicacy from the spectacle of a dishevelled and obviously lachrymose young man with one arm dangling and the other thrown negligently over the back of the leather couch. "Mr. Williams's room is ready,

Michael," she said primly. "All right, dear; thank you. I will help Williams up to bed and have his luggage sent up. He will be quite well to-morrow if he can get to sleep. You needn't bother any more, dearie. Go into the drawing-room and I will join you there presently."

Rossiter gave the rather shuddery, shivery, teeth-clacking David an arm till he saw him into the bedroom and resting on the bedroom sofa. Then he drew up a chair and said in low but distinct tones:—

"Look here. I know you want to make me an explanation. Well! It can wait. A little more of this strain and you'll be having brain fever. Sleep if you can, and eat all the breakfast Linda sends you up in the morning. Get up at eleven to-morrow and if you are fit then to drive out in my motor, return to your chambers. When you have calmed down to a normal pulse, write to me all you want to say. No one shall read it but me ... I'll burn it afterwards or send it back to you under seal. But at the present time, it may be easier for both of us if our communications are only written and not spoken. We have both been tried rather high; and both of us are human, however high-principled. If you write, register the letter.... Good-night..."

This that follows is probably what Vivie wrote to Michael. He burnt the long letter when he had finished reading it though he made excerpts in a pocket-book. But I can more or less correctly surmise how she would put her case; how she typed it herself in the solitude of two evenings; how, indeed, her nervous break-down was made the reason for fending off all clients and denying herself to all callers.

"I am not David Vavasour Williams. I am Vivien Warren, the daughter of a woman who runs a series of disreputable Private Hotels on the Continent. I had no avowed father, nor had my mother, who likewise was illegitimate. She was probably the daughter of a Lieutenant Warren who was killed in the Crimea, and *her* mother's name was Vavasour. My grandmother was probably—I can only deal with probabilities and possibilities in this undocumented past—a Welsh woman of Cardiff, and I should not be surprised if I were a sort of cousin of the man I am personating.

"He was the ne'er-do-weel, only son of a Welsh vicar, a pupil of Praed's, who went out to South Africa and died or was killed in the war.

"You have met my adopted father. He fully believes I am the bad son, the prodigal son, returned and reformed. He has grown to love me so much that it really seems to have put new life into him. I have helped him to get his affairs straight, and I think I may say he has gained by this substitution of one son for another, even though the new son is a daughter! I have taken none of his money, other than small sums he has thrust on me. I have some money of my own, earned in Honoria's firm, for I was the 'Warren' of her 'Fraser and Warren.' She has known my secret all along, hasn't quite approved, but was overborne by me in my resolve to show what a woman—in disguise, it may be—could do at the Bar.

"Michael! I started out twelve years ago—and the dreadful thing is I am now *thirty-four* in true truth! to conquer Man, and a man has conquered me! I wanted to show that woman could compete with man in all careers, and especially in the Law. So she can—have I not shown it by what I have done? But it is a drawn battle. I have realized that if some men are bad—rotten—others, like you—are supremely good. I love you as I never thought I could love any one. I cannot trust myself to write down how much I love you: it would read shamefully and be too much of a surrender of my first principle of self-respect.

"I am going to throw up the whole D.V.W. business. It has put us in a false relation which was exasperating me and puzzling you. Moreover the disguise was wearing very thin. Only those two loyal souls, Honoria Fraser and Albert Adams, were cognizant of the secret, but it was being guessed at and almost guessed right, in certain quarters. Professional jealousy was on my track. I never fainted before in my life—so far as I can remember—but I might have done so elsewhere than in your dear house, after the strain of such an effort as I made to save that worthless woman—she was your cousin, which is why I fought for her so hard—How often is not justice deflected by Love! I might, somewhere else, when over-strained have had a fit of hysterics; and my disguise would have been penetrated by eyes less merciful than yours. Then would have come exposure and its consequences—damaging to You (*I* should not have mattered), to my poor old 'father' down in Wales—whom I sincerely love—to Praddy, to Honoria....

"Let me be thankful to get off so easily! *Somme toute*, I have had a glorious time, have seen the world from the man's point of view—and I can assure you that from his point of view it is a jolly place to live in—*He* can walk up and down the Strand and receive no insult.

"Well now, to relieve your anxieties, I will tell you, that after a brief visit to South Wales to recuperate from the exertions of that trial, Mr. David Williams the famous young barrister at the Criminal Bar will go abroad to investigate the White Slave Traffic. Miss Vivien Warren privately believes—and hopes—that the horrors of this traffic in British womanhood are greatly exaggerated. The lot in life of many of these young women is so bad in their native land that they cannot make it worse by going abroad, no matter in what avowed

Sir Harry Johnston

career. But Mr. David Williams takes rather a higher line and is resolved in any case to get at the Truth. Miss Warren, nathless, has her misgivings anent her old mamma, and would like to know what that old lady is doing at the present time, and whether she is past reform. Miss Warren even has her moments of doubt as to the flawless perfection of her own life: whether the path of duty in 1897 did not rather lie in the direction of a serious attempt to be a daughter to her wayward mother and reclaim her then, instead of going off at a tangent as the mannish type of New Woman, to whom applicable Mathematics are everything and human affections very little. I suppose the truth, the commonplace truth is, that rather late in life, Vivien Warren has fallen in love in the old-fashioned way—How Nature mocks at us!—and now sees things somewhat differently. At any rate, David and Vivie, fused into one personality, are going abroad for a protracted period ... going out of your life, my dearest, for it is better so. Linda has every right to you and Science is a jealous mistress. Moreover poor, outcast Vivie has her own bitter pride. She is resolved to show that a woman *can* cultivate strength of character and an unflinching sobriety of conduct, even when born of such doubtful stock as mine, even when devoid of all religious faith. I know you love me, I glory in the knowledge, but I know that you likewise are more strongly bound by principles of right conduct because like myself you have no sham theology....

"Michael! *why* are we tortured like this? Why mayn't we love where we please? Is this discipline necessary to the improvement of the race? I only know that if we sinned against these human laws and conventions, your great career in Science—and again, why in Science? Lightness in love does not seem to affect the career of orchestral conductors, actors, singers, play-wrights and house painters—why weren't you one of these, and not a High Priest of the only real religion? I only know also that if I fell, so many people would have the satisfaction of saying: 'There! *what* did I say? What's bred in the bone comes out in the flesh. *That's* how the Woman's Movement's goin' to end, you take my word for it! They'll get a man somewhere, somehow, and then they'll clear out of it.'"

"I think I said before—I meant to say, at any rate, so as to ease your mind: I'm all right as regards financial matters. I have a life annuity and some useful savings. I shall give Bertie Adams a year's salary; and if you feel, dear friend, you *must* put forth your hand to help me, help *him* instead to get another position. He has a wife and a young family, and for his class is just about as good a chap as I have ever met—this is 'David' speaking! If you can do nothing you may be sure Vivie will, even if she has to borrow unclean money from her wicked old mother to keep Bertie Adams from financial anxiety and his pretty young wife and the child they are so proud of....

"I must finish this gigantic letter somewhere, though I'm not going to stop writing to you. I couldn't—I should lose all hold on life if I did. For the purpose of correspondence and finishing up things, I shall be 'David Williams' for some time longer. You know his address in Wales? Pontystrad Vicarage, Pontyffynon, Glamorgan, if you've forgotten it. He'll be there till April, and then begin his foreign tour and write to you at intervals from the Continent. As to Vivie, I think she won't return to life and activity till the autumn and *then* she'll make things hum. She'll throw all the energy of frustrated love into the Woman's Cause, and get 'em the Vote somehow...!"

Early in the genesis of the book. I appointed a jury of matrons to judge each chapter before it went to the Press, and to decide whether it was suited to the restrictions of the circulating library, and whether it would cause real distress or perturbation to three persons whom we chose as representative readers of decent fiction: Admiral Broadbent, Lady Percy Mountjoye, and old Mrs. Bridges (Mrs. Bridges was said to have had a heart attack after reading THE GAY-DOMBEYS—I did not wish her to have another). This jury of broad-minded women of the world decided that Rossiter's reply to Vivie's very long epistle should not see the light. He himself would probably—had he known we were discussing his affairs—have been thankful for this decision; because twelve hours after he had written it he was heartily ashamed of his momentary lapse from high principles, ashamed that the woman in the case should have shown herself truer metal. He resolved, so far as our poor human resolves are worth anything, to remain inflexibly true to his devoted Linda and to his career in biological Science. He knew too well that if he were caught in adultery it would be all over with the great theories he was working to establish. The Royal Society would condemn them. Besides, so fine a resolve as Vivie's, to live on the heights must be respected.

At the same time, it is certain that for the next three months he muddled his experiments, confused his arguments, lost his temper with a colleague on the Council of the Zoological Society, kicked the pugs—even caused the most unbearable two of them to be poisoned by his assistant—and lied in attributing their deaths to other causes. He promised the weeping Linda a Pom instead; he said "Hell!" when the macaw interrupted them with raucous screams. He let pass all sorts of misprints in his article on the Ductless Glands for the *Encyclopaedia Scotica*, he was always losing the thread of his discourse in his lectures at the London Institution and University College; and he spent too much of his valuable time writing hugely long letters on all sorts of subjects to David Williams.

David—or Vivie—replied much more laconically. In the

first place he—she—had had her say in the one big out-pouring from which I have quoted so freely; in the second she did not wish to stoke up these fires lest they should become volcanic and break up a happy home and a great career. She wrote once saying: "If ever you were in trouble of any kind; if Linda should die before me, for example, I would come back to you from the ends of the earth and even if I were legitimately married to the Prince of Monaco; come back and serve you as a drudge, as a butt for your wit, as a sick nurse. But meantime, Michael, you must play the game."

And so after this three months' frenzy was past, he did. It was not always easy. Linda's devotion was touching. She perceived—though she hardly liked admitting it—that her husband missed the society of "that" Mr. Williams, in whom she, for one, never could see anything particularly striking, and who was now travelling abroad on a quest it would be indelicate to particularize, and one that in *her* opinion should have been taken up by a far older man, the father of a grown-up family. She strove to replace Williams as an intelligent companion in the Library and even in the Laboratory. She gave up works of charity and espionage in Marylebone and many of her trips into Society, to sit more often with the dear Professor, and was a little distressed by his groans which seemed to be quite unprovoked by her remarks or her actions. However as the months went by, Rossiter buckled down more to his work, and Mrs. Rossiter noticed that he engaged a new assistant at L300 a year to take charge of his enormous correspondence. Mr. Bertie Adams seemed a nice young man, though also afflicted at times with something that gave melancholy to his gaze. But he had a good little wife who came to make a home for him in Marylebone. Mrs. Rossiter being a kindly woman went to call on her and was entirely taken up with their one child whom she frequently asked to tea and found much more interesting than the new

Pom. "But it's got such a funny name, Michael; I mean funny for their station in life. It's a girl and they call it 'Vivvy,' which is short for Vivien. I told Mrs. Adams she must have been reading Tennyson's *Idylls of the King*; but she said 'No, she wasn't much of a reader: Adams was, and it was some lady's name in a story that had stuck in his head, and that as her mother's name was Susan and his was Jane, she hadn't minded.'"

CHAPTER XI

DAVID GOES ABROAD

David Williams had an enthusiastic greeting when he went home to Pontystrad for the Easter of 1909. It was an early Easter that year, whether you like it or not; it suits my story better so, because then David can turn up in Brussels at the end of April, and yet have attended to a host of necessary things before his departure on a long absence.

He first of all devoted himself to making the old Vicar happy for a few weeks in a rather blustery, showery March-April. His father was full of wonderment and exultation over the honourable publicity his barrister son had attained. "You'll be a Judge, Davy; at any rate a K.C., before I'm dead! But marry, boy, *marry*. *That's* what you must do now. Marry and give me grandchildren." The burly curate privately thought David a bit morbid in his passionate devotion to the Woman's Cause, and this White Slave Traffic all rot. He had worked sufficiently in the bad towns of the South Welsh coast and had had an initiation into the lower-living parts of Birmingham and London to be skeptical about the existence of these poor, deluded virgins, lured from their humble respectable homes and thrust by Shakespearean procuresses, bawds, and bullies into an impure life. If they went to these places abroad it was probably with the hope of greater gains,

Sir Harry Johnston

better food, and stricter medical attention. However, he kept most of these thoughts to himself and his wife, the squire's daughter; who as she somehow thought David *ought* to have married *her*, was a little bit sentimental about him and considered he was a Galahad.

Old Nannie remained as usual wistfully puzzled, half fearing the explanation of the enigma if it ever came.

Returned to London and Fig Tree Court—which he was soon vacating—David obtained through his and her bankers a passport for himself and another for Miss Vivien Warren, thirty-four, British subject, and so forth, travelling on the Continent, a lady of independent means. He re-arranged all David's and Vivie's money matters, stored such of Vivie's property and his own as was indispensable at Honoria Armstrong's house in Kensington, and left a box containing a complete man's outfit in charge of Bertie Adams; bade farewell as "David Williams" and "Uncle David" to Honoria and her two babies, and to the still unkindly-looking Colonel Armstrong (who very much resented the "uncle" business, which was perhaps why Honoria out of a wholesome *taquinage* kept it up); and called in for a farewell chat with dear old Praddy—beginning to look a bit shaky and rather too much bossed by his parlour-maid. Honoria had said as he departed "Do try to run up against Vivie somewhere abroad and tell her I shan't be happy till she returns and takes up her abode among us once more. 'Army' is *longing* to know her." ('Army' didn't look it.) "Now pettums! Wave handikins to Uncle David. He's goin' broadies. 'Army' dear, would you ask them to whistle for a taxi? I know David doesn't want to walk all the way back to the Temple in those lovely button boots."

Praed told him all he wanted to know about the localities of the Warren Private Hotels; most of all, that at which Vivie's mother resided in the Rue Royale, Brussels.

So at this establishment a well but plainly dressed English lady, scarcely looking her age (thirty-four) turned up one morning, and sent in a card to the lady-proprietress, Mme. Varennes. This card was closely scanned by a heavy-featured Flemish girl who took it upstairs to an *appartement* on the first floor. She read:

> *Miss Vivien Warren*

and vaguely noted the resemblance of the two names Varennes and Warren, and the fact that the establishment in which she earned a lucrative wage was one of the "Warren" Hotels.

With very short delay, Vivie was invited to ascend in a lift to the first floor and was shown in to a gorgeously furnished bedroom which, through an open door, gave a glimpse of an attractive boudoir or sitting-room beyond, and beyond that again the plane trees of a great boulevard breaking into delicate green leaf. A woman of painted middle age in a *descente de lit* that in its opulence matched the hangings and furniture of the room, had been reclining on a sofa, drinking chocolate and reading a newspaper. She rose shakily to her feet, when the door closed behind Vivie, tottered forward to meet her, and exclaimed rather theatrically "My *daughter* ... come back to me ... after all these years!" (a few tears ran down the rouged cheeks).

"Steady on, mother," said Vivie, propping her up, and feeling oh! so clean and pure and fresh and wholesome by contrast with this worn-out woman of pleasure. "Lie down again on your sofa, go on with your *petit dejeuner*—which is surely rather late? There were signs and appetizing smells of the larger meal being imminent as I passed through the hotel.

Now just lie down until you want to dress—if you like, I'll help you dress" (swallowing hard to choke down a little shudder of repulsion). "I'm not in any hurry. I've come to Brussels to go into matters thoroughly. For the present, I am staying at the Hotel Grimaud."

Mrs. Warren was convulsively sobbing and ruining the complexion she had just made up, before she changed out of her *descente de lit*: "Why not stop here, dearie? Don't laugh! There's *lots* that do and never suspect for one minute it ain't like any other hotel; though from all I see and hear, *all* hotels are pretty much the same now-a-days, whether they're called by my name or not. Of course a man might find out pretty quick, but not a woman who wasn't in the business herself. Why we actually *encourage* decent women to come here when we ain't pressed for room. They give the place a better tone, don't you know. There's two clergyman's sisters come here most autumns and stop and stop and don't notice anything. They come in here and chat with me, and once they said they liked foreign gentlemen better than their own fellow-countrymen: 'their manners are so *affable*.' Why it was partly through people like that, that I got to hear every now and then what *you* was up to. Oh, I wasn't taken in long by that David Williams business. Praddy didn't give you away—to speak of, when I sent you that thousand pounds— Lord, I was glad you kept it! But what fixed me was your portrait in the *Daily Mirror* a couple of years ago as 'the Brilliant young Advocate, Mr. David Vavasour Williams.' Somehow the 'Vavasour' seemed to fit in all right, though what you wanted with my—ahem—maiden name, with what was pore mother's *reel* name, before she lived with your grandfather—Well as I say, I soon saw through the whole bag o' tricks—But *what* a lark! Beat anythink *I* ever did. What have you done with your duds? Gone back to bein' Vivie once more?—"

Vivie: "I'll tell you all about it in good time. But I would rather not stay here all the same. I've found a quiet hotel near the station. I will come and see you if you can make it easy for me; but what I should very much prefer, if you can only get away from this horrid place, is that you should come and see *me*. Why shouldn't you give yourself a fortnight's holiday and go off with me to Louvain ... or to Spa ... or some other quiet place where we can talk over everything to our heart's content?"

Mrs. Warren: "Not a bad idea. Do me a lot of good. I was feeling awfully down, Vivie, when you came. I wasn't altogether taken aback at your coming, dearie, 'cos Praddy had given me a kind of a hint you might turn up. But somehow, though everything goes well in business—we seldom had so busy a time as during this last Humanitarian Congress of the Powers—all the diplomats came here— mostly the old ones, the old and respectable—oh we *all* like respectability—yet I never 'ad such low spirits. My gals used to come in here and find me cryin' as often as not.... 'Comment, Madame,' they used to say, 'pourquoi pleurez vous? Tout va si bien! *Quelle* clientele, et pas chiche'—I suppose you understand French? However about this trip to the country, look on it as *settled*. I'll pack up now and away we go in the afternoon. And not to any of your measly Hotels or village inns. Why I've got me *own* country place and me *own* auto. Villa de Beau-sejour, a mile or so beyond the lovely beech woods of Tervueren. Ain't so far from Louvain, so's I can send you on there one day—Ah! There's some one you'd like to see in Louvain, if I mistake not! You always was one for findin' out things, and maybe I'll tell you more, now you've come back to me, than what I'd a done with you standing up so stiff and proud and me unfit to take up the hem of your skirt.... How I do ramble. Suppose it's old age comin' on" (shudders). "About this Villa de Beau-sejour ... It was once a farm house, and even now it's the farm where I get me eggs and milk and butter an' the fruit and vegetables for this hotel. *He* gave it to me—you know whom I mean by '*He*'? ... don't do to talk too loud in a place like this.... They say he's pretty bad just now, not likely to live much longer. I was his mistress once, years ago—at least I was more a confidante than anything else. *How* he used to laugh at my stories! 'Que tu es une drolesse,' he used to say. I never used to mince matters and we were none the worse for that. Bless you, he wasn't as bad as they painted him, 'long of all this fuss about the blacks. As I say, he gave me the Villa de Beau-sejour, and used to say if I behaved myself he might some day make me 'Baronne de Beau-sejour.' How'd you have liked that, eh? Sort of morganatic Queen? I lay I'd have put some good management into the runnin' of those places. Aie! How they used to swindle 'im, and he believing himself always such a sharp man of business! When that Vaughan hussy..."

Vivie: "Very well. We'll go to Villa Beau-sejour. But don't give me too many of your reminiscences or I may leave you after all and go back to England. Whilst I'm with you, you must give up rouge and patchouli and the kind of conversation that goes with them. I'm out here trying to do my duty and duty is always unpleasant. I don't want to be a kill-joy, but don't give me more of that side of your character than you can help. It—it makes me sick, mother..."

[Mrs. Warren—or Madame Varennes—whimpers a little, but soon cheers up, rings the bell for her maid preparatory to dressing and being the business woman over her preparations for departure. She notes the address of Vivie's hotel and promises to call for her there in the *auto* at three o'clock. Vivie leaves her, descends the richly carpeted stairs—the lift is worked by an odiously pretty, little, plump soubrette dressed as a page boy—and goes out into the street. Several lounging men stare hard at her, but decide she is too English, too plainly dressed, and a little too old to neddle with. This last consideration is apparent to Vivie's intelligence and she muses on it with a wistful little smile, half humour, half regret. She will at her leisure write a whole description of the scene to Michael.]

Those who come after us will never realize how delightful was foreign travel before the War, before that War which installed damnable Dora in power in all the countries of Europe, especially France, Belgium, Switzerland, Italy, and Holland. They will not conceive it possible that the getting of a passport (as a mere means of rapidly establishing one's identity at bank or post-office) was a simple transaction done through a banker or a tourist agency, the enclosing of stamps and the payment of a shilling or two; that there was no question of *visas* entailing endless humiliation and back-breaking delays, waiting about in ante-rooms and empty apartments of squalid, desolating ugliness situate always in the most odious parts of a town. But the Foreign Offices of Europe were agreed on one topic, and this was that having got their feet back on the necks of the people, their serfs of the glebe should not, save under circumstances hateful, fatiguing, unhealthy and humiliating, travel through the lands that once were beautiful and bountiful and are so no longer.

So: Vivie, never having consciously been abroad before (though she was later to learn she had actually been born in Brussels), began to experience all the delights of travel in a foreign land. She woke up the next morning to the country pleasures of Villa Beau-sejour, a preposterous chateau-villa it might be, but attached to a charming Flemish farm; with cows and pigs, geese and ducks, plump poultry and white pigeons, with clumps of poplars and copses of hawthorns and wild cherry trees which joined the little domain on to the splendid forest of Tervueren. There were the friendly, super-intelligent big dogs, like bastard St. Bernards or mastiffs in breed, that drew the little carts which carried the produce of the farm to the markets or to Brussels. There were cheery Flemish farm servants and buxom dairy or poultry women, their wives; none of them particularly aware that there was anything discreditable about Madame Varennes. They may have vaguely remembered she had once lived under High protection, but that, if anything, added to her prestige in their eyes. She was an English lady who for purposes of business and may be of *la haute politique* chose to live in Belgium. She was a kind mistress and a generous *patronne*. Vivie as her daughter was assured of their respect, and by her polite behaviour won their liking as well.

"You know, Viv, old girl," said Mrs. Warren one day, "if you played your cards all right, this pretty place might be yours after I'd gone. Why don't yer pick up a decent husband somewhere and drop all this foolishness about the Suffragettes? He needn't know too much about me, d'yer see? And if you looked at things sensible-like, you'd come in for a pot of money some day; and whilst I lived I'd make you a good allowance—"

"It's no use, dear mother"—involuntarily she said "dear": her heart was hungry for affection, Wales was rapidly passing out of her sphere, David's business must soon be wound up in that quarter and where else had she to go? "So long as you keep on with those Hotels I can't touch a penny. I oughtn't to have kept that thousand, only Praddy assured me it was 'clean' money."

Mrs. W.: "So it was. I won it at Monte. I don't often gamble now, I hate losing money. But we'd had a splendid season at Roquebrune and I sat down one day at the tables, a bit reckless-like. Seemed as if I couldn't lose. When I got up and left I had won Thirty thousand francs. So I says to myself: 'This shall go to my little girl: I'll send it through Praddy and he'll pay it into her bank. Then I shan't feel anxious about her.'"

"Mother! what a strange creature you are! Such a mixture of good and bad—for I suppose it *is* bad, I feel somehow it *is* bad, trafficking in women's bodies, as they put it sensationally. Towards me you have always been compact of kindness; you took every precaution to have me brought up well, out of knowledge of any impurity; and well and modernly educated. You left me quite free to marry whom I liked ... but ... but ... you stuck to this horrible career..."

"Well, Vivie. I did. But did you make any great effort to turn me from it? Besides, *is* it horrible? I won't promise much for Berlin and Buda-Pest or even Vienna, because I haven't been in those directions for ever so long, and the Germans are reg'lar getting out of hand, they are, working up for something. I dessay if you looked in at the Warren Hotels in those places you might find lots to say against 'em. But you couldn't say the places I supervise here and at Roquebrune are so bad? *I* won't stop your looking into 'em. The girls are treated right down well. Looked after if they fall sick and given every encouragement to marry well. I even call those two places—I've giv' up me Paris house this ten years—I even call them my 'marriage markets.' Ah! an' I've given in my time not a few *dots* to decent girls that had found a good husband *dans la clientele*. Why they're no more than what you might call hotels a bit larkier than what other Hotels are. I've never in all my twenty years of Brussels management had a row with the police.... And as to all this rot about the White Slave Traffic that you seem so excited about ... well I'm not saying there's nothin' in it.... Antwerp, Hamburg, Rotterdam—you'd hear some funny stories there ... but only if you went as David Williams in your man's kit—My! what a wheeze that's bin!... And from all they tell me, that place in South America—Buenos Aires, is a reg'lar Hell. But ... God bless my soul ... there's nothin' to fuss about here. Our young ladies would take on like anything if you forced them to go away from my care. It's gettin' near the time when we close our Roquebrune establishment for the summer, an' the girls'll all be goin' back to their homes in the mountains and fattenin' up on new milk; still if you go there before the middle of May you'll see things pretty much as they are in the season; and what's more you'll see plenty of perfectly respectable people stoppin' there. Of course the prices are high. But look at the luxury! What that wicked Bax used to call 'All the Home Comforts.' He liked 'is joke. I hear he's settlin' down at home with his old Dutch. She's bin awful good to him, I must say. *I* couldn't stand 'im long. I don't often lose me temper but I did with him, after he got licked by Paul Dombey, and I threw an inkpot at his head and ain't seen him for a matter of thirteen or fourteen year. He sold out all his shares in the Warren Hotels when he came a cropper."

"Well, mother, I'll have a look round. I'm truly glad you're quit of the German and Austrian horrors, though you must bear the blame for having organized them in the first place. I will presently put on David Williams's clothes and see what I *can* see of them. But if you want me to be a daughter to you, you'll take the first and the readiest opportunity of removing your name from these—*ach!*—these legacies of the Nineteenth century. You'll wind up the Warren Hotels' Company, and as to the two houses you've got here and at Roquebrune, you'll turn them now into decent places where no indecency is tolerated."

Mrs. Warren: "I'll think it over and I don't say as I won't give in to you. I'm tired of a rackety life and I'm proud of you and ... and ... (cries) ... ashamed of meself ... ashamed whenever I look at you. Though I've never bin what I call *bad*. I've helped many a lame dog over a stile.... That's partly how you came into existence—almost the only time I've ever been in love—Many years ago—why, girl, you must be—getting on for thirty-five—let me see ... (muses). Yes, it was in the winter of '73-74. I'd bin at Ostende with a young barrister from London ... him I told you about once, who used to write plays, and we came on to Brussels because he had some business with the Belgian Government. He left me pretty much to myself just then, though quite open-handed, don't you know.... One day I was walking through one of the poorer streets where the people was very Flemish, and I stood looking up at an old doorway—Dunno' why—S'pose I thought it picturesque—reminded me of Praddy's drawin's. And an old woman comes up and says in French, 'Madame est Anglaise?' In those days I couldn't hardly speak a word o' French, but I said 'Oui.' Then she wants me to come upstairs but I thought it was some trap. However as far as I could make out there was a young Irishman there, she said, lying very sick of a fever and seemingly had no friends.

"Well: I took down the address and the next day I came there with the concierge of the hotel where we were staying, and under his protection we went upstairs. My! it was a beastly place—and your poor father—for he *was* your father—was tossing about and raving, with burning cheeks and huge eyes, just like yours. Well! I had plenty of money just then, so with the help of that concierge we found a decent lodging—they wasn't so partic'lar then about infection or they didn't think typhoid infectious—I took him there in an ambulance, engaged a nurse, and in a fortnight he was recovering. He turned out to be a seminarist—I think they called it—from Ireland who was going to be trained for the priesthood at Louvain—lots of Irish used to come there in those days. And somehow a fit of naughtiness had overcome him—he was only twenty—and he thought he'd like to see a bit of the world. So he'd sloped from his college and had a bit of a spree at Brussels and Ostende. Then he was took with this fever—

"His name was Fergus O'Conor and he always said he was descended from the real old Irish Kings, and he was some kind of a Fenian. I mean he used to go on something terrible against the English, and say he would never rest till they were drove out of Ireland. When he got well again he was that handsome—well I've never seen any one like him, unless it's you. I expect when you dress up as David Williams you're the image of what he was when I fell in love with him.

"And I did. And when me barrister friend—Mr. Fitz-Simmons—teased me about it, and wanted me—he having finished his business—to return with him to London I refused. Bein' a bit free with me speech in those days I dessay I said 'Go to Hell.' But he only laughed and left me fifty pounds.

"Well, I lived with this young student for a matter of six months. A lovely time we had, till he began gettin' melancholy—matter of no money partly. He tried bein' a journalist.

"Then the Church got him back. There came about a reg'lar change in him, and just at the time when *you* was comin' along. He woke up one night in a cold sweat and said he was eternally damned. 'Nonsense,' I says, 'it's them crayfish; you ought never to eat that bisque soup...'"

"But he meant it. He went back to Louvain—where I'm goin' to take you in a day or two—and I suppose they made him do all sorts of penances before they gave him absolution. But he stuck to it. In due time he became a priest and entered one of them religious houses. They think a lot of him at Louvain. I've seen him once or twice but I can't bear to meet his eyes—they're somethin' like yours—make me feel a reg'lar

Jezebel. And as to you? Well, when he left me I hadn't got much money left; so, before I begged a passage back to England, I called in at the very hotel where you found me the other day, and where me an' my barrister friend had been stayin'. I'd got to know the proprietress a little—real kind-'earted woman she was. She said to me 'See here. You stop with me and help me in the bureau and have your baby. I'll look after you. And when you can get about again, stop on and help me in my business. I reckon you're the type of woman I've bin looking out for this long while.' And that's how the first of the Warren Hotels was started and that's where you were born ... in October, Eighteen—seventy—five—"

(Vivie gave a little shudder, but her mother's thoughts were so intent on the past that she did not perceive it.)

Mrs. Warren: "Dj'ever see yer Aunt Liz?"

Vivie told her of the grim experiences already touched on in Chapter I.

Mrs. Warren: "Well she dropped *me*—*com*pletely—from the time she married that Canon. And I respected her. She was comfortably off, her past was dead and done with. D'yer think *I* wanted to bother 'er? Not I. It depends so much on the way you was born and brought up. If Liz had been the child of a respectable married couple that could give her a good start in life, 'probability is she'd have run straight from the first. Dunno about me. I was always a bit larky. And yet d'you know, I think if yer father hadn't been a sort of young god, with his head in the skies, and no reg'lar income, if he'd a married me and been kind to me ... I should have been an honest woman all the rest of me life...."

"What do *you* feel about morality? You don't seem to have

much faith in religion, yet you've always taken a high line—and somehow I'm glad you have—about things that never seemed to me to matter much. We're given these passions and desires—and my! don't it hurt, falling in love!—and then the clergy, though they're awful humbugs, tells us we must deny our cravings..."

Vivie: "In the main the clergy are right in what they preach though they give the wrong reasons. We must try to regulate our passions or they will master us, stifle what is really good in us. My solution of this problem which I am so sick of discussing.... But let's finish with it while we are about it—my solution is that the State and the Community should do their utmost to encourage, subsidize, reward early marriages; and at the same time facilitate in a reasonable degree divorce. Apply both these remedies and you would go far to wipe out prostitution, which I think perfectly horrible—I—I should like to penalize it. Perhaps it is the Irish ascetic in my constitution. A good many early marriages might be failures. Well then, at the end of ten years these should be dissolvable, with proper provision made for the children. I think many a couple if they knew that after a time and without scandal their partnership could be dissolved wouldn't, when the time came, want it. While on the other hand if you made the tie not everlastingly binding, young people—especially if they hadn't to trouble about means—would get married without hesitation or delay. I should not only encourage that, but I should give every woman a heavy bonus for bringing a living child into the world.... Now let's talk of something else. When are you going to take me to Louvain?"

* * * * *

They went to Louvain a few days later and Vivie's newly awakened senses for the beautiful in art revelled in the glorious architecture, so much of which was afterwards wrecked in the War.

Walking beneath the planes in a narrow street between monastic buildings, they descried a gaunt, stately figure of a Father Superior of some great Order. "There!" said Mrs. Warren; "that's him, that's your father." They quickened their pace and were presently alongside him. He flashed his great, grey eagle eyes for a contemptuous second on the face of Mrs. Warren, who was all of a tremble and could not meet the gaze. Vivie, he scarcely glanced at as he strode towards a doorway which engulfed him, though the eyes she had inherited would have met his unflinchingly.

*   *   *   *   *

David Williams duly visited Antwerp, Rotterdam, Hamburg, Berlin, Vienna, and Buda-Pest. Much of what he saw disgusted, even revolted, him, but he found few of his fellow-countrywomen held captive and crying to be delivered from a life of infamy. On his return to England in the autumn of 1909, he published the results of his observations; but they had very little effect on continental public opinion.

However Mrs. Warren in due course turned her two establishments into hotels that gradually acquired a well-founded character of propriety and were in time included amongst those recommended to quiet, studious people by first class tourist agencies. Their names were changed respectively from Hotel Leopold II to Hotel Edouard-Sept, from The Homestead, Roquebrune, to Hotel du Royaume-Uni. Mrs. Warren or Mme. Varennes retired completely from the management, but arranged to retain for her own use the magnificently furnished *appartement* on the first floor of the Hotel Edouard-Sept at Brussels, where Vivie had seen her in the late spring of 1909. She still continued to receive a certain income from these two admirably managed hostelries.

Constrained by Vivie she bestowed large donations on charitable and educational institutions affecting the welfare of women and established a fund of Ten thousand pounds for the promotion of Woman Suffrage in Great Britain, which fund was to be at Vivie's disposal. But even with these sacrifices to *bienseance* she remained a lady of considerable fortune.

She resisted however all invitations to make her home in England. "No, dear; I've got used to foreign ways. I hate my own people; they're such damned hypocrites; and the cooking don't suit my taste, accustomed to the best."

But she gave up brandy except as a very occasional *chasse* after the postprandial coffee. She no longer dyed her hair and used very little rouge and no scent but lavender. Her hair turned a warm white colour, and dressed a la Pompadour made her look what she probably was at heart—quite a decent sort.

CHAPTER XII

VIVIE RETURNS

Honoria Armstrong, faithful in friendship and purpose as few people are (though she abated never a whit her love for her dear, fierce, blue-eyed, bristly-moustached, battle-scarred, bullying husband) prepared for Vivie's return in the autumn of 1909 by securing for her occupancy a nice little one-storeyed house in a Kensington back street; one of those houses—I doubt not, now tenanted by millionaires who don't want a large household, just a roof over their heads—that remain over from the early nineteenth century, when Kensington was emerging from a country village into villadom. The broad, quiet road, named after our late dear Queen, has nothing but these detached or semi-detached little *cottages ornes*, one-storeyed villas with a studio behind, or two-storeyed components of "terraces," for about a quarter of a mile; and just before the War, building speculators were wont to pace its pavements with a hungry gaze directed to left and right buying up in imagination all this wasted space, pulling down these pretty stucco nests, and building in their place castles of flats, high into the air. I don't suppose this district will escape much longer the destruction of its graceful flowering trees and vivid gardens, its air of an opulent village; it will match with the rest of Kensingtonia in huge, handsome buildings and be much sought after by the

Sir Harry Johnston

people who devote their lives—till they commit suicide—to illicit love and the Victory Balls at the Albert Hall. But in 1909—would that we were all back in 1909!—it was as nice a part of London as a busy, energetic, sober-living spinster, in the movement, yet liking home retirement and lilac-scented privacy—could desire to inhabit, at the absurd rental of fifty pounds a year, with comparatively low rates, and the need for only one hard-working, self-respecting Suffragette maid, with the monthly assistance of a charwoman of advanced views.

There Vivie took up her abode in November of the year indicated. Honoria lived not far away, next door but one to the Parrys in Kensington Square. She—Vivie—was aware that Colonel Armstrong did not altogether like her, couldn't "place" her, felt she wasn't "one of us," and therefore despite Honoria's many invitations to run in and out and not to mind dear old "Army" who was *always* like that at first, just as their Chow was—she exercised considerable discretion about her frequentation of the Armstrong household, though she generally attended Honoria's Suffrage meetings, held whenever the Colonel was called away to Aldershot or Hythe.

Honoria by this time—the close of 1909—was the mother of four lovely, healthy, happy children. She would give birth to a fifth the following June (1910), and then perhaps she would stop. She often said about this time—touching wood as she did so—"could any woman be happier?" She was so happy that she believed in God, went sometimes to St. Mary Abbott's or St. Paul's, Knightsbridge—the music was so jolly—and gave largely to cheerful charities as well as to the Suffrage Cause. She would in the approach to Christmas, 1909, look round and survey her happiness: could any one have a more satisfactory husband? Of course he was a man and had silly mannish prejudices, but then without them he would not be so lovable. Her children—two boys and two girls—could you find greater darlings if you spent a week among the well-bred childern playing round the Round Pond? Such *natural* children with really original remarks and untrained ideas; not artificial Peter Pans who wistfully didn't want to grow up; not slavish little mimics of the Children's stories in vogue, pretending to play at Red Indians—when every one knew that Red Indians nowadays dressed like all the other citizens of the United States and Canada and sat in Congress and cultivated political "pulls" or sold patent medicines; or who said "Good hunting" and other Mowgli shibboleths to mystified relations from the mid-nineteenth century country towns; nor children who teased the cat or interfered with the cook or stole jam or did anything else that was obsolete; or decried Sullivan's music in favour of Debussy's or of Scarlatini's 17th century *tiraliras*; or wore spectacles and had to have their front teeth in gold clamps. Just clear-eyed, good-tempered, good-looking, roguish and spontaneously natural and reasonably self-willed children, who adored their parents and did not openly mock at the Elishas that called on them.

Then there were Honoria's friends. I gave a sort of list of them in Chapter II—which I am told has caused considerable offence, not by what was put *in* but to those who were left out. But they needn't mind: if the protesters were nice people according to my standard, you may be sure Honoria knew them. But of all her friends none was dearer and closer— save her husband—than Vivie Warren—pal of pals, brave comrade of the unflinching eyes. And somehow Vivie (since she fell in love with Michael Rossiter) was ten times dearer than she had been before: she was more understanding; she had a brighter eye, a much greater sense of humour; she was tenderer; she liked children as she never had done in bygone years, and was soon adopted by the four children in Kensington Square as "Aunt Vivie" (They also—the two elder ones—had a vague remembrance of an Uncle David who had brought them toys and sweetmeats in a dim past). Aunt Vivie and Mummie used to get up the most amusing Suffrage meetings in the long, narrow garden behind the house; or they combined forces with Lady Maud Parry, and spoke in lilting contralto or mezzo-soprano (with the compliant tenor or baritone of here and there a captive man) across the two gardens. Or somehow they commandeered the Square Garden on the pretext of a vast Garden Party, at which every one talked and laughed at once over their Suffrage views.

Yes: Honoria was happy then, as indeed she had been during most of her life, except when her brother died and her mother died. What did she lack for happiness? Nothing that this world can give in the opening twentieth century ... not even a very good pianola or a motor. I feel somehow it was almost unfair (in my rage at the inequality of treatment meted out by the Powers Beyond). Shall not General Sir Petworth Armstrong die in the great debacle of the world-wide War? I shall see, later. And yet I feel that this nucleus of pure happiness housed in Kensington Square—or at Petworth Manor—was to the little world that revolved round the Armstrongs like a good radiator in a cold house. It warmed many a chilly nature into fructification; it healed many a scar, it brightened many a humble life, like that of Bertie Adams's hard-working, washerwoman mother, or the game-keeper's crippled child at Petworth or the newest, suburbanest little employe of *Fraser and Claridge's* huge establishment in the Brompton Road. It pulled straight the wayward life of some young subaltern, about to come a cropper, but who after a talk or two with that jolly Mrs. Armstrong took quite a different course and made a decent marriage. It conjoined with many of the social activities for good of one who might have been her twin sister—Suzanne Feenix—only that Suzanne was twenty years older and

perhaps an inch or two shorter. Dear woman! My remembrance flashes a kiss to your astral cheek—which in reality I
should never have dared to salute, so great was my awe of
Colonel Armstrong's muscles—as, at any reasonable time
before or after the birth of your last child in June, 1910, you
stand in the hall of your sunny, eighteenth century house,
with the gold and green glint of the Kensington garden
behind you: saying with your glad eyes and bonny mouth
"Come to our Suffrage Party? *Such* a lark! We've got Mrs.
Pankhurst here and the Police daren't raid us; they're so
afraid of 'Army.' Of course he's away, but he knows *perfectly
well* what I'm doing. He's *quite* given in. Now Michael, you
show Sir Harry and Lady Johnston to the front seats..."

(I looked round for the rather gloomy presence of Michael
Rossiter, but it was his little golden-haired god-son she
meant.)

You shall have your general back safe from the wars, with a
wound that gives only honour, a reasonable number of well-
earned decorations, and a reputation for rather better strategy
than Aldershot generally produces; and he shall live out his
wholesome life alongside yours, still dispensing happiness,
even under a Labour Government: till, as Burton used to
wind up his Arabian Nights love stories, "there came to them
the Destroyer of delight and the Sunderer of societies."

 Honoria acted towards the Suffrage movement somewhat as
in older-fashioned days of Second Empire laxity well-to-do
people evaded military service under conscription by paying
a substitute to take their place in the fighting line. On
account of her husband, and the children she had just had or
was going to have, she did not throw herself into the physical
struggle; but she still continued out of her brother's ear-
marked money to subsidize the cause. Rather regretfully, she
looked on from a motor, a balcony, a front window or the

safe plinth of some huge statue, whilst her comrades, with less to risk physically and socially, matched their strength of will, their trained muscles, their agility, astuteness and feminine charm (seldom without some effect) against the brute force and imperturbability of the Police.

The struggle waxed hot and fierce in the early months of 1910. Vivie held herself somewhat in the background also, not wishing to strike publicly and effectively until she was sure for what principle she endangered her life and liberty. Nevertheless she became a resource of rising importance to the Suffrage cause. She was known to have had a clever barrister cousin who for some reasons best known to himself had of late kept in the background—ill-health, said some; an unfortunate love affair, said another. But his pamphlet on the White Slave Traffic on the Continent showed that he was still at work. Vivie was thought to be fully equal in her knowledge of the law to her cousin, though not allowed to qualify for the Bar. Case after case was referred to her with the hope that if she could not solve it, she might submit it to her cousin's judgment. In this way, excellent legal advice was forthcoming which drove the Home Office officials from one quandary to another.

But Vivie in the spring of 1910, looking back on nearly twelve months of womanly life (save for David's summer of continental travel) decided that she didn't like being a woman, so far as Woman was dressed in 1910 and for three or four hundred years previously.

As "David" this had been more or less her costume: an undershirt (two, in very cold weather), a pair of pants coming down to the ankle, and well-fitting woollen socks on the feet. A shirt, sometimes in day-time all of one piece with its turn-over collar; at worst with a separate collar and a tie passed through it. Braces that really braced and held up the nether garment of trousers; a waistcoat buttoning fairly high up (no pneumonia blouse)—two waistcoats if she liked, or a dandy slip buttoned innocently inside the single vest to suggest the white lie of a second inner vest. Over the waistcoat a coat or jacket. On the head a hat which fitted the head in thirty seconds (allowing for David's shock of hair). Lace-up or button boots, with perhaps at most six buttons; gloves with one button; spats—if David wanted to be very dressy—with three buttons. On top of all this a warm, easily-fitting overcoat or a mackintosh. If you were really dressing to kill (as a man) it might take half an hour; if merely to go about your business and not be specially remarked for foppishness, twenty minutes. To divest yourself of all this and get into paijamas and so to bed: ten minutes. But when Vivie returned to herself and went about the world of 1909-1910, and merely wished to pass as an inconspicuous, modest woman she had to spend *hours* in dressing and undressing, and this is what she had to wear and waste so much of her time in adjusting and removing:—

Next the skin, merino combinations, unwieldy garments requiring a contortionist's education to put on without entangling your front and hind limbs. The "combies" were specially buttoned with an infinitude of small, scarcely visible buttons, which always wanted sewing on and replacing, and were peevish about remaining in the button hole. Often, too, the "combies" (I really can't keep writing the full name) had to be tied here and there with little white ribbons which preferred getting into a knot (no wonder the average woman has a temper!). When the "combies" went to the wash, all these ribbonlets had to be taken out, specially washed, specially ironed, and ingeniously threaded back into position.

Next to the combinations, proceeding outwards, came the corset, a most serious affair. This exceedingly expensive instrument of torture was compounded chiefly of silk (which easily frayed) and whale-bone. Many good women of the middle class have gone to their graves for three hundred years believing that Almighty God had specially created toothless whales of the Family *Balaenidae* solely for the purpose of providing women with the only possible ingredient for a corset; and for three hundred years, brave seamen of the Dutch, British and Basque nations had gone to a watery grave to procure for women this indispensable aid to correct clothing. But these filaments of horny palatal processes are unamiable. Though sheathed in silk or cotton, they, after the violent movements of a Suffragette or a charwoman, break through the restraining sheath and run into the body under the fifth rib, or press forward on to the thigh. Which is why you often see a woman's face in an omnibus express severe pain and her lips utter the excla-mation "Aie, Aie." Then this confounded corset had to be laced with pink ribbons at the back and in front and both lacings demanded unusual suppleness of arms and sense of touch in finger-tips; and when the corset went to the wash the ribbons had to be drawn out, washed, ironed, and threaded again.

From the front of the corset hung two elastic suspenders as yet awaiting their prey. But first must be drawn on the silk or stockinette knickerbockers which in the 1910 woman replaced the piteously laughable drawers of the Victorian period. Then the suspenders clutched the rims of the stockings with an arrangement of nickel and rubber which no *man* would have tolerated for its inefficiency but would have thrown back in the face of the shopman and have been charged with assault. In times of stress, at public meetings the suspenders would release the stockings from their hold, and the latter roll about the ankles of the embarrassed pleader for Woman's Rights ("Who would be free, themselves must strike the blow," and first of all throttle the modiste, thought Vivie).

Then there was the camisole that concealed the corset and had to be "pinned" in with safety pins. The knickerbockers might not seek the aid of braces; but they must be kept up by an elastic band. Over the camisole, in 1910, came a blouse, pernickety and shiftless about its waist fastening; and finally a hobble skirt, chiefly kept up by safety pins, and so cut below as to hamper free movement of the limbs as much as possible.

Day-boots often had as many as twenty-one buttons—and, mind you, not *sham*, buttons, as I used to think, out of swagger; but every button demanded entrance into a practicable button hole. Or the boots themselves were mere shoes with many buttoned spats drawn over them. All the boots had high heels and the woman walked so as to put a severe strain on her arched instep in order that she might bring on by degrees "flat foot" for surgical treatment.

Who shall describe the hats of 1910?—and before and since—in all but the very poorest women? They were enormous; and so were the hat-boxes; and they could only be held on to the head by running hatpins through wisps of hair.

I will not portray the evening dresses that it sometimes takes a kindly husband an hour to fasten, with "press-buttons" and hooks and eyes; and poor Vivie had no husband and depended on her suffragette maid because at all costs she mustn't look dowdy or the woman's cause might suffer at Mrs. Pethick Lawrence's receptions.

As to night gear: of course Vivie being a free agent slept in David's paijamas. She had long ago cut the Gordian knots of her be-ribboned, girdled night gowns in favour of the Indian garment. But can you wonder after this true recital of the

Sir Harry Johnston

simplest forms of a decent woman's costume in 1909-1910 and even now (a recital drawn from a paper on *Woman's dress* delivered by David on one of the last occasions in which he appeared at the Debating Society of the Inner Temple—and checked by my jury of matrons)—can you wonder that Vivie took very hardly to giving up a man's life in the clothes of David Williams? How she vowed to herself —fruitlessly, because now she is one of the best-dressed women in town (in a quiet way)—that she would one day enfranchise women in their costume as in their citizenship? This will never be done until the modistes of Paris, in some great popular uprising, are strangled and burnt on the Place de la Concorde.

At the 1910 (January) Election, Michael Rossiter had been returned as M.P. for one of the Midland Universities. His Science had certainly suffered from his suppressed love for Vivie, a passion which secretly tortured him, yet for which he dared ask no respite. He thought it was about time that *real* men of Science entered Parliament to check the utter mismanagement of public affairs which had been going on since 1900. He proposed to himself to make a succession of brilliant speeches (he really was an admirable and fluent lecturer) on Anthropology, Chemistry—Chemistry ought to appeal, even to City men because it made such a lot of money—Ethnology, Hygiene, Geography, Economic Botany, Regional Zoology, Germ Diseases, Agriculture, etc., etc.; *and* the absolute necessity of giving Woman the same electoral privileges as Man. He was always well inclined that way, but after he realized that David was Vivie he became almost an embittered Suffragist.

The Speaker took care that he had little scope for his Anthropology, Economic Botany, Chemistry, Hygiene, etc., on Votes of Supply: but he got in some nasty blows in the Woman's cause, and in fact was so strangely rancorous that

Ministers looked at him evilly and arranged that he was not placed on the committee of the Conciliation Bill; that amusing farce with which the Liberal Ministry sought in 1910 to stave off the Suffrage dilemma.

Rossiter and Vivie seldom met except at public receptions. Every now and again he came to Suffrage meetings when she was going to speak; and how well she spoke then! How real it all seemed to her! How handsome she looked (even at 36) and how near she was to tears and a breakdown; while his eyes burned; and when he got home poor little Linda was in despair over her poor distraught Michael, who could find no happiness or contentment in Ten Thousand a year, great fame as the chief inventor of the Ductless Glands, and the man who had issued a taxonomic classification of the *Bovidae* which even satisfied *me*.

What a cruel force is Love! Or is the cruelty in human disciplinary laws? Here were two persons eminently suited to be mates, calculated while still in the prime of life to procreate offspring that would be a credit to the nation, who asked for nothing more in life than to lie in each other's arms—after which no doubt they would have arisen and performed the most wonderful feats in inductive science or in embroidery or mathematics. And they were inwardly raging, losing their appetites, sleeping very badly yet eschewing drugs, pursuing will-of-the-wisps in politics, wasting the best years of their lives ... from a sense of duty, that sense of duty which has made the Nordic White man the dominant race on the earth. "We suffer individually but we gain collectively," Rossiter said to himself.

In May, 1910, King Edward died, and all these gladiators, male and female, willingly declared a Truce in the Suffrage battle, to obtain a much needed rest in the weary conflict. As soon as political activities were resumed, the Conciliation

Bill by the energies of the Liberal Whips was talked out (wasn't it?). At any rate it came to nothing for that Session. Vivie took this as a decision. She openly declared that the Vote never would be given by the House of Commons or House of Lords until it was wrung from the Legislature by a complete dislocation of public affairs, the nearest approach to a revolution women could bring about without rifles and cannon.

Meantime she refused to be duped by Ministers or by amiable go-betweens. She resolved instead, perhaps for the last time, to resume the clothes and status of David Williams, go down to Wales, and stay with her father who was dying by slow degrees.

The letters which the curate had written from time to time to D.V. Williams, Esq., care of Michael Rossiter, Esq., F.R.S., and usually forwarded on by Bertie Adams, had told David how much the Revd. Howel Williams had failed since the cold spring of 1909, and how in the colder spring of 1910 he had once or twice narrowly survived influenza. In July, 1910, he was dying of heart failure. Nevertheless the return of David, his well-beloved, brought to him a flicker of renewed life, a little pink in the cheeks, and some garrulity.

He could hardly bear his darling son out of his sight, except for the narrowest margin of necessary sleep; and often David slept sitting up in an arm-chair in the Vicar's bedroom. The Revd. Howel said nothing more about grandchildren; often—with a finer sense—spoke to him not as though he were a son, but as a beloved daughter. At last he died in his sleep one night, holding David's hand, looking so ineffably happy that the impostor inwardly gloried in his imposture as in one of the best deeds of his chequered life.

*　*　*　*　*

The will, of course, had not been changed, and David inherited all his "father's" property. Out of it he settled L500 on the miner's—or rather Jenny's—son who probably *was* the offspring of the real David Williams's boyish amour. He provided a handsome annuity for poor, shaken, old Nannie; and the rest of the money after paying all expenses he laid out on the endowment of a Village Hall for games and study, social meetings and political discussions, together with provision for an annual stipend of a hundred pounds for the Vicar or curate of the parish who should run this Hall: which was to be a lasting memorial to the Reverend Howel Vaughan Williams, so learned in the lore of Wales.

Having settled all these matters to his satisfaction, and certainly to that of the Revd. Cadwalladr Jones (who succeeded as Vicar of Pontystrad by a wise nudging and monetary pressure on the part of the late Vicar's son), David returned to London at the close of 1910, took off his clothes and shed his personality. It was bruited that he had gone abroad to nurse a health that was seriously impaired through his incredible exertions over the Shillito case. He left his cousin Vivie free to espouse the Suffrage cause, even unto the extremest militancy.

CHAPTER XIII

THE SUFFRAGE MOVEMENT

The Conciliation Bill which was intended to give the Parliamentary Vote to a little over one million women had passed its Second reading on July 12, 1910, by a majority of 110 votes; in spite of the bitter opposition of the Premier, the Chancellor of the Exchequer, the Home Secretary, the President of the Board of Trade, and the Secretary for the Colonies. The Premier's arguments against it were, firstly, that "Women were Women"—this of course was a deplorable fact—and that "the balance of power might fall into their hands without the physical force necessary to impose their decisions, etc., etc."; and finally "that in Force lay the ultimate appeal" (rather a dangerous incitement to the sincere militants). The Chancellor of the Exchequer took up a more subtle attitude than the undisguised, grumpy hostility of his leader.

His arguments at the time reminded me of an episode in East Africa thirty years ago. A certain independent Chief tolerated the presence on his territory of a plucky band of missionary pioneers. He did not care about Christianity but he liked the trade goods the missionaries brought to purchase food and pay for labour in the erection of a station. These trade goods they kept in a storehouse made of wattle and daub. But this temporary building was not proof against cunning attempts at burglary on the part of the natives. The missionaries at length went to the Chief (who was clothed shamelessly in the stolen calicoes) and sought redress. "All right," said the potentate, who kept a fretful realm in awe, "*But* you have no proof it *is* my people who break in and steal. You just catch one in the act, and *then* you'll see what I'll do."

So the Oxford and Cambridge athletic missionaries sat up night after night under some camouflage and at last their patience was rewarded by the capture of a naked, oily-skinned negro who emerged from a tunnel he had dug under the store-foundations. Then they bore him off to the Yao chieftain.

"*Now* we know where we are," said the Chief. "You've proved your complaint. We'll have him burnt to death, after lunch, in the market place. I presume you've brought a lunch-basket?"

"Oh no!" said the horrified propagandists: "We don't want such a penalty as *that*..."

"Very good" said the Chief, "then we'll behead him..." "No! No!"

"Crucify him?"—"No! No!"—"Peg him down over a Driver Ants' nest?" "No! No!"

"Then, if you don't want *any* rational punishment, he shall go free." And free he went.

In the same way the Chancellor of the Exchequer of those days was so hard to please over Suffrage measures that none brought forward was democratic enough, far-reaching and overwhelming enough to secure his adhesion. He was therefore forced to torpedo the Conciliation Bill, to snatch away the half-loaf that was better than no bread at all. He spoke and voted against these tentative measures of feminine enfranchisement, with tongue in cheek, no doubt, and hand linked in that of Lulu Grandcourt whose opposition to any vote being given to woman and whole attitude towards the sex was so bitter that he had to be reminded by Lord Aloysius Brinsley (who like his brother Robert was a convinced Suffragist) that after all he, Lulu Grandcourt, had deigned to be born of a woman, had even—maybe—been spanked by one.

The Speaker had hinted on the occasion of the second reading of the Concilition Bill and at a later raising of the same question that there might arise all sorts of obstacles to wreck the Woman's Franchise measure in Committee; obstacles that apparently need not be taken into account as dangerous to any measure affecting male interests. Therefore many of the M.P.'s timorously voted for the second reading of the Conciliation Bill in order to stand well with their Constituencies, yet looked to the Premier to trip it up by some adroit use of Parliamentary jiu-jitsu. They were not disappointed in their ideal politician. The Bill after it had passed its second reading by a large majority was referred to a Committee of the whole House, which seemingly is fatal to any measure that seeks to become law.

So the stale summer of 1910 wore itself away in recriminations, hopings against probability that the newer types of Liberal statesmen were honest men, keepers of promises, not merely—as Vivie said in one of the many speeches that got her into trouble—"Bridge-players, first and foremost, golf-players when they couldn't play bridge, or speculators on the Stock Exchange, champagne drinkers; and prone to eat at their Lucullus banquets, public and private, till they sometimes fainted with indigestion."

My! But she was bitter in her Hyde Park speeches and at her Albert Hall meetings against this band of mock-liberals who had seized the impulse of the country towards reform which had grown up under the Chamberlain era to instal themselves in power with the financial backing of great America-German-Jewish internationalists, who in those early years of the Twentieth century were ready to stake their dollars on the Free Trade British Empire if they might guide its policy.

[Very likely if they had obtained the complete guidance they sought for they might have staved off this ruinous war by telling Germany bluntly she must keep her hands off France and Belgium; they might also have seen to it that the War Office *was* reformed and the British army ready to fulfil Lord Haldane's promises; for there is no doubt they had ability even if they despised the instruments they worked with.]

But as I say, Vivie was a bitter and most effective speaker. She inflamed to action many a warm-hearted person like myself, like Rossiter (who got into trouble—though it was hushed up—in 1910-1911 for slapping the face of a Secretary of State who spoke slightingly of the women Suffragists and their motives). Yet I seem to be stranded now, with a few others, in my pre-war enthusiasm over the woman's cause, or, later, my horror at the German treatment of Belgium.

Where are the snows of yester-year; where is the animosity which in the years between the burking of the Conciliation Bill and the spring of 1914 grew up between the disinterested Reformers who wanted Woman enfranchised and the Liberal ministers who fought so doggedly, so unscrupulously, against such a rational completion of representative government? The other day I glanced at a newspaper and saw that Sir Michael and Lady Rossiter had been dining at the Ritz with the Grandcourts, Princess Belasco, Sir Abel Batterby, the great Police Surgeon, knighted for his skill and discretion in forcible feeding, and the George Bounderbys (G.B. was the venomous Private Secretary of a former Chancellor of the Exchequer and put him up to most of his anti-suffrage dodges); and meeting Vivien Rossiter soon afterwards I said, "How *could* you?" "How could I what?" "Dine with the people you once hated." "Oh I don't know, it's all past and done with; we've got the Vote and somehow after those years in Brussels I seem to have no hates and few loves left"—However this is anticipating. I only insert this protest because I may seem to be expressing a bitterness the protagonists have ceased to feel, a triumph at the victory of their cause which produces in them merely a yawn.

Where is Mrs. Pankhurst? Somehow one thought she would never rest till she was in the Cabinet. And Christabel? And Annie Kenney? Married perchance to some permanent under Secretary of State and viewing "direct action" with growing disapproval.

And the Pethick Lawrences? Some one told me the other day that they'd almost forgotten what it felt like to be forcibly fed.

But in November, 1910, we all—we that were whole-hearted reformers, true Liberals, not wolves in sheep's clothing, took very much to heart what happened on the 18th of that month, when the Prime Minister of the time announced that the Conference between the House of Lords and the House of Commons on the Veto question having broken down he had advised His Majesty to dissolve Parliament. This meant that the Conciliation Bill was *finally* done for; while the declaration of the Prime Minister as to the future Programme of the Liberal Party, if it was returned to power, excluded any mention of a Woman's enfranchisement Bill.

On Black Friday, November 18th, Vivie was present at the meeting in Caxton Hall when Mrs. Pankhurst explained the position to the Suffragist women assembled there. Her blood was fired by the recital of their wrongs and she was prominent among the four hundred and fifty volunteers who came forward to accompany Mrs. Pankhurst, Dr. Garret Anderson and Susan Knipper-Totes (the two last, infirm old ladies) when they proposed to march to the Houses of Parliament to exercise their right of presenting a petition.

The women proceeded to Parliament Square in small groups so as to keep within the letter of the law. Some like Vivie carried banners with pitiful devices—"Where there's a Bill there's a Way," "Women's Will Beats Asquith's Skill," and so on.... She wished she had given more direct attention to these mottoes, but much of this procedure had been got up on impulse and little preparation made. It was near to four o'clock on a fine November afternoon when the four hundred and fifty women began their movement towards Parliament Square. A red sun was sinking behind the House of Lords, the blue of the misty buildings and street openings was enhanced by the lemon yellow lights of the newly-lit lamps. The avenues converging on the Houses of Parliament were choked with people, and vehicles had to be diverted from the streets. The men in the watching crowd covered the pavements and island "refuges," leaving the roadways to the little groups of struggling women, and the large force—a thousand or more—of opposing police.

It was said at the time that the Government of the day, realizing by their action or inaction in the House of Commons they had provoked this movement of Mrs. Pankhurst's, had prepared the policy with which to meet it. As on the eve of a General Election it might be awkward if they made many arrests of women—perchance Liberal women—on their way to the House to present a petition or escort a deputation, the police should be instructed instead to repel the Suffragists by force, to give them a taste of that "frightfulness" which became afterwards so familiar a weapon in the Prussian armoury. Some said also that the Government looked to the crowd which was allowed to form unchecked on the pavements, the crowd of rough men and boys—costers from Lambeth, longshore men from the barges on the unembanked Westminster riverside, errand boys, soldiers, sailors, clerks returning home, warehouse-men, the tag-rag and bob-tail generally of London when a row is brewing—looked to this crowd to catch fire from the brutality of the police (uniformed and in plain clothes) and really give the women clamouring for the Vote "what for"; teach them a lesson as to what the roused male can do when the female passes the limits of domestic license. A few deaths might result (and did), and many injuries, but the treatment they received would make such an impression on Mrs. Pankhurst's followers that they would at last realize the futility of measuring their puny force against the muscle of man. Force, as the Premier had just said, must be the decisive factor.

But unfortunately for these calculations the large male crowd took quite a different line. The day had gone by when men and boys were wont to cry to some expounding Suffragette: "Go home and mind yer biby." Dimly these toilers and moilers, these loafers and wasters now understood that women of a courage rarely matched in man were fighting for the cause of all ill-governed, mal-administered, swindled, exploited people of either sex. The mass of men, *in* the mass, is chivalrous. It admires pluck, patience, and persistency. So the crowd instead of aiding the police to knock sense into the women began to take sides with the buffeted, brutalized and bleeding Suffragettes.

Fortunately before the real fighting began, and no doubt as a stroke of policy on the part of some Police Inspector, Mrs. Pankhurst convoying the two frail old ladies—Dr. Garret Anderson and Susan Knipper-Totes—champions of the Vote when Woman Suffrage was outside practical politics—had reached the steps of the Strangers' entrance to the House of Commons. From this point of 'vantage a few of the older leaders of the deputation were able to witness the four or five hours' struggle in and around Parliament Square, the Abbey, Parliament Street, Great George Street which made Black Friday one of the note-worthy days in British history—though, *more nostro*, it will be long before it is inserted in school books.

Here, while something like panic signalized the Legislative Chamber and Cabinet ministers scurried in and out like flurried rabbits and finally took refuge in their private rooms—here was fought out the decisive battle between physical and moral force over the suffrage question. The women were so *exaltees* that they were ready to face death for their cause. The police were so exasperated that they saw red and some went mad with sex mania. It was a horrible spectacle in detail. Men with foam on their moustaches were gripping women by the breasts, tearing open their clothing, and proceeding to rabid indecencies. Or, if not sex-mad, they twisted their arms, turned back their thumbs to dislocation, rained blows with fists on pale faces, covering them with blood. They tore out golden hair or thin grey locks with equal disregard. Mounted police were summoned to overawe the crowd, which by this time whether suffragist and female, or neutral, non-committal and male, was giving the police on foot a very nasty time. The four hundred and fifty women of the original impulse had increased to several thousand. Dusk had long since deepened into a night lit up with arc lamps and the golden radiance of great gas-lamp clusters. Flares were lighted to enable the police to see better what they were doing and who were their assailants. But the women showed complete indifference to the horses; and the horses with that exquisite forbearance that the horse can show to the distraught human, did their utmost not to trample on small feet and outspread hands.

Here and there humanity asserted itself. One policeman—helmetless, his fair, blond face scratched and bleeding—had in berserkr rage felled a young woman in the semi-darkness. He bore his senseless victim into the shelter of some nook or cloister and turned on her his bull's eye lantern. She was a beautiful creature, in private life a waitress at a tea shop. Her hat was gone and her hair streamed over her drooping face and slender shoulders. The policeman overcome with remorse exclaimed—mentioning the Home Secretary's name "—be damned; this ain't the job for a decent man." The Suffragette revived under his care. He escorted her home, resigned from the police force, married her and I believe has lived happily ever afterwards, if he was not killed in the War.

Vivie had struggled for about two hours to reach the precincts of the House, with or without her banner. Probably without, because she had freely used its staff as a weapon of defence, and her former skill in fencing stood her in good stead. But at last she was gripped by two constables, one of them an oldish man and the other a plain-clothes policeman, whom several spectators had singled out for his pleasure in needless brutalities.

These men proceeded to give her "punishment," and involuntarily she shrieked with mingled agony of pain and outraged sex-revolt. A man who had paused irresolutely on the kerb of a street refuge came to her aid. He dealt the grey-haired constable a blow that sent him reeling and then seized the plain-clothes man by his coat collar. A struggle ensued which ended in the intervener being flung with such violence on the kerb stone that he was temporarily stunned. Presently he found himself being dragged along with his heels dangling, while Vivie, described in language which my jury of matrons will not allow me to repeat, was being propelled alongside him, her clothes nearly torn off her, to some police station where they were placed under arrest. As soon as they had recovered breath and complete consciousness, had wiped the blood from cut heads, noses, and lips, they looked hard at each other. "Thank you *so* much," said Vivie, "it *was* good of you." "That's enough," said her defender, "it wanted the voice to make me sure; but somehow I thought all along it *was* Vivie. Don't you know me? Frank Gardner!"

While waiting for the formalities to be concluded and their transference to cells in which they were to pass the night, Frank told Vivie briefly that he had returned from Rhodesia a prosperous man on a brief holiday leaving his wife and children to await his return. Hearing there was likely to be an unusual row that evening over the Suffrage question he had sauntered down from the Strand to see what was going on and had been haunted by the conviction that he would meet Vivie in the middle of the conflict. But when he rushed to her defence his action was instinctive, the impulse of any red-blooded man to defend a woman that was being brutally maltreated.

The next morning they were haled before the magistrate. Michael Rossiter was in court as a spectator, feverishly anxious to pay Vivie's fine or to find bail, or in all and every way to come to her relief. He seemed rather mystified at the sight of Frank Gardner arraigned with her. But presently the prosecuting counsel for the Chief Commissioner of Police arrived and told the astonished magistrate it was the wish of the Home Secretary that the prisoners in the dock should all be discharged, Vivie and Frank Gardner among them. At any rate no evidence would be tendered by the prosecution.

So they were released, as also was each fresh batch of prisoners brought in after them. Vivie went in a cab to her house in the Victoria Road; Frank back to his hotel. Both had promised to foregather at Rossiter's house in Portland Place at lunch.

Hitherto Vivie had refrained from entering No. 1 Park Crescent. She had not seen it or Mrs. Rossiter since David's attack of faintness and hysteria in February, 1909, nearly two years ago. Why she went now she scarcely knew, logically. It was unwise to renew relations too closely with Rossiter, who showed his solicitude for her far too plainly in his face. The introduction to Linda Rossiter in her female form would be embarrassing and would doubtless set that good lady questioning and speculating.

Yet she felt she must see Rossiter—writing was always dangerous and inadequate—and reason with him; beg him not to spoil his own chances in life for her, not lose his head in politics and personal animosities on her behalf, as he seemed likely to do. Already people were speaking of him as a parallel to—, and—, and—(you can fill the blanks for yourself with the names of great men of science who have become ineffective, quarrelsome, isolated members of Parliament); saying it was a great loss to Science and no gain to the legislature.

As to Frank Gardner, she was equally eager for a long explanatory talk with him. Except that her life had inured her to surprises and unexpected meetings, it was sufficiently amazing that Frank and she, who had not seen each other or touched hands for thirteen years, should meet thus in a dangerous scuffle in a dense struggling crowd outside the Houses of Parliament. She must so arrange matters after lunch that Frank should not prevent her hour's talk with Rossiter, yet should have the long explanation he himself deserved. An idea. She would telephone to Praddy and invite herself and Frank to tea at his studio after she had left the Rossiters.

Mrs. Rossiter was used to unexpected guests at lunch. People on terms of familiarity dropped in, or the Professor detained some colleague or pupil and made him sit down to the meal which was always prepared and seated for four. Therefore she was not particularly taken aback when her husband appeared at five minutes to one in the little drawing-room and after requesting that the macaw and the cockatoo might be removed for the nonce to a back room—as they made sustained conversation impossible, announced that he expected momently—ah! there was the bell—two persons whose acquaintance he was sure Linda would like to make. One was Captain Frank Gardner, who owned a big ranch in Rhodesia, and—er—the other—oh no! no relation—was Miss Warren....

"What, one of the Warrens of Huddersfield? Well, I never! And where did you pick her up? Strange she shouldn't have written to me she was coming up to town! I could—"

"No, this is a Miss Vivien Warren—"

"Vivien? How curious, why that is the name of the Adams's little girl—"

"A Miss Vivien Warren," went on Rossiter patiently—"a well-known Suffragist who—"

"Oh Michael! *Not* a Suffragette!" wailed Mrs. Rossiter, imagining vitriol was about to be thrown over the surviving pug and damage done generally to the furniture—But at this moment the butler announced: "Captain Frank Gardner and Miss Warren."

Gardner was well enough, a lean soldierly-looking man, brown with the African sun, with pleasant twinkling blue eyes, a thick moustache and curly hair, just a little thin on the top. His face was rather scarred with African adventure and did not show much special trace of his last night's tussle with the police. There was a cut at the back of his head where he had fallen on the kerb stone but that was neatly plastered, and you do not turn your back much on a hostess, at any rate on first introduction.

But Vivie had obviously been in the wars. She had—frankly —a black eye, a cut and swollen lip, and her ordinarily well-shaped nose was a trifle swollen and reddened. But her eyes likewise were twinkling, though the bruised one was bloodshot.

"I'm sorry, Mrs. Rossiter, to be introduced to you like this. I don't know *what* you will think of me. It's the first time I've been in a really bad row.... We were trying to get to the House of Commons, but the police interfered and gave us the full privileges of a man as regards their fists. Captain Gardner here—who is an old friend of mine—intervened, or I'm afraid I shouldn't have got off as cheaply as I did. And your husband kindly came to the police court to testify to our good character, and then invited us to lunch."

Mrs. Rossiter: "Why how your voice reminds me of some one who used to come here a good deal at one time—a Mr. David Williams. I suppose he isn't any relation?"

Vivie (while Frank Gardner looks a little astonished): "Oh— my cousin. I knew you knew him. He has often talked to me about you. I'll tell you about David by and bye, Frank."

At this interchange of Christian names Mrs. Rossiter thinks she understands the situation: they are engaged, have been since last night's rescue. But what *extraordinary* people the dear Professor *does* pick up! Have *they* got ductless glands, she wonders?

Rossiter who has been fidgeting through this dialogue considers that lunch is ready, so they proceed to the small dining-room, "the breakfast-room." Mrs. Rossiter was always very proud of having a *small* drawing-room (otherwise, "me boudwor") and a *small* dining-room. It prepared the way for greater magnificence at big parties and also enabled one to be cosier with a few friends.

At luncheon:

Mrs. Rossiter to *Frank Gardner*, archly: "I suppose you've come home to be married?"

Frank: "Oh no! I'm not a bigamist, I've got a wife already and four children, and jolly glad I shall be to get back to 'em. I can't stand much of the English climate, after getting so used to South African sunshine. No. I came on a business trip to England, leaving my old dear out at the farm near Salisbury, with the kids—we've got a nice English governess who helps her to look after 'em. A year or two hence I hope to bring 'em over to see the old country and we may have to put the eldest to school: children run wild so in South Africa. As to Miss Warren, she's an old friend of mine and a very dear one. I hadn't seen her for—for—thirteen years, when the sound of her voice—She's got one of those voices you never forget—the sound of her voice came up out of that beastly crowd of gladiators yesterday, and I found her being hammered by two policemen. I pretty well laid one out, though I hadn't used my fists for a matter of ten years. Then I got knocked over myself, I passed a night in a police cell feeling pretty sick and positively maddened at not being able to ask any questions. Then at last morning came, I had a

Sir Harry Johnston

wash and brush up—the police after all aren't bad chaps, and most of 'em seemed jolly well ashamed of last night's doin's—Then I met Vivie in Court and your husband too. He took me on trust and I'm awfully grateful to him. I've got a dear old mater down in Kent—Margate, don't you know—my dad's still alive, Vivie!—and she'd have been awfully cut up at hearing her son had been spending the night in a police cell and was goin' to be fined for rioting, only fortunately the Home Secretary said we weren't to be punished.... But Professor Rossiter's coming on the scene was a grand thing. Besides being an M.P., I needn't tell *you*, Mrs. Rossiter, he has a world-wide reputation. Oh, we read your books, sir, out in South Africa, *I* can tell you—Well—er—and here we are—and I'm monopolizing the conversation."

Vivie sat opposite her old lover, and near to the man who loved her now with such ill-concealed passion that his hand trembled for her very proximity. She felt strangely elated, strangely gay, at times inclined to laugh as she caught sight of her bruised and puffy face in an opposite mirror, yet happy in the knowledge that notwithstanding the thirteen years of separation, her repeated rejection of his early love, her battered appearance, Frank still felt tenderly towards her, still remembered the timbre of her voice. Her mouth was too sore and swollen to make eating very pleasant. She trifled with her food but she felt young and full of gay adventure. Mrs. Rossiter a little overwhelmed with all the information Gardner had poured out, a little irritated also at the dancing light in Vivie's eyes, turned her questionings on her.

Mrs. Rossiter: "I suppose you are the Miss Warren who speaks so much. I often see your name in the papers, especially in *Votes for Women* that the Professor takes in. Isn't it funny that a man should care so much about women getting the vote? I'm sure *I* don't want it. I'm *quite* content to exercise *my* influence through *him*, especially now he's in

Parliament. But then I have my home to look after, and I'm *much* too busy to go out and about and mix myself up in politics. I'm quite content to leave all that to the menfolk."

Vivie: "Quite so. In your position no doubt I should do the same; but you see I haven't any menfolk. There is my mother, but she prefers to live abroad, and as she is comfortably off she can employ servants to look after her." (This hint of wealth a little reassured Mrs. Rossiter, who believed most Suffragettes to be adventuresses.) "So, as I have no ties I prefer to give myself up to the service of women in general. When they have the vote and other privileges of men, then of course I can attend to my private interests and pursuits—mathematical calculations, insurance risks—"

Mrs. Rossiter: "It is *extraordinary* how like your voice is to your cousin's. If I shut my eyes I could think he was back again. Not," (she added hastily) "that he has not, no doubt, *plenty* to do abroad. Do you ever see him now? Why does he not marry and settle down? One never hears of him now as a barrister. But then he used to *feel* his cases too much. The last time he was here he fainted and had to stay here all night.

"And yet he had won his case and got his—what do you say? client? off—I dare say you remember it? She was my husband's cousin though we hardly liked to say so at the time: it is so unpleasant having a murder in the family. Fortunately she was let off; I mean, the jury said 'not guilty,' though personally I—However that is neither here nor there, and since then she's married Colonel Kesteven—Won't you have some pheasant? No? I remember your cousin used to have a very poor appetite, especially when one of his cases was on. *How* he used—excuse my saying so—how he used to tire poor Michael—Mr. Rossiter! Talk, talk, talk! in the evenings, and I knew the Professor had his lectures to prepare, but hints were thrown away on Mr. David."

Rossiter broke in:

"Now what would you like to do in the afternoon, Miss Warren? And Gardner? You, by the bye, have the first claim on our hospitality. You have just arrived from Africa and the only thing we have done for you, so far, is to drag you into a disgraceful row."

Frank: "Well, *I* should like a glimpse of the Zoo. I'm quite willing to pay my shilling and give no more trouble, but if Vivie is going there too we could all walk up together. After that I'm going to revisit an old acquaintance of mine and Vivie's, Praed the architect—lives somewhere in Chelsea if I remember right—"

Vivie: "In Hans Place. I don't particularly want to go to the Zoo. I look so odd I might over-excite the monkeys. I think I should like to try a restful visit to the Royal Botanic. I'm so fond of their collection of weird succulent plants—things that look like stones and suddenly produce superb flowers."

Mrs. Rossiter: "We belong to the Botanic as well as to the Zoo. *I* could take you there after lunch."

Rossiter: "You forget, dearie, you've got to open that Bazaar in Marylebone Town Hall—"

Linda: "Oh, have I? To be sure. But it's Lady Goring that does the opening, I'm *much* too nervous. Still I promised to come. Would Miss Warren care to come with me?"

Vivie: "I should have liked to awfully: I love bazaars; but just at this moment I'm thinking more of those succulent plants ... and my battered face."

Rossiter: "I'll make up your minds for you. We'll *all* drive to the Zoo in Linda's motor. Gardner shall look at the animals and then find his way to Hans Place. I'll escort Miss Warren to the Botanic, and then come on and pick you up, Linda, at the Town Hall."

That statement seemed to satisfy every one, so after coffee and a glance round the laboratory and the last experiments, they proceeded to the Zoo, with at least an hour's daylight at their disposal.

Rossiter and Vivie were at last alone within the charmed circle of the Botanic Gardens. They made their way slowly to the great Palm House and thence up twisty iron steps to a nook like a tree refuge in New Guinea, among palm boles and extravagant aroid growths.

"Now Michael," said Vivie—despite her bruised face she looked very elegant in her grey costume, grey hat, and grey suede gloves, and he had to exercise great self-restraint, remember that he was known by sight to most of the gardeners and to the ubiquitous secretary, in order to refrain from crushing her to his side: "Now Michael: I want a serious talk to you, a talk which will last for another eighteen months—which is about the time that has elapsed since we had our last—You're *not* keeping the pact we made."

"What was that?"

"Why you promised me that your—your—love—No! I won't misuse that word—Your friendship for me should not spoil your life, your career, or make Linda unhappy. Yet it is doing all three. You've lived in a continual agitation since you got into Parliament, and now you'll be involved in more electioneering in order to be returned once more. Meantime your science has come to a dead stop. And it's so far more important for us than getting the Vote. All this franchise agitation is on a much lower plane. It amuses and interests me. It keeps me from thinking too much about you. Besides, I am naturally rather combative; I secretly enjoy these rough-and-tumbles with constituted authority. I also really *do* think it is a *beastly* shame, this preference shown for man, in most of the careers and in the franchise. But don't you worry *yourself* unduly about it. If I really thought that you cared so much about me that it was turning you away from *our* religion, scientific research, I'd go over to Brussels to my mother and stay there. I really would; and I really will if you don't stop following me about from meeting to meeting and going mad over the Suffrage question in the House. Is it true that you struck a Cabinet minister the other day? Mr.—?"

Rossiter: "Yes, it's true, and he asked for it. If I am unreasonable what are *they*?—,—, *and*—? Why have they such a bitter feeling against your sex? Have they had no mothers, no sweethearts, no sisters, no wives? If I'd never met you I should still have been a Suffragist. I think I *was* one, as a boy, watching what my mother suffered from my father, and how he collared all her money—I suppose it was before the Married Woman's Property Act—and grudged her any for her dress, her little comforts, her books, or even for proper medical advice. And to hear these Liberal Cabinet Ministers—*Liberal*, mind you—talk about women, often with the filthy phrases of the street—Well: he got a smack on the jaw and decided to treat the incident as a trifling one ... his private secretary patched it up somehow, but I expressed no regret....

"Well, darling, I'll try to do as you wish. I'll try to shut you out of my thoughts and return to my experiments, when I'm not on platforms or in the House. I think I shall get in again—it's a mere matter of money, and thanks to Linda that isn't wanting. I'm not going to withdraw from politics, you bet, however disenchanted I may be. It's because the decent, honest, educated men withdraw that legislation and administration are left to the case-hardened rogues ... and the uneducated ... and the cranks. But don't make things *too* hard for me. Keep out of prison ... keep off hunger strikes—If you're going to be man-handled by the police—Ah! *why* wasn't *I* there, instead of in the House? Gardner had all the luck.... I was glad to hear he was married."

Vivie: "Oh you needn't be jealous of poor Frank. And he'll soon be back in South Africa. You needn't be jealous of *any* one. I'm all yours—in spirit—for all time. Now we must be going: it's getting dusk and we should be irretrievably ruined if we were locked up in this dilapidated old palm house. Besides, I'm to meet Frank at Praddy's studio in order to tell him the history of the last thirteen years."

As they walked away: "You know, Michael, I'm still hoping we may be friends without being lovers. I wonder whether Linda would get to like me?"

At Praed's studio. Lewis Maitland Praed is looking older. He must be now—November, 1910—about fifty-eight or fifty-nine. But he has still a certain elegance, the look of a lesser Leighton about him. Frank has been there already for half an hour, and the tea-table has been, so to speak, deflowered. Vivie accepts a cup, a muffin, and a marron glace. Then says, "Now, dear Praddy, summon your mistress, *dons l'honnete sens du mot*, and have this tea-table cleared so that we can have a hugely long and uninterrupted talk. I have got to give Frank a summary of all that I've done in the past thirteen years. Meanwhile Frank, as your record, I feel convinced, is so blameless and normal that it could be told before any parlour-maid, you start off whilst she is taking away the tea, fiddling with the stove, and prolonging to the uttermost her services to a master who has become her slave."

The parlour-maid enters, and casts more than one searching glance at Vivie's bruised features, but performs her duties in a workmanlike manner.

Frank: "My story? Oh well, it's a happy one on the whole—very happy. Soon as the war was over, I got busy in Rhodesia and pitched on a perfect site for a stock and fruit farm. The B.S.A. Co. was good to me because I'd known Cecil Rhodes and Dr. Jim; and by nineteen four I was going well, they'd made me a magistrate, and some of my mining shares had turned out trumps. Then Westlock came out as Governor General, and Lady Enid had brought out with her a jolly nice girl as governess to her children. She was the daughter of a parson in Hertfordshire near the Brinsley estates. Well, I won't say—bein' the soul of truth—that I fell in love with her—straight away—because I don't think I ever fell deep in love—straight away—with any girl but you, Vivie. But I did feel, as it was hopeless askin' you to marry me, here was the wife I wanted. She was good enough to accept me and the Westlocks were awfully kind and made everything easy. Lady Enid's a perfect brick—and, by the bye, she's a great Suffragist too. Well: we were married at Pretoria in 1904, and now we've got four children; a sturdy young Frank, a golupshous Vivie—oh, I told Muriel everything, she's the sort of woman you can—And the other two are called Bertha after my mother and Charlotte after Mrs. Bernard Shaw. I sent you, Vivie—a newspaper with the announcement of my marriage—Dj'ever get it?"

Vivie: "Never. But I was undergoing a sea-change of my own, just then, which I will tell you all about presently."

Frank: "Well then. I came back to England on a hurried visit. You remember, Praddy? But you were away in Italy and I couldn't find Vivie anywhere. I called round at where your office was—Fraser and Warren—where we parted in 1897—and there was no more Fraser and Warren. Nobody knew anything about what had become of you. P'raps I might have found out, but I got a bit huffy, thought you might have written me a line about my marriage. I did write to Miss Fraser, but the letter was returned from the Dead Letter office," (*Vivie*: "She married Colonel Armstrong.") "Well, there it is! By some devilish lucky chance I had no sooner got to London from Southhampton, day before yesterday, than some one told me all about the expected row between the Suffragettes and the police. Thought I'd go and see for myself what this meant. No idea before how far the thing had gone, or what brutes the police could be. Had a sort of notion, don't know why, that dear old Viv would be in it, up to the neck. Got mixed up in the crowd and helped a woman or two out of it. Lady Feenix—they said it was—picked up some and took 'em into her motor. And then I heard a cry which could only be in Vivie's voice—dear old Viv—(leans forward with shining eyes to press her hand) and ... there we are. How're the bruises?"

Vivie: "Oh, they ache rather, but it is such *joy* to have such friends as you and Praddy and Michael Rossiter, that I don't mind *what* I go through..."

Frank: "But I say, Viv, about this Rossiter man. He seems awfully gone on you...?"

Vivie (flushing in the firelight): "Does he? It's only friend-ship. I really don't see them often but he came to my assistance once at a critical time. And now that Praddy's all-powerful parlour-maid's definitely left us, I will tell you *my* story."

So she does, between five and half-past six, almost without

interruption from the spell-bound Frank—who says it licks any novel he ever read, and she ought to turn it into a novel—with a happy ending—or from Praed who is at times a little somnolent. Then at half-past six, the practical Frank says:

"Look here, you chaps, I could go on listening till midnight, but what's the matter with a bit of dinner? I dare say Praddy's parlour-maid might turn sour if we asked her at a moment's notice to find dinner for three. Why not come out and dine with me at the Hans Crescent Hotel? Close by. I'll get a quiet table and we can finish our talk there. To-morrow I must go down to Margate to see the dear old mater, and it may be a week before I'm up again."

They adjourn to the hostelry mentioned.

Over coffee and cigarettes, Vivie makes this appeal to Frank: "Now Frank, you know all my story. Tell me first, what really became of the real David Williams, the young man you met in the hospital and wrote to me about?"

Frank: "'Pon my life I don't know. I never heard one word about him after I got clear of the hospital myself. You know it fell into Boer hands during that rising in Cape Colony. I expect the 'real' David Williams, as you call him, died from neglected wounds or typhoid—or recovered and took to drink, or went up country and got knocked on the head by the natives for interfering with their women—Good riddance of bad rubbish, I expect. What do you want me to do? I'll swear to anything in reason."

Vivie: "I want you to do this. Run down one day before you go back to Africa, to South Wales, to Pontystrad—It's not far from Swansea—And call at the Vicarage on the pretext that you've come to enquire about David Vavasour Williams whom you once knew in South Africa. It'll give verisimilitude to my stories. They'll probably say they haven't seen him for ever so long, but that you can hear of him through Professor Rossiter. I dare say it's a silly idea of mine, but what I fear sometimes—is that if the fact comes out that *I* was David Williams, some Vaughan or Price or other Williams may call the old man's will in question and get it put into Chancery, get the money taken away from poor old Bridget Evanwy and the village hall which I've endowed. That's all. If it wasn't that I've disposed of my supposed father's money in the way I think he would have liked best, I shouldn't care a hang if they found out the trick I'd played on the Benchers. D'you see?"

Frank: "I see."

The next day Vivie wisely spent in bed, healing her wounds and resting her limbs which after the mental excitement was over ached horribly. Honoria came round and listened, applauded, pitied, laughed and concurred.

But she was well enough on the following Tuesday after Black Friday to attend another meeting of the W.S.P.U. at Caxton Hall, to hear one more ambiguous, tricky, many-ways-to-be-interpreted promise of the then Prime Minister. Mrs. Pankhurst pointing out the vagueness of these assurances announced her intention then and there of going round to Downing Street to ask for a more definite wording. Vivie and many others followed this dauntless lady. Their visit was unexpected, the police force was small and the Suffragettes had two of the Cabinet Ministers at their mercy. They contented themselves by shaking, hustling, frightening but not otherwise injuring their victims before the latter were rescued and put into taxi-cabs.

CHAPTER XIV

MILITANCY

The Lilacs,
Victoria Road, S.W.
December 31, 1910.

DEAR MICHAEL,—

I'm so glad you got returned all right by your University. I feared very much your championship of the Woman's Cause might have told against you. But these newer Universities are more liberal-minded.

I am keeping my promise to tell you of any important move I am making. So this is to inform you, *in very strict confidence*, of my latest dodge. For the effective organization of my particular branch of the W.S.P.U. activities, I must have an office. "The Lilacs" is far too small, and besides I shrink from having my little home raided or too much visited even by confederates. I learned the other day that the old Fraser and Warren offices on the top floor of 88-90 Chancery Lane were vacant. The Midland Insurance Co. that occupied nearly all the building has cleared out and the block is to be given over to a multitude of small undertakings. Well: I secured our old rooms! Simply splendid, with the two safes that Honoria, untold ages ago, fitted into the walls, and hid so cleverly that if there is no treachery it would be hard for the police to find them and raid them. The Midland Insurance Co. did not behave well to Fraser and Warren, so Beryl Storrington, when she was clearing out said nothing about the safes, which were not noticed by the Company. Honoria kept the keys and now hands them over to me.

The W.S.P.U. has taken—also under an alias—other offices on the same side of the way, at No. 94, top storey. We find we can, by using the fire escape, pass over the intervening roofs and reach the parapet outside the "partners' room" at the 88-90 building. I shall once again make use of the little room next the partners' office as a bedroom or rather, "tiring" room, where I can if necessary effect changes of costume. I have taken the new offices in the name of Mr. Michaelis[1] for a special reason; and with some modifications of David's costume I have appeared in person to assume possession of them. I generally enter No. 94 dressed as Vivie Warren. All this may sound very silly to you, like playing at conspiracy. But these precautions seem to be necessary. The Government is beginning to take Suffragism seriously, and a whole department at New Scotland Yard has been organized to cope with our activities.

[Footnote 1: Michaelis, I believe, was a Greek merchant dealing with sponges, emery powder, coral, and other products of the Mediterranean shores whose acquaintance Vivie had originally made when interested in the shares of that Levantine house, Charles Davis and Co. Of Ionian birth he had become a naturalized British subject, but having grown wealthy had decided to transfer himself to Athens and enter political life. He had consented amusedly to Vivie's adoption of his name for her new tenancy and had given her an old passport, which you could do in the days that knew not Dora—she resembling him somewhat in appearance. He was aware of her Suffragist activities and guessed she might want it occasionally for eluding the police on trips abroad.— H.H.J.]

One reason I have in writing this letter—a letter I hope you will burn after you have read and noted its contents—is to ask you to lend me for a while the services of Bertie Adams as clerk. Of course I shall insist on paying his salary whilst I employ him, and indemnifying him for anything he may suffer in my service—that of the W.S.P.U. I am fairly well off for money now. Besides the funds the W.S.P.U. places at my disposal, I have the interest on mother's Ten Thousand pounds, and she would give me more if I asked for it. She has quite taken to the idea of spending her ill-gotten gains on the Enfranchisement of Women! (I am going over to see her for a week or so, when it is not quite so cold.)

What business am I going specially to undertake in Mr. Michaelis's office on the top storey of 88-90? I will tell you. Scotland Yard is getting busy about us, the Suffragists, trying to find out all it can that is detrimental to our personal characters, our upbringing, our progeniture, our businesses and our relations; whether we had a forger in the family, whether I am the daughter of the "notorious" Mrs. Warren, whether Mrs. Canon Burstall is really my aunt and whether she couldn't be brought to use her private influence on me to keep me quiet, in case it came out that Kate Warren was her sister, and that she led Kate into that way of life wherein she earned her shameful livelihood. I have had one or two covert hints from Aunt Liz promising to open up relations *if* only I'll behave myself! Scotland Yard has already had the sorry triumph of causing one or two of our most prominent workers to retire from the ranks because they were not properly married or had been married after the eldest child was born; or had once "been in trouble," over some peccadillo, or had had a son or a sister who though now upright and prosperous had once been in the clutches of the law.

Now my idea is to turn the tables on all this. I myself am impeccable in a real court of equity. My avatar as David Williams was by way of being a superb adventure. I only retired from the harmless imposture lest I might compromise you, and you are so far gone in politics now that the revelation—if it came about—that you were deceived by me and by my "father"—would do you no harm. For a number of reasons I know pretty well that the Benchers would not make themselves ridiculous by having the story of my successful entry into their citadel told in open court. I have in fact, through a devious channel, received the assurance that if I do not resume this character (of D.V.W.) nothing more will be said. What, then, have I to fear? My mother *s'est bien rangee*. She leads a life of the most respectable. If they challenge her, she can counter with some of the most piquant scandals of the last thirty years.

My own careful study of criminology and the assiduous searchings of Albert Adams in the same direction; my mother's anecdotes of the lives of statesmen, police-magistrates, prosecuting counsel, judges, press-editors— many of whom have enjoyed her hospitality abroad—have given me numerous hints in what direction to pursue my researches. Consequently the office of Mr. Michaelis will be the Criminal Investigation Department of the W.S.P.U. I feel instinctively I am touching pitch and that you will disapprove ... but if we are to fight with clean hands, *que Messieurs les Assassins commencent*! If Scotland Yards drops slander and infamous suggestions as a weapon we will let our poisoned arrows rust in the armoury.

How *beastly* all this is! *Why* do they drive us to these extremes? I know already enough to blast the characters of several among our public men. Yet I know in so doing I should wreck the life-happiness of faithful wives, believing sisters or daughters, or bright-faced children. Perhaps I won't, when it comes to the pinch. But somehow, I think, if they guess I have this knowledge in my possession, they will leave David Williams and Kate Warren alone.

Sometimes, d'you know, I wake up in the middle of the night at the Lilacs or in my reconstituted bedroom at 88-90, and wish I were quit of all this Suffrage business, all this vain struggle against predominant man—and away with you on a Pacific Island. Then I realize that we should have large cockroaches and innumerable sand fleas in our new home, that we should have broken Linda's heart, have set back the Suffrage cause as much as Parnell's adultery postponed Home Rule; and above all that I am already thirty-five and shall soon be thirty-six and that it wouldn't be very long before you in comfort-loving middle age sighed for the well-ordered life of No. 1, Park Crescent, Portland Place!

On the whole, I think the most rational line I can take is to continue resolutely this struggle for the Vote. With the Vote must come the opening of Parliament to women. I'm not too old to aspire to be some day Secretary of State for Home Affairs. Because the General Post Office has already become interested in my correspondence, and because this is really a "pivotal" letter I am not trusting it to the post but am calling with it at No. 1 and handing it personally to your butler. I look to you to destroy it when you have read its contents—if you go to that length.

Yours,
VIVIE.

Rossiter read this letter an hour or so after it had been delivered, frowned a good deal, made notes in one of his memorandum books; then tore the sheets of typewriting into four and placed them on the fire. Having satisfied himself that the flames had caught them, he went up with a sullen face to dress for dinner: Linda was giving a New Year's Eve dinner to friends and relations and he had to play the part of host with assumed heartiness.

In the perversity of fate, one piece of the typewritten letter escaped the burning except along the edge. A puff of air from the chimney or the opened door, as Linda entered the room, lifted it off the cinders and deposited it on the hearth. Linda had dressed early for the party, had felt a little hurt at the locked door of Michael's dressing-room, and had come with some vague intention into his study, to see perhaps if the fire was burning brightly: because to avoid unnecessary journies upstairs they would receive their guests to-night in the study and thence pass to the dining-room. But the fire had gone sulky, as fires do sometimes even with well-behaved chimneys and first-class coal. She noted the charred portion of paper lying untidily on the hearth, with typewriting on its upper surface. Picking it up she read inside the scorched margin:

ria kept the keys and now   them over to me.
W.S.P.U. has taken—also under an alias—other of
same side of the way, at No. 94, top storey. We
using the fire-escape, pass over the intervening r
reach the parapet outside the "partners' room" at the
ding.   I shall once again make use of the little room
tners' office as a bedroom or rather "tiring" room, w
if necessary effect changes of costume. I have tak
ces in the name of Mr. Michaelis for a special reas
ome modifications of David's costume I have appeared in p

ssume possession of them. I generally enter No. 94 dressed
a Warren. All this may sound very silly to you, like pla

"Warren!" That name stood out clear. Did it mean the
suffragette, Vivien Warren, who had sometimes been here,
and in whose adventures her husband seemed so unbeco-
mingly interested? One of the great ladies who were Anti-
Suffragists and had already decoyed Mrs. Rossiter within
their drawing-rooms had referred with great disapproval to
Miss Warren as the daughter of a most notorious woman
whom their husbands wouldn't hear mentioned because of
her shocking past. And David, David of course must be that
tiresome David Williams, supposed to be a cousin of Vivien
Warren, but really seeming in these allusions to be a disguise
in which this bold female deceived people. And "Mr.
Michaelis?" Could that be her own Michael? The shameless
baggage! She choked at the thought. Was it a conspiracy into
which they were luring her husband, already rather compromised as a man of science by his enthusiasm for the Suffrage
cause? People used to speak of Michael almost with awe, he
was so clever, he made such wonderful discoveries. Now,
since he had become a politician he had many enemies, and
several ladies of high title referred to him contemptuously
even in her hearing and cut *her* without compunction, though
she had Ten thousand a year. She felt all the same a profound
conviction that Michael was the most honourable of men.
Yet why all this mystery? The W.S.P.U.? Those letters stood
for some more than usually malignant Suffrage Society. She
had seen the letters often in "Votes for Women."...

Her musings here were stayed by the sound of her husband's
steps in the passage. Hastily she thrust the half sheet of
charred paper into her corsage and brushed off the fragments
of the burnt edges from her laces; then turned and affected to
be tidying the writing table as Michael came in.

Rossiter: "Linda! Surely not putting my papers in order—or rather disorder? I thought you were far too intimate with my likes and dislikes to do that!... Why, what's the matter?"

Linda: "Oh nothing. I was only seeing if they had made up your fire. I—I—haven't touched anything."

(Rossiter looked anxiously at the grate, but was relieved to see nothing but burnt, shrivelled squares of paper. He poked the fire fiercely and at any rate demolished the remains of Vivie's letter.)

Rossiter: "Yes: it isn't very cheerful. They must brighten it while we are at dinner; though as we shall go to the drawing-room afterwards we shan't need a huge fire here. There! It looks better after that poke. I threw some papers on it to start a flame just before I went up to dress.... Why dearie! What cold hands and what flushed cheeks!"...

Linda: "Oh Michael! You'll always love me, won't you? I—I know I'm not clever, not half clever enough for you. But I *do* try to help you all I can. I—I—" (Sobs.)

Rossiter (really distressed): "*Of course* I love you! What silly notion have you got into your head?" (He asks himself anxiously "Surely all that letter was burnt before she came in?") "Come! Pull yourself together. Be worthy of that dress. It is such a beauty."

Linda: "I thought you'd like it. I remembered your saying that blue always became me." (Dabs at her eyes with a small lace handkerchief.)

Loud double knocks begin to sound. Dinner guests are soon announced. Linda and Michael receive them heartily. Rossiter—as many a public man does and has to do—shoves his vain regrets, remorse, anxiety, weary longing for the unattainable—somewhere to the back of his brain, where these feelings will not revive till he lies awake at three in the morning; and prepares to entertain half-a-dozen hearty men and buxom women who are easily impressed by a little spoon-fed science. Linda is soon distracted from the scrap of paper in her bosom and gives all her attention to her cousins and grown-up school friends from Bradford and North-allerton who are delighted to see the New Year in amid the gaieties of London.

But before she rings for her maid and undresses that night, she locks the burnt fragment in a secret drawer of her desk.

 The Ministry which was returned to power in December, 1910, had to plan during the first half of 1911 to keep the Suffragists becalmed with promises and prevent their making any public protest which might mar the Coronation festivities. So various Conciliation Bills were allowed to be read to the House of Commons and to reach Second readings at which they were passed with huge majorities. Then they came to nothingness by being referred to a Committee of the whole House. Still a hope of some solution was dangled before the oft-deluded women, who could hardly believe that British Ministers of State would be such breakers of promises and tellers of falsehoods. In November, 1911, there being no reason for further dissembling, the Government made the announcement that it was contemplating a Manhood Suffrage Bill, which would override altogether the petty question as to whether a proportion of women should or should not enjoy the franchise. This new electoral measure was to be designed for men only, but—the Government opined—it might be susceptible of amendment so as to admit women likewise.

[Probably the Government had satisfied itself beforehand

that, acting on some unwritten code of Parliamentary procedure, the Speaker would rule out such an amendment as unconstitutional. At any rate, this is what he did in 1913.]

The wrath of the oft-deluded women flamed out with immediate resentment when the purport of this trick was discerned. Led by Mrs. Pethick Lawrence a band of more than a thousand women and men (and some of the presumed men were, like Vivie, women in men's clothes, as it enabled them to move about with more agility and also to escape identification) entered Whitehall and Parliament Street armed with hammers and stones. They broke all the windows they could in the fronts of the Government offices and at the residences of Ministers of State. Vivie found herself shadowed everywhere by Bertie Adams though she had given him no orders to join the crowd, indeed had begged him to mind his own business and go home. "This *is* my business," he had said curtly, and for once masterfully, and she gave way. Though Vivie for her own reasons carried no hammer or stone and as one of the principal organizers of the militant movement had been requested by the inner Council of the W.S.P.U. to keep out of prison as long as possible, she could not help cheering on the boldest and bravest in the mild violence of their protest. To the angry police she seemed merely an impertinent young man, hardly worth arresting when they could barely master the two hundred and twenty-three arch offenders with glass-breaking weapons in their hands. So a constable contented himself with marching on her feet with all his weight and thrusting his elbows violently into her breast.

She well-nigh fainted with the pain; in fact would have fallen in the crowd but for the interposition of Adams who carried her out of it to the corner of Parliament Street, where he pounced on one of the many taxis that crawled about the outskirts of the shouting, swaying crowd, sure of a fare from either police or escaping Suffragists. Feeling certain that some policeman had not left the disguised Vivie entirely unobserved—indeed Bertie had half thought he caught the words above the din: "That's David Williams, that is," he told the taxi man to drive along the Embankment to the Temple. By the time they had reached the nearest access on that side of Fountain Court, Vivie was sufficiently recovered from her semi-swoon to get out, and leaning heavily on Bertie's arm, limp slowly through the intricacies of the Temple and out into Fleet Street by Sergeant's Inn. Then with fresh efforts and further halts they made their way to 94, Chancery Lane.

Some one was sitting up here with one electric light on, ready for any development connected with W.S.P.U. work that night. To her—fortunately it was a woman—Bertie handed over his stricken chief, and then made his way home to his little house in Marylebone and a questioning and not too satisfied wife. The Suffragette in charge of the top storey at 94 knew something, fortunately, of first aid, was deft of hands and full of sympathy. Vivie's—or Mr. Michaelis's— lace-up boots were carefully removed and the poor crushed and bleeding toes washed with warm water. The collar was taken off and the shirt unbuttoned revealing a terrible bruise on the sternum where the policeman's elbow had struck her—better however there, though it had nearly broken the breastbone, than on either side, as such a blow might have given rise to cancer. As it was, Vivie when she coughed spat blood.

A cup of hot bovril and an hour's rest on a long chair and she was ready, supremely anxious indeed, to try the last adventure: an excursion across the roofs and up and down fire-escapes on to the parapet of her own especial dwelling, the old offices of Fraser and Warren at No. 88-90. The great window of the partners' room opened to her manipulations—

it had been carefully left unbolted before her departure for Caxton Hall; and aided cautiously and cleverly by her suffragette helper, Vivie at last found herself—or Mr. Michaelis did—in the snug little bedroom that knew her chiefly in her male form.

Here she was destined to lie up for several weeks till the feet and the chest were healed and sound again. Hither by the normal entrance came a woman suffragette surgeon to heal, and Vivie's woman clerk to act as secretary; whilst Adams typed away in the outer office on Mr. Michaelis's business or went on long and mysterious errands. Hither also came the little maid from the Lilacs, bringing needed changes of clothes, letters, and messages from Honoria. A stout young man with a fresh colour went up in the lift at No. 94 to the flat or office of "Algernon Mainwaring," and then skipped along the winding way between the chimney stacks and up and down short iron ladders till he too reached the parapet, entered through the opened casement, and revealed himself as a great W.S.P.U. leader, costumed like Vivie as a male, but in reality a buxom young woman only waiting for the Vote to be won to espouse her young man—shop steward— and begin a large family of children. From this leader, Vivie received humbly the strictest injunctions to engage in no more disabling work for the present, to keep out of police clutches and the risk of going to prison or of attracting too much police attention at 88-90 Chancery Lane. "You are our brain-centre at present. Our offices for show and for raiding by the police have been at Clifford's Inn and are now in Lincoln's Inn. But the really precious information we possess is ... well, you know where it is: walls may have ears ... your time for public testimony hasn't come yet ... we'll let you know fast enough when it has and *you* won't flinch, *I'm* quite sure..."

As a matter of fact, though Vivie's intelligence and

inventiveness, her knowledge of criminal law, of lawyers and of city business, her wide education, her command of French (improved by the frequent trips to Brussels—where indeed she deposited securely in her mother's keeping some of the funds and the more remarkable documents of the Suffrage cause) and her possession of monetary supplies were not to be despised: as a figure-head, she was of doubtful value. There was always that mother in the background. If Vivie was in court for a suffrage offence of a grave character the prosecuting Counsel would be sure to rake up the "notorious Mrs. Warren" and drag in the White Slave Traffic, to bewilder a jury and throw discredit on the militant side of the Suffrage cause. Of course if the true story of Vivie were fully known, she would rise triumphant from such a recital.... Still ... throw plenty of mud and some of it will stick.... And what *was* her full, true story? Even in the pure passion of the fight for liberty among these young and middle-aged women, the tongue of scandal occasionally wagged in moments of lassitude, discouragement, undeception. At such times some weaker sister with a vulgar mind, or a mind with vulgar streaks in it, might hint at the great interest taken in Vivie by a distinguished man of science who had become an M.P. and a raging suffragist. Or indecorum would be hinted in the relations between this enigmatic woman, so prone seemingly to don male costume, and the burly clerk who attended her so faithfully and had brought her home on the night of Mrs. Pethick Lawrence's spirited raid.

So much so, that Vivie with a sigh, as soon as she attained convalescence was fain to send for Bertie and tell him with unanswerable decision that he must return to his work with Rossiter and thither she would send from time to time special instructions if he could help her business in any way.

This was done in January, 1912. Vivie's feet were now

healed and the woman surgeon was satisfied that she could walk on them without displacing the reset bones. The slight fracture in the breastbone had repaired itself by one of Nature's magic processes. So one day our battered heroine doffed the invalid garments of Michaelis and donned those of any well-dressed woman of 1912, including a thick veil. Thus attired she passed from the parapet to the fire-escape (recalling the agony these gymnastics had caused her the previous November), and from the fire-escape to the roof of No. 92 (continuous with the roof of 94), and past the chimney stacks, into the top storey of 94, and so on down to the street, where a taxi was waiting to convey her to the Lilacs.

(The W.S.P.U., by the bye, to bluff Scotland Yard had added to the name of "Algernon Mainwaring, 5th Floor," the qualification of "Hygienic Corset-maker," as an explanation—possibly—of why so many women found their way to the top storey of No. 94.)

Arrived at the Lilacs, Vivie took up for a brief spell the life of an ordinary young woman of the well-to-do middle class, seriously interested in the suffrage question but non-militant. She attended several of Honoria's or Mrs. Fawcett's suffrage parties or public meetings and occasionally spoke and spoke well. She also went over to Brussels twice in 1912 to keep in touch with her mother. Mrs. Warren had had one or two slight warnings that a life of pleasure saps the strongest constitution.[1] She lived now mainly at her farm, the Villa Beau-sejour, and only occasionally occupied her *appartement* in the Rue Royale. She must have been about fifty-nine in the spring of 1912, and was beginning to "soigner son salut," that is to say to take stock of her past life, apologize for it to herself and see how she could atone reasonably for what she had done wrong. A decade or two earlier she would have turned to religion, inevitably to that most attractive and

Sir Harry Johnston

logical form, the religion expounded by the Holy Roman Catholic and Apostolic Church. She would have confessed her past, slightly or very considerably *gazee*, to some indulgent confessor, have been pardoned, and have presented a handsome sum to an ecclesiastical charity or work of piety. But she had survived into a skeptical age and she had conceived an immense respect for her clever daughter. Vivie should be her spiritual director; and Vivie's idea put before her at their reconciliation three years previously had seemed the most practical way of making amends to Woman for having made money in the past out of the economic and physiological weakness of women. She had fined herself Ten Thousand pounds then; and out of her remaining capital of Fifty or Sixty thousand (all willed with what else she possessed to her daughter) she would pay over more if Vivie demanded it as further reparation. Still, she found the frequentation of churches soothing and gave much and often to the mildly beseeching Little Sisters of the Poor when they made their rounds in town or suburbs.

[Footnote 1: Or so the observers say who haven't had a life of pleasure.]

"What do you think about Religion, Viv old girl?" she said one day in the Eastertide of 1912, when Vivie was spending a delicious fortnight at Villa Beau-sejour.

"Personally," said Vivie, "I hate all religions, so far as I have had time to study them. They bind up with undisputed ethics more or less preposterous theories concerning life and death, the properties of matter, man, God, the universe, the laws of nature, the food we should eat, the relations of the sexes, the quality of the weekly day of rest. Gradually they push indisputable ethics on one side and are ready to apply torture, death, or social ostracism to the support of these preposterous theories and explanations of God and Man. Such theories"—went on Vivie, though her mother's attention had wandered to some escaped poultry that were scratching disastrously in seed beds—"Such theories and explanations, mark you—*do* listen, mother, since you asked the question..."

"I'm listenin', dearie, but you talk like a book and I don't know what some of your words mean—What's ethics?"

"Well 'ethics' means er—er—'morality'; it comes from a Greek word meaning 'character.'"

Mrs. Warren: "You talk like a book—"

Vivie: "I do sometimes, when I remember something I've read. But now I've lost my thread.... What I meant to finish up with was something like this 'Such theories and explanations were formulated several hundred, or more than two thousand years ago, in times when Man's knowledge of himself, of his surroundings, of the earth and the universe was almost non-existent, yet they are preserved to our times as sacred revelations, though they are not superior to the fancies and fetish rites of a savage.' There! All that answer is quoted from Professor Rossiter's little book (*Home University Library*, "The Growth of the Human Mind")."

Mrs. Warren: "Rossiter! Is that the man you're sweet on?"

Vivie: "Don't put it so coarsely. There is a great friendship between us. We belong to a later generation than you. A man and a woman can be friends now without becoming lovers."

Mrs. Warren: "Go *on*! Don't humbug me. Men and women's the same as when I was young. I'm sorry, all the same, dear girl. There are you, growin' middle-aged and not married to some good-'earted chap as 'd give you three-four children I could pet in me old age. Wodjer want to go fallin' in love with some chap as 'as got a wife already? *I* know your principles. There's iron in yer blood, same as there is in that proud priest, your father. I know you'd break your 'eart sooner 'n have a good time with the professor. My! It seems to me Love's as bad as Religion for bringin' about sorrer!"

Vivie: "If you mean that it is answerable for the same intense happiness and even more intense *un*happiness, I suppose you're right. I'm *miserable*, mother, and it's some relief to me to say so. If I could become honourably the wife of Michael Rossiter I'm afraid I should let Suffrage have the go-by. But as I can't, why this struggle for the vote is the only thing that keeps me going. I shall fight for it for another ten years, and by that time certain physiological changes may have taken place in me, and my feelings towards Rossiter will have calmed down."

(Here Mrs. Warren proceeded to call out rather disharmoniously in Flemish to the poultry woman, and asked why the something-or-other she let the Houdans spoil the seed beds.)

Mrs. Warren resuming: "Well it's clear you're your father's daughter. 'E'd 'ave gone on—*did* go on—in just such a way. 'Im and me were jolly well suited to one another. I'd got to reg'lar love 'im. I'd 'a bin a true wife to him, and 'ave worked my fingers to the bone for 'im, and you bet I'd 'ave made a livin' somehow. And he'd have written some jolly good books and 'ave made lots of money. But no! This beastly Religion comes in with its scare of Hell fire and back 'e goes to the priests and 'is prayers and 'is penances. The last ten years or so 'e's bin filled up with pride. 'Is passions 'ave died down and 'e thinks 'imself an awful swell as the head of his Order. And they do say as 'e's got 'is fingers in several pies and is a reg'lar old conspirator, working up the Irish to do something against England. Yer know since I've made my peace with you.... *Ain't* it a rum go, by the bye? Ten or twenty years ago it'd 'a bin 'my peace with God.' I dunno nothin' about God—can't see 'im at the end of a telescope, anyways. But I *can* see you, Vivie, and there's no one livin' I respect more" (speaks with real feeling).... "Well, as I was sayin', since I'd set myself right with you and wound up the business of the hotels I ain't so easy cowed by 'is looks as I used to be. So every now and then it amuses me to run over in my auto to Louvain and stroll about there and watch 'im as 'e comes out for 'is promenade, pretendin' to be readin' a breviary or some holy book. I know it riles 'im....

"Well, but for high principles, 'e and I might 'a bin as 'appy as 'appy and 'ad a large family. And there was nothin' to stop 'im a-marryin' me, if that was all he wanted to feel comfortable about it. But jus' see. He's had a life that seems to me downright sterile, and I—well, I ain't been *really* happy till we made it up three years ago" (leans over, and kisses Vivie a little timorously).

"Now there's you, burning yourself out 'cos your high principles won't let you go for once in a way on the spree with this Rossiter—s'posin' 'e's game, of course.... You've too much pride to throw yourself at his head. But if he loves you as bad as you loves 'im, why don't you ask him" (instinctively the old ministress of love speaks here) "ask 'im to take you over to Paris for a trip? I'll lay 'e 'as to go over now'n again to the Sorbonne or one of them scientific institutes. *She'd* never come to 'ear of it. An' after one or two such honeymoons you'd soon get tired of 'im, specially now you're gettin' on a bit in years, and may be you'd settle down quietly after that. Or if you ain't reg'lar set on *'im*, why not giv' up this suffrage business and live a bit with me here? There's plenty of upstanding, decent, Belgian men in good positions as'd like to have an English wife. *They* wouldn't look too shy at my money..."

Vivie: "Get thee behind me, Satan! Mother, you oughtn't to make such propositions. Don't you understand, we must all have a religion somewhere. Some principle to which we sacrifice ourselves. Rossiter would be horrified if he could hear you. His mistress is Science, besides which he is really devoted to his wife and would do nothing that could hurt her. You don't know England, it's clear. Supposing for one moment I could consent—and I couldn't—we should be found out to a certainty, and then Michael's career would be ruined.

"My religion, though I sometimes weary of it and sneer at it, is Women's Rights: women must have precisely the same rights as men, no disqualification whatever based merely on their being women. Did you read those disgusting letters in the *Times* by the surgeon, the midwifery man, Sir Wrigsby Blane? Declaring that the demand for the Vote was based on immorality, and pretending that once a month, till they were fifty, and for several years *after* they were fifty, women were not responsible for their actions, because of what he vaguely called 'physiological processes.' What poisonous rubbish! You know as well as I do that in most cases it makes little or no difference; and if it does, what about men? Aren't *they* at certain times not their normal selves? When they're full up with wine or beer or whiskey, when they're courting, when they're pursuing some illicit love, when after fifty they get a little odd in their ways through this, that and the other internal trouble or change of function? What's true of the one sex is equally true of the other. Most men and women between twenty and sixty jolly well know what they want, and generally they want something reasonable. We don't legislate for the freaks, the unbalanced, the abnormal; or if we do restrict the vote in those cases, let's restrict it for males as well as females—But don't you see at the same time what a text I should furnish to this malign creature if I ran away to Paris with Michael, and made the slightest false step ... even though it had no bearing on the main argument?..."

At this juncture Vivie, whose obsession leads her more and more to address every one as a public meeting—is interrupted by the smiling *bonne a tout faire* who announces that *le dejeuner de Madame est servi*, and the two women gathering up books and shawls go in to the gay little *saile-a-manger* of the Villa Beau-sejour.

On Vivie's return to London, after her Easter holiday, she threw herself with added zest into the Suffrage struggle. The fortnight of good feeding, of quiet nights and lazy days under her mother's roof had done her much good. She was not quite so thin, the dark circles under her grey eyes had vanished, and she found not only in herself but even in the most middle-aged of her associates a delightful spirit of tomboyishness in their swelling revolt against the Liberal leaders. It was specially during the remainder of 1912 that Vivie noted the enormous good which the Suffrage movement had done and was doing to British women. It was producing a splendid camaraderie between high and low. Heroines like Lady Constance Lytton mingled as sister with equally heroic charwomen, factory girls, typewriteresses, waitresses and hospital nurses. Women doctors of Science, Music, and Medicine came down into the streets and did the bravest actions to present their rights before a public that now began to take them seriously. Debutantes, no longer quivering with fright at entering the Royal Presence, modestly but audibly called their Sovereign's attention to the injustice of Mr. Asquith's attitude towards women, while princesses of the Blood Royal had difficulty in not applauding. Many a tame cat had left the fire-side and the skirts of an inane old mother (who had plenty of people to look after her selfish wants) and emerged, dazed at first, into a world that was unknown to her. Such had thrown away their crochet hooks, their tatting-shuttles and fashion articles, their Church almanacs, and Girl's Own Library books, and read and talked of social, sexual, and industrial problems that have got to be faced and solved. Colour came into their cheeks, assurance into their faded manners, sense and sensibility into their talk; and whatever happened afterwards they were never crammed back again into the prison of Victorian spinsterhood. They learnt rough cooking, skilled confectionery, typewriting, bicycling, jiu-jitsu perhaps. "The maidens came, they talked, they sang, they read; till she not fair began to gather light, and she that was became her former beauty treble" sang in prophecy, sixty years before, the greatest of poets and the poet-prophet of Woman's Emancipation. Many a woman has directly owed the lengthened, happier, usefuller life that became hers from 1910-1911-1912 onwards to the Suffrage movement for the Liberation of Women.

The crises of 1912 moreover were not so acute as bitterly to envenom the struggle in the way that happened during the two following years. There was always some hope that the Ministry might permit the passing of an amendment to the Franchise Bill which would in some degree affirm the principle of Female Suffrage. It is true that a certain liveliness was maintained by the Suffragettes. The W.S.P.U. dared not relax in its militancy lest Ministers should think the struggle waning and Woman already tiring of her claims. The vaunted Manhood Suffrage Bill had been introduced by an anti-woman-suffrage Quaker Minister and its Second reading been proposed by an equally anti-feminist Secretary of State—this was in June-July, 1912; and no member of the Cabinet had risen to say a word in favour of the Women's claims. Still, something might be done in Committee, in the autumn Session—if there were one—or in the following year. There was a simmering in the Suffragist ranks rather than any alarming explosion. In March, before Vivie went to Brussels, Mrs. Pankhurst had carried out a window-smashing raid on Bond Street and Regent Street and the clubs of Piccadilly, during which among the two hundred and nineteen arrests there were brought to light as "revolutionaries" two elderly women surgeons of great distinction and one female Doctor of Music. In revenge the police had raided the W.S.P.U. offices at Clifford's Inn, an event long foreseen and provided against in the neighbouring Chancery Lane.

The Irish Nationalist Party had shown its marked hostility to the enfranchisement of women in any Irish Parliament and so a few impulsive Irish women had thrown things at Nationalist M.P.'s without hurting them. Mr. Lansbury had spoken the plain truth to the Prime Minister in the House of Commons and had been denied access to that Chamber where Truth is so seldom welcome.

In July the slumbering movement towards resisting the payment of taxes by vote-less women woke up into real activity, and there were many ludicrous and pathetic scenes organized often by Vivie and Bertie Adams at which household effects were sold and bought in by friends to satisfy the claims of a tax-collector. In the autumn Vivie and others of the W.S.P.U. organized great pilgrimages—the marches of the Brown Women—from Scotland, Wales, Devon and Norfolk to London, to some goal in Downing Street or Whitehall, some door-step which already had every inch of its space covered by policemen's boots. These were among the pleasantest of the manifestations and excited great good humour in the populace of town and country. They were extended picnics of ten days or a fortnight. The steady tramp of sixteen to twenty miles a day did the women good; the food *en route* was abundant and eaten with tremendous appetite. The pilgrims on arrival in London were a justification in physical fitness of Woman's claim to equal privileges with Man.

Vivie after her Easter holiday took an increasingly active part in these manifestations of usually good-humoured insurrection. As Vivien Warren she was not much known to the authorities or to the populace but she soon became so owing to her striking appearance, telling voice and gift of oratory. All the arts she had learnt as David Williams she displayed now in pleading the woman's cause at the Albert Hall, at Manchester, in Edinburgh and Glasgow. Countess Feenix took her up, invited her to dinner parties where she found herself placed next to statesmen in office, who at first morose and nervous—expecting every moment a personal assault—gradually thawed when they found her a good conversationalist, a clever woman of the world, becomingly dressed. After all, she had been a third wrangler at Cambridge, almost a guarantee that her subsequent life could not be irregular, according to a man's standard in England of what an unmarried woman's life should be. She deprecated the violence of the militants in this phase.

But she was Protean. Much of her work, the lawless part of it, was organized in the shape and dress of Mr. Michaelis. Some of her letters to the Press were signed Edgar McKenna, Albert Birrell, Andrew Asquith, Edgmont Harcourt, Felicia Ward, Millicent Curzon, Judith Pease, Edith Spenser-Churchhill, Marianne Chamberlain, or Emily Burns; and affected to be pleas for the granting of the Suffrage emanating from the revolting sons or daughters, aunts, sisters or wives of great statesmen, prominent for their opposition to the Women's Cause. The W.S.P.U. had plenty of funds and it did not cost much getting visiting cards engraved with such names and supplied with the home address of the great personage whom it was intended to annoy. One such card as an evidence of good faith would be attached to the plausibly-worded letter. The *Times* was seldom taken in, but great success often attended these audacious deceptions, especially in the important organs of the provincial press.

Editors and sub-editors seldom took the trouble and the time to hunt through *Who's Who*, or a Peerage to identify the writer of the letter claiming the Vote for Women. No real combination of names was given, thus forgery was avoided; but the public and the unsuspecting Editor were left with the impression that the Premier's, Colonial Secretary's, Home Secretary's, Board of Trade President's, or prominent anti-suffragist woman's son, daughter, brother, sister, wife or mother-in-law did not at all agree with the anti-feminist opinions of its father, mother, brother or husband. If the politician were foolish enough to answer and protest, he was generally at a disadvantage; the public thought it a good joke and no one (in the provinces) believed his disclaimers.

Vivie generally heckled ministers on the stump and parliamentary candidates dressed as a woman of the lower middle class. It would have been unwise to do so in man's guise, in case there should be a rough-and-tumble afterwards and her sex be discovered. Although in order to avoid premature arrest she did not herself take part in those most ingenious—and from the view of endurance, heroic—stow-aways of women interrupters in the roofs, attics, inaccessible organ lofts or music galleries of public halls, she organized many of these surprises beforehand. It was Vivie to whom the brilliant idea came of once baffling the police in the rearrest of either Mrs. Pankhurst or Annie Kenney. Knowing when the police would come to the building where one or other of these ladies was to make her sensational re-appearance, she had previously secreted there forty other women who were dressed and veiled precisely similarly to the fugitive from justice. Thus, when the force of constables claimed admittance, forty-one women, virtually indistinguishable one from the other, ran out into the street, and the bewildered minions of the law were left lifting their helmets to scratch puzzled heads and admitting "the wimmen were a bit too much for us, this time, they were."

In her bedroom at 88-90 she kept an equipment of theatrical disguises; very natural-looking moustaches which could be easily applied and which remained firmly adhering save under the application of the right solvent; pairs of tinted spectacles; wigs of credible appearance; different styles of suiting, different types of women's dress. She sometimes sat in trains as a handsome, impressive matron of fifty-five, with a Pompadour confection and a tortoiseshell *face-a-main*, conversing with ministers of state or permanent officials on their way to their country seats, and saying "*Horrid* creatures!" if any one referred to the activities of the Suffragettes. Thus disguised she elicited considerable information sometimes, though she might really be on her way to organize the break-up of the statesman's public meeting, the enquiry into discreditable circumstances which might compel his withdrawal from public life, or merely the burning down of his shooting box.

This life had its risks and perils, but it agreed with her health. It was exciting and took her mind off Rossiter.

Rossiter for his part experienced a slackening in the tension of his mind during the same year 1912. He was touched by his wife's faint suspicion of his alienated affection and by her dogged determination to be sufficient to him as a companion and a helper; and a little ashamed at his middle-aged—he was forty-seven—infatuation for a woman who was herself well on in the thirties. There were times when a rift came in the cloud of his passion for Vivie, when he looked out dispassionately on the prospect of the rest of his life—he could hope at most for twenty more years of mental and bodily activity and energy. Was this all too brief period to be filled up with a senile renewal of sexual longing! He felt ashamed of the thoughts that had occupied so much of his mind since he had laid David Williams on the couch of his library, to find it was Vivie Warren whose arms were round his neck. He was not sorry this love for a woman he could not possess had sent him into Parliament. He was beginning to enjoy himself there. He had found himself, had lost that craven fear of the Speaker that paralyzes most new members. He knew when to speak and when to be silent; and when he spoke unsuspected gifts of biting sarcasm, clever characterization, convincing scorn of the uneducated minister type came to his aid. His tongue played round his victims, unequipped as they were with his vast experience of reality, vaguely discursive, on the surface as are most lawyers, at a loss for similes and tropes as are most men of business, or dull of wits as are most of the fine flowers of the public schools, stultified with the classics and scripture history. He knew that unless there was some radical change of government he could not be a minister; but he cared little for that. He was rich—thanks to his wife—he was recovering his influence and his European and American reputation as a great discoverer, a deep thinker. He enjoyed pulverizing the Ministry over their suffrage insincerities and displaying his contempt of the politician elected only for his money influence in borough, county, or in the subscription lists of the Chief Whip. Though his pulses still beat a little quicker when he held Vivie's hand in his at some reception of Lady Feenix's or a dinner party at the Gorings—Vivie as the child of a "fallen" woman had a prescriptive right of entrance to Diana's circle—he had not the slightest intention of running away with her, of nipping his career in two, just as he might be scaling the last heights to the citadel of fame: either as a politician of the new type, the type of high education, or as one of the giants of inductive science. Besides in 1912, if I mistake not, Dr. Smith-Woodward and Mr. Charles Dawson made that discovery of the remains of an ape-like man in the gravels of mid-Sussex; and the hounds of Anthropology went off on a new scent at full cry, Rossiter foremost in the pack.

Mrs. Rossiter in the same year allowed herself more and more to be tempted into anti-suffrage discussions at the houses of peers or of strong-minded, influential ladies who were on the easiest terms with peers and potentates. She still resented the line her husband had taken in politics and believed it to be chiefly due to an inexplicable interest in Vivien Warren who she began to feel was the same person as "David Williams."

If she could only master the "Anti" arguments—they sounded so convincing from the lips of Miss Violet Markham or Mrs. Humphry Ward or some suave King's Counsel with the remnants of mutton-chop whiskers—if she could wean Michael away from that disturbing nonsense—he could assign "militancy" as the justification of his change of mind...! All that was asked by Authority, so far as she could interpret hints from great ladies, was neutrality, the return of Professor Rossiter to the paths of pure science in which area no one disputed his eminence. *Then* he might receive that knighthood that was long overdue; better still his next lot of discoveries in anatomy might bring him the peerage he richly deserved and which her wealth would support. He could then rest on his oars, cease his more or less nasty investigations; they could take a place in the country and move from this much too large house which lay almost outside the limits of Society's London to a really well-appointed flat in Westminster and have a thoroughly enjoyable old age.

Honoria in these times did not see so much of Vivie as before. Her warrior husband spent a good deal of 1912 at home as he had a Hounslow command. He had come to realize—some spiteful person had told him—who Vivie's mother had been, and told Honoria in accents of finality that the "Aunt Vivie" nonsense must be dropped and Vivie must not come to the house. At the most, if she *must* meet her friend of college days—oh, he was quite willing to believe in her personal propriety, though there were odd stories in circulation about her dressing as a man and doing some very rum things for the W.S.P.U.—still if she *must* see her, it would have to be in public places or at her friends, at Lady Feenix's, if she liked. No. He wasn't attacking the cause of Suffrage. Women could have the vote and welcome so far as he was concerned: they couldn't be greater fools than the men, and they were probably less corrupt. He himself never remembered voting in his life, so Honoria was no worse off than her husband. But he drew the line in his children's friends at the daughter of a....

Here Honoria to avoid hearing something she could not forgive put her plump hand over his bristly mouth. He kissed it and somehow she couldn't take the high tone she had at first intended. She simply said "she would see about it" and met the difficulty by giving up her suffrage parties for a bit and attending Lady Maud's instead; where you met not only poor Vivie, but—had she been in London and guaranteed reformed and *rangee*—you might have met Vivie's mother; as well as the Duchess of Dulborough—American, and intensely Suffrage—the charwoman from Little Francis Street, the bookseller's wife, the "mother of the maids" from Derry and Toms; and that very clever chemist who had mended Juliet Duff's nose when she fell on the ice at Princes'—they would both be there. Honoria said nothing to Vivie and Vivie said nothing to Honoria about the inhibition, but together with her irrational jealousy of *Eoanthropos dawsoni* and irritation at the growing contentedness with things as they were on the part of Rossiter, it made her a trifle more reckless in her militancy.

And Praddy? How did he fare in these times? Praed felt himself increasingly out of the picture. He was not far gone in the sixties, sixty-one, perhaps at most. But out of the movement. In his prime the people of his set—the cultivated upper middle class, with a few recruits from the peerage—cared only about Art in some shape or form—recondite music, the themes of which were never obvious enough to be hummed, the androgyne poetry of the 'nineties, morbidities from the Yellow Book, and Scarlet Sins that you disclaimed for yourself, to avoid unpleasantness with the Criminal Investigation Department, but freely attributed to people who were not in the room; the drawings of Aubrey Beardsley and successors in audacity and ugly indecency who left Beardsley a mere disciple of Raphael Tuck; also architecture which ignored the housemaid's sink, the box-room and the fire-escape.

The people who still came to his studio because he had the reputation of being a wit and the husband of his parlour-maid (whom to her indignation they called Queen Cophetua) cared not a straw about Art in any shape or form. The women wanted the Vote—few of them knew why—the men wanted to be aviators, motorists beating the record in speed on French trial trips, or Apaches in their relations with the female sex or prize-fighters—Jimmy Wilde had displaced Oscar, to the advantage of humanity, even Praddy agreed.

To Praed however Vivie took the bitterness, the disillusions which came over her at intervals:

"I feel, Praddy, I'm getting older and I seem to be at a loose end. D'you know I'm on the verge of thirty-seven—and I have no definite career? I'm rather tired of being a well-meaning adventuress."

"Then why," Praddy would reply, "don't you go and live with your mother?"

"Ugh! I couldn't stand for long that life in Belgium or elsewhere abroad. They seem miles behind us, with all our faults. Mother only seems to think now of good things to eat and a course of the waters at Spa in September to neutralize the over-eating of the other eleven months. There is no political career for women on the Continent."

"Then why not marry and have children? That is a career in itself. Look at Honoria, how happy she is."

"Yes—but there is only one man I could love, and he's married already."

"Pooh! nonsense. There are as many good fish in the sea as ever came out of it. If you won't do as Beryl did—by the bye isn't she a swell in these days! And *strict* with her daughters! She won't let 'em come here, I'm told, because of some silly story some one set abroad about me! And that humbug, Francis Brimley Storrington—by the bye he's an A.R.A. now and scarcely has enough talent to design a dog kennel, yet they've given him the job of the new stables at Buckingham Palace. Well if you won't share some one else's husband, pick out a good man for yourself. There must be plenty going—some retired prize-fighter. They seem all the rage just now, and are supposed to be awfully gentlemanly out of the ring."

"Don't be perverse. You know exactly how I feel. I'm wasting the prime of my life. I see no clear course marked out before me. Sometimes I think I would like to explore Central Africa or get up a Woman's Expedition to the South Pole. Life has seemed so flat since I gave up being David Williams. Then I lived in a perpetual thrill, always on my guard. I tire every now and then of my monkey tricks, and the praise of all these women leaves me cold. I wish I were as simple minded as most of them are. To them the Vote seems the beginning of the millennium. They seem to forget that after we've *got* the Vote we shall have another fight to be admitted as members to the House. You may be sure the men will stand out another fifty years over *that* surrender. I alternate in my moods between the reckless fury of an Anarchist and the lassitude of Lord Rosebery. To think that I was once so elated and conceited about being a Third Wrangler...!"

With the closing months of 1912, however, there was a greater tenseness, a sharpening of the struggle which once more roused Vivie to keen interest. When she returned from an autumn visit to Villa Beau-sejour she found there had been a split between the "Peths" and the "Panks." The Girondist section of the women suffragists had separated from those who could see no practical policy to win the Vote but a regime of Terrorism—mild terrorism, it is true—somewhat that of the Curate in *The Private Secretary* who at last told his persecutors he should *really have to give them a good hard knock*. The Peths drew back before the Pankish programme (mild as this would seem, to us of Bolshevik days and of Irish insurrection). *Votes for Women* returned to the control of the Pethick Lawrences, and the Pankhurst party to which Vivie belonged were to start a new press organ, *The Suffragette*.

The Panks, it seemed, had a more acute fore-knowledge than the Peths. The latter had felt they were forcing an open door; that the Liberal Ministry would eventually squeeze a measure of Female Suffrage into the long-discussed Franchise Bill; and that too much militancy was disgusting the general public with the Woman's cause. The former declared all along that Women were going to be done in the eye, because all the militancy hitherto had got very little in man's way, had only excited smiles, and shoulder-shrugs. Ministers of the Crown in 1912 had compared the hoydenish booby-traps and bloodless skirmishes of the Suffragettes with the grim fighting, the murders, burnings, mob-rule of the 1830's, when MEN were agitating for Reform; or the mutilation of cattle, the assassinations, dynamite outrages, gun-powder plots, bombs and boycotting of the long drawn-out Irish agitation for Home Rule. An agitation which was now resulting in the placing on the Statute Book of a Home Rule Bill, while another equally deadly agitation—in promise—was being worked up by Sir Edward Carson, the Duke of This and the Marquis of That, and a very rising politician, Mr. F.E. Smith, to defeat the operation of Home Rule for Ireland. In short, if one might believe the second-rate ministers who were not repudiated by their superiors in rank, the Vote for Women could only be wrung from the reluctance of the tyrant man, *if* the women made life unbearable for the male section of the community.

It was a dangerous suggestion to make, or would have proved so, had these sneering politicians been provoking men to claim their constitutional rights: bloodshed would almost certainly have followed. But the leaders of the militant women ordered (and were obeyed) that no attacks on life should be part of the Woman's militant programme. Property might be destroyed, especially such as did not impoverish the poor; but there were to be no railway accidents, no sinking of ships, no violent deeds dangerous to life. At the height and greatest bitterness of militancy no statesman's life was in danger.

The only recklessness about life was in the militant women. They risked and sometimes lost their lives in carrying out their protests. They invented the Hunger Strike (the prospect of which as an inevitable episode ahead of her, filled Vivie with tremulous dread) to balk the Executive of its idea of turning the prisons of England into Bastilles for locking up these clamant women who had become better lawyers than the men who tried them. But think what the Hunger Strike and its concomitant, Forcible Feeding, meant in the way of pain and danger to the life of the victim. The Government were afraid (unless you were an utterly unknown man or woman of the lower classes) of letting you die in prison; so to force them to release you, you had first to refuse for four days all food—the heroic added all drink. Then to prevent your death—and being human you, the prisoner, must have hoped they were keeping a good look-out on your growing weakness—the prison doctor must intervene with his forcible feeding. This was a form of torture the Inquisition would have been sorry to have overlooked, and one no doubt that the Bolsheviks have practised with great glee. The patient was strapped to a chair or couch or had his—usually her—limbs held down by warders (wardresses) and nurses. A steel or a wooden gag was then inserted, often with such roughness as to chip or break the teeth, and through the forced-open mouth a tube was pushed down the throat, sometimes far enough to hurt the stomach. This produced an apoplectic condition of choking and nausea, and as the stomach filled up with liquid food the retching nearly killed the patient. The windpipe became involved. Food entered the lungs—the tongue was cut and bruised (Think what a mere pimple on the tongue means to some of us: it keeps *me* awake half the night)—the lips were torn. Worse still—requiring really a pathological essay to which I am not equal—was feeding by slender pipes through the nose. The far simpler and painless process *per rectum* was debarred because it might have constituted an indecent assault.

Was ever Ministry in a greater dilemma? It was too old-fashioned, too antiquely educated to realize the spirit of its age, the pass at which we had arrived of conceding to Women the same rights as to men. Women were ready to die for these rights (not to kill others in order to attain them). Yet for fear of wounding the national sentimentality they must not be allowed to die; they must not be saved from suicide by any action savouring of indecency; so they must be tortured as prisoners hardly were in the worst days of the Inquisition or at the worst-conducted public school of the Victorian era.

But Vivie's gradually rising wrath was to be brought by degrees to boiling-point through the spring of 1913, and to explode at last over an incident more tragic than any one of the five or six hundred cases of forcible feeding.

Early in 1913, the Speaker intimated that any insertion of a Woman Suffrage Amendment into the Manhood Franchise Bill would be inconsistent with some unwritten code of Parliamentary procedure of which apparently he was the sole guardian and interpreter. Ministers who had probably prepared this *coup* months before went about expressing hypocritical laments at the eccentricities of our constitution; and the Franchise Act was abandoned. A little later, frightened at the renewal of arson in town and country, at interferences with their week-end golf courses, at the destruction of mails in the letter-boxes, and the slashing of Old Masters at the National Gallery (purchased at about five times their intrinsic value by a minister who would not have spent one penny of national money to encourage native art), the Cabinet let it be known that a way would be found presently to give Woman Suffrage a clear run. A private member would be allowed to bring in a Bill for conferring the franchise on women, and the opinion of the House would be sought on its merits independently of party issues. The Government Whips would be withdrawn and members of the Government be left free to vote as they pleased.

It was a fair deduction, however, from what was said at that time and later, that the strongest possible pressure—arguments *ad hominem* and in a sense *ad pecuniam*—was brought to bear on Liberals and on Irish Nationalists to vote against the Bill. Had the Second reading been carried, the

Government would have resigned and a Home Rule Bill for Ireland have been once more postponed.

The rejection of Mr. Dickinson's measure by a majority of forty-seven convinced the Militants that Pharaoh had once more hardened his heart; and the hopelessness of the Woman's cause at that juncture inspired one woman with a resolution to give her life as a protest in the manner most calculated to impress the male mind of the British public.

CHAPTER XV

IMPRISONMENT

Prior to the Derby day of 1913, Vivie had heard of Emily
Wilding Davison as a Northumbrian woman, distantly
related to the Rossiters and also to the Lady Shillito she had
once defended. She came from Morpeth in Northumberland
and had had a very distinguished University career at Oxford
and in London, of which latter university she was a B.A. The
theme of the electoral enfranchisement of Women had
gradually possessed her mind to the exclusion of all other
subjects; she became in fact a fanatic in the cause and a
predestined martyr to it. In 1909 she had received her first
sentence of imprisonment for making a constitutional
protest, and to escape forcible feeding had barricaded her
cell. The Visiting Committee had driven her from this
position by directing the warders to turn a hose pipe on her
and knock her senseless with a douche of cold water; for
which irregularity they were afterwards fined and mulcted in
costs. Two years later, for another Suffragist offence (setting
fire to a pillar box after giving warning of her intention) she
went to prison for six months. Here the tortures of forcible
feeding so overcame her reason—it was alleged—that she
flung herself from an upper gallery, believing she would be
smashed on the pavement below and that her death under
such circumstances might call attention to the agony of

Sir Harry Johnston

forcible feeding and the reckless disregard of consequences which now inspired educated women who were resolved to obtain the enfranchisement of their sex. But an iron wire grating eight feet below broke her fall and only cut her face and hands. The accident or attempted suicide, however, procured the shortening of her sentence.

Vivie and she often met in the early months of 1913, and on the first day of June she confided to a few of the W.S.P.U. her intention of making at Epsom a public protest against public indifference to the cause of the Woman's Franchise. This protest was to be made in the most striking manner possible at the supreme moment of the Derby race on the 4th of June. Probably no one to whom she mentioned the matter thought she contemplated offering up her own life; at most they must have imagined some speech from the Grand Stand, some address to Royalty thrown into the Royal pavilion, some waving of a Suffrage Flag or early-morning placarding of the bookies' stands.

Vivie however had been turning her thoughts to horse-racing as a field of activity. She was amused and interested at the effect that had been produced in ministerial circles by her interference with the game of golf. If now something was done by the militants seriously to impede the greatest of the sports, the national form of gambling, the protected form of swindling, the main interest in life of the working-class, of half the peerage, all the beerage, the chief lure of the newspapers between October and July, and the preoccupation of princes, she might awaken the male mind in a very effectual way to the need for settling the Suffrage question.

So she determined also to see the running of the Derby, as a preliminary to deciding on a plan of campaign. She had become hardened to pushing and scrouging, so that the struggle to get a seat in one of the fifty or sixty race trains leaving Waterloo or Victoria left her comparatively calm. She was dressed as a young man and had no clothing impediments, and as a young man she was better able to travel down with racing rascality. In that guise she did not attract too much attention. Rough play may have been in the mind of the card-playing, spirit-drinking scoundrels that occupied the other seats in the compartment, but Vivie in her man's dress created a certain amount of suspicion and caution. "Look's like a 'tec,'" one man whispered to another. So the card-playing was not thrust on her as a round-about form of plunder, and the stories told were more those derived from the spicy columns of the sporting papers, in words of double meaning, than the outspoken, stable obscenity characteristic of the race-course rabble.

Vivie arriving early managed to secure a fairly good seat on the Grand Stand, to which she could have recourse when the crowd on the race course became too repulsive or too dangerous. She wished as much as possible to see all aspects of the premier race meeting. Indeed, meeting a friend of Lady Feenix's, a good-natured young peer who halted irresolute between four worlds—the philosophic, the political, the philanthropic, and the sporting, she introduced herself as "David Williams"—hoping no Bencher was within hearing—said "Dare say you remember me? Lady Feenix's? Been much abroad lately—really feel quite strange on an English race course," and persuaded him to take her round before the great people of the day were all assembled. She was shown the Royal pavilion being got ready for the King and Queen, the weighing room of the jockeys, the paddock and temporary stables of the horses that were to race that day. Here was a celebrated actress in a magnificent lace dress and a superb hat, walking up and down on the sun-burnt, trodden turf, in a devil of a temper. Her horse—for with her lovers' money she kept a racing stable—had been scratched for the race—I really can't tell you why, not having been able to study all the *minutiae* of racing. [Talking of that, *how* annoying it is—or was—when one cared about things of great moment, to take up an evening newspaper's last edition and read in large type "Official Scratchings," with a silly algebraic formula underneath about horses being withdrawn from some race, when you thought it was a bear fight in the Cabinet.] Vivie gathered from her guide that to-day would be rather a special Derby, because it did not often happen that a King-Emperor was there to see a horse from his own racing stables running in the classic race.

Then, thanking the pleasant soldier-peer for his information, Vivie (David Williams) left him to his duties as equerry and member of the Jockey-Club and entered the dense crowd on either side of the race course. It reminded her just slightly of Frith's Derby Day. There were the gypsies, the jugglers, the acrobats, the costers with their provision barrows; the grooms and stable hands; the beggars and obvious pick-pockets; the low-down harlots—the high-up ones were already entering the seats of the Grand Stand or sitting on the four-in-hand coaches or in the open landaulettes and Silent Knights. But evidently the professional betting men were a new growth since the mid-nineteenth century. They were just beginning to assemble, wiping their mouths from the oozings of the last potation; some, the aristocrats of their calling, like sporting peers in dress and appearance; others like knock-about actors on the music-hall stage. The generality were remarkably similar to ordinary city men or to the hansom-cab drivers of twenty years ago.

In the very front of the crowd on the Grand Stand side, leaning with her elbows on the wooden rail, she descried Emily Davison. Vivie edged and sidled through the crowd and touched her on the shoulder. Emily looked up with a start, surprised at seeing the friendly face of a young man, till she recognized Vivie by her voice. "Dear Emily," said Vivie, "you look so tired. Aren't you over-trying your strength? I don't know what you have in hand, but why not postpone your action till you are quite strong again?"

"I shall never be stronger than I am to-day and it can't be postponed, cost me what it will," was the reply, while the sad eyes looked away across the course.

"Well," said Vivie, "I wanted you to know that I was close by, prepared to back you up if need be. And there are others of our Union about the place. That young man over there talking to the policeman is really A—K—though she is supposed to be in prison. Mrs. Tuke is somewhere about, Mrs. Despard is on the Grand Stand, and Blanche Smith is selling *The Suffragette*."

"Thank you," said Miss Davison, turning round for an instant, and pressing Vivie's hand, "Good-bye. I hope what I am going to do will be effectual."

Vivie did not like to prolong the talk in case it should attract attention. Individual action was encouraged under the W.S.P.U., and when a member wished to do something on her own, her comrades did not fuss with advice. So Vivie returned to the Grand Stand.

Presently there was the stir occasioned by the arrival of the Royal personages. Vivie noted with a little dismay that while she was wearing a Homburg hat all the men near her wore the black and glistening topper which has become—or had, for the tyranny of custom has lifted a little since the War— the conventional head-gear in which to approach both God and the King. There was a great raising of these glistening hats, there were grave bows or smiling acknowledgments from the pavilion. Then every one sat down and the second event was run.

Still Emily Wilding Davison made no sign. Vivie could just descry her, still in the front of the crowd, still gazing out over the course, pressed by the crowd against the broad white rail.

*   *   *   *   *

The race of the day had begun. The row of snickering, plunging, rearing, and curvetting horses had dissolved, as in a kaleidoscope, into a bunch, and a pear-shaped formation with two or three horses streaming ahead as the stem of the pear. Then the stem became separated from the pear-shaped mass by its superior speed, and again this vertical line of horses formed up once more horizontally, leaving the mass still farther behind. Then the horses seen from the Grand Stand disappeared—and after a minute reappeared—three, four, five—and the bunch of them, swerving round Tattenham Corner and thundering down the incline towards the winning post.... The King's horse seemed to be leading, another few seconds would have brought it or one of its rivals past the winning post, when ... a slender figure, a woman, darted with equal swiftness from the barrier to the middle of the course, leapt to the neck of the King's horse, and in an instant, the horse was down, kneeling on a crumpled woman, and the jockey was flying through the air to descend on hands and knees practically unhurt. The other horses rushed by, miraculously avoiding the prostrate figures. Some horse passed the winning post, a head in front of some other, but no one seemed to care. The race was fouled. Vivie noted thirty seconds—approximately—of amazed, horrified silence. Then a roar of mingled anger, horror, enquiry went up from the crowd of many thousands. "It's the Suffragettes" shouted some one. And up to then Vivie had not thought of connecting this unprecedented act with the purposed protest of Emily Wilding Davison. She sprang to her feet, and shouting to all who might have tried to stop her "I'm a friend of the lady. I am a doctor"—she didn't care what lie she told—she was soon authoritatively pushing through the ring of police constables who like warrior ants had surrounded the victims of the protest—the shivering, trembling horse, now on its legs, the pitifully crushed, unconscious woman—her hat hanging to the tresses of her hair by a dislodged hat-pin, her thin face stained with blood from surface punctures. The jockey was being carried from the course, still unconscious, but not badly hurt.

A great surgeon happening to be at Epsom Race course on a friend's drag, had hurried to offer his services. He was examining the unconscious woman and striving very gently to straighten and disentangle her crooked body. Presently there was a respectful stir in the privileged ring, and Vivie was conscious by the raising of hats that the King stood amongst them looking down on the woman who had offered up her life before his eyes to enforce the Woman's appeal. He put his enquiries and offered his suggestions in a low voice, but Vivie withdrew, less with the fear that her right to be there and her connection with the tragedy might be questioned, as from some instinctive modesty. The occasion was too momentous for the presence of a supernumerary. Emily Wilding Davison should have her audience of her Sovereign without spectators.

Returning with a blanched face to the seething crowd, and presently to the Grand Stand, Vivie's mood altered from awe to anger. The "bookies" were beside themselves with fury. She noted the more frequent of the nouns and adjectives they applied to the dying woman for having spoilt the Derby of 1913, but although she went to the trouble, in framing her indictment of the Turf, of writing down these phrases, my jury of matrons opposes itself to their appearance here, though I am all for realism and completeness of statement. After conversing briefly and in a lowered voice with such

Suffragettes as gathered round her, so that this one could carry the news to town and that one his to communicate with Miss Davison's relations, Vivie—recklessly calling herself to any police questioner, "David Williams" and eliciting "Yes, sir, I have seen you once or twice in the courts," reached once more the Grand Stand with its knots of shocked, puzzled, indignant, cynical, consternated men and women. Most of them spoke in low tones; but one—a blond Jew of middle age—was raving in uncontrolled anger, careless of what he said or of who heard him. He was short of stature with protruding bloodshot eyes, an undulating nose, slightly prognathous muzzle and full lips, and a harsh red moustache which enhanced the prognathism. His silk hat tilted back showed a great bald forehead, in which angry, bluish veins stood out like swollen earth worms. "Those Suffragettes!" he was shouting or rather shrieking in a nasal whine, "if I had *my* way, I'd lay 'em out along the course and have 'em— by—. The—'s!"

The shocked auditory around him drew away. Vivie gathered he was Mr.—well, perhaps I had better not give his name,[1] even in a disguised form. He had had a chequered career in South America—Mexico oil, Peruvian rubber, Buenos Aires railways, and a corner in Argentine beef—but had become exceedingly rich, a fortune perhaps of twenty millions. He had given five times more than any other aspirant in benefactions to charities and to the party chest of the dominant Party, but the authorities dared not reward him with a baronetcy because of the stories of his early life which had to be fought out in libel cases with Baxendale Strangeways and others. But he had won through these libel cases, and now devoted his vast wealth to improving our breed of horses by racing at Newmarket, Epsom, Doncaster, Gatwick, Sandown and Brighton. Racing had, in fact, become to him what Auction Bridge was to the Society gamblers of those days, only instead of losing and winning tens and hundreds of pounds, his fluctuations in gains and losses were in thousands, generally with a summing up on the right side of the annual account. But whether on the Turf, at the billiard table, or in the stock market he was or had become a bad loser. He lost his temper at the same time. On this occasion Miss Davison's suicide or martyrdom would leave him perhaps on the wrong side in making up his day's book to the extent of fifteen hundred pounds. Viewed in the right proportion it would be equivalent to our—you and me—having given a florin to a newspaper boy as the train was moving, instead of a penny. But no doubt her unfortunate impulse had spoiled the day for him in other ways, upset schemes that were bound up with the winning of the King's horse. Yet his outburst and the shocking language he applied to the Suffrage movement made history: for they fixed on him Vivie's attention when she was looking out for some one or something on whom to avenge the loss of a comrade.

[Footnote 1: He died in 1917. My jury of matrons has excised his phrases.]

She forthwith set out for London and wrote up the dossier of Mr.—. In the secret list of buildings which were to be destroyed by fire or bombs, with as little risk as possible to human or animal life, she noted down the racing stables, trainers' houses and palaces of Mr.—at Newmarket, Epsom, the Devil's Dyke, and the neighbourhood of Doncaster.

Rossiter and Vivie met for the first time for a year at Emily Davison's funeral. Rossiter had been profoundly moved at her self-sacrifice; she was moreover a Northumbrian and a distant kinswoman. Perhaps, also, he felt that he had of late been a little lukewarm over the Suffrage agitation. His motor-brougham, containing with himself the very unwilling Mrs. Rossiter, followed in the procession of six thousand persons which escorted the coffin across London from Victoria station to King's Cross. A halt was made outside a church in Bloomsbury where a funeral service was read.

Mrs. Rossiter thought the whole thing profoundly improper. In the first place the young woman had committed suicide, which of itself was a crime and disentitled you to Christian burial; in the second she had died in a way greatly to inconvenience persons in the highest society; in the third she had always understood that racing was a perfectly proper pastime for gentlemen; and in the fourth this incident, touching Michael through his relationship with the deceased, would bring him again in contact with that Vivie Warren—*there* she was and there was *he*, in close converse—and make a knighthood from a nearly relenting Government well-nigh impossible. Rossiter, after the service, had begged Vivie to come back to tea with them in Park Crescent and give Mrs. Rossiter and himself a full account of what took place at Epsom. Vivie had declined. She had not even spoken to the angry little woman, who had refused to attend the service and had sat fuming all through the half hour in her electric brougham, wishing she had the courage and determination to order the chauffeur to turn round and run her home, leaving the Professor to follow in a taxi. But perhaps if she did that, he would go off somewhere with that Warren woman.

Michael presently re-entered the carriage and in silence they returned to Portland Place.

The next day his wife meeting one of her Anti-Suffrage friends said:

"Er—supposing—er—you had got to know something about these dreadful militant women, something which might help the police, yet didn't want to get *too* much mixed up with it yourself, and *certainly* not bring your husband into it—the Professor *thoroughly* disapproves of militancy, even though he may have foolish ideas about the Vote—er—what would you do?"

"Well, what is it?"

"It's part of a letter."

"Well, I should just send it to the Criminal Investigation Department, New Scotland Yard, and tell them under what circumstances it came into your possession. You needn't even give your name or address. They'll soon know whether it's any use or not." So Mrs. Rossiter took from her desk that scrap of partly burnt paper with the typewritten words on it which she had picked out of the grate two and a half years before, and posted it to the Criminal Investigation Department, with the intimation that this fragment had come into the possession of the sender some time ago, and seemed to refer to a militant Suffragist who called herself "Vivie Warren" or "David Williams," and perhaps it might be of some assistance to the authorities in tracking down these dangerous women who now stuck at nothing. She posted the letter with her own hands in the North West district. Park Crescent, Portland Place, she always reflected, was still in the *Western* district, though it lay perilously near the North West border line, beyond which Lady Jeune had once written, no one in Society thought of living. This was a dictum that at one time had occasioned Mrs. Rossiter considerable perturbation. It was alarming to think that by crossing the Marylebone Road or migrating to Cambridge Terrace you had passed out of Society.

It took the police a deuce of a time—two months—to make use effectively of the information contained in Mrs. Rossiter's scrap of burnt paper; though the statement of their anonymous correspondent that Vivie Warren and David Williams were probably the same person helped to locate Mr. Michaelis's office. It was soon ascertained that Miss Vivien Warren, well known as a sort of Society speaker on Suffrage, lived at the Lilacs in Victoria Road, Kensington. But when a plain-clothes policeman called at Victoria Road he was only told by the Suffragette caretaker (whose mother now usually lived with her to console her for her mistress's frequent absences) that Miss Warren was away just then, had recently been much away from home, probably abroad where her mother lived. (Here the enquirer registered a mental note: Miss Warren has a mother living abroad: could it be *the* Mrs. Warren?). Polite and respectful calls on Lady Feenix, Lady Maud Parry, and Mrs. Armstrong—Vivie's known associates—elicted no information, till on leaving the last-named lady's house in Kensington Square the detective heard Colonel Armstrong come in from the garden and call out "Ho-no-ria." "'—ria," he said to himself, "'-ria kept the keys, and now—' Honoria. What was her name before she married Colonel Armstrong?—why—" He soon found out—"Fraser." "Wasn't there once a firm, *Fraser and Warren*, which set up to be some new dodge for establishing women in a city career?—Accountancy? Stockbroking? Where did *Fraser and Warren* have their office? Fifth floor of Midland Insurance office in Chancery Lane. What was that building now called? No. 88-90." Done.

These two sentences run over a period of—what did I say? Two months?—in their deductions and guesses and consultation of out-of-date telephone directories. But on one day in September, 1913, two plain-clothes policemen made their way up to the fifth floor of 88-90 Chancery Lane and found the outer door of Mr. Michaelis's office locked and a notice board on it saying "Absent till Monday." Not deterred by this, they forced open the door—to the thrilling interest of a spectacled typewriteress, who had no business on that landing at all, but she usually made assignations there with the lift man. And on the writing table in the outer office they found a note addressed to Miss Annie Kenney, which said inside: "Dear Annie. If you should chance to look in between your many imprisonments and find me out, you will know I am away on the Firm's business, livening up the racing establishments of the Right Honble Sir—, Bart. Bart. No one knows anything about this at No. 94."

(This note was purely unnecessary—a bit of swagger perhaps, lest Miss Kenney should think Vivie never did anything dangerous, but only planned dangerous escapades for others. Like the long letter of Vivie to Michael Rossiter, written on the last day of December, 1910, which he had imperfectly destroyed, it was a reminder of that all-too-true saying: "Litera scripta manet.")

If the outer door of Michaelis's office was locked how could Miss Kenney be expected to call and find this note awaiting her? Why, *here* came in the "No. 94" of the scrap of paper. There was an over-the-roofs communication between the block of 88-90 and House No. 94. The policemen in fact found that the large casement of the partners' room was only pulled to, so that it was easily opened from the outside. From the parapet they passed to the fire-escapes and through the labyrinth of chimney stacks to a similar window leading into the top storey of 94, the office of Mr. Algernon Mainwaring, Hygienic Corset-maker. This office at the time of their unexpected entry was fairly full of Suffragettes planning all sorts of direful things. So the plain-clothes policemen had a rare haul that day and certainly had Mrs. Rossiter to thank for rising to be Inspectors and receiving some modest Order of later days. It was about the worst blow the W.S.P.U. had; before the outbreak of War turned suddenly the revolting women into the stanchest patriots and the right hands of muddling ministers. For in addition to many a rich find in

No. 94 and a dozen captives caught red-handed in making mock of the Authorities, the plain-clothes policemen made themselves thoroughly at home in Mr. Michaelis's quarters till the following Monday. And when in the fore-noon of that day, Mr. Michaelis entered his rooms, puzzled and perturbed at finding the outer door ajar, he was promptly arrested on a multiform charge of arson ... and on being conveyed to a police station and searched he was found to be Miss Vivien Warren.

At intervals in the summer and early autumn of 1913 the male section of the public had been horrified and scandalized at the destruction going on in racing establishments, particularly those of Sir George Crofts and of a well-known South American millionaire, whose distinguished services to British commerce and immense donations to Hospitals and Homes would probably be rewarded by a grateful government. If these outrages were not stopped, horse-racing and race-horse breeding must come to a stand-still; and we leave our readers to realize what *that* would mean! There would be no horses for the plough or the gig, or the artillery gun-carriage; no—er—fox-hunting, and without fox-hunting and steeple-chasing and point-to-point races you could have no cavalry and without cavalry you could have no army. If we neglected blood stock we would deal the farmer a deadly blow, we should—er—

You know the sort of argument? Reduced to its essentials it is simply this:—That a few rich people are fond of gambling and fond of the excitement that is concentrated in the few minutes of the horse race. Some others, not so rich, believe that by combining horse-racing with a certain amount of cunning and bold cheating they can make a great deal of money. A few speculators have invested funds in spaces of open turf, and turn these spaces into race courses. Having no alternative, no safer method of gambling offered them, and being as fond of gambling as other peoples of the world, the men of the labouring classes and a few of their women, the publicans and their frequenters, army officers, farmers, and women of uncertain virtue stake their money on horses they have never seen, who may not even exist, and thus keep the industry going. And the chevaliers of this "industry," the go-betweens, the parasites of this sport, are the twelve thousand professional book-makers and racing touts.

Somehow the Turf has during the last hundred years, together with its allies the Distillers and Brewers, the Licensed Victuallers and the Press that is supported by these agencies, acquired such a hold over the Government Departments, the Labour Party, the Conservative Party, and Liberal politicians who are descended from county families, that it has more interest with those who govern us than the Church, the Nonconformist Conscience, the County Palatine of Lancaster or any other body of corporate opinion. So that when in September, 1913, representatives of the Turf (and no doubt of the Trade Unions) went to the Home Secretary in reference to the burning and bombing of racing stables, trainers' houses, Grand Stands and the residences of racing potentates, and said "Look here! This has GOT TO STOP," the Home Secretary and the Cabinet knew they were up against no ordinary crisis. At the same time Sir Edward Carson, the Marquis of Londonderry, the Duke of Abercorn, Mr. F.E. Smith and nearly a third of the Colonels in the British Army of Ulster descent were actively organizing armed resistance to any measure of Home Rule; while Keltiberian Ireland was setting up the Irish Volunteers to start a Home Rule insurrection. You can therefore imagine for yourselves the mental irritability of members of the Liberal Cabinet in the autumn of the sinister year 1913. I have been told that there were days at the House of Commons during the Autumn Session of that year when the leading ministers would just shut themselves up in their

Private Rooms and scream on end for a quarter of an hour....
Of course an exaggeration, a sorry jest.

In retrospect one feels almost sorry for them: the Great War
must have come almost as a relief. Not one of them was what
you would call a bad man. Some of them suffered over
forcible feeding and the Cat and Mouse Act as acutely as
does the loving father or mother who says to the recently
spanked child, "You *know*, dear, it hurts *me* almost as much
as it hurts *you*." If one met them out at dinner parties, or in
an express train which they could not stop by pulling the
communication cord, and sympathized with their dilemma,
they would ask plaintively *what* they could do. They could
not yield to violence and anarchy; yet they could not let
women die in prison.

Of course the answer was this, but it was one they waved
aside: "Dissolve Parliament and go to the Country on the one
question of Votes for Women. If the Country returns a great
majority favourable to that concession, you must bring in a
Bill for eliminating the sex distinction in the suffrage. If on
the other hand, the Country votes against the reform, then
you must leave it to the women to make a male electorate
change its mind. And meantime if men and women, to
enforce some principle, rioted and were sent to prison for it,
and then started to abstain from food and drink, why they
must please themselves and die if they wanted to."

But this was just what the Liberal Ministry of those days
would not do; at all costs they must stick to office,
emoluments, patronage, the bestowal of honours, and the
control of foreign policy. They clung to power, in fact, at all
costs; even inconsistency with the bedrock principle of
Liberalism: no Taxation without Representation.

It was decided in the innermost arcana of the Home Office

that an example should be made of Vivie. They had evidently in her got hold of something far more dangerous than a Pankhurst or a Pethick Lawrence, a Constance Lytton or an Emily Davison. The very probable story—though the Benchers were loth to take it up—that she had actually in man's garb passed for the Bar and pleaded successfully before juries, appalled some of the lawyer-ministers by its revolutionary audacity. They might not be able to punish her on that count or on several others of the misdemeanours imputed to her; but they had got her, for sure, on Arson; and on the arson not of suburban churches, which occurred sometimes at Peckham or in the suburbs of Birmingham and made people laugh a little in the trains coming up to town and say there were far too many churches, seemed to them; *but* the burning down of racing establishments. *That* was Bolshevism, indeed, they would have said, had they been able to project their minds five years ahead. Being only in 1913 they called Vivie by the enfeebled term of Anarchist, the word applied by *Punch* to Mr. John Burns in 1888 for wishing to address the Public in Trafalgar Square.

So it was arranged that Vivie's trial should take place in October at the Old Bailey and that a judge should try her who was quite certain he had never stayed at a Warren Hotel; who would be careful to keep great names out of court; and restrain counsel from dragging anything in to the simple and provable charge of arson which might give Miss Warren a chance to say something those beastly newspapers would get hold of.

I am not going to give you the full story of Vivie's trial. I have got so much else to say about her, before I can leave her in a quiet backwater of middle age, that this must be a story which has gaps to be filled up by the reader's imagination. You can, besides, read for yourself elsewhere— for this is a thinly veiled chronicle of real events—how she was charged, and how the magistrate refused bail though it was offered in large amounts by Rossiter and Praed, the latter with Mrs. Warren's purse behind him. How she was first lodged in Brixton Prison and at length appeared in the dock at the Old Bailey before a Court that might have been set for a Cinematograph. There was a judge with a full-bottomed wig, a scarlet and ermine vesture, there was a jury of prosperous shopkeepers, retired half pay officers, a hotelkeeper or two, a journalist, an architect, and a builder. A very celebrated King's Counsel prosecuted—the Cabinet thus said to the Racing World "We've done *all* we can"—and Vivie defended herself with the aid of a clever solicitor whom Bertie Adams had found for her.

From the very moment of her arrest, Bertie Adams had refused—even though they took away his salary—to think of anything but Vivie's trial and how she might issue from it triumphant. He must have lost a stone in weight. He was ready to give evidence himself, though he was really quite unconcerned with the offences for which Vivie was on trial; prepared to swear to anything; to swear he arranged the conflagrations; that Miss Warren had really been in London when witness had seen her purchasing explosives at Newmarket (both stories were equally untrue). Bertie Adams only asked to be allowed to perjure himself to the tune of Five Years' penal servitude if that would set Vivie free. Yet at a word or a look from her he became manageable.

The Attorney General of course began something like this. "I am very anxious to impress on you," he said, addressing the jury, "that from the moment we begin to deal with the facts of this case, all questions of whether a woman is entitled to the Parliamentary franchise, whether she should have the same right of franchise as a man are matters which in no sense are involved in the trial of this issue. All you have to decide is whether the prisoner in the dock committed or procured and assisted others to commit the very serious acts of arson of which she is accused..."

Nevertheless he or the hounds he kept in leash, the lesser counsel, sought subtly to prejudice the jury's mind against Vivie by dragging in her parentage and the eccentricities of her own career. As thus:—

Counsel for the prosecution: "We have in you the mainspring of this rebellious movement..."

Vivie: "Have you?"

Counsel: "Are you not the daughter of the notorious Mrs. Warren?"

Vivie: "My mother's name certainly is Warren. For what is she notorious?"

Counsel: "Well—er—for being associated abroad with—er—a certain type of hotel synonymous with a disorderly house—"

Vivie: "Indeed? Have you tried them? My mother has managed the hotels of an English Company abroad till she retired altogether from the management some years ago. It was a Company in which Sir George Crofts—"

Judge, interposing: "We need not go into that—I think the Counsel for the prosecution is not entitled to ask such questions."

Counsel: "I submit, Me Lud, that it is germane to my case that the prisoner's upbringing might have—"

Vivie: "I am quite willing to give you all the information I possess as to my upbringing. My mother who has resided mainly at Brussels for many years preferred that I should be educated in England. I was placed at well-known boarding schools till I was old enough to enter Newnham. I passed as a Third Wrangler at Cambridge and then joined the firm of Fraser and Warren. As you seem so interested in my relations, I might inform you that I have not many. My mother's sister, Mrs. Burstall, the widow of Canon Burstall, resides at Winchester; my grandfather, Lieutenant Warren, was killed in the Crimea—or more likely died of neglected wounds owing to the shamefully misconducted, man-conducted Army Medical Service of those days. My mother in early days was better known as Miss Kate Vavasour. She was the intimate friend of a celebrated barrister who—"

Judge, intervening: "We have had enough of this discursive evidence which really does not bear on the case at all. I must ask the prosecuting counsel to keep to the point and not waste the time of the court."

Prosecuting Counsel (who has meantime received three or four energetic notes from his leader, begging him to remember his instructions and not to be an ass): "Very good M'Lud." (To Vivie) "Do you know Mr. David Vavasour Williams, a barrister?"

Vivie: "I have heard of him."

Counsel: "Have you spoken of him as your cousin?"

Vivie: "I may have done. He is closely related to me."

Counsel: "I put it to you that *you* are David Williams, or at any rate that you have posed as being that person."

Judge, interposing with a weary air: "*Who* is David Williams?"

Counsel: "Well—er—a member of the Bar—well known in the criminal courts—Shillito case—"

Judge: "Really? I had not heard of him. Proceed."

Counsel (to Vivie): "You heard my questions?"

Vivie: "I have never posed as being other than what I am, a woman much interested in claiming the Parliamentary Franchise for Women; and I do not see what these questions have to do with my indictment, which is a charge of arson. You introduce all manner of irrelevant matter—"

Counsel: "You decline to answer my questions?"

(Vivie turns her head away.)

Judge, to Counsel: "I do not quite see the bearing of your enquiries."

Counsel: "Why, Me Lud, it is common talk that prisoner is the well-known barrister, David Vavasour Williams; that in this disguise and as a pretended man she passed the necessary examinations and was called to the Bar, and—"

Judge: "But what bearing has this on the present charge, which is one of Arson?"

Counsel: "I was endeavouring by my examination to show that the prisoner has often and successfully passed as a man, and that the evidence of witnesses who affirmed that they only saw *a young man* at or near the scene of these incendiary fires, that a young man, supposed to have set the stables alight, once dashed in and rescued two horses which had been overlooked, might well have been the prisoner who is alleged to have committed most of these crimes in man's apparel—"

Judge: "I see." (To Vivie) "Are you David Vavasour Williams?"

Vivie: "Obviously not, my Lord. My name is Vivien Warren and my sex is feminine."

Judge, to Counsel: "Well, proceed with your examination—" (But here the Leader of the prosecution takes up the role and brushes his junior on one side).

Vivie of course was convicted. The case was plain from the start, as to her guilt in having organized and carried out the destruction of several great Racing establishments or buildings connected with racing. There had been no loss of life, but great damage to property—perhaps two or three hundred thousand pounds, and a serious interruption in the racing fixtures of the late summer and early autumn. The jury took note that on one occasion the prisoner in the guise of a young man had personally carried out the rescue of two endangered horses; and added a faintly-worded recommendation to mercy, seeing that the incentive to the crimes was political passion.

But the judge put this on one side. In passing sentence he said: "It is my duty, Vivien Warren, to inflict what in my opinion is a suitable and adequate sentence for the crime of which you have been most properly convicted. I must point out to you that whatever may have been your motives, your deeds have been truly wicked because they have exposed hard-working people who had done you no wrong to the danger of being burnt, maimed or killed, or at the least to the loss of employment. You have destroyed property of great value belonging to persons in no way concerned with the granting or withholding of the rights you claim for women. In addition, you have for some time past been luring other people—young men and young women—to the committal of crime as your assistants or associates. I cannot regard your case as having any political justification or standing, or as being susceptible of any mitigation by the recommendation of the jury. The least sentence I can pass upon you is a sentence of Three years' penal servitude."

Vivie took the blow without flinching and merely bowed to the judge. There was the usual "sensation in Court." Women's voices were heard saying "Shame!" "Shame!" "Three cheers for Vivie Warren," and a slightly ironical "Three cheers for David Whatyoumay-callem Williams." The judge uttered the usual unavailing threats of prison for those who profaned the majesty of the Court; Honoria, Rossiter, Praed (in tears), Bertie Adams, looking white and ill, all the noted Suffragists who were out of prison for the time being and could obtain admittance to the Court, crowded round Vivie before the wardresses led her away from the dock, assuring her they would move Heaven and Earth, first to get the sentence mitigated, and secondly to have her removed to the First Division.

But on both points the Government proved adamant. An interview between Rossiter and the Home Secretary nearly ended in a personal assault. All the officials concerned refused to see Honoria, who almost had a serious quarrel with her husband, the latter averring that Vivien Warren had only got what she asked for. Vivien was therefore taken to Holloway to serve her sentence as a common felon.

"Didn't she hunger-strike to force the Authorities to accord her better prison treatment?" She did. But she was very soon, and with extra business-like brutality, forcibly fed; and that and the previous starvation made her so ill that she spent weeks in hospital. Here it was very plainly hinted to her that between hunger-striking and forcible feeding she might very soon die; and that in her case the Government were prepared to stand the racket. Moreover she heard by some intended channel about this time that scores of imprisoned suffragists were hunger-striking to secure her better treatment and were endangering if not their lives at any rate their future health and validity. So she conveyed them an earnest message—and was granted facilities to do so—imploring them to do nothing more on her account; adding that she was resolved to go through with her imprisonment; it might teach her valuable lessons.

The Governor of the prison fortunately was a humane and reasonable man—unlike some of the Home Office or Scotland Yard officials. He read the newspapers and reviews of the day and was aware who Vivie Warren was. He probably made no unfair difference in her case from any other, but so far as he could mould and bend the prison discipline and rules it was his practice not to use a razor for stone-chipping or a cold-chisel for shaving. He therefore put Vivie to tasks co-ordinated with her ability and the deftness of her hands—such as book-binding. She had of course to wear prison dress—a thing of no importance in her eyes— and her cell was like all the cells in that and other British prisons previous to the newest reforms—dark, rather damp, cruelly cold in winter, and disagreeable in smell; badly ventilated and oppressively ugly. But it was at any rate clean. She had not the cockroaches, bugs, fleas and lice that the earliest Suffragists of 1908 had to complain of. Five years of outspoken protests on the part of educated, delicate-minded women had wrought great reforms in our prisons—the need for which till then was not apparent to the perceptions of Visiting Magistrates.

The food was better, the wardresses were less harsh, the chaplains a little more endurable, though still the worst feature in the prison personnel, with their unreasoning Bibliolatry, their contemptuous patronage, their lack of Christian pity—Christ had never spoken to *them*, Vivie often thought—their snobbishness. The chaplain of her imprisonment became quite chummy when he learnt that she had been a Third Wrangler at Cambridge, knew Lady Feenix, and had lived in Kensington prior to committing the offences for which she was imprisoned. However this helped to alleviate her dreary seclusion from the world as he occasionally dropped fragments of news as to what was going on outside, and he got her books through the prison library that were not evangelical pap.

One day when she had been in prison two months she had a great surprise—a visit from her mother. Strictly speaking this was only to last fifteen minutes, but the wardress who had conceived a liking for her intimated that she wouldn't look too closely at her watch. Honoria came too—with Mrs. Warren—but after kissing her friend and leaving some beautiful flowers (which the wardress took away at once with pretended sternness and brought back in a vase after the visitors had left) Honoria with glistening eyes and a smile that was all tremulous sweetness, intimated that Mrs. Warren had so much to say that she, Honoria, was not going to stay more than that *one* minute.

Mrs. Warren had indeed so much to impart in the precious half hour that it was one long gabbled monologue.

"When I heard you'd got into trouble, my darling, I *was* put about. Some'ow I'd never thought of your being pinched and acshally sent to prison. It was in the Belgian papers, and a German friend of mine—Oh! quite proper I assure you! He's a Secretary of their legation at Brussels and ages ago he used to be one of my clients when the Hotel had a different name. Well, he was full of it. 'Madam,' 'e said, 'your English women are splendid. They're going to bring about a revolt, you'll see, and that, an' your Ulster movement 'll give you a lot of trouble next year.'"

"Well: I wrote at once to Praddy, givin' him an order on my London agents, 'case he should want cash for your defence. I offered to come over meself, but he replied that for the present I'd better keep away. Soon as I heard you was sent to prison I come over and went straight to Praddy. My! He *was* good. He made me put up with him, knowin' I wanted to live quiet and keep away from the old set. 'There's my parlour-maid,' 'e says, 'sort of housekeeper to me—good sort too, but wants a bit of yumourin.' You'll fix it up with her,' he says. And I jolly soon did. I give her to begin with a good tip, an' I said: 'Look 'ere, my gal—she's forty-five I should think—Every one's in trouble *some* time or other in their lives, and *I'm* in trouble now, if you like. And the day's come,' I said, 'when all women ought to stick by one another.' 'Pears she's always had the highest opinion of you; very different, you was, from *some* of 'er master's friends. I says 'Right-o; then *now* we know where we are.'"

"Praddy soon got into touch with the authorities, but for some reason they wouldn't pass on a letter or let me come and see you, till to-day. But here I am, and here I'm goin' to stay—with Praddy—till they lets you out. I'm told that if you be'ave yourself they'll let me send you a passel of food, once a week. Think of that! My! won't I find some goodies, and pate de foie gras. I'll come here once a month, as often as they'll let me, till I gets you out. 'N after that, we'll leave this 'orrid, 'yprocritical old country and live 'appily at my Villa, or travel a bit. Fortunately I've plenty of money. Bein' over here I've bin rearranging my investments a bit. Fact is, I 'ad a bit of a scare this autumn. They say in Belgium, War is comin'. Talkin' to this same German—He's always pumpin' me about the Suffragettes so I occasionally put a question or so to 'im, 'e knowing 'what's, what' in the money market—'e says to me just before I come over, 'What's your English proverb, Madame Varennes, about 'avin' all your eggs in one basket? Is all your money in English and Belgian securities?' I says 'Chiefly Belgian and German and Austrian, and some I've giv' to me daughter to do as she likes with.' 'Well' 'e says, 'friend speakin' to friend, you've giv' me several good tips this autumn,' he says. 'Now I'll give you one in return. Sell out your Austrian investments—there's goin' to be a big war in the Balkans next year and as like as not *we* shall be here in Belgium. Sell out most of yer Belgian stock and put all your money into German funds. They'll be safe there, come what may.' I thanked 'im; but I haven't quite done what he suggested. I'm takin' all my money out of Austrian things and all but Ten thousand out of Belgian funds. I'm leavin' my German stock as it was, but I'm puttin' Forty thousand pounds—I've got Sixty thousand altogether—all yours some day—into Canadian Pacifics and Royal Mail—people 'll always want steamships—and New Zealand Five per cents. I don't like the look of things in old England nor yet on the Continent. Now me time's up. Keep up your heart, old girl; it'll soon be over, specially if you don't play the fool and rile the prison people or start that silly hunger strike and ruin your digestion. G—good-bye; and G-God b-bless you, my darlin'" added Mrs. Warren relapsing into tears and the conventional prayer, of common humanity, which always hopes there *may* be a pitiful Deity, somewhere in Cosmos.

Going out into the corridor, she attempted to press a sovereign into the wardress's hard palm. The latter indignantly repudiated the gift and said if Mrs. Warren tried on such a thing again, her visits would be stopped. But her indignation was very brief. She was carrying Honoria's flowers at the time, and as she put them on the slab in Vivie's cell, she remarked that say what you liked, there was nothing to come up to a mother, give her a mother rather than a man any day.

On other occasions Bertie Adams came with Mrs. Warren; even Professor Rossiter, who also went to see Vivie's mother at Praed's, and conceived a whimsical liking for the unrepentant, outspoken old lady.

Vivie's health gradually recovered from the effects of the forcible feeding; the prison fare, supplemented by the weekly parcels, suited her digestion; the peace of the prison life and the regular work at interesting trades soothed her nerves. She enjoyed the respite from the worries of her complicated toilettes, the perplexity of what to wear and how to wear it; in short, she was finding a spell of prison life quite bearable, except for the cold and the attentions of the chaplain. She gathered from the fortnightly letter which her industry and good conduct allowed her to receive, and to answer, that unwearied efforts were being made by her friends outside to shorten her sentence. Mrs. Warren through Bertie Adams had found out the cases where jockeys and stable lads had lost their effects in the fires or explosions which had followed Vivie's visits to their employers' premises, and had made good their losses. As to their employers, they had all been heavily insured, and recovered the value of their buildings; and as to the insurance companies *they* had all been so enriched by Mr. Lloyd George's legislation that the one-or-two hundred thousand pounds they had lost, through Vivie's revenge for the seemingly-fruitless death of Emily Wilding Davison, was a bagatelle not worth bothering about. But all attempts to get the Home Office to reconsider Miss Warren's case or to shorten her imprisonment (except by the abridgment that could be earned in the prison itself) were unavailing. So long as the Cabinet held Vivie under lock and key, the Suffrage movement—they foolishly believed—was hamstrung.

So the months went by, and Vivie almost lost count of time and almost became content to wait. Till War was declared on August 4th, 1914. A few days afterwards followed the amnesty to Suffragist prisoners. From this the Home Office strove at first to exclude Vivien Warren on the plea that her crime was an ordinary crime and admitted of no political justification; but at this the wrath of Rossiter and the indignation of the W.S.P.U. became so alarming that the agitated Secretary of State—not at all sure how we were going to come out of the War—gave way, and an order was signed for Vivie's release on the 11th of August; on the understanding that she would immediately proceed abroad; an understanding to which she would not subscribe but which in her slowly-formed hatred of the British Government she resolved to carry out.

Mrs. Warren, assured by Praed and Rossiter that Vivie's release was a mere matter of a few days, had left for Brussels on the 5th of August. If—as was then hoped—the French and Belgian armies would suffice to keep the Germans at bay on the frontier of Belgium, she would prefer to resume her life there in the Villa de Beau-sejour. If however Belgium was going to be invaded it was better she should secure her property as far as possible, transfer her funds, and make her way somehow to a safe part of France. Vivie would join her as soon as she could leave the prison.

Sir Harry Johnston

CHAPTER XVI

BRUSSELS AND THE WAR: 1914

The Lilacs in Victoria Road had been disposed of—through Honoria—as soon as possible, after the sentence of Three years' imprisonment had been pronounced on Vivie; and the faithful Suffragette maid had passed into Honoria's employ at Petworth, a fact that was not fully understood by Colonel Armstrong until he had become General Armstrong and perfectly indifferent to the Suffrage agitation which had by that time attained its end. So when Vivie had come out of prison and had promised to write to all the wardresses and to meet them some day on non-professional ground; had found Rossiter waiting for her in his motor and Honoria in hers; had thanked them both for their never-to-be-forgotten kindness, and had insisted on walking away in her rather creased and rumpled clothes of the previous year with Bertie Adams; she sought the hospitality of Praddy at Hans Place. The parlour-maid received her sumptuously, and Praddy's eyes watered with senile tears.

But Vivie would have no melancholy. "Oh Praddy! If you only knew. It's worth going to prison to know the joy of coming out of it! I'm so happy at thinking this is my last day in England for ever so long. When the War is over, I think I shall settle in Switzerland with mother—or perhaps all three of us—you with us, I mean—in Italy. We'll only come back here when the Women have got the Vote. Now to-night you shall take me to the theatre—or rather I'll take *you*. I've thought it all out beforehand, and Bertie Adams has secured the seats. It's *The Chocolate Soldier* at the Adelphi, the only war piece they had ready; there are two stalls for us and Bertie and his wife are going to the Dress Circle. My Cook's ticket is taken for Brussels and I leave to-morrow by the Ostende route."

"To-morrow" was the 12th of August, and Dora was not yet in being to interpose every possible obstacle in the way of the civilian traveller. Down to the Battle of the Marne in September, 1914, very little difficulty was made about crossing the Channel, especially off the main Dover-Calais route.

So in the radiant noon of that August day Vivie looked her last on the brown-white promontories, cliffs and grey castle of Dover, scarcely troubling about any anticipations one way or the other, and certainly having no prevision she would not recross the Channel for four years and four months, and not see Dover again for five or six years.

British war vessels were off the port and inside it. But there was not much excitement or crowding on the Ostende steamer or any of those sensational precautions against being torpedoed or mined, which soon afterwards oppressed the spirits of cross-Channel passengers. Vessels arriving from Belgium were full of passengers of the superior refugee class, American and British tourists, or wealthy people who though they preferred living abroad had begun to think that the Continent just now was not very healthy and England the securest refuge for those who wished to be comfortable.

Vivie being a good sailor and economical by nature, never

Sir Harry Johnston

thought of securing a cabin for the four or five hours' sea-journey. She sat on the upper deck with her scanty luggage round her. A nice-looking young man who had a cabin the door of which he locked, was walking up and down on the level deck and scrutinizing her discreetly. And when at last they worked their way backwards into Ostende—the harbour was full of vessels, chiefly mine-dredgers and torpedo boats—she noticed the obsequiousness of the steamer people and how he left the ship before any one else.

She followed soon afterwards, having little encumbrances in the way of luggage; but she observed that he just showed a glimpse of some paper and was allowed to walk straight through the Douane with unexamined luggage, and so, on to the Brussels train.

But she herself had little difficulty. She put her hand luggage—she had no other—into a first-class compartment, and having an hour and a half to wait walked out to look at Ostende.

Summer tourists were still there; the Casino was full of people, the shops were doing an active trade; the restaurants were crowded with English, Americans, Belgians taking tea, chocolate, or liqueurs at little tables and creating a babel of talk. Newspapers were being sold everywhere by ragamuffin boys who shouted their head-lines in French, Flemish, and quite understandable English. A fort or two at Liege had fallen, but it was of no consequence. General Leman could hold out indefinitely, and the mere fact that German soldiers had entered the town of Liege counted for nothing. Belgium had virtually won the war by holding up the immense German army. France was overrunning Alsace, Russia was invading East Prussia and also sending uncountable thousands of soldiers, via Archangel, to England, whence they were being despatched to Calais for the relief of Belgium.

"It looks," thought Vivie, after glancing at the *Independance Belge*, "As though Belgium were going to be extremely interesting during the next few weeks; I may be privileged to witness—from a safe distance—another Waterloo."

Then she returned to the train which in her absence had been so crowded with soldiers and civilian passengers that she had great difficulty in finding her place and seating herself. The young man whom she had seen pacing the deck of the steamer approached her and said: "There is more room in my compartment; in fact I have selfishly got one all to myself. Won't you share it?"

She thanked him and moved in there with her suit case and rugs. When the train had started and she had parried one or two polite enquiries as to place and ventilation, she said: "I think I ought to tell you who I am, in case you would not like to be seen speaking to me—I imagine you are in diplomacy, as I noticed you went through with a Red passport.—I am Vivien Warren, just out of prison, and an outlaw, more or less."

"'The outlaws of to-day are the in-laws of to-morrow,' as the English barrister said when he married the Boer general's daughter. I have thought I recognized you. I have heard you speak at Lady Maud's and also at Lady Feenix's Suffrage parties. My name is Hawk. I suppose you've been in prison for some Suffrage offence? So has my aunt, for the matter of that."

Vivie: "Yes, but in her case they only sentenced her to the First Division; whereas *I* have been doing nine months' hard."

Hawk: "What was your crime?"

Vivie: "I admit nothing, it is always wisest. But I was accused of burning down Mr.—'s racing stables—and other things..."

Hawk: "*That* beast. Well, I suppose it was very wrong. Can't quite make up my mind about militancy, one way or the other. But here we are up against the biggest war in history, and such peccadilloes as yours sink into insignificance. By the bye, my aunt was amnestied and so I suppose were you?"

Vivie: "Yes, but not so handsomely. I was requested to go away from England for a time, so here I am, about to join my mother in Brussels—or in a little country place near Brussels."

Hawk: "Well, I've been Secretary of Legation there. I'm just going back to—to—well I'm just going back."

At Bruges they were told that the train would not leave for Ghent and Brussels for another two hours—some mobilization delay; so Hawk proposed they should go and see the Memlings and then have some dinner.

"Don't you think they're perfectly wonderful?"—*apropos* of the pictures in the Hospital of St. Jean.

Vivie: "It depends on what you mean by 'wonderful.' If you admire the fidelity of the reproduction in colour and texture of the Flemish costumes of the fifteenth century, I agree with you. It is also interesting to see the revelations of their domestic architecture and furniture of that time, and the types of domestic dog, cow and horse. But if you admire them as being true pictures of life in Palestine in the time of Christ, or in the Rhineland of the fifth century, then I think they—like most Old Masters—are perfectly rotten. And have you ever remarked another thing about all paintings prior to the seventeenth century: how *plain*, how *ugly* all the people are? You never see a single good-looking man or woman. Do let's go and have that dinner you spoke of. I've got a prison appetite."

At Ghent another delay and a few uneasy rumours. The Court was said to be removing from Brussels and establishing itself at Antwerp. The train at last drew into the main station at Brussels half an hour after midnight. Vivie's mother was nowhere to be seen. She had evidently gone back to the Villa Beau-sejour while she could. It was too late for any tram in the direction of Tervueren. There were no taxis owing to the drivers being called up. Leaving most of her luggage at the cloak-room—it took her about three-quarters of an hour even to approach the receiving counter—Vivie walked across to the *Palace Hotel* and asked the night porter to get her a room. But every room was occupied, they said— Americans, British, wealthy war refugees from southern Belgium, military officers of the Allies. The only concession made to her—for the porter could hold out little hope of any neighbouring hotel having an empty room—was to allow her to sit and sleep in one of the comfortable basket chairs in the long atrium. At six o'clock a compassionate waiter who knew the name of Mrs. Warren gave her daughter some coffee and milk and a *brioche*. At seven she managed to get her luggage taken to one of the trams at the corner of the Boulevard du Jardin Botanique. The train service to Tervueren was suspended—and at the Porte de Namur she would be transferred to the No. 45 tram which would take her out to Tervueren.

Even at an early hour Brussels seemed crowded and as the tram passed along the handsome boulevards the shops were being opened and tourists were on their way to Waterloo in

Sir Harry Johnston

brakes. Every one seemed to think in mid-August, 1914, that Germany was destined to receive her *coup-de-grace* on the field of Waterloo. It would be so appropriate. And no one— at any rate of those who spoke their thoughts aloud—seemed to consider that Brussels was menaced.

Leaving her luggage at the tram terminus, Vivie sped on foot through forest roads, where the dew still glistened, to the Villa Beau-sejour. Mrs. Warren was not yet dressed, but was rapturous in her greeting. Her chauffeur had been called up, so the auto could not go out, but a farm cart would be sent for the luggage.

"I believe, mother, I'm going to enjoy myself enormously," said Vivie as she sat in the verandah in the morning sunshine, making a delicious *petit dejeuner* out of fresh rolls, the butter of the farm, a few slices of sausage, and a big cup of frothing chocolate topped with whipped cream. The scene that spread before her was idyllic, from a bucolic point of view. The beech woods of Tervueren shut out any horizon of town activity; black and white cows were being driven out to pasture, a flock of geese with necks raised vertically waggled sedately along their own chosen path, a little disturbed and querulous over the arrival of a stranger; turkey hens and their half-grown poults and a swelling, strutting turkey cock, a peacock that had already lost nearly all his tail and therefore declined combat with the turkey and was, moreover, an isolated bachelor; guinea-fowls scratching and running about alternately; and plump cocks and hens of mixed breed covered most of the ground in the adjacent farm yard and the turf of an apple orchard, where the fruit was already reddening under the August sun. Pigeons circled against the sky with the distinct musical notes struck out by their wings, or cooed and cooed round the dove cots. The dairy women of the farm laughed and sang and called out to one another in Flemish and Wallon rough chaff about their men-folk who were called to the Colours. There was nothing suggestive here of any coming tragedy.

This was the morning of the 13th of August. For three more days Vivie lived deliriously, isolated from the world. She took new books to the shade of the forest, and a rug on which she could repose, and read there with avidity, read also all the newspapers her mother had brought over from England, tried to master the events which had so rapidly and irresistibly plunged Europe into War. Were the Germans to blame, she asked herself? Of course they were, technically, in invading Belgium and in forcing this war on France. But were they not being surrounded by a hostile Alliance? Was not this hostility on the part of Servia towards Austria stimulated by Russia in order to forestal the Central Powers by a Russian occupation of Constantinople? Why should the Russian Empire be allowed to stretch for nine millions of square miles over half Asia, much of Persia, and now claim to control the Balkan Peninsula and Asia Minor? If England might claim a large section of Persia as her sphere of influence, and Egypt likewise and a fourth part of Africa, much of Arabia, and Cyprus in the Mediterranean, why might not Germany and Austria expect to have their little spheres of influence in the Balkans, in Asia Minor, in Mesopotamia? We had helped France to Morocco and Italy to Tripoli; why should we bother about Servia? It might be unkind, but then were we not unkind towards her father's country, Ireland? Were we very tender towards national independence in Egypt, in Persia?

Yet this brutal invasion of France, this unprovoked attack on Liege were ugly things. France had shown no disposition to egg Servia on against Austria, and Sir Edward Grey in the last days of June—she now learnt for the first time, for she had seen no newspapers in prison, where it is part of the dehumanizing policy of the Home Office to prevent their

Sir Harry Johnston

entry, or the dissemination of any information about current events—Sir Edward Grey had clearly shown Great Britain did not approve of Servian intrigues in Bosnia. Well: let the best man win. Germany was just as likely to give the Vote to her women as was Britain. The Germans were first in Music and in Science. She for her part didn't wish to become a German subject, but once the War was over she would willingly naturalize herself Belgian or Swiss.

And the War must soon be over. Europe as a whole could not allow this devastation of resources. America would intervene. Already the Germans realized their gigantic blunder in starting the attack. Their men were said to be—she read—much less brave than people had expected. The mighty German Armies had been held up for ten days by a puny Belgian force and the forts of Liege and Namur. There would presently be an armistice and Germany would have to make peace with perhaps the cession to France of Metz as a *solatium*, while Germany was given a little bit more of Africa, and Austria got nothing....

Meantime the Villa Beau-sejour seemed after Holloway Prison a paradise upon earth. Why quarrel with her fate? Why not drop politics and take up philosophy? She felt herself capable of writing a Universal History which would be far truer if more cynical than any previous attempt to show civilized man the route he had followed and the martyrdom he had undergone.

On the 17th of August she took the tram into Brussels. It seemed however as if it would never get there, and when she reached the Porte de Namur she was too impatient to wait for the connection. She could not find any gendarme, but at a superior-looking flower-shop she obtained the address of the British Legation.

She asked at the lodge for Mr. Hawk; but there was only a Belgian coachman in charge, and he told her the Minister and his staff had followed the Court to Antwerp. Mr. Hawk had only left that morning. "What a nuisance," said Vivie to herself. "I might have found out from him whether there is any truth in the rumours that are flying about Tervueren."

These rumours were to the effect that the Germans had captured all the forts of Liege and their brave defender, General Leman; that they were in Namur and were advancing on Louvain. "I wonder what we had better do?" pondered Vivie.

In her bewilderment she took the bold step of calling at the Hotel de Ville, gave her name and nationality, and asked the advice of the municipal employe who saw her as to what course she and her mother had better pursue: leave Tervueren and seek a lodging in Brussels; or retreat as far as Ghent or Bruges or even Holland? The clerk reassured her. The Germans had certainly occupied the south-east of Belgium, but dared not push as far to the west and north as Brussels. They risked otherwise being nipped between the Belgian army of Antwerp and the British force marching on Mons.... He directed her attention to the last *communique* of the Ministry of War: "La situation n'a jamais ete meilleure. Bruxelles, a l'abri d'un coup de main, est defendue par vingt mille gardes civiques armes d'un excellent fusil," etc.

Vivie returned therefore a trifle reassured. At the same time she and her mother spent some hours in packing up and posting valuable securities to London, via Ostende, in packing for deposit in the strong rooms of a Brussels bank Mrs. Warren's jewellery and plate. The tram service from Tervueren had ceased to run. So they induced a neighbour to drive them into Brussels in a chaise: a slow and wearisome journey under a broiling sun. Arrived in Brussels they found the town in consternation. Placarded on the walls was a notice signed by the Burgomaster—the celebrated Adolphe Max—informing the Bruxellois that in spite of the resistances of the Belgian army it was to be feared the enemy might soon be in occupation of Brussels. In such an event he adjured the citizens to avoid all panic, to give no legitimate cause of offence to the Germans, to renounce any idea of resorting to arms! The Germans on their part were bound by the laws of war to respect private property, the lives of non-combatants, the honour of women, and the exercise of religion.

Vivie and her mother found the banks closed and likewise the railway station. They now had but one thought: to get back as quickly as possible to Villa Beau-sejour, and fortunately for their dry-mouthed impatience their farmer friend was of the same mind. Along the Tervueren road they met numbers of peasant refugees in carts and on foot, driving cattle, geese or pigs towards the capital; urging on the tugging dogs with small carts and barrows loaded with personal effects, trade-goods, farm produce, or crying children. All of them had a distraught, haggard appearance and were constantly looking behind them. From the east, indeed, came the distant sounds of explosions and intermittent rifle firing. Mrs. Warren was blanched with fear, her cheeks a dull peach colour. She questioned the people in French and Flemish, but they only answered vaguely in raucous voices: "Les Allemands!" "De Duitscher."

One old woman, however, had flung herself down by the roadside, while her patient dog lay between the shafts of the little cart till she should be pleased to go on. She was more communicative and told Mrs. Warren a tale too horrible to be believed, about husband, son, son-in-law all killed, daughter violated and killed too, cottage in flames, livestock driven off. Recovering from her exhaustion she rose and shook herself. "I've no business to be here. I should be with *them*. I was just packing this cart for the market when it happened. Why did I go away? Oh for shame! I'll go back—to *them*..." And forthwith she turned the dog round and trudged the same way they were going.

At last they came opposite the courtyard of the Villa and saw the lawn and gravel sweep full of helmeted soldiers in green-grey uniform, their bodies hung with equipment—bags, great-coats, rolled-up blankets, trench spades, cartridge bandoliers. Vivie jumped down quickly, said to her mother in a low firm voice: "Leave everything to me. Say as little as possible." Then to the farmer: "Nous vous remercions infiniment. Vous aurez mille choses a faire chez vous, je n'en doute. Nous reglerons notre compte tout-a l'heure.... Pour le moment, adieu." She clutched the handbags of valuables, slung them somehow on her left arm, while with her other she piloted the nearly swooning Mrs. Warren into the court.

They were at once stopped by a non-commissioned officer who asked them in abrupt, scarcely understandable German what they wanted. Vivie guessing his meaning said in English—she scarcely knew any German: "This is our house. We have been absent in Brussels. We want to see the officer in command." The soldier knew no English, but likewise guessed at their meaning. He ordered them to wait where they were. Presently he came out of the Villa and said the Herr Oberst would see them. Vivie led her mother into the gay little hall—how pleasant and cool it had looked in the early morning! It was now full of surly-looking soldiers. Without hesitating she took a chair from one soldier and placed her mother in it. "You rest there a moment, dearest, while I go in and see the officer in command." The corporal she had first spoken with beckoned her into the pretty sitting-room at the back where they had had their early breakfast that morning.

Here she saw seated at a table consulting plans of Brussels and other papers a tall, handsome man of early middle age, who might indeed have passed for a young man, had he not looked very tired and care-worn and exhibited a bald patch at the back of his head, rendered the more apparent because the brown-gold curls round it were dank with perspiration. He rose to his feet, clicked his heels together and saluted. "An English young lady, I am told, rather ... a ... surprise ... on ... the ... outskirts ... of Brussels..." (His English was excellent, if rather staccato and spaced.) "It ... is ... not ... usual ... for ... Englishwomen ... to ... be owners ... of chateaux ... in Belgium. But I ... hear ... it ... is ... your mother ... who is the owner ... from long time, and you are her daughter newly arrived from England? Nicht wahr? Sie verstehen nicht Deutsch, gnaediges Fraulein?"

"No," said Vivie, "I don't speak much German, and fortunately you speak such perfect English that it is not necessary."

"I have stayed some time in England," was the reply; "I was once military attache in London. Both your voice and your face seem—what should one say? Familiar to me. Are you of London?"

"Yes, I suppose I may say I am a Londoner, though I believe I was born in Brussels. But I don't want to beat about the bush: there is so much to be said and explained, and all this time I am very anxious about my mother. She is in the hall outside—feels a little faint I think with shock—might she— might I?"—

"But my dear Miss—?"

"Miss Warren—"

"My dear Miss Warren, of course. We are enemies—pour le moment—but we Germans are not monsters. ("What about those peasants' stories?" said Vivie to herself.) Your lady mother must come in here and take that fauteuil. Then we can talk better at our ease."

Vivie got up and brought her mother in.

"Now you shall tell me everything—is it not so? Better to be quite frank. A la guerre comme a la guerre. First, you are English?"

"Yes. My mother is Mrs. Warren, I am her daughter, Vivien Warren. My mother has lived many years in Belgium, though also in other places, in Germany, Austria and France. Of late, however, she has lived entirely here. This place belongs to her."

"And you?"

"I? I have just been released from prison in London, Holloway Prison..."

"My dear young lady! You are surely joking—what do you say? You pull my leg? But no; I see! You have been Suffragette. Aha! *I* understand you are *the* Miss Warren, the Miss Warren who make the English Government afraid, nicht wahr? You set fire to Houses of Parliament..."

Vivie (interrupting): "No, no! Only to some racing stables..."

Oberst: "I understand. But you are rebel?"

Vivie: "I hate the present British Government—the most hypocritical, the most..."

Oberst: "But we are in agreement, you and I! This is splendid. But now we must be praktisch. We are at war, though we hope here for a peaceful occupation of Belgium. You will see how the Flaemisch—Ah, you say the Fleming?—the Flemish part of Belgium will receive us with such pleasure. It is only with the Waelsch, the Wallon part we disagree.... But there is so much for me to do—we must talk of all these things some other time. Let us begin our business. I must first introduce myself. I am Oberst Gottlieb von Giesselin of the Saxon Army. (He rose, clicked heels, bowed, and sat down.) I see you have three heavy bags you look at often. What is it?"

Vivie (taking courage): "It is my mother's jewellery and some plate. She fears—"

Von G.: "I understand! We have a dr-r-eadful reputation, we poor Germans! The French stuff you up with lies. But we are better than you think. You shall take them in two—three days to Brussels when things are quiet, and put them in some bank. Here I fear I must stay. I must intrude myself on your hospitality. But better for you perhaps if I stay here at present. I will put a few of my men in your—your—buildings. Most of them shall go with their officers to Tervueren for billet." (Turning to Mrs. Warren.) "Madam, you must cheer up. I foresee your daughter and I will be great friends. Let us now look through the rooms and see what disposition we can make. I think I will have to take this room for my writing, for my work. I see you have telephone here. *Gut*!"

Leaving Mrs. Warren still seated, but a little less stertorous in breathing, a little reassured, Vivie and Oberst von Giesselin then went over the Villa, apportioning the rooms. The Colonel and his orderly would be lodged in two of the bedrooms. Vivie and her mother would share Mrs. Warren's large bedroom and retain the salon for their exclusive occupation. They would use the dining-room in common with their guest.

Vivie looking out of the windows occasionally, as they passed from room to room, saw the remainder of the soldiery strolling off to be lodged at their nearest neighbour's, the farmer who had driven them in to Brussels that morning. There were perhaps thirty, accompanying a young lieutenant. How would he find room for them, poor man? They were more fortunate in being asked only to lodge six or seven in addition to the Colonel's orderly and soldier-clerk. Before sunset, the Villa Beau-sejour was clear of soldiers, except the few that had gone to the barn and the outhouses. The morning room had been fitted up with a typewriter at which the military clerk sat tapping. The Colonel's personal luggage had been placed in his bedroom. A soldier was even sweeping up all traces of the invasion of armed men and making everything tidy. It all seemed like a horrid dream that was going to end up happily after all. Presently Vivie would wake up completely and there would even be no Oberst, no orderly; only the peaceful life of the farm that was going on yesterday. Here a sound of angry voices interrupted her musings. The cows returning by themselves from the pasture were being intercepted by soldiers who were trying to secure them. Vivie in her indignation ran out and ordered the soldiers off, in English. To her surprise they obeyed silently, but as they sauntered away to their quarters she was saddened at seeing them carrying the bodies of most of the turkeys and fowls and even the corpse of the poor tailless peacock. They had waited for sundown to rob the hen-roosts.

Very much disillusioned she ran to the morning room and burst in on the Colonel's dictation to his clerk. "Excuse me, but if you don't keep your soldiers in better order you will have very little to eat whilst you are here. They are killing and carrying off all our poultry."

The Colonel flushed a little at the peremptory way in which she spoke, but without replying went out and shouted a lot of orders in German. His orderly summoned soldiers from the barn and together they drove the cows into the cow-sheds. All the Flemish servants having disappeared in a panic, the Germans had to milk the cows that evening; and Vivie, assisted by the orderly, cooked the evening meal in the kitchen. He was, like his Colonel, a Saxon, a pleasant-featured, domesticated man, who explained civilly in the Thuringian dialect—though to Vivie there could be no discrimination between varieties of High German—that the Sachsen folk were "Eines guetes leute" and that all would go smoothly in time.

Nevertheless the next morning when she could take stock she found nearly all the poultry except the pigeons had disappeared; and most of the apples, ripe and unripe, had vanished from the orchard trees. The female servants of the farm, however, came back; and finding no violence was offered took up their work again. Two days afterwards, von Giesselin sent Vivie into Brussels in his motor, with his orderly to escort her, so that she might deposit her valuables at a bank. She found Brussels, suburbs and city alike, swarming with grey-uniformed soldiers, most of whom looked tired and despondent. Those who were on the march, thinking Vivie must be the wife of some German officer of high rank, struck up a dismal chant from dry throats with a refrain of "Gloria, Viktoria, Hoch! Deutschland, Hoch!" At the bank the Belgian officials received her with deference. Apart from being the daughter of the well-to-do Mrs. Warren, she was English, and seemed to impose respect even on the Germans. They took over her valuables, made out a receipt, and cashed a fairly large cheque in ready money. Vivie then ventured to ask the bank clerk who had seen to her business if he had any news. Looking cautiously round, he said the rumours going through the town were that the Queen of Holland, enraged that her Prince Consort should have facilitated the crossing of Limburg by German armies, had shot him dead with a revolver; that the Crown Prince of Germany, despairing of a successful end of the War, had committed suicide at his father's feet; that the American Consul General in Brussels—to whom, by the bye, Vivie ought to report herself and her mother, in order to come under his protection—had notified General Sixt von Arnim, commanding the army in Brussels, that, *unless he vacated the Belgian capital immediately*, England would bombard Hamburg and the United States would declare war on the Kaiser. Alluring stories like these flitted through despairing Brussels during the first two months of German occupation, though Vivie, in her solitude at Tervueren, seldom heard them.

After her business at the bank she walked about the town. No one took any notice of her or annoyed her in any way. The restaurants seemed crowded with Belgians as well as Germans, and the Belgians did not seem to have lost their appetites. The Palace Hotel had become a German officers' club. On all the public buildings the German Imperial flag hung alongside the Belgian. Only a few of the trams were running. Yet you could still buy, without much difficulty at the kiosques, Belgian and even French and British newspapers. From these she gathered that the German forces were in imminent peril between the Belgian Antwerp army on the north and the British army advancing from the south; and that in the plains of Alsace the French had given the first public exhibition of the new "Turpin" explosive. The results had been *foudroyant* ... and simple. Complete regiments of German soldiers had been destroyed in *one minute*. It seemed curious, she thought, that with such an arm as this the French command did not at once come irresistibly to the rescue of Brussels....

However, it was four o'clock, and there was her friend the enemy's automobile drawn up outside the bank, awaiting her. She got in, and the soldier chauffeur whirled her away to the Villa Beau-sejour, beyond Tervueren.

On her return she found her mother prostrate with bad news. Their nearest neighbour, Farmer Oudekens who had driven them into Brussels the preceding day had been executed in his own orchard only an hour ago. It seemed that the lieutenant in charge of the soldiers billeted there had disappeared in the night, leaving his uniform and watch and chain behind him. The farmer's story was that in the night the lieutenant had appeared in his room with a revolver and had threatened to shoot him unless he produced a suit of civilian clothes. Thus coerced he had given him his eldest son's Sunday clothes left behind when the said son went off to join the Belgian army. The lieutenant, grateful for the assistance, had given him as a present his watch and chain.

On the other hand the German non-commissioned officers insisted their lieutenant had been made away with in the night. The farmer's allegation that he had deserted (as in fact he had) only enhanced his crime. The finding of the court after a very summary trial was "guilty," and despite the frantic appeals of the wife, reinforced later on by Mrs. Warren, the farmer had been taken out and shot.

The evening meal consequently was one of strained relations. Colonel von Giesselin came to supper punctually and was very spruce in appearance. But he was gravely polite and uncommunicative. And after dessert the two ladies asked permission to retire. They lay long awake afterwards, debating in whispers what terror might be in store for them. Mrs. Warren cried a good deal and lamented futilely her indolent languor of a few days previously. *Why* had she not, while there was yet time, cleared out of Brussels, gone to Holland, and thence regained England with Vivie, and from England the south of France? Vivie, more stoical, pointed out it was no use crying over lost opportunities. Here they were, and they must sharpen their wits to get away at the first opportunity. Perhaps the American Consul might help them?

The next morning, however, their guest, who had insensibly turned host, told Vivie the tram service to Brussels, like the train service, was suspended indefinitely, and that he feared they must resign themselves to staying where they were. Under his protection they had nothing to fear. He was sorry the soldiers had helped themselves so freely to the livestock; but everything had now settled down. Henceforth they would be sure of something to eat, as he himself had got to be fed. And all he asked of them was their agreeable society.

Two months went by of this strange life. Two months, in which Vivie only saw German newspapers—which she read with the aid of von Giesselin. Their contents filled her with despair. They made very little of the Marne rebuff, much of the capture of Antwerp and Ostende, and the occupation of all Belgium (as they put it). Vivie noted that the German Emperor's heart had bled for the punishment inflicted on Louvain. (She wondered how that strange personality, her father, had fared in the destruction of monastic buildings.) But she had then no true idea of what had taken place, and the far-reaching harm this crime had done to the German reputation. She noted that the German Press expressed disappointment that the cause of Germany, the crusade against Albion, had received no support from the Irish Nationalists, or from the "revolting" women, the Suffragettes, who had been so cruelly maltreated by the administration of Asquith and Sir Grey.

This point was discussed by the Colonel, but Vivie found herself speaking as a patriot. How *could* the Germans expect British women to turn against their own country in its hour of danger?

"Then you would not," said von Giesselin, "consent to write some letters to your friends, if I said I could have them sent safely to their destination?—only letters," he added hastily, seeing her nostrils quiver and a look come into her eyes—"to ask your Suffrage friends to bring pressure to bear on their Government to bring this d-r-r-eadful War to a just peace. That is all we ask." But Vivie said "with all her own private grudge against the present ministry she felt *au fond* she was *British*; she must range herself in time of war with her own people."

Mrs. Warren went much farther. She was not very voluble nowadays. The German occupation of her villa had given her a mental and physical shock from which she never recovered. She often sat quite silent and rather huddled at meal times and looked the old woman now. In such a conversation as this she roused herself and her voice took an aggressive tone. "My daughter write to her friends to ask them to obstruct the government at such a time as this? *Never!* I'd disown her if she did, I'd repudiate her! She may have had her own turn-up with 'em. I was quite with her there. But that, so to speak, was only a domestic quarrel. We're British all through, and don't you forget it—sir—(she added deprecatingly): British *all through* and we're goin' to beat Germany yet, *you'll* see. The British navy never *has* been licked nor won't be, this time."

Colonel von Giesselin did not insist. He seemed depressed himself at times, and far from elated at the victories announced in his own newspapers. He would in the dreary autumn evenings show them the photographs of his wife—a sweet-looking woman—and his two solid-looking, hand-some children, and talk with rapture of his home life. Why, indeed, was there this War! His heart like his Emperor's bled for these unhappy Belgians. But it was all due to the Macchiavellian policy of "Sir Grey and Asquiss." If Germany had not felt herself surrounded and barred from all future expansion of trade and influence she would not have felt forced to attack France and invade Belgium. Why, see! All the time they were talking, barbarous Russia, egged on by England, was ravaging East Prussia!

Then, in other moods, he would lament the war and the policy of Prussia. How he had loved England in the days when he was military attache there. He had once wanted to marry an Englishwoman, a Miss Fraser, a so handsome daughter of a Court Physician.

"Why, that must have been Honoria, my former partner," said Vivie, finding an intense joy in this link of memory. And she told much of her history to the sentimental Colonel, who was conceiving for her a sincere friendship and camaraderie. They opened up other veins of memory, talked of Lady Feenix, of the musical parties at the Parrys, of Emily Daymond's playing, of this, that and the other hostess, of such-and-such an actress or singer.

The Colonel of course was often absent all day on military duties. He advised Vivie strongly on such occasions not to go far from Mrs. Warren's little domain. "I am obliged to remind you, dear young lady, that you and your mother are my prisoners in a sense. Many bad things are going on— things we cannot help in war—outside this quiet place..."

In November, however, there was a change of scene, which in many ways came to Vivie and her mother with a sense of great relief. Colonel von Giesselin told them one morning he had been appointed Secretary to the German Governor of Brussels, and must reside in the town not far from the Rue de la Loi. He proposed that the ladies should move into Brussels likewise; in fact he delicately insisted on it. Their pleasant relations could thus continue—perhaps—who knows?—to the end of this War, "to that peace which will make us friends once more?" It would in any case be most unsafe if, without his protection, they continued to reside at this secluded farm, on the edge of the great woods. In fact it could not be thought of, and another officer was coming here in his place with a considerable suite. Eventually compensation would be paid to Mrs. Warren for any damage done to her property.

The two women readily agreed. In the curtailment of their movements and the absence of normal means of communication their life at Villa Beau-sejour was belying its name. Their supply of money was coming to an end; attempts must be made to regularize that position by drawing on Mrs. Warren's German investments and the capital she still had in Belgian stock—if that were negotiable at all.

Where should they go? Mrs. Warren still had some lien on the Hotel Edouard-Sept (the name, out of deference to the Germans, had been changed to Hotel Imperial). With the influence of the Government Secretary behind her she might turn out some of its occupants and regain the use of the old "appartement." This would accommodate Vivie too. And there was no reason why their friend should not place his own lodging and office at the same hotel, which was situated conveniently on the Rue Royale not far from the Governor's residence in the Rue de la Loi.

So this plan was carried out. And in December, 1914, Mrs. Warren had some brief flicker of happiness once more, and even Vivie felt the nightmare had lifted a little. It was life again. Residence at the Villa Beau-sejour had almost seemed an entombment of the living. Here, in the heart of Brussels, at any rate, you got some news every day, even if much of it was false. The food supply was more certain, there were 700,000 people all about you. True, the streets were very badly lit at night and fuel was scarce and dear. But you were in contact with people.

In January, Vivie tried to get into touch with the American Legation, not only to send news of their condition to England but to ascertain whether permission might not be obtained for them to leave Belgium for Holland. But this last plea was said by the American representative to be unsustainable. For various reasons, the German Government would not permit it, and he was afraid neither Vivie nor her mother would get enough backing from the British authorities to strengthen the American demand. She must stop on in Brussels till the War came to an end.

"But how are we to live?" asked Vivie, with a catch in her throat. "Our supply of Belgian money is coming to an end. My mother has considerable funds invested in England. These she can't touch. She has other sums in German securities, but soon after the War they stopped sending her the interest on the plea that she was an 'enemy.' As to the money we have in Belgium, the bank in Brussels can tell me nothing. What are we to do?" The rather cold-mannered American diplomatist—it was one of the Secretaries of Legation and he knew all about Mrs. Warren's past, and regarded Vivie as an outlaw—said he would try to communicate with her friends in England and see if through the American Relief organization, funds could be transmitted for their maintenance. She gave him the addresses of Rossiter, Praed, and her mother's London bankers.

Vivie now tried to settle down to a life of usefulness. To

increase their resources she gave lessons in English to Belgians and even to German officers. She offered herself to various groups of Belgian ladies who had taken up such charities as the Germans permitted. She also asked to be taken on as a Red Cross helper. But in all these directions she had many snubs to meet and little encouragement. Scandal had been busy with her name—the unhappy reputation of her mother, the peculiar circumstances under which she had left England, the two or three months shut up at Tervueren with Colonel von Giesselin, and the very protection he now accorded her and her mother at the Hotel Imperial. She felt herself looked upon almost as a pariah, except among the poor of Brussels in the Quartier des Marolles. Here she was only regarded as a kind English-woman, unwearied in her efforts to alleviate suffering, mental and bodily.

And meantime, silence, a wall of silence as regarded England—England which she was beginning to look upon as the paradise from which she had been chased. Not a word had come through from Rossiter, from Honoria, Bertie Adams, or any of her Suffrage friends. I can supply briefly what she did not know.

Rossiter at the very outbreak of War had offered his services as one deeply versed in anatomy and in physiology to the Army Medical Service, and especially to a great person at the War Office; but had been told quite cavalierly that they had no need of him. As he persisted, he had been asked—in the hope that it might get rid of him—to go over to the United States in company with a writer of comic stories, a retired actor and a music-hall singer, and lecture on the causes of the War in the hope of bringing America in. This he had declined to do, and being rich and happening to know personally General Armstrong (Honoria's husband) he had been allowed to accompany him to the vicinity of the front and there put his theories of grafting flesh and bone to the test; with the ultimate results that his work became of enormous beneficial importance and he was given rank in the R.A.M.C. Honoria, racked with anxiety about her dear "Army," and very sad as to Vivie's disappearance, slaved at War work as much as her children's demands on her permitted; or even put her children on one side to help the sick and wounded. Vivie's Suffrage friends forgot she had ever existed and turned their attention to propaganda, to recruiting for the Voluntary Army which our ministers still hoped might suffice to win the War, to the making of munitions, or aeroplane parts, to land work and to any other work which might help their country in its need.

And Bertie Adams?

When he realized that his beloved and revered Miss Warren was shut off from escape in Belgium, could not be heard of, could not be got at and rescued, he went nearly off his nut.... He reviewed during a succession of sleepless nights what course he might best pursue. His age was about thirty-two. He might of course enlist in the army. But though very patriotic, his allegiance lay first at the feet of Vivie Warren. If he entered the army, he might be sent anywhere but to the Belgian frontier; and even if he got near Belgium he could not dart off to rescue Vivie without becoming a deserter. So he came speedily to the conclusion that the most promising career he could adopt, having regard to his position in life and lack of resources, was to volunteer for foreign service under the Y.M.C.A., and express the strongest possible wish to be employed as near Belgium as was practicable. So that by the end of September, 1914, Bertie was serving out cocoa and biscuits, writing paper and cigarettes, hot coffee and sausages and cups of bovril to exhausted or resting soldiers in the huts of the Y.M.C.A., near Ypres. Alternating with these services, he was, like other Y.M.C.A. men in the same district and at the same time, acting as stretcher bearer to bring in the wounded, as amateur chaplain with the dying, as amateur surgeon with the wounded, as secretary to some distraught officer in high command whose clerks had all been killed; and in any other capacity if called upon. But always with the stedfast hope and purpose that he might somehow reach and rescue Vivie Warren.

CHAPTER XVII

THE GERMANS IN BRUSSELS: 1915-1916

In the early spring of 1915, Vivie, anxious not to see her mother in utter penury, and despairing of any effective assistance from the Americans (very much prejudiced against her for the reasons already mentioned), took her mother's German and Belgian securities of a face value amounting to about L18,000 and sold them at her Belgian bank for a hundred thousand francs (L4,000) in Belgian or German bank notes. She consulted no one, except her mother. Who was there to consult? She did not like to confide too much to Colonel von Giesselin, a little too prone in any case to "protect" them. But as she argued with Mrs. Warren, what else were they to do in their cruel situation? If the Allies were eventually victorious, Mrs. Warren could return to England. There at least she had in safe investments L40,000, ample for the remainder of their lives. If Germany lost the War, the German securities nominally worth two hundred thousand marks might become simply waste paper; even now they were only computed by the bank at a purchase value of about one fifth what they had stood at before the War. If Germany were victorious or agreed to a compromise peace, her mother's shares in Belgian companies might be unsaleable. Better to secure now a lump sum of four thousand pounds in bank notes that would be legal

Sir Harry Johnston

currency, at any rate as long as the German occupation lasted. And as one never knew what might happen, it was safer still to have all this money (equivalent to a hundred thousand francs), in their own keeping. They could live even in war time, on such a sum as this for four, perhaps five years, as they would be very economical and Vivie would try to earn all she could by teaching. It was useless to hope they would be able to return to Villa Beau-sejour so long as the German occupation lasted, or during that time receive a penny in compensation for the sequestration of the property.

The notes for the hundred thousand francs therefore were carefully concealed in Mrs. Warren's bedroom at the Hotel Imperial and Vivie for a few months afterwards felt slightly easier in her mind as to the immediate future; for, as a further resource, there were also the jewels and plate at the bank.

They dared hope for nothing from Villa Beau-sejour. Von Giesselin, after more entreaty than Vivie cared to make, had allowed them with a special pass and his orderly as escort to go in a military motor to the Villa in the month of April in order that they might bring away the rest of their clothes and personal effects of an easily transportable nature. But the visit was a heart-breaking disappointment. Their reception was surly; the place was little else than a barrack of disorderly soldiers and insolent officers. Any search for clothes or books was a mockery. Nothing was to be found in the chests of drawers that belonged to them; only stale food and unnameable horrors or military equipment articles. The garden was trampled out of recognition. There had been a beautiful vine in the greenhouse. It was still there, but the first foliage of spring hung withered and russet coloured. The soldiers, grinning when Vivie noticed this, pointed to the base of the far spreading branches. It had been sawn through, and much of the glass of the greenhouse deliberately smashed.

On their way back, Mrs. Warren, who was constantly in tears, descried waiting by the side of the road the widow of their farmer-neighbour, Madame Oudekens. She asked the orderly that they might stop and greet her. She approached. Mrs. Warren got out of the car so that she might more privately talk to her in Flemish. Since her husband's execution, the woman said, she had had to become the mistress of the sergeant-major who resided with her as the only means, seemingly, of saving her one remaining young son from exile in Germany and her daughters from unbearably brutal treatment; though she added, "As to their virtue, *that* has long since vanished; all I ask is that they be not half-killed whenever the soldiers get drunk. Oh Madame! If you could only say a word to that Colonel with whom you are living?"

Mrs. Warren dared not translate this last sentence to Vivie, for fear her daughter forced her at all costs to leave the Hotel Imperial. Where, if she did, were they to go?

The winter of 1914 had witnessed an appalling degree of frightfulness in eastern Belgium, the Wallon or French-speaking part of the country more especially. The Germans seemed to bear a special grudge against this region, regarding it as doggedly opposed to absorption into a Greater Germany; whereas they hoped the Flemish half of the country would receive them as fellow Teutons and even as deliverers from their former French oppressors. Thousands of old men and youths, of women and children in the provinces south of the Meuse had been shot in cold blood; village after village had been burnt. Scenes of nearly equal horror had taken place between Brussels and Antwerp, especially around Malines. Von Bissing's arrival as Governor General was soon signalized by those dreaded Red Placards on the walls of Brussels, announcing the verdicts of courts-martial, the condemnation to death of men and women who had contravened some military regulation.

Yet in spite of this, life went on in Brussels once more—by von Bissing's stern command—as though the country were not under the heel of the invader. The theatres opened their doors; the cinemas had continuous performances; there was Grand Opera; there were exhibitions of toys, or pictures, and charitable bazaars. Ten days after the fall of Antwerp *char-a-bancs* packed with Belgians drove out of Brussels to visit the scenes of the battles and those shattered forts, so fatuously deemed impregnable, so feeble in their resistance to German artillery.

Vivie, even had she wished to do so, could not have joined the sight-seers. As the subjects of an enemy power she and her mother had had early in January to register themselves at the Kommandantur and were there warned that without a special passport they might not pass beyond the limits of Brussels and its suburbs. Except in the matter of the farewell visit to the farm at Tervueren, Vivie was reluctant to ask for any such favour from von Giesselin, though she was curious to see the condition of Louvain and to ascertain whether her father still inhabited the monastic house of his order—she had an idea that he was away in Germany in connection with his schemes for raising the Irish against the British Government. Von Giesselin however was becoming sentimentally inclined towards her and she saw no more of him than was necessary to maintain polite relations. Frau von Giesselin, for various reasons of health or children, could not join him at Brussels as so many German wives had done with other of the high functionaries (to the great embitterment of Brussels society); and there were times when von Giesselin's protestations of his loneliness alarmed her.

The King of Saxony had paid a visit to Brussels in the late autumn of 1914 and had invited this Colonel of his Army to

a fastuous banquet given at the Palace Hotel. The King—
whom the still defiant Brussels Press, especially that
unkillable *La Libre Belgique*, reminded ironically of his
domestic infelicity, by enquiring whether he had brought
Signor Toselli to conduct his orchestra—was gratified that a
subject of his should be performing the important duties of
Secretary to the Brussels Government, and his notice of von
Giesselin gave the latter considerable prestige, for a time; an
influence which he certainly exercised as far as he was able
in softening the edicts and the intolerable desire to annoy and
exasperate on the part of the Prussian Governors of province
and kingdom. He even interceded at times for unfortunate
British or French subjects, stranded in Brussels, and sometimes asked Vivie about fellow-countrymen who sought this
intervention.

This caused her complicated annoyances. Seeing there was
some hope in interesting her in their cases, these English
governesses, tutors, clerks, tailors' assistants and cutters,
music-hall singers, grooms appealed to Vivie to support their
petitions. They paid her or her mother a kind of base court,
on the tacit assumption that she—Vivie—had placed Colonel
von Giesselin under special obligations. If in rare instances,
out of sheer pity, she took up a case and von Giesselin
granted the petition or had it done in a higher quarter, his
action was clearly a personal favour to her; and the very
petitioners went away, with the ingratitude common in such
cases, and spread the news of Vivie's privileged position at
the Hotel Imperial. It was not surprising therefore that in the
small circles of influential British or American people in
Brussels she was viewed with suspicion or contempt. She
supported this odious position at the Hotel Imperial as long
as possible, in the hope that Colonel von Giesselin when he
had realized the impossibility of using herself or her mother
in any kind of intrigue against the British Government would
do what the American Consul General professed himself

unable or unwilling to do: obtain for them passports to proceed to Holland.

Von Giesselin, from December, 1914, took up among other duties that of Press Censor and officer in charge of Publicity. After the occupation of Brussels and the fall of Antwerp, the "patriotic" Belgian Press had withdrawn itself to France and England or had stopped publication. Its newspapers had been invited to continue their functions as organs of news-distribution and public opinion, but of course under the German Censorate and martial law. As one editor said to a polite German official: "If I were to continue the publication of my paper under such conditions, my staff and I would all be shot in a week."

But the large towns of Belgium could not be left without a Press. Public Opinion must be guided, and might very well be guided in a direction favourable to German policy. The German Government had already introduced the German hour into Belgian time, the German coinage, the German police system, and German music; but it had no intention, seemingly, of forcing the German speech on the old dominions of the House of Burgundy. On the contrary, in their tenure of Belgium or of North-east France, the Germans seemed desirous of showing how well they wrote the French language, how ready they were under a German regime to give it a new literature. Whether or not they enlisted a few recreants, or made use of Alsatians or Lorrainers to help them, it is never-the-less remarkable how free as a rule their written and printed French was from mistakes or German idioms; though their spoken French always remained Alsatian. It suffered from that extraordinary misplacement and exchange in the upper and lower consonants which has distinguished the German people—that nation of great philologists—since the death of the Roman Empire. German officers still said "Barton, die fous brie," instead of "Pardon, je vous prie" (if they were polite), but they were quite able to contribute *articles de fond* to a pretended national Belgian press. Besides there was a sufficiency of Belgian "Sans-Patries" ready to come to their assistance: Belgian nationals of German-Jewish or Dutch-Jewish descent, who in the present generation had become Catholic Christians as it ranged them with the best people. They were worthy and wealthy Belgian citizens, but presumably would not have deeply regretted a change in the political destinies of Belgium, provided international finance was not adversely affected. There were also a few Belgian Socialists—a few, but enough—who took posts under the German provisional government, on the plea that until you could be purely socialistic it did not matter under what flag you drew your salary.

Von Giesselin was most benevolently intentioned, in reality a kind-hearted man, a sentimentalist. Not quite prepared to go to the stake himself in place of any other victim of Prussian cruelty, but ready to make some effort to soften hardships and reduce sentences. (There were others like him—Saxon, Thuringian, Hanoverian, Wuerttembergisch— or the German occupation of Belgium might have ended in a vast Sicilian Vespers, a boiling-over of a maddened people reckless at last of whether they died or not, so long as they slew their oppressors.) He hoped through the pieces played at the theatres and through his censored, subsidized press to bring the Belgians round to a reasonable frame of mind, to a toleration of existence under the German Empire. But his efforts brought down on him the unsparing ridicule of the Parisian-minded Bruxellois. They were prompt to detect his attempts to modify the text of French operettas so that these, while delighting the lovers of light music, need not at the same time excite a military spirit or convey the least allusion of an impertinent or contemptuous kind towards the Central Powers. Thus the couplets

Sir Harry Johnston

"Dans le service de l'Autriche
Le militaire n'est pas riche"

were changed to

"Dans le service de la Suisse
Le militaire n'est pas riche."

These passionate lines of a political exile:

"A l'etranger un pacte impie
Vendait mon sang, liait ma foi,
Mais a present, o ma patrie
Je pourrai done mourir pour toi!"

were rendered harmless as

"A l'etranger, en reverie
Chaque jour je pleurais sur toi
Mais a present, o ma patrie
Je penserai sans cesse a toi!"

The pleasure he took in recasting this doggerel—calling in Vivie to help him as presumably a good scholar in French—got on her nerves, and she was hard put to it to keep her temper.

Sometimes he proposed that she should take a hand, even become a salaried subordinate; compose articles for his subsidized paper, "*L'Ami de l'Ordre*" (nicknamed "L'Ami de L'Ordure" by the Belgians), "*La Belgique,*" "*Le Bruxellois,*" "*Vers la Paix.*" He would allow her a very free hand, so long as she did not attack the Germans or their allies or put in any false news about military or naval successes of the foes of Central Europe. She might, for instance, dilate on the cruel manner in which the Woman Suffragists had been persecuted in England; give a description of forcible feeding or of police ferocity on Black Friday.

Vivie declined any such propositions. "I have told you already, and often," she said, "I am deeply grateful for all you have done for my mother and me. We might have been in a far more uncomfortable position but for your kindness. But I cannot in any way associate myself with the German policy here. I cannot pretend for a moment to condone what you do in this country. If I were a Belgian woman I should probably have been shot long ago for assassinating some Prussian official—I can hardly see von Bissing pass in his automobile, as it is, without wishing I had a bomb. But there it is. It is no business of mine. As I can't get away, as you won't let us go out of the country—Switzerland, Holland—and as I don't want to go mad by brooding, find something for me to do that will occupy my thoughts: and yet not implicate me with the Germans. Can't I go and help every day in your hospitals? If you'll continue your kindness to mother—and believe me"—she broke off—"I *do* appreciate what you have done for us. I shall *never* forget I have met *one true German gentleman*—if you'll continue to be as kind as before, you will simply give instructions that mother is in no way disturbed or annoyed. There are Germans staying here who are odious beyond belief. If they meet my mother outside her room they ask her insulting questions—whether she can give them the addresses of—of—light women ... you know the sort of thing. I have always been outspoken with you. All I ask is that mother shall be allowed to stay in her own room while I am out, and have her meals served there. But the hotel people are beginning to make a fuss about the trouble, the lack of waiters. A word from you—And then if my mind was at ease about her I could go out and do some good with the poor people. They are getting very restive in the Marolles quarter—the shocking bad bread, the lack of fuel—Most of all I should like to help in the hospitals. My own countrywomen will not have me in theirs. They suspect me of being a spy in German pay. Besides, your von Bissing has ordered now that all Belgian, British, and French wounded shall be taken to the German Red Cross. Well: if you want to be kind, give me an introduction there. Surely it would be bare humanity on your part to let an Englishwoman be with some of those poor lads who are sorely wounded, dying perhaps"—she broke down—"The other day I followed two of the motor ambulances along the Boulevard d'Anspach. Blood dripped from them as they passed, and I could hear some English boy trying to sing 'Tipperary—'"

"My *tear* Miss Warren—I will try to do all that you want— You will not do *anything I* want, but never mind. I will show you that Germans can be generous. I will speak about your mother. I am sorry that there are bad-mannered Germans in the hotel. There are some—what-you-call 'bounders'— among us, as there are with you. It is to be regretted. As to our Red Cross hospitals, I know of a person who can make things easy for you. I will write a letter to my cousin—like me she is a Saxon and comes from Leipzig—Minna von Stachelberg. She is but a few months widow, widow of a Saxon officer, Graf von Stachelberg who was killed at Namur. Oh! it was very sad; they were but six months married. Afterwards she came here to work in our Red Cross—I think now she is in charge of a ward..."

So Vivie found a few months' reprieve from acute sorrow and bitter humiliation. Graefin von Stachelberg was as kind in her way as her cousin the Colonel, but much less sentimental. In fact she was of that type of New German woman, taken all too little into account by our Press at the time of the War. There were many like her of the upper middle class, the professorial class, the lesser nobility to be found not only in Leipzig but in Berlin, Hamburg, Frankfort, Halle, Bonn, Muenchen, Hannover, Bremen, Jena, Stuttgart,

Cologne—nice to look at, extremely modern in education and good manners, tasteful in dress, speaking English marvellously well, highly accomplished in music or with some other art, advocates of the enfranchisement of women. The War came just too soon. Had Heaven struck down that epilept Emperor and a few of his ministers, had time been given for the New German Woman to assert herself in politics, there would have been no invasion of Belgium, no maltreatment of Servia. Germany would have ranged herself with the Western powers and Western culture.

Minna von Stachelberg read her cousin's note and received the worn and anxious-looking Vivie like a sister ... like a comrade, she said, in the War for the Vote ... "which we will resume, my dear, as soon as this dreadful Man's war is over, only we won't fight with the same weapons."

But though kind, she was not gushing and she soon told Vivie that in nursing she was a novice and had much to learn. She introduced her to the German and Belgian surgeons, and then put her to a series of entirely menial tasks from which she was to work her way up by degrees. But if any English soldier were there and wanted sympathy, she should be called in to his ward ... From that interview Vivie returned almost happy.

In the hot summer months she would sometimes be allowed to accompany Red Cross surgeons and nurses to the station, when convoys of wounded were expected, if there was likelihood that British soldiers would be amongst them. These would cheer up at the sound of her pleasant voice speaking their tongue. Yet she would witness on such occasions incongruous incidents of German brutality. Once there came out of the train an English and a French soldier, great friends evidently. They were only slightly wounded and the English soldier stretched his limbs cautiously to relieve himself of cramp. At that moment a German soldier on leave came up and spat in his face. The Frenchman felled the German with a resounding box on the ear. Alarums! Excursions! A German officer rushed up to enquire while the Frenchman was struggling with two colossal German military policemen and the Englishman was striving to free him. Vivie explained to the officer what had occurred. He bowed and saluted: seized the soldier-spitter by the collar and kicked him so frightfully that Vivie had to implore him to cease.

Moreover the Red Placards of von Bissing were of increasing frequency. As a rule Vivie only heard what other people said of them, and that wasn't very much, for German spies were everywhere, inviting you to follow them to the dreaded Kommandantur in the Rue de la Loi—a scene of as much in the way of horror and mental anguish as the Conciergerie of Paris in the days of the Red Terror. But some cheek-blanching rumour she had heard on a certain Monday in October caused her to look next day on her way home at a fresh Red Placard which had been posted up in a public place. The daylight had almost faded, but there was a gas lamp which made the notice legible. It ran:

CONDAMNATIONS

Par jugement du 9 Octobre, 1915, le tribunal de campagne a prononce les condamnations suivantes pour trahison commise pendant l'etat de guerre (pour avoir fait passer des recrues a l'ennemi):

1 deg. Philippe BAUCQ, architecte a Bruxelles;

2 deg. Louise THULIEZ, professeur a Lille;

3 deg. Edith CAVELL, directrice d'un institut medical

a Bruxelles;

4 deg. Louis SEVERIN, pharmacien a Bruxelles;

5 deg. Comtesse JEANNE DE BELLEVILLE, a Montignies.

A LA PEINE DE MORT

* * * * *

Vivie then went on to read with eyes that could hardly take in the words a list of other names of men and women condemned to long terms of hard labour for the same offence—assisting young Belgians to leave the Belgium that was under German occupation. And further, the information that of the five condemned to death, *Philip Bauck* and *Edith Cavell* had already been *executed*.

* * * * *

The monsters! Oh that von Bissing. How gladly she would die if she might first have the pleasure of killing him! That pompous old man of seventy-one with the blotched face, who had issued orders that wherever he passed in his magnificent motor he was to be saluted with Eastern servility, who boasted of his "tender heart," so that he issued placards about this time punishing severely all who split the tongues of finches to make them sing better. Edith Cavell—she did not pause to consider the fate of patriotic Belgian women—but Edith Cavell, directress of a nursing home in Brussels, known far and wide for her goodness of heart. She had held aloof from Vivie, but was that to be wondered at when there was so much to make her suspect—living, seemingly, under the protection of a German official? But the very German nurses and doctors at the Red Cross hospital had spoken of her having given free treatment in her Home to Germans who needed immediate operations, and for whom there was no room in the military hospitals—And for such a trivial offence as *that*—and to kill her before there could be any appeal for reconsideration or clemency. Oh *what* a nation! She would tend their sick and wounded no more.

She hurried on up the ascent of the Boulevard of the Botanic Garden on her way to the Rue Royale. She burst into von Giesselin's office. He was not there. A clerk looking at her rather closely said that the Herr Oberst was packing, was going away. Vivie scarcely took in the meaning of his German phrases. She waited there, her eyes ablaze, feeling she must tell her former friend and protector what she thought of his people before she renounced any further relations with him.

Presently he entered, his usually rather florid face pale with intense sorrow or worry, his manner preoccupied. She burst out: "*Have* you seen the Red Placard they have just put up?"

"What about?" he said wearily.

"The assassination by your Government of Edith Cavell, a crime for which England—yes, and America—will *never* forgive you.... From this moment I—"

"But have you not heard what has happened to *me*? I am *dismissed* from my post as Secretary, I am ordered to rejoin my regiment in Lorraine—It is very sad about your Miss Cavell. I knew nothing of it till this morning when I received my own dismissal—And *oh* my dear Miss, I fear we shall never meet again."

"Why are they sending you away?" asked Vivie drily,

compelled to interest herself in his affairs since they so closely affected her own and her mother's.

"Because of this," said von Giesselin, nearly in tears, pulling from a small portfolio a press cutting. "Do you remember a fortnight ago I told you some one, some Belgian had written a beautiful poem and sent it to me for one of our newspapers? I showed it to you at the time and you said— you said 'it was well enough, but it did not seem to have much point.'" Vivie did remember having glanced very perfunctorily at some effusion in typewriting which had seemed unobjectionable piffle. She hadn't cared two straws whether he accepted it or not, only did not want to be too markedly indifferent. Now she took it up and still read it through uncomprehendingly, her thoughts absent with the fate of Miss Cavell. "Well! what is all the fuss about? I still see nothing in it. It is just simply the ordinary sentimental flip-flap that a French versifier can turn out by the yard."

"It is *far* worse than that! It is a horrible—what the French call 'acrostiche,' a deadly insult to our people. And I never saw it, the Editor never saw it, and you, even, never guessed its real meaning![1] The original, as you say, was in typewriting, and at the bottom was the name and address of a very well-known homme de lettres: and the words: 'Offert a la redaction de l'Ami de L'Ordre.' He say now, *never never* did he send it. It was a forgery. When we came to understand what it meant all the blame fall on me. I am sent back to the Army—I shall be killed before Verdun, so good-bye dear Miss—We have been good friends. Oh this War: this d-r-r-eadful War—It has spoilt everything. Now we can never be friends with England again."

[Footnote 1: I have obtained a copy and give it here as it had an almost historical importance in the events of the German occupation. But the reader must interpret its meaning for himself.

LA GUERRE

Ma soeur, vous souvient-il qu'aux jours de notre enfance,
En lisant les hauts fails de l'histoire de France,
Remplis d'admiration pour nos freres Gaulois,
Des generaux fameux nous vantions les exploits?

En nos ames d'enfants, les seuls noms des victoires
Prenaient un sens mystique evocateur de gloires;
On ne revait qu'assauts et combats; a nos yeux
Un general vainqueur etait l'egal des dieux.

Rien ne semblait ternir l'eclat de ces conquetes.
Les batailles prenaient des allures de fetes
Et nous ne songions pas qu'aux hurrahs triomphants
Se melaient les sanglots des meres, des enfants.

Ah! nous la connaissons, helas, l'horrible guerre:
Le fleau qui punit les crimes de la terre,
Le mot qui fait trembler les meres a genoux
Et qui seme le deuil et la mort parmi nous!

Mais ou sqnt les lauriers que reserve l'Histoire
A celui qui demain forcera la Victoire?
Nul ne les cueillira: les lauriers sont fletris
Seul un cypres s'eleve aux torubes de nos fils.]

He gave way to much emotion. Vivie, though still dazed
with the reverberating horror of Edith Cavell's execution,
tried to regain her mind balance and thank him for the
kindness he had shown them. But it was now necessary to
see her mother who might also be undergoing a shock. As
she walked up to their bedroom she reflected that the
departure of von Giesselin would have to be followed by

their own exile to some other lodging. They would share in his disgrace.

The next morning in fact the Belgian manager of the hotel with many regrets gave them a month's warning. The hotel would be required for some undefined need of the German Government and he had been told no one could be lodged there who was not furnished with a permit from the Kommandantur.

For three weeks Vivie sought in vain for rooms. Every suitable place was either full or else for reasons not given they were refused. She was reduced to eating humble pie, to writing once more to Graefin von Stachelberg and imparting the dilemma in which they were placed. Did this kind lady know where a lodging could be obtained? She herself could put up with any discomfort, but her mother was ill. If she could help them, Vivie would humbly beg her pardon for her angry letter of three weeks ago and resume her hospital work. Minna von Stachelberg made haste to reply that there were some things better not discussed in writing: if Vivie could come and see her at six one evening, when she had a slight remission from work—

Vivie went. Out of hearing, Graefin von Stachelberg—who, however, to facilitate intercourse, begged Vivie to call her "Minna,"—"We may all be dead, my dear, before long of blood-poisoning, bombs from your aeroplanes, a rising against us in the Marolles quarter—" said very plainly what she thought of Edith Cavell's execution. "It makes me think of Talleyrand—was it not?—who said 'It is a blunder; worse than a crime' ... these terrible old generals, they know nothing of the world outside Germany." As to her cousin, Gottlieb von Giesselin—"Really dear, if in this time of horrors one *dare* laugh at anything, I feel—oh it is too funny, but also, too 'schokking,' as we suppose all English women say. Yet of course I am sad about him, because he is a good, kind man, and I know his wife will be very very unhappy when she hears—And it means he will die, for certain. He must risk his life to—to—regain his position, and he will be shot before Verdun in one of those dreadful assaults." Then she told Vivie where she might find rooms, where at any rate she could use her name as a reference. Also: "Stay away at present and look after your mother. When she is quite comfortably settled, come back and work with me—here—it is at any rate the only way in which you can see and help your countrymen."

One day in November when their notice at the hotel was nearly expired, Vivie proposed an expedition to her mother. They would walk slowly—because Mrs. Warren now got easily out of breath—up to the Jardin Bontanique; Vivie would leave her there in the Palm House. It was warm; it was little frequented; there were seats and the Belgians in charge knew Mrs. Warren of old time. Vivie would then go on along the inner Boulevards by tram and look at some rooms recommended by Minna von Stachelberg in the Quartier St. Gilles.

Mrs. Warren did as she was told. Vivie left her seated in one of the long series of glass houses overlooking Brussels from a terrace, wherein are assembled many glories of the tropics: palms, dracaenas, yuccas, aloes, tree-ferns, cycads, screw-pines, and bananas: promising to be back in an hour's time.

Somehow as she sat there it seemed to Mrs. Warren it was going for her to be the last hour of fully conscious life—fully conscious and yet a curious mingling in it of the past and present. She had sat here in the middle of the 'seventies with Vivie's father, the young Irish seminarist, her lover for six months. He had a vague interest in botany, and during his convalescence after his typhoid fever, when she was still his nurse, not yet his mistress, she used to bring him here to rest and to enjoy the aspect of these ferns and palms. What a strange variety of men she had known. Some she had loved, more or less; some she had exploited frankly. Some—like George Crofts and Baxendale Strangeways—she had feared, though in her manner she had tried to conceal her dread of their violence. Well! she had taken a lot of money off the rich, but she had never plundered the poor. Her greatest conquest—and that when she was a woman of forty—was the monarch of this very country which now lay crushed under the Kaiser's heel. For a few months he had taken a whimsical liking to her handsome face, well-preserved figure, and amusing cockney talk. But he had employed her rather as the mistress of his menus plaisirs, as his recruiting agent. He had rewarded her handsomely. Now it was all in the dust: her beautiful Villa Beau-sejour a befouled barrack for German soldiers. She herself a homeless woman, repudiated by the respectable British and Americans more or less interned in this unhappy city.

Not much more than a year ago she had been one of the most respected persons in Brussels, with a large income derived from safe investments. Now all she had for certain was something over three thousand pounds in bank notes that might turn out next month to be worthless paper. And was she certain even of them? Had Vivie before they left the hotel remembered to put some, at least, of this precious sum on her person? Suppose, whilst they were out, looking for a fresh dwelling place, the hotel servants or the police raided her bedroom and found the little hoard of notes? This imagined danger made her want to cry. They were so friendless now, she in particular felt so completely deserted. Had she deserved this punishment by Fate? Was there after all a God who minded much about the sex foolishnesses and punished you for irregularities—for having lovers in your youth, for selling your virtue and inducing other women to sell theirs? Was she going to die soon and was there a hereafter?' She burst out crying in an abandonment of grief.

An elderly gardener who had been snipping and sweeping in the next house came up and vaguely recognized her as a well-known Bruxelloise, a good-natured lady, a foreigner who, strange to say, spoke Flemish. "Ach," he said, looking out where he thought lay the source of her tears, at the dim view of beautiful Brussels through the steamy glass, "Onze arme, oude Bruessel." Mrs. Warren wept unrestrainedly. "Madame is ill?" he enquired. Mrs. Warren nodded—she felt indeed very ill and giddy. He left her and returned shortly with a small glass of Schnapps. "If Madame is faint—?" She sipped the cordial and presently felt better. Then they talked of old times. Madame had kept the Hotel Leopold II in the Rue Royale? Ah, *now* he placed her. A *superb* establishment, always well-spoken of. Her self-respect returned a little. "Yes," she said, "never a complaint! I looked after those girls like a mother, indeed I did. Many a one married well from there." The gardener corroborated her statement, and added that her *clientele* had been of the most chic. He had a private florist's business of his own and he had been privileged often to send bouquets to the pensionnaires of Madame. But Madame was not alone surely in these sad times. Had he not seen her come here with a handsome English lady who was said to have been—to have been—fortunately—*au mieux* with one of the German officials?

"*That* was my daughter," Mrs. Warren informed him with pride.... "She is a lady who has taken a high degree at an English University. She has been an important person in the English feminist movement. When this dreadful war is over, I and my daughter will—"

At this juncture Vivie entered. "*Mother*, I hope you haven't missed me, haven't been unwell?" she said, looking rather questioningly at the little glass of Schnapps, only half of which had been drunk.

"Well yes, dear, I have. *Terrible* low spirits and all swimmy-like. Thought I was going to faint. But this man here has been so kind "—her tears flowed afresh—"We've bin talking of old times; he used to know me before—"

Vivie: "Quite so. But I think, dear, we had better be going back. I want to talk to you about the new rooms I've seen. Are you equal to walking? If not perhaps this kind man would try to get us a cab...?"

But Mrs. Warren said it was no distance, only round the corner, and she could well walk. When they got back she would go and lie down. Vivie, reading her mother's thoughts, pressed a five-franc note into the gardener's not reluctant palm, and they regained the Rue Royale.

But just as they were passing through the revolving door of the Hotel Imperial, a German who had been installed as manager came up with two soldiers and said explosively: "Heraus! Foutez-nous le camp! Aout you go! Don't show your face here again!"

"But," said Vivie, "our notice doesn't expire till the end of this week...!"

"Das macht nichts. The rooms are wanted and I won't have you on the premises. Off you go, or these soldiers shall take you both round to the Kommandantur."

"But our luggage? *Surely* you will let me go up to our room and pack it—and take it away? We..."

"Your luggage has been packed and is in the corridor. If you send round for it, it shall be delivered to your messenger. But you are not to stop on the premises another minute. You understand?" he almost shrieked.

"But—"

For answer, the soldiers took them by the shoulders and whirled them through the revolving door on to the pavement, where a crowd began to collect, as it does in peace or war if you cough twice or sneeze three times in Brussels. "Englische Hure! Englische Kuepplerin," shouted the soldiers as they retreated and locked the revolving door. Mrs. Warren turned purple and swayed. Vivie caught her round the waist with her strong arm.... Thus was Mrs. Warren ejected from the once homely inn which she had converted by her energy, management and capital into the second most magnificent hostelry of Brussels; thus was Vivie expelled from the place of her birth....

Hearing the shouting and seeing the crowd a Belgian gendarme came up. To him Vivie said, "Si vous etes Chretien et pas Allemand—" "Prenez garde, Madame," he said warningly—"Vous m'aiderez a porter ma mere a quelqu' endroit ou elle peut se remettre..."

He assisted her to carry the inert old woman across the street and a short distance along the opposite pavement. Here, there was a pleasant, modest-looking tea-shop with the name of Walcker over the front, and embedded in the plate glass were the words "Tea Rooms." These of course dated from long before the war, when the best Chinese tea was only four francs the demi-kilo and the fashion for afternoon tea had become established in Brussels. Vivie and her mother had often entered Walcker's shop in happier days for a cup of tea and delicious forms of home-made pastry. Besides the cakes, which in pre-war times were of an excellence rarely equalled, they had been drawn to the pleasant-looking serving woman. She was so English in appearance, though she only spoke French and Flemish. Behind the shop was a cosy little room where the more intimate clients were served with tea; a room with a look-out into a little square of garden. Thither Mrs. Warren was carried or supported. She regained consciousness slightly as she was placed on a chair, opened her eyes, and said "Thank you, my dears." Then her head fell over to one side and she was dead—seemingly....

The *agent de police* went away to fetch a doctor and to disperse the crowd of *ketjes*[1] and loafers which had transferred itself from the hotel to the tea-shop. The shop woman, who was one of those angels of kindness that turn up unexpectedly in the paths of unhappy people, called in a stout serving wench from the kitchen, and the three of them carried Mrs. Warren out of the inner tea-room into the back premises and a spare bedroom. Here she was laid on the bed, partially undressed and all available and likely restoratives applied.

[Footnote 1: Street urchins of Brussels. How they harassed the Germans and maddened them by mimicking their military manoeuvres!]

The doctor when he came pronounced her dead, thought it was probably an effusion of blood on the brain but couldn't be certain till he had made an autopsy.

"What *am* I to do?" said Vivie thinking aloud....

"Why, stay here till all the formalities are over and you can find rooms elsewhere," said Mme. Trouessart, the owner-servant of the tea-shop. "I have another spare room. For the moment my locataires are gone. I know you both very well by sight, you were clients of ours in the happy days before the War. Madame votre mere was, I think, the gerante of the Hotel Edouard-Sept when I first came to manage here. Since then, you have often drunk my tea. Je me nomme 'Trouessart' c'est le nom de mon mari qui est ... qui est—Vous pouvez diviner ou il est, ou est a present tout Belge loyal qui peut servir. Le nom Walcker? C'etait le nom de nom pere, et de plus est, c'etait un nom Anglais transforme un peu en Flamand. Mon arriere-grand-pere etait soldat Anglais. Il se battait a Waterloo. For me, I spik no English—or ver' leetle."

She went on to explain, whilst the doctors occupied themselves with their gruesome task, and Vivie was being persuaded to take some nourishment, that her great grandfather had been a soldier servant who had married a Belgian woman and settled down on the site of this very shop a hundred years ago. He and his wife had even then made a specialty of tea for English tourists. She, his great grand-daughter, had after her marriage to Monsieur Trouessart carried on the business under the old name— Walker, made to look Flemish as Walcker.

Vivie when left alone suddenly thought of the money question. She remembered then that before going out to look for rooms she had transferred half the notes from their hiding-place to an inner pocket. They were still there. But what about her luggage and her mother's, and the remainder of the money? In her distress she wrote to Graefin von Stachelberg. Minna came over from her hospital at half past six in the evening. By that time the doctor had given the necessary certificate of the cause of death, and an undertaker had come on the scene to make his preparations.

Minna went over to the Hotel Imperial with Vivie. Appearing in her Red Cross uniform, she was admitted, announced herself as the Graefin von Stachelberg, and demanded to know what justification the manager could offer for his extraordinary brutality towards these English ladies, the result of which had been the death of the elder lady. The manager replied that inasmuch as the All Highest himself was to arrive that very evening to take up his abode at the Hotel Imperial, the hotel premises had been requisitioned, etc., etc. He still refused absolutely to allow Vivie to proceed to her room and look for her money. She might perhaps be allowed to do so when the Emperor was gone. As to her luggage he would have it sent over to the tea-shop. (The money, it might be noted, she never recovered. There were many things also missing from her mother's trunks and no satisfaction was ever obtained.)

So there was Vivie, one dismal, rainy November evening in 1915; homeless, her mother lying dead in a room of this tea-shop, and in her own pocket only a matter of thirty thousand francs to provide for her till the War was over. A thousand pounds in fluctuating value was all that was left of a nominal twenty thousand of the year before.

But the financial aspect of the case for the time being did not concern her. The death of her mother had been a stunning shock, and when she crossed over to the hotel—what irony, by the bye, to think she had been born there thirty-nine years ago, in the old inn that had preceded the twice rebuilt hotel!—when she crossed the street with Minna, it had been with blazing, tearless eyes and the desire to take the hotel manager and his minions by the coat collar, fling *them* into the street, and assert her right to go up to her room. But now her violence was spent and she was a broken, weeping woman as she sat all night by the bedside of her dead mother, holding the cold hand, imprinting kisses on the dead face which was now that of a saintly person with nothing of the reprobate in its lineaments.

* * * * *

Sir Harry Johnston

The burial for various reasons had to take place in the Cemetery of St. Josse-ten-Noode, near the shuddery National Shooting Range where Edith Cavell and numerous Belgian patriots had recently been executed. Minna von Stachelberg left her hospital, with some one else in charge, and insisted on accompanying Vivie to the interment. This might have been purely "laic"; not on account of any harsh dislike to the religious ceremony on Vivie's part; only due to the fact that she knew no priest or pastor. But there appeared at the grave-side to make a very suitable and touching discourse and to utter one or two heartfelt prayers, a Belgian Baptist minister, a relation of Mme. Trouessart.

Waterloo left many curious things behind it. Not only a tea-shop or two; but a Nonconformist nucleus, that intermarried, as Sergeant Walker or Walcker had done, with Belgian women and left descendants who in the third generation—and by inherent vigour, thrift, matrimony and conversion—had built up quite a numerous congregation, which even grew large enough and rich enough to maintain a mission of its own in Congoland. Kind Mme. Trouessart (nee Walcker), distressed and unusually moved at the sad circumstances of Mrs. Warren's death, had called in her uncle the Baptist pastor (who also in some unexplained way seemed to hold a brief for the Salvation Army). He prayed silently by the death-bed which, under the circumstances, was more tactful than open intercession. He helped greatly over all the formalities of the funeral, and he took upon himself the arrangement of the ceremony, so that everything was done decorously, and certainly to the satisfaction of the Belgians, who attended. Such people would be large-minded in religion—you might be Protestant, if you were not Catholic, or you might be Jewish; but a funeral without some outward sign of faith and hope would have puzzled and distressed them.

To Vivie's great surprise, there was a considerable attendance at the ceremony. She had expected no more than the company of Minna—an unprofessing but real Christian, if ever there were one, and the equally Christian if equally hedonist Mme. Trouessart. But there came in addition quite a number of shopkeepers from the Rue Royale, the Rues de Schaerbeek, du Marais, de Lione, and de l'Association, with whom Mrs. Warren had dealt in years gone by. "C'etait une dame *tres* convenable," said one purveyor, and the others agreed. "Elle me paya ecus sonnants," said another, "et toujours sans marchander." There was even present a more distinguished acquaintance of the past: a long-retired Commissaire de Police of the Quartier in which Mrs. Warren's hotel was situated.

He appeared in the tightly-buttoned frock-coat of civil life, with a minute disc of some civic decoration in his button hole, and an incredibly tall chimney-pot hat. He came to render his *respectueux hommages* to the maitresse-femme who had conducted her business within the four corners of the law, "sans avoir maille a partir avec la police des moeurs."

Mrs. Warren at least died with the reputation of one who promptly paid her bills; and the whole *assistance*, as it walked slowly back to Brussels, recalled many a deed of kindness and jovial charity on the part of the dead Englishwoman.

*　*　*　*　*

Vivie, on sizing up her affairs, got Monsieur Walcker, the Baptist pasteur, to convey a letter to the American Consulate General. Walcker was used to such missions as these, of which the German Government was more or less cognizant. The Germans, among their many contradictory features, had a great respect for religion, a great tolerance as to its forms. They not only appreciated the difference between Jews and Christians, Catholics and Lutherans, but between the Church of England and the various Free Churches of Britain and America. The many people whom they sentenced to death must all have their appropriate religious consolation before facing the firing party. Catholics, Lutherans and Calvinists were all provided for; there was a Church of England chaplain for the avowed Anglicans; but what was to be done for the Free Churches and Nonconformist sects of the Anglo-Saxons? They were not represented by any captive pastor; so in default this much respected Monsieur Walcker, the Belgian Baptist, was called in to minister to the Nonconformist mind in its last agony. He therefore held a quasi-official position and was often entrusted with missions which would have been dealt with punitorily on the part of any one else. Consequently he was able to deliver Vivie's communication to the American Consul-General with some probability of its being sent on. It contained no further appeal to American intervention than this: that the Consul-General would try to convey to England the news of her mother's death to such-and-such solicitors, and to Lewis Maitland Praed A.R.A. in Hans Place.

She went to the Brussels bank a fortnight after her mother's death whilst still availing herself of the hospitality of Madame Trouessart: to withdraw the jewellery and plate which she had deposited there on her mother's account. But there she found herself confronted with the red tape of the Latin which is more formidable, even, than that of the land of Dora at the present day. These deposited articles were held on the order of Mrs. Warren; they could not be given up till her will was proved and letters of administration had been granted. So *that* small resource in funds was withheld, at any rate till some time after peace had been declared. However she had a thousand pounds (in notes) between her and penury, and the friendship of Minna von Stachelberg. She would resume her evening lessons in English—Madame Trouessart had found her several pupils—and she would lodge—as they kindly invited her to do—with the Baptist pastor and his wife in the Rue Haute. And she would help Minna at the hospital, and hope to be rewarded with the opportunity of bringing comfort and consolation to the wounded British prisoners.

Thus, with no unbearable misery, she passed the year 1916. There were short commons in the way of food, and the cold was sometimes cruel. But Madame Walcker was a wonderful cook and could make soup from a sausage skewer, and heaped *edredons* on Vivie's bed. Vivie sighed a little over the Blue Placards which announced endless German victories by land and sea; and she gasped over the dreadful Red Placards with their lists of victims sentenced to death by the military courts. She ground her teeth over the announce-ment of Gabrielle Petit's condemnation, and behind the shut door of Minna's small sitting-room—and she only shut the door not to compromise Minna—she raved over the judicial murder of this Belgian heroine, who was shot, as was Edith Cavell, for nothing more than assisting young Belgians to escape from German-occupied Belgium.

She witnessed the air-raids of the Allies, when only comforting papers were dropped on Brussels city, but bombs on the German aerodromes outside; and she also saw the Germans turn their guns from the aeroplanes—which soared high out of their reach or skimmed below range—on to thickly-inhabited streets of the poorer quarters, to teach them to cheer the air-craft of the Allies!

She beheld—or she was told of—many acts of rapine, considered cruelty and unreasoning ferocity on the part of German officials or soldiers; yet saw or heard of acts and episodes of unlooked-for kindness, forbearance and sympathy from the same hated people. Von Giesselin, after all, was a not uncommon type; and as to Minna von Stachelberg, she was a saint of the New Religion, the Service of Man.

CHAPTER XVIII

THE BOMB IN PORTLAND PLACE

Mrs. Rossiter said to herself in 1915 that she had scarcely known a happy day, or even hour, since the War began. In the first place Michael had again shown violence of temper with ministers of state over the release from prison of "that" Miss Warren—"a convict doing a sentence of hard labour." And then, when he had got her released, and gone himself with their beautiful new motor—whatever *could* the chauffeur have thought?—to meet her at the prison gates, *there* he was, afterwards, worrying himself over the War: not content as she was, as most of her friends were, as the newspapers were, to leave it all to Lord Kitchener and Mr. Asquith, Sir Edward Grey, and even Mr. Lloyd George— though the latter had made some rather foolish and exaggerated speeches about Alcohol. Michael, if he went on like this, would *never* get his knighthood!

Then when Michael had at last, thanks to General Armstrong, found his right place and was accomplishing marvels—the papers said—as a "mender of the maimed"— here was she left alone in Portland Place with hardly any one to speak to, and all her acquaintances—she now realized they were scarcely her friends—too much occupied with war work to spend an afternoon in discussing nothing very important over a sumptuous tea, still served by a butler and footman.

Presently, too, the butler left to join the Professor in France and the footman enlisted, and the tea had to be served by a *distraite* parlour-maid, with her eye on a munitions factory—so that she might be "in it"—and her heart in the keeping of the footman, who, since he had gone into khaki, was irresistible.

Mrs. Rossiter of course said, in 1914, that she would take up war work. She subscribed most handsomely to the Soldiers' and Sailors' Families' Association, to the Red Cross, to the Prince of Wales's Fund (one of the unsolved war-time mysteries ... what's become of it?), to the Cigarette Fund, the 1914 Christmas Plum Pudding Fund, the Blue Cross, the Purple Cross, the Green Cross funds; to the outstandingly good work at St. Dunstan's and at Petersham—(I am glad she gave a Hundred pounds each to *them*); and to the French, Belgian, Russian, Italian, Serbian, Portuguese and Japanese Flag Days and to Our Own Day; besides enriching a number of semi-fraudulent war charities which had alluring titles.

But if, from paying handsomely to all these praise-worthy endeavours to mitigate the horrors of war, she proceeded to render personal service, she became the despair of the paid organizers and business-like workers. She couldn't add and she couldn't subtract or divide with any certainty of a correct result; she couldn't spell the more difficult words or remember the right letters to put after distinguished persons' names when she addressed envelopes in her large, childish handwriting; she couldn't be trusted to make enquiries or to detect fraudulent appeals. She lost receipts and never grasped the importance of vouchers; she forgot to fill up counterfoils, or if reminded filled them up "from memory" so that they didn't tally; she signed her name, if there was any choice of blank spaces, in quite the wrong place.

So, invariably, tactful secretaries or assistant secretaries were told off to explain to her—ever so nicely—that "she was no business woman" (this, to the daughter of wholesale manufacturers, sounded rather flattering), and that though she was invaluable as a "name," as a patroness, or one of eighteen Vice Presidents, she was of no use whatever as a worker.

She had no country house to place at the disposal of the Government as a convalescent home. Michael after a few experiments forbade her offering any hospitality at No. 1 Park Crescent to invalid officers. Such as were entrusted to her in the spring of 1915 soon found that she was—as they phrased it—"a pompous little, middle-class fool," wielding no authority. They larked in the laboratory with Red Cross nurses, broke specimens, and did very unkind and noisy things ... besides smoking in both the large *and* the small dining-rooms. So, after the summer of 1915, she lived very much alone, except that she had the Adams children from Marylebone to spend the day with her occasionally.

Poor Mrs. Adams, though a valiant worker, was very downcast and unhappy. She confided to Mrs. Rossiter that although she dearly loved her Bert—"and a better husband I defy you to find"—he never seemed all hers. "Always so wrapped up in that Miss Warren or 'er cousin the barrister." And no sooner had war broken out than off he was to France, as a kind of missionary, she believed—the Young Men's Christian Something or other; "though before the War he didn't seem particular stuck on religion, and it was all she could do to get him sometimes to church on a Sunday morning. Oh yes: she got 'er money all right; and she couldn't say too much of Mr. and Mrs. Rossiter's kindness. There was Bert, not doin' a stroke of work for the Professor, and yet his pay going on all the same. Indeed she was putting money by, because Bert was kep' out there, and all found."

However his two pretty children were some consolation to Mrs. Rossiter, whom they considered as a very grand lady and one that was lavishly kind.

Mrs. Rossiter tried sometimes in 1915 having working parties in her house or in the studio; and if she could attract workers gave them such elaborate lunches and plethoric teas that very little work was done, especially as she herself loved a long, aimless gossip about the Royal Family or whether Lord Kitchener had ever *really* been in love. Or she tried, since she was a poor worker herself—her only jersey and muffler were really finished by her maid—reading aloud to the knitters or stitchers, preferably from the works of Miss Charlotte Yonge or some similar novelist of a later date. But that was found to be too disturbing to their sense of the ludicrous. For she read very stiltedly, with a strange exotic accent for the love passages or the death scenes. As Lady Victoria Freebooter said, she would have been *priceless* at a music-hall matinee which was raising funds for war charities, if only she could have been induced to read passages from Miss Yonge in *that* voice for a quarter of an hour. Even the Queen would have had to laugh.

But as that could not be brought off, it was decided that working parties at her house led to too much giddiness from suppressed giggles or torpor from too much food. So she relapsed once more into loneliness. Unfortunately air-raids were now becoming events of occasional fright and anxiety in London, and this deterred Cousin Sophie from Darlington, Cousin Matty from Leeds, Joseph's wife from Northallerton or old, married schoolfellows from other northern or midland towns coming to partake of her fastuous hospitality. Also, they all seemed to be busy, either over their absent husbands' business, or their sons', or because they were plunged in war work themselves. "And really, in these times, I couldn't stand Linda for more than five minutes," one of them said.

As to the air-raids, she was not greatly alarmed at them. Of course it was very uncomfortable having London so dark at night, but then she only went out in the afternoon, and never in the evening. And the Germans seemed to be content and discriminating enough not to bomb what she called "the residential" parts of London. The nearest to Portland Place of their attentions was Hampstead or Bloomsbury. "We are protected, my dear, by the open spaces of Regent's Park. They wouldn't like to waste their bombs on poor me!"

However her maid didn't altogether like the off chance of the Germans or our air-craft guns making a mistake and trespassing on the residential parts of London, so she persuaded her mistress to spend part of the winter of 1915-16 at Bournemouth. Here she was not happy and far lonelier even than in London. She did not like to send all that way for the Adams children, she had a parlour suite all to herself at the hotel, and was timid about making acquaintances outside, since everybody now-a-days wanted you to subscribe to something, and it was so disagreeable having to say "no." She was not a great walker so she could not enjoy the Talbot woods; the sea made her feel sad, remembering that Michael was the other side and the submarines increasingly active: in short, air-raids or no air-raids, she returned home in March, and her maid, who had been with her ten years, gave her warning.

But then she had an inspiration! She engaged Mrs. Albert Adams to take her place, and although the parlour-maid at this took offence and cut the painter of domestic service, went off to the munitions till Sergeant Frederick Summers should get leave to come home and marry her; and they were obliged to engage another parlour-maid in her place at double the wages: Mrs. Rossiter had done a very wise thing. "Bert" had been home for three weeks in the preceding February, and the recently bereaved Mrs. Adams had united her tears with Mrs. Rossiter's on the misery of the War which separated attached husbands and wives. It now alleviated the sorrows of both that they should be together as mistress and maid. The cook—a most important factor—had always liked Bertie and adored his "sweet, pretty little children." "If you'll let 'em sleep in the spare room on the fourth floor, next their mother, and play in the day-time in the servants' 'all, they'll be no manner of difficulty *nor* bother to me and the maids. We shall love to 'ave 'em, the darlin's. And they'll serve to cheer you up a bit ma'am till the Professor comes back."

Mrs. Adams was a very capable person who hated dust and grime. The big house wanted some such intervention, as since the butler's departure it had become rather slovenly, save in the portions occupied by Mrs. Rossiter. Charwomen were got in, and spring cleanings on a gigantic scale took place, so that when Rossiter did return he thought it had never looked so nice, or his Linda been so cheery and companionable.

But before this happy confirmation of her wisdom in engaging Nance Adams as maid and factotum, Mrs. Rossiter had several waves of doubt and distress to breast. There was the Suffrage question. Once converted by Mrs. Humphry Ward, Miss Violet Markham, Sir Almroth Wright—whose *prenom* she could not pronounce—the late Lord Cromer, and the impressive Lord Curzon, to the perils of the Woman's Vote, Mrs. Rossiter was hard to move from her uncompromising opposition to the enfranchisement of her sex. Some adroit champion of the Wrong had employed the argument that *once* Women got the vote, *the Divorce Laws would be greatly enlarged.* This would be part of the scheme of the wild women to get themselves all married; that and *the legalisation of Polygamy* which would follow the Vote *as surely as the night the day*. Linda had an undefined terror that her Michael might take advantage of such licentiousness to depose her, like the Empress Josephine was put aside in favour of a child-producing rival; or if polygamy came into force, that Miss Warren might lawfully share the Professor's affections.

She was therefore greatly perturbed in the course of 1916 at the sudden throwing up of the sponge by the Anti-suffragists. However, there it was. The long struggle drew to a victorious close. Example as well as precept pointed to what women could do and were worth; sound arguments followed the inconveniences of militancy, and the men were convinced. Or rather, the men in the mass and the fighting, working men had for some time been convinced, but the great statesmen who had so obstinately opposed the measures were now weakening at the knees before the results of their own mismanagement in the conduct of the War.

A further perplexity and anxiety for Mrs. Rossiter arose over the German spy mania. She had been to one of Lady Towcester's afternoon parties "to keep up our spirits." Lady Towcester collected for at least six different charities and funds, and Mrs. Rossiter was a generous subscriber to all six. Touching the wood of the central tea-table, she had remarked to Lady Victoria and Lady Helen Freebooter how fortunate they (who lived within the prescribed area defined by Lady Jeune) had been in so far escaping air-raids.

"But don't you know why?" said Lady Victoria.

Mrs. Rossiter didn't.

"Because in Manchester Square, in Cavendish—Grosvenor —Hanover Squares, in Portland Place—a few doors off your own house—in Harley Street and Wigmore Street: there are special friends of the Kaiser living. They *may* call themselves by English names, they may even be ex-cabinet-ministers; but they are working for the Kaiser, all the same. And *he* wouldn't be such a fool as to have them bombed, would he?"

"Especially as it is well known that there *is a wireless installation* on a house in Portland Place which communicates with a similar installation in the Harz Mountains," added Lady Helen.

This was a half-reassuring, half-terrifying statement. It was comfortable to know that you lived under the Kaiser's wing—Mrs. Rossiter hoped the aim of the aeronauts was accurate, and their knowledge of London topography good. At the same time it was alarming to feel that you might be involved in that final blow up of the villains which must bring such scoundreldom to a close. But if Lady Vera and Lady Helen knew all this for a fact, why not tell the Police? "What would be the good? They'd deny everything and we should only be sued for libel."

However to form some conception of how English home life was undermined with plots, she was advised to go and see Mr. Dennis Eadie in *The Man That Stayed at Home*. She did, taking Mrs. Adams with her to the Dress Circle for a matinee. Both were very much impressed, and on their return expected the fireplaces to open all of a piece and reveal German spies with masked faces and pistols, standing in the chimney.

At last these and other nightmares were dispelled by the arrival of Rossiter on leave of absence in the autumn of 1916. He had the rank of Colonel in the R.A.M.C., and wore the khaki uniform—Mrs. Rossiter proudly thought—of a

General. He had shaved off his beard and trimmed his moustache and looked particularly soldierly. The butler who came with him though not precisely a soldier but a sort of N.C.O. in a medical corps, also looked quite martial, and had so much to say for himself that Mrs. Rossiter felt he could never become a butler again. But he did all the same, and a most efficient one though a little breezy in manner.

Linda now entered on an aftermath of matrimonial happiness. Rossiter was to take quite a long leave so that he could pursue the most important researches in curative surgery—bone grafting and the like; not only in his own laboratory but at the College of Surgeons and the Zoological Gardens Prosectorium. With only occasional week-ends at home he had been away from London since September, 1914; had known great hardships, the life of the trenches and the bomb-proof shelter, stewed tea and bad tinned milk, rum and water, bully beef, plum and apple jam, good bread, it is true, but shocking margarine for butter. He had slept for weeks together on an old sofa more or less dressed, kept warm by his great-coat and two Army blankets of woven porcupine quills (seemingly) the ends of which tickled his nose and scratched his face. He had been very cold and sweatingly hot, furiously hungry with no meal to satisfy his healthy appetite, madly thirsty and no long drink attainable; unable to sleep for three nights at a time owing to the noise of the bombardment; surfeited with horrible smells; sickened with butchery; shocked at his own failures to retrieve life, yet encouraged by an isolated victory, here and there, over death and disablement. So the never-before-appreciated comfort of his Park Crescent home filled him with intense gratitude to Linda.

Had he known, he owed some of his acknowledgment to Mrs. Adams; who had worked both hard and tactfully in her undefined position of lady's-maid-housekeeper-companion.

But naturally he didn't know, though he praised his wife warmly for her charity of soul in taking pity on the poor little woman and her two children. He could only give the slightest news about Bertie, but said he was a sort of jack-of-all-trades for the Y.M.C.A. As to Vivie—"that Miss Warren"—he answered his wife's questions neither with the glowering taciturnity nor suspicious loquacity of former times. "Miss Warren? Vivie? I fancy she's still at Brussels, but there is no chance of finding out. There is a story that her mother is dead. P'raps now they'll let her come away. She must be jolly well sick of Brussels by now. When I last heard of Adams he was still hoping to get into touch with her. I hope he won't take any risks. She's a clever woman and I dare say can take care of herself. I hope we shall all meet again when the War is over."

He seemed very pleased to hear of the new Conciliation Bill, the general agreement all round on the Suffrage question and the enlargement of the electorate. He had always told Linda it was bound to come. "And after it has come, dearie, you mark my words: things will go on pretty much as before." But his real, intense, absorbing interest lay in the new experiments he was about to make in bone grafting and cartilage replacing, and the functions of the pituitary body and the interstitial glands. To carry these out adequately the Zoological Society had accumulated troops of monkeys and baboons. At a certain depot in Camden Town dogs were kept for his purposes. And the vaults and upper floors of the Royal College of Surgeons were at Rossiter's disposal, with Professor Keith to co-operate. Never had his house in Portland Place—to be accurate the Park Crescent end thereof—seemed so conveniently situated, or its studio-laboratory so well designed. "Air-raids? Pooh! Just about one chance in a million we should be struck. Besides: can't think of that, when so much is at stake. That's a fine phrase, 'Menders of the Maimed.' Just what we want to be! No more artificial limbs if we can help you to grow your own new legs and arms—perhaps. At any rate, mend up those that are a hopeless mash. Grand work! Only bright thing in the War. Now dear, are you ready with that lymph?"

And she was. Never had Linda been so happy. She overcame her disgust at the sight of blood, at monkeys, dogs, and humans under anaesthetics, at yellow fat, gleaming sinew, and blood-stained bone. She was careful as a washer-up. The services of Mrs. Adams were enlisted, and she was more deft even than her mistress; and the butler, who was by this time a regular hospital dresser, greatly admired her pretty arms when they were bared to the elbow, and her flushed cheeks when she took a humble part in some tantalizing adjustment.

"I'm some use to you after all," Linda would say when they retired from the studio for a rest and she made the tea. "Some *use*? I should think so!" said Rossiter (whether truly or not). And he reproached himself that twenty years ago he had not trained and developed her to help him in his work, to be a real companion in his studies.

He was really fond of her through the winter of 1916. And so jovial and lover-like, so boyish in his fun, so like the typical Tommy home from the trenches. When he was overjoyed at the success of some uncovered and peeped-at experiment, he would sing, "When *I* get me civvies on again, an' it's Home Sweet Home once more"; and ask for the ideal cottage "with rowses round the door—And a nice warm bottle in me nice warm bed, An' a nice soft pillow for me nice soft 'ead..." Mrs. Rossiter began to think there was a good side to the War, after all. It made some men more conscious of their home comforts and less exigent for intellectuality in their home companions.

They went out very little into Society. Rossiter held that

war-time parties were scandalous. He poohpoohed the idea that immodest dancing with frisky matrons or abandoned spinsters was necessary to restore the shell-shocked nerves of temporary captains, locally-ranked majors, or the recently-joined subaltern. He was far too busy for twaddly tea-fights and carping at hard-worked generals who were doing their best and a good best too. He and Linda did dine occasionally with Honoria, but the latter felt she could not let herself go about Vivie in the presence of Mrs. Rossiter and seemed a little cold in manner.

Ordinarily, after working hard all day while the daylight lasted they much preferred an evening of complete solitude. Rossiter's new robustness of taste included love of a gramophone. Money being no consideration with them, they acquired a tip-top one with superlative records; not so much the baaing, bellowing and shrieking of fashionable singers, but orchestral performances, heart-melting duets between violin and piano (*what* human voice ever came up to a good violin or violoncello?), racy comic songs, inspiriting two steps, xylophone symphonies, and dreamy, sensuous waltzes. This gramophone Linda learnt to work; and while Michael read voraciously the works of Hunter, Hugh Owen Thomas, Stromeyer, Duchenne, Goodsir, Wolff, and Redfern on bones, muscles, ligaments, tendons, cartilage, periosteum and osteogenesis—or, more often, Keith's compact and lucid analysis of their experiments and conclusions—Linda let loose in the scented air of a log fire these varied melodies which attuned the mind to extraordinary perceptibility.

The little Adamses were allowed to steal in and listen, on condition they never uttered a word to break the spell of Colonel Rossiter's thoughts.

I think also Rossiter felt his wife had been unjustly snubbed by the great ladies and the off-hand, harum-scarum young war-workers; so he flatly declined to have any of them messing around his studio or initiated into his research work. It was intimated that the Rossiter Thursday afternoons of long ago would not be resumed until after the peace. Linda therefore derived much consolation and satisfaction for past injuries to her pride when Lady Vera—or Victoria— Freebooter called one day just before Christmas and said "Oh—er—mother's let our house till February and thinks we'd better—I mean the Marrybone Guild of war-workers— meet at *your* house instead"; and she, Linda, had the opportunity of replying: "Oh, I'm sorry, *but* It's QUITE impossible. The Professor—I mean, Colonel Rossiter—and I are so *very* busy ... we are seeing *no* one just now. Indeed we've enlisted all the servants to help the Colonel in his work, so I can't even offer you a cup of tea.... I must *rush* back at once.... You'll excuse me?"

"That Rossiter woman is quite off her head with grandeur," said Lady Vera to Lady Helen. "I expect Uncle Algy has let out that her husband is in the New Year's honours."

And so he was. But Uncle Algy, though he might have babbled to his nieces, had not written a word to the Rossiters. So they just enjoyed Christmas—too much, they thought, more than any Christmas before—in the simple satisfaction of being Colonel and Mrs. Rossiter, all in all to each other, but rendered additionally happy by making those about them happy. The little Adamses staggered under their presents and had a Christmas Tree to which they were allowed to ask their two grannies—Mrs. Laidly from Fig Tree Court and Mrs. Adams from the Kilburn Laundry—and numerous little friends from Marylebone, who had been washed and curled and crimped and adjured not to disgrace their parents, *or* father—in the trenches—would be told "as sure as I stand here."

(The little Adamses were also warned that if they *ever* again were heard calling Mrs. Rossiter "Gran'ma," they'd—but the threat was too awful to be uttered, especially as their mother at this time was always on the verge of tears, either at getting no news of Bert or at the unforgettable kindness of Bert's employer.)

Mrs. Rossiter, quite unaware that she was soon to be a Dame, gave Christmas entertainments at St. Dunstan's, at the Marylebone Workhouse, and to all the wounded soldiers in the parish. And on December 31, 1916, Michael received a note from the Prime Minister to say that His Majesty, in recognition of his exceptional services in curative surgery at the front, had been pleased to bestow on him a Knight Commandership of the Bath. "So that, Linda, you can call yourself Lady Rossiter, and you will have to get some new cards printed for both of us."

Linda didn't feel quite that ecstasy over her title that she had expected in her day-dreams. She was getting a little frightened at her happiness. Generations of Puritan forefathers and mothers had left some influence of Calvinism on her mentality. She was brought up to believe in a jealous God, whose Providence when you felt too happy on earth just landed you in some unexpected disaster to fit you for the Kingdom of Heaven—a Kingdom which all healthy human beings shrink from entering with the terror of the unknown and a certain homeliness of disposition which is humbly content with this cosy planet and a corporeal existence.

However it was very nice to leave cards of calling on Lady Towcester—even though she was out of town on account of air-raids—and on others, inscribed: "Lady Rossiter, Colonel Sir Michael Rossiter, Sir Michael and Lady Rossiter;" and to see printed foolscap envelopes for Michael arrive from the War Office and lie on the hall table, addressed: Colonel Sir

Michael Rossiter K.C.B. etc., etc., etc., etc.

And later on, in January or February, for some very good reason, Sir Michael and Lady Rossiter were received in audience by the King and Queen at Buckingham Palace. The King had already watched Sir Michael at work in his laboratory just behind the French front; so they two, as Linda timidly glanced at them, had no lack of subjects for conversation. But the Queen! Linda had thought she could *never* have talked to a Queen without swooning, and indeed had arrived primed with much sal volatile. Yet there, as in some realistic dream, she was led on to talk about her war charities and Sir Michael's experiments without trembling, and found herself able to listen with intelligence to the Queen's practical suggestions about war work and the application of relief funds in crowded districts. "*We actually compared notes!*" said a flushed and triumphant Linda to her Michael, as they drove away through the blue twilight of St. James's Park.

And so far from being puffed up by this, people said they had always thought Lady Rossiter was kind, but they really before had never imagined there was so much in her. She was even allowed to preside as Vice President, in the absence of Lady Towcester; and got through it quite creditably—kind hearts being more than coronets—and made a little speech to which cook and Nance Adams called out "Hear, *Hear!*" and roused quite a hearty response.

Of course it was an awful wrench when Michael had to return to France. But he would be back in the autumn, and meantime she must remember she was a soldier's wife. So the summer was got through with cheerfulness, especially as she was now treated with much more regard in the different committees whereof she was Vice President. On these committees she met Honoria Armstrong, and the longing to renew the old friendship and talk about Michael's superlative qualities to one who had long known them, took her over to Kensington Square, impulsively. Honoria perceived the need instinctively. The coldness engendered by Linda's silly Anti-suffragism disappeared. They both talked by the hour together of their respective husbands and their outstanding virtues and charming weaknesses. The Armstrong children took to calling her Aunt Linda—Michael and Petworth, after all, were brothers-in-arms and friends from youth. Lady Rossiter was delighted, and lavished presents on them, till Honoria reminded her it was war-time and extravagance in all things was reprehensible, even in British-made toys.

They discussed the Vote, soon to be theirs, and how it should be exercised. From that—by some instinct—Honoria passed on to a talk about Vivien Warren ... a selective talk. She said nothing about David Williams, but enlarged on Vivie's absolute "straightness," especially towards other women; her business capacities, her restoration of her mother to the ranks of the respectable; till at last it seemed as though the burning down of racing stables was a meritorious act ... "ridding England of an evil that good might come." And there was poor Vivie, locked up in Brussels, if indeed she were still living.

Linda felt shocked at her own treachery to the Woman's Cause in having betrayed that poor, well-meaning Miss Warren to the police. Never could she confess this to Lady Armstrong (Sir Petworth had just been knighted for a great success in battle), tell her about the fragment of letter she had forwarded anonymously to Scotland Yard. Perhaps she might some day tell Michael, when he returned. In any case she would say at the next opportunity that as soon as Miss Warren reappeared in England, he might ask her to the house as often as he liked—even to stay with them if she were in want of a home.

She said as much to Michael when he came back in September, 1917, to make some further investigations into bone grafting. He seemed genuinely pleased at her broad-mindedness, and said it would indeed be delightful when the War was over—and it *surely* must be over soon—now Mr. Lloyd George and Clemenceau and President Wilson had taken it in hand—it would indeed be delightful to form a circle of close friends who had all been interested in the Woman's Movement. As to Vivie ... if she were not dead ... he should advise her to go in for Parliament.

He had had no news of her since ever so long; what was worse, he had now very great misgivings about Bertie Adams. During the autumn of 1916 he had disappeared in the direction of La Bassee. There were stories of his having joined some American Relief Expedition at Lille—a most dangerous thing to do; insensate, if it were not a mad attempt to get through to Brussels in disguise to rescue Miss Warren. No one in the Y.M.C.A. believed for a moment that he had done anything dishonourable. Most likely he had been killed—as so many Y.M.C.A. people were just then, assisting to bring in the wounded or going up to the trenches with supplies. Mrs. Adams had better be prepared, cautiously, for a bereavement. Rossiter himself was very sad about it. He had missed Bertie's services much these last three years. He had never known a better worker—turn his hand to anything—Such a good indexer, for example.

Linda wondered whether *she* could do any indexing? Three years ago Michael would have replied: "*You?* Nonsense, my dear. You'd only make a muddle of it. Much better stick to your housekeeping" (which as a matter of fact was done in those days by cook, butler and parlour-maid). But now he said, thoughtfully:

"Well—I don't know—perhaps you might. There's no reason

Sir Harry Johnston

you shouldn't try."

And Linda began trying.

But she also worked regularly in the laboratory now, calling it at his suggestion the lab, and stumbling no more over the word. She wore a neat overall with tight sleeves and her hair plainly dressed under a little white, pleated cap. She never now caught anything with her sleeve and switched it off the table; she never let anything drop, and was a most judicious duster and wiper-up.

Rossiter in this autumn of 1917 was extremely interested in certain crucial experiments he was making with spiculum in sponge-cells; with scleroblasts, "mason-cells," osteoblasts, and "consciousness" in bone-cells. Most of the glass jars in which these experiments were going on (those of the sponges in sea-water) required daylight for their progress. There was no place for their storage more suitable than that portion of his studio-laboratory which was above ground; and the situation of his house in regard to air attacks, bombs, shrapnel seemed to him far more favourable than the upper rooms at the College of Surgeons. That great building was often endangered because of its proximity to the Strand and Fleet Street; and the Strand and Fleet Street, being regarded by the Germans as arteries of Empire, were frequently attacked by German air-craft.

But in Rossiter's studio there was an under-ground annex as continuation of the house cellars; and the household was instructed that if, in Rossiter's absence, official warnings of an air-raid were given, certain jars were to be lifted carefully off the shelves and brought either into the library or taken down below in case, through shrapnel or through the vibration of neighbouring explosions, the glass of the studio roof was broken.

One day in October, 1917, the German air fleet made a determined attack on London. It was intended this time to belie the stories of the heart of the Western district being exempted from punishment because Lady So-and-so lived there and had lent her house in East Anglia to the Empress and her children in 1912, or because Sir Somebody-else was really an arch spy of the Germans and had to go on residing in London. So the aeroplanes this time began distributing their explosives very carefully over the residential area between Regent's Park and Pall Mall, the Tottenham Court Road and Selfridge's.

Lady Rossiter in her overall was disturbed at her indexing by the clamour of an approaching daylight raid; by the maroons, the clanging of bells, the hooters, the gunfire; and finally by the not very distant sounds of exploding bombs. She called and rang for the servants, and then rushed from the library into the studio to commence removing the more important of the jars to a place of greater safety. She had seized two of them, one under each arm, and was making for the library door, when there came the most awful crash she had ever heard, and resounding bangs which seemed to echo indefinitely in her ears....

Rossiter was working in the Prosectorium at the Zoo when the daylight air-raid began. It seemed to be coming across the middle of London; so, hastily doffing his overall, he left the Gardens and walked rapidly towards Portland Place. He had hardly got past the fountain presented by Sir Jamsetjee Jeejeebhoy in wasted benevolence, than he heard the deafening report of the bomb which had wrecked his studio, reduced it to a tangle of iron girders and stanchions, strewn its floor with brick rubble and thick dust, and left his wife a human wreck, lying unconscious with a broken spine, surrounded by splinters of glass, broken jars, porcelain trays, and nasty-looking fragments of sponge and vertebrate anatomy. With an almost paralyzing premonition of disaster he ran as quickly as possible towards Park Crescent. The Marylebone Road was strewn with glass, and a policeman—every one else had taken shelter—was ringing and knocking at his front door to ascertain the damage and possible loss of life. Michael let both of them in with his latch-key. In the hall the butler was lying prone, stunned by a small statue which had been flung at him by the capricious violence of the explosion. All the mirrors were shivered and most of the pictures were down. At the entrance to the library cook was standing, all of a tremble. The two little Adamses rushed up to him: "Oh Sir Michael! Mummie is dead and Gran'ma is awfully hurted."

But Mummie—Mrs. Adams—was not dead; neither was the expensive parlour-maid. Both had fainted or been stunned by the explosion on their way to help their mistress. Both lay inanimate on the library floor. The library glass door was shivered to dangerous jagged splinters, but the iron frame-work—"Curse it"—remained a tangled, maddening obstacle to his further progress. He could see through the splinters of thick glass something that looked like Linda, lying on her back—and—something that looked like blood. The police-man who followed him was strong and adroit. Together they detached the glass splinters and wrenched open the framework, with space enough, at any rate, to pass through without the rending of clothes into the studio.

Linda Rossiter was regaining consciousness for just a few more minutes of sentient life. She was aware there had been a dreadful accident to some one; perhaps to herself. But she fully believed she had first of all saved the precious jars. No doubt they had put her to bed, and as there was something warm (her blood, poor thing) round her body, they must have packed her with hot water bottles. Some idea of Michael's no doubt. How *kind* he was!

She would soon get right, with him to look after her. She opened her eyes to meet his, as he bent over her, and said with the ghost of an arch smile: "I—have been—of some use—to you, haven't—I? ... (then the voice faltered and trailed away) ... I ... saved—your—specimens—"

CHAPTER XIX

BERTIE ADAMS

One day, early in April, 1917, Vivie was standing in a corridor of the Hopital de St. Pierre talking to Minna von Stachelberg. She had just come from the railway station, where in common with the few British and Americans who remained in Brussels she had been to take a respectful and grateful farewell of the American Minister and his wife, who were leaving Belgium for Holland, prior to the American declaration of war. American diplomacy had done little for her or her mother, but it had been the shield, the salvation, the only hope of Belgium. Moreover, the break-off of diplomatic relations initiated the certain hope of a happier future. American intervention in the war *must* lead to Peace and Freedom. Germany *must* now be beaten and Belgium set free.

So she had contributed her mite to the fund which purchased spring flowers—hothouse-grown, for this April was a villainous prolongation of winter—with which to strew the approach to the station and fill the reserve compartment of the train.

As Vivie was nearing the end of her description—and Minna was hoping it *was* the end, as she wanted to get back to her patients—two German policemen marched up to Vivie, clicked their heels, saluted, and said in German, "Mademoiselle Varennes, nicht wahr? Be good enough to accompany us to the Kommandantur."

At this dread summons, Vivie turned pale, and Minna dismayed began to ask questions. The Polizei answered that they had none to give.... Might she accompany her friend? She might not. Then followed a ride in a military motor, with the two silent policemen.

They arrived outside the Kommandantur.... More clanking, clicking, and gruff conversation in German. She got out, in response to a tight pressure on her arm, a grip in fact, and accompanied her grim guide through halls and corridors, and at last entered a severely furnished office, a kind of magistrate's court, and was confronted with—Bertie Adams! A whiskered, bearded, moustached, shabbily dressed (in a quasi-military uniform) Bertie Adams: lean, and hollow-eyed, but with the love-light in his eyes. He turned on her such a look of dog-like fealty, of happy recognition that although, by instinct and for his safety, she was about to deny all knowledge of him, she could not force her eyes or tongue to tell the lie.

"Oh miss, oh my dear Miss Warren! *How* I have hungered and thirsted for a sight of you all these months and years! To see you once more is worth all and more I've gone through to get here. They may shoot me now, if they've got the heart— Not that I've done anything to deserve it—I've simply had one object in view: To come here and help you."

He looked around as if instinctively to claim the sympathy of the policemen. To say he met with none would be to make them out more inhuman than they were. But as all this speech was in English they understood but little of what he had said. They guessed he loved the woman to whom he spake, but he may have been pleading with her not to give him away, to palliate his acts of espionage.

Vivie replied:

"*Dear* Bertie! You can't be gladder to see me than I am you. I greet you with all my heart. But you must be aware that in coming here like this you—" her words stuck in her throat— she knew not what to say lest she might incriminate him farther—

A police officer broke in on her embarrassment and said in German: "Es ist genug—You recognize him, Madame? He was arrested this morning at the Hotel Imperial, enquiring for you. Meantime, you also are under arrest. Please follow that officer."

"May I communicate with my friends?" said Vivie, with a dry tongue in a dry mouth.

"Who are your friends?"

"Graefin von Stachelberg, at the Hopital de St. Pierre; le Pasteur Walcker, Rue Haute, 33—"

"I will let them know that you are arrested on a charge of high treason—in league with an English spy," he hissed.

Then Vivie was pushed out of the room and Bertie was seized by two policemen—

They did not meet again for three days. It was a Saturday, and a police agent came into the improvised cell where Vivie was confined—who had never taken off her clothes since her arrest and had passed three days of such mental distress as she had never known, unable to sleep on the bug-infested pallet, unable to eat a morsel of the filthy food—and invited her to follow him. "By the grace of the military governor of the prison of Saint-Gilles"—he said this in French as she understood German imperfectly—"you are permitted to proceed there to take farewell of your English friend, the prisoner A-dams, who has been condemned to death."

Bertie had been tried by court-martial in the Senate, on the Friday. He followed all the proceedings in a dazed condition. Everything was carried on in German, but the parts that most concerned him were grotesquely translated by a ferocious-looking interpreter, who likewise turned Bertie's stupid, involved, self-condemnatory answers into German—no doubt very incorrectly. Bertie however protested, over and over again, that Miss Warren knew *nothing* of his projects, and that his only object in posing as an American and travelling with false passports was to rescue Miss Warren from Brussels and enable her to pass into Holland, "or get out of the country *some* 'ow." As to the Emperor, and taking his life—"why lor' bless you, *I* don't want to take *any one's* life. I 'ate war, more than ever after all I've seen of it. Upon my honour, gentlemen, all I want is Miss Warren." Here one member of the court made a facetious remark in German to a colleague who sniggered, while, with his insolent light blue eyes, he surveyed Bertie's honest, earnest face, thin and hollowed with privations and fatigue....

He was perfunctorily defended by a languid Belgian barrister, tired of the invidious role of mechanical pleading for the lives of prisoners, especially where, as in this case, they were foredoomed, and eloquence was waste of breath, and even got you disliked by the impatient ogres, thirsty for the blood of an English man or woman.... "Du reste," he said to a colleague, "agissait-il d'un Belge, mon cher, tu sais que l'on se sentirait force a risquer le deplaisir de ces ogres:

tandis que, pour un pauvre bougre d'Anglais...? Et qu'ont-ils fait pour nous, les Anglais? Nous avons tache de leur boucher le trou a Liege—et—il—nous—ont—abandonne. Enfin—allons boire un coup—"

Verdict: as translated by the ferocious interpreter:—

"Ze Court faind you Geeltee. You are condemned to Dess, and you will be shot on Monday."

In the prison of Saint-Gilles—as I believe elsewhere in Belgium—though there might be a military governor in control who was a German, the general direction remained in the hands of the Belgian staff which was there when the German occupation began. These Belgian directors and their subordinates were as kind and humane to the prisoners under their charge as the Germans were the reverse. Everything was done at Saint-Gilles to alleviate the mental agony of the condemned-to-death. The German courts tried to prolong and enhance the agony as much as possible, by sentencing the prisoners three days, six days, a week before the time of execution (though for fear of a reprieve this sentence was not immediately published) and letting them know that they had just so many days or hours to live: consequently most of them wasted away in prison with mind-agony, inability to sleep or eat; and even opiates or soporifics administered surreptitiously by the Belgian prison doctors were but slight alleviations.

Bertie when first placed in his cell at Saint-Gilles asked for pen, ink, and paper. They were supplied to him. He was allowed to keep on the electric light all night, and he distracted his mind—with some dreadful intervals of horror at his fate—by trying to set forth on paper for Vivie to read an explanation and an account of his adventures. He intended to wind up with an appeal for his wife and children.

Vivie never quite knew how Bertie had managed to cross the War zone from France into Belgium, and reach Brussels without being arrested. When they met in prison they had so little time to discuss such details, in face of the one awful fact that he was there, and was in all probability going to die in two days. But from this incomplete, tear-stained scribble that he left behind and from the answers he gave to her few questions, she gathered that the story of his quest was something like this:—

He had planned an attempt to reach her in Brussels or wherever she might be, from the autumn of 1914 onwards. The most practicable way of doing so seemed to be to pass as an American engaged in Belgian relief work, in the distribution of food. Direct attempts to be enrolled for such work proved fruitless, only caused suspicion; so he lay low. In course of time he made the acquaintance of one of those American agents of Mr. Hoover—a tousle-haired, hatless, happy-go-lucky, lawless individual, who made mock of laws, rules, precedents, and regulations. He concealed under a dry, taciturn, unemotional manner an intense hatred of the Germans. But he was either himself of enormous wealth or he had access to unlimited national funds. He spent money like water to carry out his relief work and was lavishly generous to German soldiers or civilians if thereby he might save time and set aside impediments. He took a strong liking to Bertie, though he showed it little outwardly. The latter probably in his naivete and directness unveiled his full purpose to this gum-chewing, grey-eyed American. When the news of Mrs. Warren's death had reached Bertie through a circuitous course—Praed-Honoria-Rossiter—he had modified his scheme and at the same time had become still more ardent about carrying it into execution. In fact he felt that Mrs. Warren's death was opportune, as with her still living and impossible to include in a flight, Vivie would probably have refused to come away.

Sir Harry Johnston

Therefore in the summer of 1916, he asked his American friend to obtain two American passports, one for himself and one for "his wife, Mrs. Violet Adams." Mr. Praed had sent him a credit for Five hundred pounds in case he could get it conveyed to Vivie. Bertie turned the credit into American bank notes. This money would help him to reach Brussels and once there, if Vivie would consent to pass as his wife, he might convey her out of Belgium into Holland, as two Americans working under the Relief Committee.

It had been excessively difficult and dangerous crossing the War zone and getting into occupied Belgium. There was some hint in his talk of an Alsatian spy who helped him at this stage, one of those "sanspatries" who spied impartially for both sides and sold any one they could sell (Fortunately after the Armistice most of these Judases were caught and shot). The spy had probably at first blackmailed him when he was in Belgium—which is why of the Five hundred pounds in dollar notes there only remained about a third in his possession when he reached Brussels—and then denounced him to the authorities, for a reward.

But his main misfortune lay in the long delay before he reached Brussels. During that time, the entire American diplomatic and consular staff was leaving Belgium; and the Emperor was arriving more or less secretly in Brussels (it was said in the hope that a personal talk with Brand Whitlock might stave off the American declaration of war).

Bertie on his arrival dared not to go to the American legation for fear of being found out and disavowed. So he had asked his way in very "English" French, and wearing the semi-military uniform of an American Relief officer—to the Hotel "Edward-Sett," where he supposed Vivie would be or could be heard of. When he reached the Hotel Imperial and asked for "Miss Warren," he had been at once arrested. Indeed probably his steps had been followed all the way from the railway station to the door of the hotel by a plain-clothes German policeman. The Germans were convinced just then that many Englishmen and some American cranks were out to assassinate the Kaiser. They took Bertie's appearance at the door of the Hotel Imperial as a proof of his intention. They considered him to have been caught red-handed, especially as he had a revolver concealed on his person and was obviously travelling with false passports.

"Ah, Bertie," said Vivie, when they first met in his cell at Saint-Gilles prison. "If *only* I had not led you into this! I am mad with myself..."

"Are you, miss? But 'oo could 'a foreseen this war would come along! We thought all we 'ad to fight was the Police and the 'Ome Office to get the Vote. And *then*, you'd 'a bin able to come out into the open and practise as a barrister— and me, again, as your clerk. It was our damned Government that made you go abroad and get locked up 'ere. And once I realized you couldn't get away, thinks I to meself, *I'll* find a way..."

It was here that Vivie began questioning him as to how he had reached Brussels from the War zone; and as, towards the end of his story—some of which he said she would find he had written down in case they wouldn't let him see her—the reference to the Emperor came in, she sprang up and tried the door of the cell. It was fastened without, but a face covered the small, square opening through which prisoners were watched; and a rough voice asked her what she wanted. It was the German police agent or spy, who, perched on a stool outside, next this small window, was there to listen to all they said. As they naturally spoke in English and the rough creature only knew "God-dam," and a few unrepeatable words, he was not much the wiser for his vigil.

"I want—I *must* see the Director," said Vivie.

Presently the Director came.

"Oh, sir," said Vivie, "give me paper and an envelope, I *implore* you. There is pen and ink here and I will write a letter to the Emperor, a petition. I will tell him briefly the true story of this poor young man; and *then*, if you will only forward it he may grant a reprieve."

The Director said he would do his best. After all, you never knew; and the Kaiser, though he said he hated them always, had a greater regard for the English than for any other nation. As he glanced from Vivie and her face of agonized appeal to the steadfast gaze which Bertie fixed on her, as on some fairy godmother, his own eyes filled with tears—as indeed they did many, many times over the tragic scenes of the German Terror.

Another request. Could Vivie see or communicate with Graefin von Stachelberg?—with Pasteur Walcker?

Here the police agent intervened—"Nothing of the kind! You're not going to hold a salon here. Far too many concessions already. Much more fuss and trouble, and I shall take you back to the Kommandantur and report. Write your letter to the All Highest, who may deign to receive it. As to Pastor Walcker, he shall come to-morrow, Sunday, to prepare the Englishman for his death, on Monday—"

Vivie wrote her letter—probably in very incoherent language. It was handed to the German police agent. He smiled sardonically as he took it in his horny hand with its dirty broken nails. The Governor General disliked these appeals to the All Highest. Indeed, in most cases executions that were intended to take place were only announced at the same time as the condemnation, to obviate the worry of these appeals. Besides, he knew the Emperor had left that morning for Charleville, after having bestowed several decorations on the police officials who told him they had just frustrated an English plot for his assassination.

Vivie and Bertie were at length alone, for the police agent was bored, couldn't understand their talk, and gave himself an afternoon off. In this prison of Saint-Gilles, the cells were in many ways superior to those of English prisons. They were well lit through a long window, not so high up but that by standing on a chair you could look out on the prison garden. Through this window the rays of the sun could penetrate into and light up the cell. There was no unpleasant smell—one of the horrors of Holloway. The floor was a polished parquet. The bed was comfortable. There was a table, even a book-shelf. The toilet arrangements were in no way repulsive or obvious.

Vivie insisted on Bertie lying down on the bed; she would sit on the chair by his side. He must be so exhausted....

"And what about *you*, miss? I'll lay you ain't slept these last three nights. *What* a mess I've made of the 'ole thing!"

"Bertie! *Why* did you do this? *Why* did you risk your life to come here; *oh why, oh why*?" wailed Vivie.

"Because I loved you, because I've always loved you, better'n any one else on earth—since I was a boy of fourteen and you spoke so kind to me and encouraged me to get on and improve myself; and giv' me books, and encouraged me about me cricket. I suppose I'm going to die, so I ain't got any shame about tellin' you all this. Though if I thought I was goin' to live, I'd cut my tongue out sooner'n offend you—Oh,"—he gave a kind of groan—"When the news come about Mrs. Warren bein' dead an' you p'raps without money and at the mercy of these Germans ... well!—all I wonder at is I didn't steal an airyplane, and come in that. I tell you I had to exercise great self-control to stay week after week fiddling with the food distribution and pretendin' to be an American....

"Well! There it is! We must all die sooner or later. It's a wonder I ain't dead already. I've bin in some tight places since I come out for the Y.M.C.A....

"And talkin' about the Y.M.C.A., miss, I do *beg* of you, if you get out of this—an' I'm sure you will—they'll never kill *you*," said Bertie adoringly, looking up at the grave, beautiful face that bent over him—"I do *beg* of you to make matters right with the Y.M.C.A. I ain't taken away one penny of their money—I served 'em faithfully up to the last day before I saw my chance of hooking it across the lines—They must think me dead—and so must poor Nance, my wife. For I haven't dared to write to any one since I've bin in Belgium. But I did send her a line 'fore I started, sayin', 'Don't be surprised if you get no letter from me for some time. I'll turn up all right, you bet your boots—'

"That may 'ave kept 'er 'opin'. An' soon you'll be able to let 'er know. Who can say? *I* dunno! But Peace, you'd think, must come soon—Seems like our poor old world is comin' to an end, don't it? *What* times we've 'ad—if you don't mind me puttin' it like that! I remember when I had to be awful careful always to say 'Sir' to you, and 'Mr. David' or 'Mr. Williams'" —and a roguish look, a gleam of merriment came into Bertie's eyes, and he laughed a laugh that was half sob. "If you was to write your life, no one 'ud believe it, miss. It licks any novel I ever read—and I've read a tidy few, looking after the Y.M.C.A. libraries....

"My! But you was wonderful as a pleader in the courts! I used sometimes to reg'lar cry when I heard you takin' up the case of some poor girl as 'ad bin deserted by 'er feller, and killed 'er baby. 'Tricks of the trade,' says some other barrister's clerk, sneerin' because you wasn't 'is boss. An' then I'd punch 'is 'ead.... An' I don't reckon myself a soft-'earted feller as a rule.... Reklect that Shillito Case—?"

"*Don't*, Bertie! *Don't* say such things in praise of me. I'm not *worth* such love. I'm just an arrogant, vain, quarrelsome woman.... Look how many people I've deceived, what little good I've really done in the world—"

"Rub—bish! You done good wherever you went ... to my pore mother—wonder, by the bye, what *she* thinks and 'ow *she's* gettin' on? Sons are awful ungrateful and forgettin'. What with you—and Nance—and the little 'uns, I ain't scarcely give a thought to poor mother. But you'll let her know, won't you, miss?...

"Think 'ow good you was to your old father down in Wales, 'im as you called your father—an' 'oo's to say 'e wasn't? You never know.... Miss Warren! what a pity it is you never married. There's lots was sweet on you, I'll bet. Yet I remember I used to 'ate the idea of your doin' so, and was glad you dressed up as a man, an' took 'em all in.... I may tell you all, miss, now I'm goin' to die, day after to-morrow. My poor Nance! She see there was some one that always occupied my mind, and she used to get jealous-like, at times. But never did I let on it was you. Why I wouldn't even 'av said it to myself—I respected you more than—than—"

And Bertie, at a loss for a parallel, ceased speaking for a time, and gulped down the sobs that were mastering him.

Then, after this pause—"I haven't a word to say against

Nance. No one could 'a bin a better wife. I know, miss, if you get away from here you'll look after her and my kids? I ain't bin much of a father to 'em lately. P'raps this is a punishment for neglecting my home duties—As they used to say to you when you was Suffragin'." He gave a bitter laugh—"Two such *nice* kids.... I ain't seen 'em since last February twelve-month ... more'n a year ago ... I got a bit of leave then.... There's little Vivie—the one we called after you.... She's growin' up so pretty ... and Bert! 'E'll be a bigger and a better man than me, some day. 'E's started in life with better chances. I 'ope 'e'll be a cricketer. There's no game comes up to cricket, in my opinion..."

At this juncture, the Belgian Directeur of the jail opened the door and asked Vivie to follow him, telling Bertie she would return in the afternoon. At the same time, a warder escorting two good conduct prisoners who did the food distribution proceeded to place quite an appetizing meal in Bertie's cell. "Dear miss," said the Directeur in French, "You are so wise, I know, you will do what I wish...?"

(Vivie bowed.)

"I shall not send you back to the Kommandantur. I will take that on myself. But I must regard you while here as my prisoner"—he smiled sadly—"Come with me. I will give you a nice cell where you shall eat and sleep, and—yes—and my wife shall come and see you..."

In the evening of that day, Vivie was led back to Bertie's cell. There she found kind Pasteur Walcker. In some way he had heard of Bertie's condemnation—perhaps seen it posted up on a Red Placard—and in his quiet assumption that whatever he did was right, had not waited for an official summons but had presented himself at the prison of Saint-Gilles and asked to see the Directeur. He constituted himself

Bertie's spiritual director from that time onwards.... He spoke very little English but he was there more to sympathize than to preach—

"Ce n'est pas, chere Mamselle que je suis venu le troubler sur les questions de religion. J'ai voulu le rassurer—et vous aussi—que j'ai deja mis en train tous les precedes possibles, et que je connais, pour obtenir sa grace.... But," he went on, "I have spoken to the prison doctor and begged him meantime to give the poor young man an injection or a dose of something to make him sleep a little while..."

Then he withdrew.

The daylight turned pink and faded to grey whilst Vivie sat by the bed holding the left hand of the sleeping man. Exhausted with emotion, she dropped off to sleep herself, slid off the chair on to the parquet, laid her head on the angle of his pillow and slept likewise....

The electric light suddenly shone out from a globe in the angle of the wall which served two cells. She awoke; Bertie awoke. He was still happy in some opiate dream and his eyes in his haggard face looked at her with a sleepy, happy affection. Loth to awaken him to reality she kissed him on the cheek and withdrew from the cell—for the Directeur, out of delicacy, had withdrawn and left the door ajar. She rejoined him in the corridor and he led her to her own quarters for the night; where, worn out with sorrow and fatigue, she undressed and slept dreamlessly.

But the hour of the awakening on that wintry Sunday morning! It was snowing intermittently and the sky, seen from the high window, was lead-coloured. Owing to the scarcity of fuel, the cell was unwarmed. She dressed hurriedly, feeling still untidy and dishevelled when she had finished. Her breakfast, and with it a little packet of white powder from the prison doctor, to be taken with the breakfast. She swallowed it. If it were poison sent by the German Government, what matter? But it was in reality some drug which took the edge off sorrow.

Bertie had evidently been given a similar dose. They spent the morning and the afternoon of that Sunday together, almost happily. With intervals of dreamy silence, they talked of old times. Neither would have been surprised had the cell walls dissolved as in a transformation scene and they had been able to step out into the Fountain Court of the Temple or into the cheerful traffic of Chancery Lane.

When however she returned to his cell after her evening meal, his mood had changed; the effect of the drug had passed. He had moods of despair and wild crying. No response had come, no answer to Vivie's appeal, no result from Monsieur Walcker's activities. Bertie reproached himself for cowardice ... then the doctor came in. "An injection in the arm? So! He will sleep now till morning. Esperons toujours! Et vous, ma pauvre Mademoiselle. Vous etes excedee. Permettez que je vous fasse la meme piqure?"

But she thanked him and said she wanted all her wits about her, though she promised "se maitriser"—to keep calm.

What a night! Her ears had a sense of hearing that was preternaturally acute. The most distant step in the corridors was audible. Was it a reprieve? One such sound multiplied itself into the footsteps of two men walking, coming ever nearer—nearer—nearer till they stopped outside her cell door. With a clank it was opened. She sprang up. Fortunately she had not undressed. "You've brought a reprieve?" she gasped. But the Directeur and Monsieur Walcker only stood with downcast faces. "It will soon be morning," the Directeur said. "There is no hope of a reprieve. He is to be executed at seven at the Tir National. All we have secured for you is permission to accompany him to the end. But if you think *that* too painful, too great a strain, I would suggest that you—"

"Nothing could overstrain me," said Vivie, "or rather I don't care if anything kills me. I will go with him and stay with him, till the very last moment, stay with him till he is buried if you permit!"

She made some hasty toilette, more because she wanted to look a fit companion for him, and not a wretched derelict. They summoned her, proffering a cup of acorn coffee, which she waved aside. The bitter cold air of the snowy April morning braced her. She entered the shuttered, armoured prison taxi in which Bertie and a soldier were placed already. Bertie had his arms tied, but not too painfully. He was shivering with the cold, but as he said, "*Not* afraid, miss. It'll come out allright, some'ow. That Mr. Walcker, 'e done me a lot of good. At any rate I'll show how an Englishman can die. 'Sides 'e says reprieves sometimes comes at the last moment. They takes a pleasure in tantalizin' you. And the doctor put somethin' in me cup of coffee, sort of keeps me spirits up."

But for Vivie, that drive was an unforgettable agony. They went through suburbs where the roads had been unrepaired or torn up by shrapnel. The snow lay in places so thickly that it nearly stopped the motor. Still, it came to an end at last. The door on one side was wrenched open; she was pulled out rather unceremoniously; then, the pinioned Bertie, who was handed over to a guard; and the soldier escort after him, who took his place promptly by his side. Vivie had just time to note the ugly red-brick exterior of the main building of the Tir National. It reminded her vaguely of some hastily-constructed Exhibition at Earl's Court or Olympia. Then she was pushed inside a swinging door, into a freezing corridor; where the Prison Directeur and Monsieur Walcker were standing—irresolute, weeping....

"Where is Bertie?" she asked.

"He is being prepared for the shooting party," they answered. "It will soon be over ... dear dear lady ... try to be calm—"

"I will be as calm as you like," she said, "I will behave with the utmost correctitude or whatever you call it, if you—if they—the soldiers—the officer—will let me see him—as you promised—up to the last, the very last. But by God—if there *is* a God—if you or they prevent me, I'll—"

Inexplicably, sheer mind-force prevailed, without the need for formulating the threat the poor grief-maddened woman might have uttered—she moved unresisted to a swing door which opened on to a kind of verandah. Here was drawn up the firing party, and in front of them, fifteen feet away on snow-sodden, trampled grass, stood Bertie. He caught sight of Vivie passing in, behind the firing party, and standing beyond them at the verandah rail. He straightened himself; ducked his head aside from the handkerchief with which they were going to bandage his eyes, and shouted "Take away your blasted handkerchief! *I* ain't afraid o' the guns. If you'll let me look at HER, I'll stand as quiet as quiet."

The officer in command of the firing party shrugged his shoulders. The soldier escort desisted from his attempts to blindfold the Englishman and stood aside, out of range. Bertie fixed his glowing eyes on the woman he had loved from his youth up, the rifles rang out with a reverberating bellow, and he fell out of her sight, screened by the soldiers, a crumpled body over which they threw a sheet.

What happened then to Vivie? I suppose you expect the time-worn trick of the weary novelist, anxious to put his pen down and go to his tea: "Then she seemed swallowed up in a cloud of blackness and knew no more"—till it was convenient to the narrator to begin a fresh chapter. But with me it must be the relentless truth and nothing but the truth, in all its aspects. Vivie was deafened, nearly stunned by the frightful noise of the volley in a confined space. Next, she was being unceremoniously pushed out of the verandah, into the corridor, and so out into the snow-covered space in front of the brick building; whilst the officer was examining the dead body of the fallen man, ready to give the *coup-de-grace*, if he were not dead. But he was. Vivie was next conscious that she had the most dreadful, blinding headache she had ever known, and with it felt an irresistible nausea. The prison Directeur was taking her hand and saying: "Mademoiselle: it is my duty to inform you that you are no longer under arrest. You are free to return to your lodging." Minna von Stachelberg had come from somewhere and was taking her right arm, to lead her Brussels-ward; and Pasteur Walcker was ranging himself alongside to be her escort. Unable to reply to any of them, she strode forward by herself to where under the snow lay an ill-kept grass plot, and there was violently sick. The anaesthetics and soporifics of the last two days were having their usual aftermath. After that came on a shuddering faintness and a rigor of shivers, under which her teeth clacked. Some doctor came forward with a little brandy. She put the glass to her lips, then pushed it aside, took Pasteur Walcker's proffered arm, and walked towards the tram terminus.

Then they were in the tram, going towards the heart of Brussels. How commonplace! Fat frowsy market women got in—or got out—with their baskets; clerks entered with portfolios—don't they call them "serviettes"?—under their arms; German policemen, Belgian gendarmes, German soldiers, a priest with his breviary came and went as though this Monday morning were like any other. Vivie walked quite firmly and staidly from the tram halt to the Walckers' house in the Rue Haute. There she was met by Madame Walcker, who at a sign from her husband took her upstairs, silently undressed her and put her to bed with a hot water bottle and a cup of some hot drink which tasted a little of coffee.

After that Vivie passed three days of great sickness and nausea, a furred tongue, and positively no appetite. Finally she arose a week after the execution and looked at herself in the mirror. She was terribly haggard, she looked at least fifty-five—"They must have taken me for his mother or his aunt; never for his sweetheart," she commented bitterly to herself. And her brown-gold hair was now distinctly a cinder grey.

The next day she went back to work at the hospital.

To Minna, she said: "I can *never, never, never* forget your kindness and sympathy. 'Sister' seems an insufficient name to call you by. Whatever happens, unless you cast me off, we shall be friends.... I dare say I even owe my life to you, if it is worth anything. But it is. I want to live—now—I want to live to be revenged. I want to live to help Bertie's"—her voice still shook over the name—"Bertie's wife and children. I expect but for you I should have been tried already in the Senate for complicity with ... Bertie ... and found guilty and shot..."

Minna: "I won't go so far as to say you are right. But I certainly *was* alarmed about you, when you were arrested. Of course I knew nothing—*nothing*—about that poor young man till just before his execution when Pastor Walcker came to me. Even then I could do nothing, and I understood so badly what had happened. But about you: I said to myself, if I do not do *something*, you can perhaps be sentenced to imprisonment ... and I *did* bestir myself, you can bet!" (Minna liked to show she knew a slangy phrase or two.) "So I telegraphed to the Emperor, I besieged von Bissing at the Ministere des Sciences et des Arts; wrote to him, telegraphed to him, telephoned to him, sat in his anterooms, neglected my hospital work entirely from Friday to Monday—

"I expect as a matter of fact they found nothing in that poor young's man's papers to implicate you. They just wanted—the brutes—to give you a good fright ... and I dare say ... such is the military mind—even wished you to see him shot.

"By the bye, I suppose you have heard that von Bissing is very ill? Dying, perhaps—"

Vivie: "I *hope* so. I am *so* glad. I hope it's a painful illness and that he'll die and find there really *is* a Hell, and an uncommonly hot one!"

It must not be supposed from the frequent quotations from Countess von Stachelberg's condemnations of German cruelties that she was an unpatriotic woman, repudiating, apostatizing from her own country. On the contrary: she held—mistakenly or not—that Germany had been the victim of secret diplomacy, had been encircled by a ring fence of enemies, refused the economic guarantees she required, and the colonial expansion she desired. Minna disliked the Slavs, did not believe in them, save as musicians, singers, painters, dancers, and actors. She believed Germany had a great civilizing, culture-spreading mission in South-east Europe; and that the germs of this war lay in the policy of Chamberlain, the protectionism of the United States, the revengeful spirit and colonial selfishness of France.

But she shuddered over the German cruelties in Belgium and France. The horrors of War were a revelation to her and she was henceforth a Pacifist before all things. "*Your* old statesmen and *our* old or middle-aged generals, my dear, are alike to blame. But you and I know where the *real* mischief lies. We are mis-ruled by an All-Man Government. *I,* certainly, don't want the other extreme, an All-Woman Government. What we want, and must have, is a Man-and-Woman—a Married—Government. *Then* we shall settle our differences without going to war."

Vivie agreed with her, cordially.

She—Vivie—I really ought to begin calling her "Vivien": she is forty-one by now—in resuming her duties at the Hopital de St. Pierre found no repugnance in tending wounded German soldiers—the officers she did shrink from—She realized that the soldiers were but the slaves of the officer class, of Kaiserdom. Her reward for this degree of Christianity was to have a batch of wounded English boys or men to look after. She saw again Bertie Adams in many of them, especially in the sergeants and corporals. They, in turn, thought her a very handsome, stately lady, but rather maudlin at times. "So easy to set 'er off a-cryin' as though 'er 'eart would break, poor thing.... And I says 'why ma'am, the pain's *nuthin*', nuthin' to what it use ter be.' 'Spec' she lost some son in the war. Wonder 'ow she came to be 'ere? Ain't the Germans afraid of 'er!"...

They were. The mental agony she had been through had etherialized her face, added to its look of age and gravity, but imparted likewise a sort of "awfulness." She exhaled an aura of righteous authority. She had been through the furnace, and foolishness and petulance had been burnt out of her ... though, thank goodness, she retained some sense of humour. She had probably never been so handsome from the painter's point of view, though one could not imagine a young man falling in love with her now.

Her personality was first definitely noted by the Bruxellois the day that von Bissing's funeral cortege passed through the streets of Brussels on its way to Germany. Vivien Warren was sufficiently restored to health then to stand on the steps of some monument and cry "Vive la Belgique! A bas les tyrans!" The policemen and the spies looked another way and affected deafness. They had orders not to arrest her unless she actually resorted to firearms or other lethal weapons.

It was said that her appeal for Bertie Adams did reach the Emperor, two days too late; that he pished and pshawed over von Bissing's cruel precipitancy. "Englishmen," he muttered to his entourage, "don't assassinate. The Irish do. But *how* I'm going to make peace with England, *I* don't know...!"

(His Hell on Earth must have been that few people admired the English character more than he did, and yet, unprovoked, he had blundered into war with England.)

However, though it was too late to save "this lunatic Adams," he gave orders that Vivie was to be let alone. He even, through Graefin von Stachelberg, transmitted to her his regrets that she and her mother had been treated so cavalierly at the Hotel Imperial. It was not through any orders of his.

So: Vivie became quite a power in Brussels during that last anxious year and a half of waiting, between May, 1917, and November, 1918. German soldiers, still limping from their wounds, saluted her in the street, remembering her kindness in hospital, and the letters she unweariedly wrote at their dictation to their wives and families—for she had become quite a scholar in German. The scanty remains of the British

Colony and the great ladies among the patriotic Belgians now realized how false were the stories that had circulated about her in the first year of the War; and extended to her their friendship. And the Spanish Minister who had taken the place of the American as protector of British subjects, invited her to all the fetes he gave for Belgian charities and Red Cross funds. Through his Legation she endeavoured to send information to the Y.M.C.A. and to Bertie's widow that Albert Adams of the Y.M.C.A. "had died in Brussels from the consequences of the War."

I dare say in the autumn of 1917, if Vivien Warren had applied through the Spanish Minister for a passport to leave Belgium for some neutral country, it would have been accorded to her: the German authorities would have been thankful to see her no more. She reminded them of one of the cruellest acts of their administration. But she preferred to stay for the historical revenge of seeing the Germans driven out of Belgium, and Belgian independence restored. And she could not go lest Bertie's grave should be forgotten. In common with Edith Cavell, Gabrielle Petit, Philippe Bauck, and the other forty or fifty victims of von Bissing's "Terror," he had been buried in the grassy slopes of the amphitheatre of the Rifle range, near where he had been executed. Every Sunday, wet or fine, Vivien went there with fresh flowers. She had marked the actual grave with a small wooden cross bearing his name, till the time should come when she could have his remains transferred to English soil.

One day, as she was leaving the hospital in the autumn of 1917, a shabby man pushed into her hand a soiled, way-worn copy of the *Times*, a fortnight old. "Three francs," he whispered. She paid him. It was no uncommon thing for her or one of her English or Belgian acquaintances to buy the *Times* or some other English daily at a price ranging from one franc to ten, and then pass it round the friendly circle of subscribers who apportioned the cost. On this occasion she opened her *Times* in the tram, going home, and glanced at its columns. In any one but "Mees Varennes" in these days of 1917, 1918, this would have been a punishable offence; but in her case no spy or policeman noted the infringement of regulations about the enemy press. On one of the pages she read the account of a bad air-raid on Portland Place, and a reference—with a short obituary notice elsewhere—to the death of one of the victims of the German bombs. This was "Linda, Lady Rossiter, the dearly loved wife of Sir Michael Rossiter, whose discoveries in the way of bone grafting and other forms of curative surgery had been among the outstanding achievements in etc., etc."

"Dear me!" said Vivien to herself, as the tram coursed on beyond her usual stopping place and the conductor obstinately looked the other way, "I'm glad she lived to be *Lady* Rossiter. It must have given her such pleasure. Poor thing! And to think the knowledge that he's a widower hardly stirs my pulses one extra beat. And how I *loved* that man, seven years, six years, five years ago! Hullo! Where am I? Miles from the Rue Haute! Conducteur! Arretez, s'il vous plait."

CHAPTER XX

AFTER THE ARMISTICE

The Bruxellois felt very disheartened in the closing months of 1917. The Russian revolution had brought about the collapse of Russia as an enemy of Germany; and the Germans were enabled to transport most of their troops on the Russian frontier to the west and to the Italian frontier. Italy had lost half Venetia and enormous quantities of guns in the breach of her defences at Caporetto. It seemed indeed at any moment, when the ice and snow of that dreadful winter of 1917-18 melted, as though Italy would share the fate of Rumania. Though the British army had had a grand success with their Tanks, they had, ere 1917 ended, lost nearly all the ground gained round Cambrai. Besides, the submarine menace was imperilling the British food supplies and connections with America. As to the United States: was their intervention going to be more than money loans and supplies of material? Would they really supply the fighting men, the one thing at this crisis necessary to defeat Germany?

Belgium had been divided administratively into two distinct portions, north and south of the Meuse. North of the Meuse she was to be a Dutch-speaking country either part of Germany eventually, or given to Holland to compensate her for her very benevolent neutrality towards Germany during the War. A handful of Flemish adventurers appeared at Brussels to form the Council of Flanders, and sickened the Bruxellois by their lavish praise of the German administration and servile concurrence with all German measures.

The events of the spring of 1918 accentuated the despair in the Belgian capital. When the Germans broke through the defences of the new lines which ran through Picardy and Champagne, reached the vicinity of Amiens, retook Soissons, and recrossed the Marne, it seemed as though Belgian independence had been lost; the utmost she could hope for would be the self-government of a German province.

But Vivie was not among the pessimists. She discerned a smouldering discontent among the German soldiers, even when Germany seemed near to a sweeping victory over France and Britain.

The brutality of the soldiers, their deliberate, nasty dirtiness during the first two years of the War seemed due rather to their officers' orders than to an anti-human disposition of their own. Many of the soldiers in Belgium, in Brussels, turned round—so to speak—and conceived a horror of what they had done, of what they had been told to do. Men who on the instigation of their officers—and these last, especially the Prussians, seemed fiends incarnate—had offered violence to young Belgian women, ended by offering to marry them, even showed themselves kind husbands, only too willing to become domesticated, groaning at having to leave their temporary homes and return to the terrible fighting on the Yser or in France.

There were, for example, the soldiers stationed at the Villa Beau-sejour and at the Oudekens' farm. Vivie had a growing

Sir Harry Johnston

desire to find out what had happened to her mother's property. One day, late in February, 1918, when there was a premature breath and feeling of Spring in the air, she called on her friend—as he had become—the Directeur of the Prison of Saint-Gilles, and asked him—since she herself could not deign to ask any favour or concession of the German authorities—to obtain for her a permit to proceed to Tervueren, the railway service between Brussels and that place having been reopened. She walked over—with what reminiscences the roads and paths were filled—to the Villa, and showing her pass was received, not uncivilly, by the sergeant-major in charge. Fortunately the officers had all gone, voting it very dull, with Brussels so near and yet so far. After their departure the sergeant-major and his reduced guard of men had begun to make the place more homelike. The usual German thrift had shown itself. They had reassembled the remains of Mrs. Warren's herd of cows. These had calves and were giving milk. There were once more the beginnings of a poultry yard. The rooms had been cleaned at any rate of their unspeakable filth, though the dilapidations and the ruined furniture made tears of vexation stand in Vivie's eyes. However she kept her temper and told the sergeant that it was *her* property now; that she intended to reclaim it at the end of the War, and that if he saw to it that the place was handed back to her with no further damage, she would take care that he was duly rewarded; and as an instalment she gave him a good tip. He replied with a laugh and a shrug "That may well come about." ("Das koennte wohl geschehen.")

He had already heard of the Englaenderin whom the Kommandantur was afraid to touch, and opened his heart to her; even offering to prepare her a little meal in her own *salle a manger*. With what strange sensations she sat down to it. The sergeant as he brought in the *oeufs au plat* said the soldiers were already sick of the War. Most wanted to go back to Germany, but a few were so much in love with Belgium that they hoped they might be allowed to settle down there; especially those who spoke Platt-deutsch, to whom Flemish came so easy.

From Villa Beau-sejour, Vivien Warren passed on to the Oudekens' farm, wondering what she would see—Some fresh horror? But on the contrary, Mme. Oudekens looked years younger; indeed when Vivien first stood outside the house door, she had heard really hearty laughter coming from the orchard where the farmer's widow was pinning up clothes to dry. Yet it was here that the woman's husband had been shot and buried, as the result of a field-court's sentence.

But when she answered Vivien's questions, after plying her with innumerable enquiries, she admitted with a blush that Heinrich, the German sergeant, with whom she had first cohabited by constraint, had recently married her at the Mairie, though the Cure had refused to perform the religious service. Heinrich was now invariably kind and worked hard on the farm. He hoped by diligently supplying the officers' messes in Brussels with poultry and vegetables that he and his assistants—two corporals—might be overlooked and not sent back into the fighting ranks. As to her daughters, after a few months of promiscuity—a terrible time that Mme. Oudekens wanted to forget—they had been assigned to the two corporals as their exclusive property. They were both of them about to become mothers, and if no one interfered, as soon as this accursed War was over their men would marry them. "But," said Vivie, "suppose your husband and these corporals are married already, in Germany?" "Qu'est-ce-que ca fait?" said Mme. Oudekens. "C'est si loin." By making these little concessions she had already saved her youngest son from deportation to Germany.

The enormous demands for food in Brussels, which in 1918

Sir Harry Johnston

had a floating population of over a million and where the Germans were turning large dogs into pemmican, had tripled the value of all productive farms so near the capital as those round Tervueren, especially now the railway service was reopened. Many of the peasants were making huge fortunes in complicity with some German soldier-partner.

In Brussels itself, soldiers often sided with the people against the odious "polizei," the intolerable German spies and police agents. Conflicts would sometimes occur in the trams and the streets when the German police endeavoured to arrest citizens for reading the *Times* or *La Libre Belgique*, or for saying disrespectful things about the Emperor.

The tremendous rush of the German offensive onward to the Marne, Somme, and Ypres salient in March-June, 1918, was received by the shifting garrison of Brussels with little enthusiasm. Would it not tend to prolong the War? The German advance into France was spectacular, but it was paid for by an appalling death-roll. The hospitals at Brussels were filled to overflowing with wounded and dying men. The Austrians who were brought from the Italian front to replenish the depleted battalions, quarrelled openly with the Prussians, and in some cases had to be surrounded in a barrack square and shot down.

The first real check to the German Army in its second march on Paris—that which followed its crossing of the Marne near Dormans—was prophetically greeted by the Bruxellois as the turning of the tide. The Emperor had gone thither from the Hotel Imperial in order to witness and follow the culminating march on Paris. But Foch now struck with his reserves, and the head of the tortoise was nipped off. The driving back of the Germans over the Marne coincided with the Belgian National Fete of July 21. Not since 1914 had this fete been openly observed. But on this day in 1918, the

German police made no protest when a huge crowd celebrated the fete day in every church and every street. Vivien herself, smiling and laughing as she had not done since Bertie's death, attended the service in Sainte-Gudule and joined in singing *La Brabanconne* in place of *Te Deum, laudamus*. In the streets and houses of Brussels every piano, every gramophone was enrolled to play the *Marseillaise, Vers l'Avenir*, and *La Brabanconne*, the Belgian national anthem (uninspiring words and dreary tune). From this date onwards—July 21—the German *debacle* proceeded, with scarcely one day's intermission, with never a German regain of lost ground.

When the Americans had retaken St. Mihiel on September 14, then did Belgians boldly predict that their King would be back in Brussels by Christmas. But their prophecies were outstripped by events. Already, in the beginning of October, the accredited German Press in Belgium was adjuring the Belgians not to be impatient, but to let them evacuate Belgium quietly. At the end of October, Minna von Stachelberg told Vivien that she and the other units of the German Red Cross had received instructions to leave and hand over their charges to the Belgian doctors and nurses. The two women took an affectionate farewell of each other, vowing they would meet again—somewhere—when the War was over. British wounded now began to cease coming into Brussels, so Vivie was free to attend to her own affairs.

Enormous quantities of German plunder were streaming out of Belgium by train, by motor, in military lorries, in carts and waggons. Nearly all this belonged to the officers, and the already-rebellious soldiers broke out in protestations. "Why should they who had done all the fighting have none of the loot?" So they won over the Belgian engine-drivers— delighted to see this quarrel between the hyenas—and held up the trains in the suburban stations north of Brussels. There were pitched battles which ended always in the soldiers' victory.

The soldiers then would hold auctions and markets of the plunder captured in the trains and lorries. They were in a hurry to get a little money to take back with them to Germany. Vivie, who had laid her plans now as to what to do after the German evacuation of Brussels, attended these auctions. She was nearly always civilly treated, because so many German soldiers had known her as a friend in hospital and told other soldiers. At one such sale she bought a serviceable motor-car for 750 francs; at another drums of petrol.

She had provided herself with funds by going to her mother's bank and reopening the question of the deposited jewels and plate. Now that the victory of the Allies seemed certain, the bank manager was more inclined to make things easy for her. He had the jewels and plate valued—roughly—at L3,000; and although he would not surrender them till the will could be proved and she could show letters of administration, he consented on behalf of the bank to make her a loan of 30,000 francs.

On November 10th, a German soldier who followed Vivien about with humble fidelity since she had cured him of a bad whitlow—and also because, as he said, it was a joy to speak English once more—for he had been a waiter at the Savoy Hotel—came to her in the Boulevard d'Anspach and said "The Red flag, lady, he fly from Kommandantur. With us I think it is Kaput." This was what Vivien had been waiting for. Asking the man to follow her, she first stopped outside a shop of military equipment, and after a brief inspection of its goods entered and purchased a short, not too flexible riding-whip, with a heavy handle. Then as the trams were densely crowded, she walked at a rapid pace—glancing round ever and again to see that her German soldier was following—up the Boulevard du Jardin Botanique and along the Rue Royale until she came to the Hotel Imperial. Here she halted for a minute to have the soldier close behind her; then gave the revolving door a turn and found herself and him in the marble hall once built for Mrs. Warren's florid taste. "Call the Manager," she said—trying not to pant—to two Belgian servants who came up, a porter and a lift man. The Manager—he who had ejected her and her mother in 1915— was fortunately a little while in appearing. He was really packing up with energy so as to depart with all the plunder he could transport before the way of escape was closed. This little delay enabled Vivien to get her breath and resume an impressive calm.

"Well: what you want?" the Manager said insolently, recollecting her.

"This first," she said, seizing him suddenly by his coat collar.

"I want—to—give—you—the—soundest—thrashing you have ever had..."

And before he could offer any effective resistance she had lashed him well with the riding *cravache* about the shoulders, hands, back and face. He wrenched himself free and crouched ready for a counter attack. But the Belgian servants intervened and tripped him up; and the German soldier—the ex-waiter from the Savoy—said that Madame was by nature so kind that there must some good reason for this chastisement.

"There is," she replied, now she had got her breath and was inwardly feeling ashamed at her resort to such violent methods.

"Three years ago, this creature turned my mother and myself out of this hotel with such violence that my mother died of it a few minutes afterwards. He stole our money and much of our property. I have inherited from my mother, to whom this hotel once belonged, a right over certain rooms which she used to occupy. I resume that right from to-day. I shall go to them now. As to this wretch, throw him out on to the pavement. He can afterwards send for his luggage, and what really is his he shall have."

Her orders were executed.

She then sent a message to Mme. Walcker and to the kind tea-shop woman, Mme. Trouessart, close by, explaining what she had done and why. "I shall take control of this hotel in the name of the Belgian Company that owns it, a Company in which, through my mother, I possess shares. I shall stay here till responsible persons take it over and I shall resume possession of the *appartement* that belonged to my mother." Meantime, would Madame Trouessart engage a few stout wenches to eke out the scanty hotel staff, most of which being German had already commenced its flight back to the fatherland with all the plunder it could carry off. The soldier-ex-hotel-waiter was provisionally engaged to remain, as long as the Belgian Government allowed him, and three stalwart British soldiers, until the day before prisoners-of-war, were enlisted in her service and armed with revolvers to repel any ordinary act of brigandage.

By the end of November she had the Hotel Edouard-Sept— with the old name restored—running smoothly and ready for the new guests—British, French officers and civilians who would follow the King of the Belgians on his return to his capital. The re-established Belgian authorities soon put her into possession of the Villa Beau-sejour. The German sergeant-major here had kept faith with her, and in return for handing over everything intact, including the herd of cows, received a *douceur* which amply rewarded him for this belated honesty before he, too, set his face towards Germany with the rest of the evacuating army. The motor-car she had bought enabled her to fetch supplies of food from farm to hotel and to perform many little services to Belgians who were returning to their old homes. Madame Trouessart, not as yet having any stock of tea with which to reopen her tea-shop to the first incoming of curious tourists, agreed to live with Miss Warren at the hotel and act as her deputy, if affairs took her away from Brussels.

It was at the Hotel Edouard-Sept, the place where she had been born, that Rossiter met her when he arrived in Brussels after the Armistice. She felt a little tremulous when his card was sent up to her, and kept him waiting quite five minutes while she saw that her hair was tidy and estimated before the glass the extent to which it had gone grey. She had let it grow of late years—the days of David Williams and Mr. Michaelis seemed very remote—and spent some time and consideration in arranging it. Her costume was workmanlike and that of an hotel manageress in the morning; yet distinctly set off her figure and suited her character of an able-bodied, intellectual woman.

* * * * *

"Vivie!"

"Michael!"

"My *dear*! You're handsomer than ever!"

"Michael! Your khaki uniform becomes you; and I'm *so* glad you've got rid of that beard. *Now* we can see your well-shaped chin. But still: we mustn't stand here, paying one another compliments, though this meeting is *too* wonderful: I never thought I should see you again. Let's come to realities. I suppose the real heart-felt question at the back of your mind is: *can* I let you have a room? I can, but not a bath-room suite; they're all taken..."

Michael: "Nonsense! I'm going to be put up at the Palace Hotel. Jenkins—you remember the butler of old time?—Jenkins, and my batman, a refined brigand, a polished robber, have already been there and commandeered something....

"No. I came here, firstly to find out if you were living; secondly to ask you to marry me" ... (a pause) ... "and thirdly to find out what happened to Bertie Adams. A message came through the Spanish Legation here, a year and a half ago, to the effect that he had died at Brussels from the consequences of the War. However, unless you can tell me at once this is all a mistake, we can go into his affairs later. My first question is—Oh! Bother all this cackle.... *Will* you marry me?"

Vivie: "Dear, brave Bertie, whom I shall everlastingly mourn, was shot here in Brussels by the abominable Germans, as a spy, on April 8th, 1917. He was of course no more a spy than you are or I am. The poor devoted fool—I rage still, because I shall never be worth such folly, such selfless devotion—got into Belgium with false passports—American: in the hope of rescuing me. He came and enquired here—my last address in his remembrance—and came by sheer bad luck just as the Kaiser was about to arrive. They jumped to the conclusion that—"

Rossiter: "*Awfully, cruelly* sad. But you can give me the details of it later on. You must have a long, long story of your own to tell which ought to be of poignant interest.

But ... will you marry me? I suppose you know dear Linda died—was killed by a bomb in a German air-raid last year—October, 1917. I really felt *heart-broken* about it, but I know now I am only doing what she would have wished. She came at last to talk about you *quite* differently, *quite* understanding—"

Vivie: "That's what all widowers say. They always declare the dead wife begged them to marry again, and even designated her successor. Poor Linda! Yes, I read an account of it in a copy of the *Times*; but I couldn't of course communicate with you to say how *truly, truly* sorry I was. I am glad to know she spoke nicely of me. Did she really? Or have you only made it up?"

Michael: "*Of course* I haven't. She really did. Do you know, she and I quite altered after the War began? She lost all her old silliness and inefficiency—or at any rate only retained enough of the old childishness to make her endearing. And I really grew to love her. I quite forgot you. Yes: I admit it....

"But somehow, after she was dead the old feeling for you came back ... and without any disloyalty to Linda. I felt in a way—I know it is an absurd thing for a man of science to say, for we have still no proof—I felt somehow as though she lived still. That's why I don't want to get rid of the Park Crescent house. Her presence seems to linger there. But I also knew—instinctively—that she would like us to come together.... She..."

Waiter (knocking at door and slightly opening it): "Madame! Le General Tompkins veut vous voir. Il ajoute qu'il n'est pas habitue a attendre. Il y a aussi M'sieur Emile Vandervelde, qui arrive instamment et qui n'a pas d'installation..."

Rossiter: "Damn! Let me go and settle with 'em. Tompkins! I never heard such cheek—"

Vivien: "Not at all. You forget I am Manageress." (To Waiter) "Entrez donc! Dites au General que je serai a sa disposition dans trois minutes; et montrez-lui ce que nous avons en fait de chambres. Tous les appartements avec bain sont pris. Casez M'sieur Vandervelde quelque part. Du reste, je descendrai."... (Waiter goes out) ... "Michael! It is impossible to have a sentimental conversation here, and at this hour—Eleven o'clock on a busy morning. If you want an answer to your second question, now you've seen me, meet me outside the Palm House of the Jardin Botanique, at 3 p.m. I'll get off somehow for an hour just then. Don't forget! It's close by here—along the Rue Royale. Be absolutely punctual, or else I shall think that having *seen* me, seen how changed I am, you have altered your mind. I shall *quite* understand; only I *may* come back at five minutes past three and accept General Tompkins. Acquaintances ripen quickly in Brussels."

* * * * *

In the Palm House—or rather one of its many compartments; 3.5 p.m., on a beautiful afternoon in early December. The sun is sinking over outspread Brussels in a pink and yellow haze radiating from the good-humoured-looking, orange orb. There are no other visitors to the Palm House, at any rate not to this compartment, except the superintending gardener— the same that cheered the last hours of Mrs. Warren. He recognizes Vivien and salutes her gravely. Seeing that she is accompanied by a gentleman in khaki he discreetly withdraws out of hearing and tidies up a tree fern. Vivien and Michael seat themselves on two green iron chairs under the fronds and in front of grey stems.

Vivie: "This is a favourite place of mine for assignations. I can't think why it is so little appreciated by young Brussels. These palm houses are much more beautiful than anything at Kew; they are in the heart of Brussels, over which, as you see, you have a wonderful view. It was much more frequented when the Germans were here. With all their brutality they did not injure this unequalled collection of Tropical plants. They made the Palm House an allowance of coal and coke in winter while we poor human beings went without. I used often to come in here on a winter's day to get warm and to forget my sorrows....

"Look at that superb Raphia—*what* fronds! And that Phoenix spinosa—and that Aralia—"

Rossiter: "Bother the Aralia. I haven't come here for a Botany lesson. Besides, it isn't an Aralia; it's a Gompho-carpus.... Vivie! *Will* you marry me?"

Vivie: "My dear Michael: I was forty-three last October."

Michael: "I was *fifty-three* last November, the day the Armistice was signed. But I feel more like thirty-three. Life in camp has quite rejuvenated me..."

Vivie (continuing): ... "And my hair is cinder grey—an unfortunate transition colour. And if the gardener were not looking I should say: 'Feel my elbows ... Dreadfully bony! And my face has become..." She turns her face towards him. He sees tears trembling on the lower lashes of her grey eyes, but something has come into the features, some irradiation of love—is it the light of the sunset?—which imparts a tender youthfulness to the curvature of cheek, lips and chin. Her face, indeed, might be of any age: it held the undying beauty of a goddess, in whom knowledge has sweetened to tender-ness and divinity has dissolved in a need for compassion; and the youthful assurance of a happy woman whose wish at last is won....

For a minute she looks at him without finishing her sentence. Then she sits up straighter and says explicitly: "Yes, I will."

* * * * *

The gardener managed an occasional peep at them, sitting hand in hand. He wished the idyll to last as long as the clear daylight, but the hour for closing was four o'clock—"Il n'y avait pas a nier." Either they were husband and wife, reunited, after years of war-severance; or they were mature lovers, and probably of the most respectable. In either case, the necessary hint that ecstasies must transfer themselves at sunset from the glass houses of the Jardin Botanique to the outer air was best conveyed on this occasion by a discreet gift of flowers. Accordingly he went on to where exotic lilies were blooming, picked a few blossoms, returned, came with soft padding steps up to Vivie, offered them with a bow and "Mes felicitations *sinceres*, Madame." Vivie laughed and took the lilies; Rossiter of course gave him a ten-franc note. And they sauntered slowly back to the hotel.

L'ENVOI

I am reproached by such Art Critics as deign to notice my pictures with "finishing my foregrounds over much,"— filling them with superabundant detail, making the primroses more important than the snow-peaks. And by my publishers with forgetting the price of paper and the cost of printing. My jury of matrons thinks I don't know where to leave off and that I might very well close this book on the answer that Mrs. Warren's daughter gave to Sir Michael Rossiter's proposal of marriage in the Palm House at Brussels. "The reader," they say, "can very well fill in the rest of the story for himself or herself. It is hardly likely that Vivie will cry off at the last moment, or Michael reconsider the plunge into a second marriage. Why therefore waste print and paper and our eyesight in describing the marriage ceremony, the inevitable visit to Honoria, and what Vivie did with the property she inherited from her mother?"

No doubt they are all right. Yet I am distrustful of my readers' judgment and imagination. I feel both want guiding, and I doubt their knowledge of the world and goodness of heart being equal to mine, except in rare cases.

So I throw out these indications to influence the sequels they may plan to this story.

I think that Michael and Vivie were married at the British Legation in Brussels between Christmas and the New Year of 1918-1919; before that Legation was erected into an Embassy; and that the marriage officer was kind, genial Mr. Hawk when he returned to Brussels from The Hague and proceeded to get the Legation into working order. I am sure Mr. Hawk entered into the spirit of the thing and gave an informal breakfast afterwards in the Rue de Spa to which Mons. and Mme. Walcker, Mons. and Mme. Trouessart, and the Directeur of the prison of Saint-Gilles and his wife were invited. I think the head gardener of the Jardin Botanique who had charge of the Tropical houses cribbed from the collections some of the most magnificent blooms, and presented them to Vivie on the morning of her marriage; and that afterwards she laid the bouquet on her mother's newly finished tomb in the cemetery of St. Josse-ten-Noode, where, the weather being singularly mild for the time of year, the flowers lasted fresh and blooming for several days.

I am sure she and Michael then crossed the road and passed on to the building of the Tir National; entered it and stood for a moment in the verandah from which Vivie had seen Bertie Adams executed; and passed on over the tussocky grass to the graves of Bertie Adams and Edith Cavell, where they did silent homage to the dead. I believe a few days afterwards they visited the Senate where the victims of von Bissing's "Terror" had been tried, browbeaten, insulted, mocked. And the functionary who showed them over this superb national palace is certain to have included in his exposition the once splendid carpets which the German officers prior to their evacuation of the Senate—all but the legislative chamber of which was used as a barracks for rough soldiery—had sprayed and barred, streaked and splodged with printing ink. He would also have pointed out the three-hundred-year-old tapestries they had ripped from the walls and the historical portraits they had slashed, and would again have emphasized the fact that in all these senseless devastations the officers were far worse than the men.

Also I am certain that Michael and Vivie made a pilgrimage to the prison of Saint-Gilles, and stood silently in the cell where Bertie Adams and Vivie had spent those terrible days of suspense and despair between April 6 and April 8, 1917; and that when they entered that other compartment of the prison where Edith Cavell had passed her last days before her execution, they listened with sympathetic reverence to the recital by the Directeur of verses from "l'Hymne d'Edith Cavell"—as it is now called—no other than the sad old poem of human sorrow, *Abide with me*; and that they appreciated to the full the warmth of Belgian feeling which has turned the cell of Edith Cavell into a Chapelle Ardente in perpetuity.

I think they returned to England in January, 1919, so that Michael might get back quickly to his work of mending the maimed, now transferred to English hospitals; and so that Vivie—always a practical woman—should prove her mother's will, secure her heritage and have it in hand as a fund from which to promote all the happiness she could. I doubt whether she will give much of it to "causes" rather than cases and to politics in preference to persons. I think she was awfully disgusted when she was back in the England of to-day not to find Mrs. Fawcett Prime Ministress and First Lady of the Treasury, Annie Kenney at the Board of Trade and Christabel Pankhurst running the Ministry of Health. It was disheartening after the long struggle for the Woman's Vote and the equality of the sexes in opportunity to find the same old men-muddlers in charge of all public affairs and departments of state, and the only woman on the benches of the House of Commons a millionaire peeress never before identified with the struggle for the Woman's Cause.

However I think her disenchantment did not diminish the rapture at finding herself once more in the intimacy of Honoria Armstrong. Sir Petworth, when he ran over on leave from the Army of Occupation, thought her enormously improved, though he had the tact not to say so. He frankly made the *amende honorable* for his suspicions and churlishness of the past, and himself—I think—insisted on his frank and friendly children calling her "Aunt Vivie." I am equally sure that Vivie was not long in London before she appeared at dear old Praddy's studio, beautifully gowned and looking years younger than forty-three; and I shouldn't wonder but that her presence once more in his circle will give his frame a fillip so that he may cheat Death over a few more annual outbreaks of influenza. I am convinced that he has left all his money, after providing a handsome annuity for the parlour-maid, to Vivie, knowing that in her hands, far more—and far more quickly than in those that direct princely and public charities—will his funds reach the students and the poverty-stricken artists whom he wants to benefit.

I think that after spending the first five months of 1919 in London, getting No. 1 Park Crescent tidy again and fully repaired (because Michael wished to pursue more thoroughly than ever his biological researches), Vivie and Michael went off to spend their real honeymoon in the Occupied Territory of the Rhineland, in that never-to-be forgotten June, memorable for its splendid sunshine and the beauty of its flowers and foliage. I think they did this expressly (under the guise of a visit to General Armstrong), so that Vivie and Minna von Stachelberg—now Minna Schultz—might fore-gather at Bonn. Minna had married again, an officer of no family but of means and of fine physique whom she had nursed in Brussels. His left arm had been shattered, but the skill of the Belgian surgeons and her devoted nursing had saved it from being amputated. She had wished however to have him examined by some great exponent of curative surgery at Bonn University, and the conjunction of the celebrated Sir Michael Rossiter—who in his discussions of anatomy with the Bonn professors forgot there had ever been a war between Britain and Germany—was most opportune.

I think however that Sir Michael said this was all humbug on Minna's part, and that all she wanted—her husband, Major Schultz, looking the picture of health—was to meet once more her well-beloved Vivie. At any rate I am sure they met in the Rhineland in a propitious month when you could be out of doors all day and all night; and that Minna said some time or other how happy she was in her second marriage, and that however heartily she disliked militarism and condemned War, soldiers made the nicest husbands. I think before she and Vivie parted to go their several ways, they determined to work for the building up of an Anglo-German reconciliation, and for the advocacy in both countries of a Man-and-Woman Government.

I think, nevertheless, that Vivie being a sound business woman and possessing a strong sense of justice on the lines of an eye for an eye, will claim at least Five Thousand pounds from the German Government for the devastations and thefts at the Villa Beau-sejour; and that having got it and having disposed of her mother's jewellery and plate for L3,500, she will present the Villa Beau-sejour property and an endowment of L8,000 to the Town of Brussels, as an educational orphanage for the children of Belgian soldiers who have died in the War, where they may receive a practical education in agriculture and poultry farming.

I fancy she gave a Thousand pounds to Pasteur Walcker's Congo Mission; and transferred to Mme. Trouessart all her shares in and rights over the Hotel Edouard-Sept.

I also picture to myself the Rossiters having a motor tour of pure pleasure and delight of the eyes in South Wales in September, 1919.

I imagine their going to Pontystrad and surprising the Vicar and Vicaress and puzzling them by purposely-diffuse stories of Vivie's cousin the late David Vavasour Williams, intended to convey the idea, without telling unnecessary fibs, that David died abroad during the War, but that Vivie in his memory and that of his dear old father intends to continue a strong personal interest in the Village Hall and its educational aims. I also picture Vivie going alone to Mrs. Evanwy's rose-entwined cottage. The old lady is now rather shaky and does not walk far from her little garden with its box bower and garden seat. I can foreshadow Vivie dispelling some of the mystery about David Williams and being embraced by the old Nannie with warm affection and the hearty assurances that she had guessed the secret from the very first but had been so drawn to the false David Williams and so sure of his honest purposes that nothing would have induced her to undeceive the old Vicar. I can even imagine the old lady ere—years hence—paralysis strikes her down—telling Vivie so much gossip about the Welsh Vavasours that Vivie becomes positively certain her mother came from that stock and that she really was first cousin to the boy she personated for the laudable purpose of showing how well a woman could practise at the Bar.

I like to think also that by the present year of grace—1920—the Rossiters will have become convinced that No. 1 Park Crescent, even with the Zoo and the Royal Botanic Gardens close by and the ornamental garden of Regent's Park in between, does not satisfy all their needs and ambitions: that they will have resolved even before this year began—to supplement it by a home in the country for week-ends, for summer visits, and finally for rest in their old age. That for this purpose they will acquire some ideal Grange or Priory, or ample farmstead near Petworth and the Armstrongs' home, over against the South Downs, and near the river Rother; that it shall be in no mere suburb of Petworth but in a stately little village with its own character and history going back to Roman times and a church with a Saxon body and a Norman chancel. And that in the ideal churchyard of this enviable church with ancient yews and 18th century tomb-stones, and old, old benches in the sunshine for the grandfathers and loafers of the village to sit on and smoke of a Sabbath morning, a place shall be found for the bones of Bertie Adams; reverently brought over from the grassy amphi-theatre of the Tir National to repose in this churchyard of West Sussex which looks out over one of the finest cricket pitches in the county. If, then, there is any lien between the mouldering fragments of our bodies and the inexplicable personality which has been generated in the living brain, the former office boy of *Fraser and Warren* will know that he is always present in the memory of Vivien Rossiter, that she has placed the few physical fragments still representing him in such a setting as would have delighted his honest, simple nature in his lifetime. He would also know that his children are now hers and her husband's; that his Nance very rightly married the excellent butler, Jenkins, with whom he had discussed many a cricket score; and that Love, after all, is stronger than Death.

Choose from Thousands of 1stWorldLibrary Classics By

A. M. Barnard
Ada Leverson
Adolphus William Ward
Aesop
Agatha Christie
Alexander Aaronsohn
Alexander Kielland
Alexandre Dumas
Alfred Gatty
Alfred Ollivant
Alice Duer Miller
Alice Turner Curtis
Alice Dunbar
Allen Chapman
Alleyne Ireland
Ambrose Bierce
Amelia E. Barr
Amory H. Bradford
Andrew Lang
Andrew McFarland Davis
Andy Adams
Angela Brazil
Anna Alice Chapin
Anna Sewell
Annie Besant
Annie Hamilton Donnell
Annie Payson Call
Annie Roe Carr
Annonaymous
Anton Chekhov
Archibald Lee Fletcher
Arnold Bennett
Arthur C. Benson
Arthur Conan Doyle
Arthur M. Winfield
Arthur Ransome
Arthur Schnitzler
Arthur Train
Atticus
B.H. Baden-Powell
B. M. Bower
B. C. Chatterjee
Baroness Emmuska Orczy
Baroness Orczy
Basil King
Bayard Taylor
Ben Macomber
Bertha Muzzy Bower
Bjornstjerne Bjornson

Booth Tarkington
Boyd Cable
Bram Stoker
C. Collodi
C. E. Orr
C. M. Ingleby
Carolyn Wells
Catherine Parr Traill
Charles A. Eastman
Charles Amory Beach
Charles Dickens
Charles Dudley Warner
Charles Farrar Browne
Charles Ives
Charles Kingsley
Charles Klein
Charles Hanson Towne
Charles Lathrop Pack
Charles Romyn Dake
Charles Whibley
Charles Willing Beale
Charlotte M. Braeme
Charlotte M. Yonge
Charlotte Perkins Stetson
Clair W. Hayes
Clarence Day Jr.
Clarence E. Mulford
Clemence Housman
Confucius
Coningsby Dawson
Cornelis DeWitt Wilcox
Cyril Burleigh
D. H. Lawrence
Daniel Defoe
David Garnett
Dinah Craik
Don Carlos Janes
Donald Keyhoe
Dorothy Kilner
Dougan Clark
Douglas Fairbanks
E. Nesbit
E. P. Roe
E. Phillips Oppenheim
E. S. Brooks
Earl Barnes
Edgar Rice Burroughs
Edith Van Dyne
Edith Wharton

Edward Everett Hale
Edward J. O'Biren
Edward S. Ellis
Edwin L. Arnold
Eleanor Atkins
Eleanor Hallowell Abbott
Eliot Gregory
Elizabeth Gaskell
Elizabeth McCracken
Elizabeth Von Arnim
Ellem Key
Emerson Hough
Emilie F. Carlen
Emily Bronte
Emily Dickinson
Enid Bagnold
Enilor Macartney Lane
Erasmus W. Jones
Ernie Howard Pie
Ethel May Dell
Ethel Turner
Ethel Watts Mumford
Eugene Sue
Eugenie Foa
Eugene Wood
Eustace Hale Ball
Evelyn Everett-green
Everard Cotes
F. H. Cheley
F. J. Cross
F. Marion Crawford
Fannie E. Newberry
Federick Austin Ogg
Ferdinand Ossendowski
Fergus Hume
Florence A. Kilpatrick
Fremont B. Deering
Francis Bacon
Francis Darwin
Frances Hodgson Burnett
Frances Parkinson Keyes
Frank Gee Patchin
Frank Harris
Frank Jewett Mather
Frank L. Packard
Frank V. Webster
Frederic Stewart Isham
Frederick Trevor Hill
Frederick Winslow Taylor

Friedrich Kerst
Friedrich Nietzsche
Fyodor Dostoyevsky
G.A. Henty
G.K. Chesterton
Gabrielle E. Jackson
Garrett P. Serviss
Gaston Leroux
George A. Warren
George Ade
Geroge Bernard Shaw
George Cary Eggleston
George Durston
George Ebers
George Eliot
George Gissing
George MacDonald
George Meredith
George Orwell
George Sylvester Viereck
George Tucker
George W. Cable
George Wharton James
Gertrude Atherton
Gordon Casserly
Grace E. King
Grace Gallatin
Grace Greenwood
Grant Allen
Guillermo A. Sherwell
Gulielma Zollinger
Gustav Flaubert
H. A. Cody
H. B. Irving
H.C. Bailey
H. G. Wells
H. H. Munro
H. Irving Hancock
H. R. Naylor
H. Rider Haggard
H. W. C. Davis
Haldeman Julius
Hall Caine
Hamilton Wright Mabie
Hans Christian Andersen
Harold Avery
Harold McGrath
Harriet Beecher Stowe
Harry Castlemon
Harry Coghill
Harry Houidini

Hayden Carruth
Helent Hunt Jackson
Helen Nicolay
Hendrik Conscience
Hendy David Thoreau
Henri Barbusse
Henrik Ibsen
Henry Adams
Henry Ford
Henry Frost
Henry James
Henry Jones Ford
Henry Seton Merriman
Henry W Longfellow
Herbert A. Giles
Herbert Carter
Herbert N. Casson
Herman Hesse
Hildegard G. Frey
Homer
Honore De Balzac
Horace B. Day
Horace Walpole
Horatio Alger Jr.
Howard Pyle
Howard R. Garis
Hugh Lofting
Hugh Walpole
Humphry Ward
Ian Maclaren
Inez Haynes Gillmore
Irving Bacheller
Isabel Cecilia Williams
Isabel Hornibrook
Israel Abrahams
Ivan Turgenev
J.G.Austin
J. Henri Fabre
J. M. Barrie
J. M. Walsh
J. Macdonald Oxley
J. R. Miller
J. S. Fletcher
J. S. Knowles
J. Storer Clouston
J. W. Duffield
Jack London
Jacob Abbott
James Allen
James Andrews
James Baldwin

James Branch Cabell
James DeMille
James Joyce
James Lane Allen
James Lane Allen
James Oliver Curwood
James Oppenheim
James Otis
James R. Driscoll
Jane Abbott
Jane Austen
Jane L. Stewart
Janet Aldridge
Jens Peter Jacobsen
Jerome K. Jerome
Jessie Graham Flower
John Buchan
John Burroughs
John Cournos
John F. Kennedy
John Gay
John Glasworthy
John Habberton
John Joy Bell
John Kendrick Bangs
John Milton
John Philip Sousa
John Taintor Foote
Jonas Lauritz Idemil Lie
Jonathan Swift
Joseph A. Altsheler
Joseph Carey
Joseph Conrad
Joseph E. Badger Jr
Joseph Hergesheimer
Joseph Jacobs
Jules Vernes
Julian Hawthrone
Julie A Lippmann
Justin Huntly McCarthy
Kakuzo Okakura
Karle Wilson Baker
Kate Chopin
Kenneth Grahame
Kenneth McGaffey
Kate Langley Bosher
Kate Langley Bosher
Katherine Cecil Thurston
Katherine Stokes
L. A. Abbot
L. T. Meade

L. Frank Baum
Latta Griswold
Laura Dent Crane
Laura Lee Hope
Laurence Housman
Lawrence Beasley
Leo Tolstoy
Leonid Andreyev
Lewis Carroll
Lewis Sperry Chafer
Lilian Bell
Lloyd Osbourne
Louis Hughes
Louis Joseph Vance
Louis Tracy
Louisa May Alcott
Lucy Fitch Perkins
Lucy Maud Montgomery
Luther Benson
Lydia Miller Middleton
Lyndon Orr
M. Corvus
M. H. Adams
Margaret E. Sangster
Margret Howth
Margaret Vandercook
Margaret W. Hungerford
Margret Penrose
Maria Edgeworth
Maria Thompson Daviess
Mariano Azuela
Marion Polk Angellotti
Mark Overton
Mark Twain
Mary Austin
Mary Catherine Crowley
Mary Cole
Mary Hastings Bradley
Mary Roberts Rinehart
Mary Rowlandson
M. Wollstonecraft Shelley
Maud Lindsay
Max Beerbohm
Myra Kelly
Nathaniel Hawthrone
Nicolo Machiavelli
O. F. Walton
Oscar Wilde

Owen Johnson
P.G. Wodehouse
Paul and Mabel Thorne
Paul G. Tomlinson
Paul Severing
Percy Brebner
Percy Keese Fitzhugh
Peter B. Kyne
Plato
Quincy Allen
R. Derby Holmes
R. L. Stevenson
R. S. Ball
Rabindranath Tagore
Rahul Alvares
Ralph Bonehill
Ralph Henry Barbour
Ralph Victor
Ralph Waldo Emmerson
Rene Descartes
Ray Cummings
Rex Beach
Rex E. Beach
Richard Harding Davis
Richard Jefferies
Richard Le Gallienne
Robert Barr
Robert Frost
Robert Gordon Anderson
Robert L. Drake
Robert Lansing
Robert Lynd
Robert Michael Ballantyne
Robert W. Chambers
Rosa Nouchette Carey
Rudyard Kipling
Saint Augustine
Samuel B. Allison
Samuel Hopkins Adams
Sarah Bernhardt
Sarah C. Hallowell
Selma Lagerlof
Sherwood Anderson
Sigmund Freud
Standish O'Grady
Stanley Weyman
Stella Benson
Stella M. Francis

Stephen Crane
Stewart Edward White
Stijn Streuvels
Swami Abhedananda
Swami Parmananda
T. S. Ackland
T. S. Arthur
The Princess Der Ling
Thomas A. Janvier
Thomas A Kempis
Thomas Anderton
Thomas Bailey Aldrich
Thomas Bulfinch
Thomas De Quincey
Thomas Dixon
Thomas H. Huxley
Thomas Hardy
Thomas More
Thornton W. Burgess
U. S. Grant
Upton Sinclair
Valentine Williams
Various Authors
Vaughan Kester
Victor Appleton
Victor G. Durham
Victoria Cross
Virginia Woolf
Wadsworth Camp
Walter Camp
Walter Scott
Washington Irving
Wilbur Lawton
Wilkie Collins
Willa Cather
Willard F. Baker
William Dean Howells
William le Queux
W. Makepeace Thackeray
William W. Walter
William Shakespeare
Winston Churchill
Yei Theodora Ozaki
Yogi Ramacharaka
Young E. Allison
Zane Grey